THEIR MEANT-TO-BE BABY

BY
CAROLINE ANDERSON

MILLS & BOON

Published in Great Britain 2017
By Mills & Boon, an imprint of HarperCollins*Publishers*
1 London Bridge Street, London, SE1 9GF

© 2017 Caroline Anderson

ISBN: 978-0-263-92629-3

Our policy is to use papers that are natural, renewable and recyclable
products and made from wood grown in sustainable forests. The logging
and manufacturing processes conform to the legal environmental
regulations of the country of origin.

Printed and bound in Spain
by CPI, Barcelona

THEIR MEANT-TO-BE BABY

BY
CAROLINE ANDERSON

A MUMMY FOR HIS BABY

BY
MOLLY EVANS

MILLS &
BOON

Caroline Anderson is a matriarch, writer, armchair gardener, unofficial tearoom researcher and eater of lovely cakes. Not necessarily in that order. *What Caroline loves:* Her family. Her friends. Reading. Writing contemporary love stories. Hearing from readers. Walks by the sea with coffee/ice cream/cake thrown in! Torrential rain. Sunshine in spring/autumn. *What Caroline hates:* Losing her pets. Fighting with her family. Cold weather. Hot weather. Computers. Clothes shopping. *Caroline's plans:* Keep smiling and writing!

Molly Evans has taken her experiences as a travel nurse across the USA and turned them into wondrous settings for her books. Now, living at 6,000 feet in New Mexico is home. When she's not writing, or attending her son's hockey games, she's learning to knit socks or settling in front of the kiva fireplace with a glass of wine and a good book. Visit Molly at mollyevansromance.wordpress.com for more info.

Dear Reader,

When Kate first appeared on the page in *Risk of a Lifetime* I knew she was a troubled and complicated person with a lot of love to give, but damaged by her past. I had no idea what that past might be, or who the man would be who could save her from her self-destructing course.

Enter Sam, equally damaged, equally in need of healing, but for very different reasons, and also with a lot of love to give. Getting them together was easy, but how to keep them together when all either of them wanted was to run away?

Gradually, page by page, they revealed themselves to me as I unwrapped the layers of their heartbreaking pasts and found the good and decent people underneath. I just had to help them find that in each other, but it wasn't easy. I hope as you read on and learn about them for yourself you come to love them both as much as I did.

Love,

Caroline

Huge thanks to Sheila, my long-suffering editor, whose patience and faith in me go above and beyond the course of duty, and to my equally long-suffering husband, John, who took himself off countless times to let me wrestle with Kate and Sam, and was there for me at the end of the day with a smile and a G&T to ask how I'd got on. I couldn't have done it without you.

Books by Caroline Anderson

Mills & Boon Medical Romance

From Christmas to Eternity
The Secret in His Heart
Risk of a Lifetime

Mills & Boon Cherish

The Valtieri Baby
Snowed in with the Billionaire
Best Friend to Wife and Mother?

Visit the Author Profile page at
millsandboon.co.uk for more titles.

CHAPTER ONE

'Someone bail on you?'

The low voice sent a quiver through her, making every nerve-ending tingle. She knew whose it was. He'd been sitting at the other end of the bar and he'd been watching her since she walked in.

She'd noticed him straight away—hard not to, with those killer looks and a body to die for—but she wasn't looking for that kind of trouble so she'd ignored him, even though she'd been aware of him in every cell of her body. She slid her phone into the back pocket of her jeans and tilted her head back to meet his eyes.

Close to, she could see they were blue—a pale, ice blue, strangely piercing and unsettling.

There were crow's feet at the corners that might have been from laughter, or spending a lot of time outdoors squinting into the sun. Both, maybe. He had that healthy outdoor look about him, a sort of raw masculinity that sent another shiver through her body, and she lowered her eyes a little and focused instead on a mouth that was just made for kissing…

No! No way. She pulled herself together sharply. She was done with that—with all of it. She went back to the unsettling eyes.

'Is that your best shot? I've had better chat-up lines from a ten-year-old.'

Her voice sounded more brittle than she'd meant it to, but he just laughed, a soft huff of wry humour which reeled her in just a teensy bit, and those lips tilted into a smile that creased the corners of his eyes and made them suddenly less threatening.

'Sorry. I wasn't trying to hit on you. I just read the expression on your face when you answered your phone. Sort of "so what do I do now?" which is pretty much what I was trying to work out myself.'

Unlikely. Why would anyone that gorgeous have any difficulty working out what to do on a Saturday night? Not that she was interested, or cared *at all* about this total stranger, but that sinful mouth quirked again and something inside her lurched.

'I take it your other half's busy tonight, then,' she said, telling herself it was utterly irrelevant since this was going nowhere, but his mouth firmed and for a moment she didn't think he was going to answer. Then it twitched in a rueful smile that didn't quite reach his eyes.

'No other half,' he said quietly, and his voice had a tinge of sadness which made her believe him. 'The friends I've been staying with had something else on tonight, and I've got to hang on till tomorrow so I'm just killing time in a strange town, really. How about you?'

It begged an answer, and not even she was that churlish. 'I was meeting a friend,' she offered reluctantly, 'but she's been called into work.'

'Ah. My friends are having way more fun than that. They've gone to a party, so I was well and truly trumped.'

He smiled again, a wry, easy grin this time, and hitched his lean frame onto the bar stool beside her and caught the barman's eye. 'So, can I get you a drink? Since we both seem to have time on our hands?'

She did, but she didn't want to spend it with a man, and particularly not a man with trouble written all over him. She was sworn off that type for life—and probably every other type, since she was such a lousy judge of character. And gorgeous though he was, it wasn't enough to weaken her resolve. Out of the frying pan and all that. But she had to give him full marks for persistence, and at least he was single. That was an improvement.

He was still waiting for her answer, the barman poised in suspense, and she gave a tiny shrug. She could have one drink. What harm could it do? Especially if she kept her head for a change. And it wasn't as if she had anything else to do apart from tackling the mountain of laundry in her bedroom.

She let herself meet his eyes again, those curious pale eyes that locked with hers, beautiful but unnerving, holding hers against her will. They made her feel vulnerable—raw and exposed, as if they could see things about her that no one was meant to see.

Which makes having a drink with him a really bad idea.

She mentally deleted the name of the lethal cocktail she might have shared with Petra and switched to something sensible. Something safe.

'I'll have sparkling water, please.'

One eyebrow quirked, but he nodded to the barman and asked for two. So he wasn't drinking, either.

'I'm Sam, by the way,' he said, offering his hand.

'I'm Kate,' she replied, and, because he hadn't really left her any choice, she put her hand in his and felt it engulfed in something warm and nameless that brought her whole body to life. Their eyes clashed again, and after a breathless second he released his grip and she eased away and shifted on the bar stool, resisting the urge to scrub her hand against her thigh to wipe the tingle off her palm.

'So, Kate, how come you're living in Yoxburgh?'

'What makes you think I'm not passing through like you?'

His mouth twitched. 'On the way to where? It's stuck out on a limb. And anyway, the barman knows you. He greeted you like an old friend when you walked in.'

His smile was irresistible, and she felt her lips shift without permission. 'Hardly an old friend, but fair cop. I do live here. Why is that so hard to believe?'

He shrugged, his eyes still crinkled at the corners. 'Because you're young, you're—' he glanced at her ring finger pointedly '—apparently single, and it's just a sleepy little backwater on the edge of nowhere?'

It wasn't, not really, but it had a safeness about it which was why she'd chosen it, exactly because it felt like a quiet backwater and she'd thought it might keep her heart out of trouble. Except it hadn't worked.

She ignored the comment about her being single and focused on Yoxburgh. 'Actually, it's a great place, not nearly as quiet as you'd think, and anyway I love being by the sea.'

'Yeah, me, too. It's been great staying up here for the last couple of days. I'd forgotten how much I'd missed the sea.'

'So how long are you here for?' she asked, forgetting that she wasn't supposed to be showing an interest.

'Only till tomorrow morning. I spotted a boat for sale just as I was leaving this afternoon, and the guy can't see me till the morning, so I'm staying over to see if I can strike a deal.'

'What kind of a boat?' she asked, telling herself she

was just being polite and wasn't really interested in the boat or anything else about him, like where he was staying or how he was going to pass the next twelve hours—

'An old sailing boat. A wooden Peter Duck ketch—' He broke off with a grin. 'I've lost you, haven't I?'

'Yup.' She had to laugh at his wry chuckle. 'Go on.'

'Nah, I won't bore you. If you don't know anything about *Swallows and Amazons* it won't mean a thing. Anyway, it needs work, but that's fine. It'll help pass the time, and I'm not afraid of hard physical work.'

She just stopped herself from scanning his body for tell-tale muscles.

'So what do you do when you're not rescuing old sailing boats?' she asked, against her better judgement. Not that she *had* a better judgement. Her entire life was a testament to that and she was still hurting from the last time she'd crashed and burned, but her tongue obviously hadn't learned that lesson yet.

He gave a lazy shrug, which distracted her attention from his kissable mouth to those broad, solid shoulders just made for resting her head against.

'Nothing exciting. I spend most of my life trapped indoors governed by unmeetable targets, and I sail whenever I get a chance, which isn't nearly often enough. Hence the boat. Your turn.'

'Me?' She let out a slightly strangled laugh and shifted on the bar stool. For some reason, she didn't want to tell him the truth. Maybe because she was sick of men running their latest symptoms by her or fantasising about her in uniform the second they knew she was a nurse, or maybe something to do with her latest mistake who'd moved on to someone brainless and overtly sexy when she'd found out he was married and dumped him? Whatever, she opened her mouth and said the first thing that came into her head.

'I'm a glamour model,' she lied, and his eyebrows twitched ever so slightly in surprise.

'Well, that's a first,' he murmured, and to his credit he didn't let his eyes drop and scan her body the way she'd wanted to scan his. 'Do you enjoy it?'

No. She'd hated it, for the massively short time she'd done it all those years ago, when she'd landed in the real world with a bump. Another mistake, but one forced on her by hunger and desperation.

'It pays the bills,' she said. Or it had, way back then.

He didn't bother to control his eyebrows this time. 'Lots of things pay the bills.'

'You disapprove?'

'It's not my place to disapprove. It's none of my business. I just can't imagine why someone with a brain would want to do it.'

'Maybe I don't have one?'

He snorted softly and picked up his glass. 'I don't think that's quite true.' He sat back, propping his elbow on the bar and slouching back against it. 'So, when you're not cavorting around in not a lot, what do you do for fun?'

She shrugged. 'Meet up with friends, read, go for walks, bake cakes and take them into work—'

'Cakes? You take cakes to the studio?'

Oh, hell, she was such a hopeless liar. 'Why not?' she flannelled airily. 'Everyone likes cake.'

'I thought models starved themselves.'

Ah. 'That's fashion models,' she said, ad-libbing like crazy. 'One reason why I could never do it. Glamour models are expected to have…'

She dwindled to a halt, kicking herself for engineering such a ridiculous conversation, and he finished the sentence for her.

'Curves?' he murmured, his voice lingering on the word and making her body flush slowly from the toes up.

'Exactly.'

His eyes did drop this time, and she felt the urge to suck in her stomach. She had no idea why. He wasn't looking at her stomach. He was way too busy studying her cleavage.

His eyes flicked away, and he drained his glass and set it down with a little clunk. 'Have you eaten? All this talk of cake has reminded me I'm starving.'

She was all set to lie again, but she was ravenous and if she didn't eat soon she was going to fall off the bar stool. Not a good look.

'No, I haven't eaten. Why?'

'Because I was debating getting something off the bar menu here, or going to a restaurant on my own, which frankly doesn't appeal. So what's it to be? Solitary scampi and chips here, or shall we go somewhere rather nicer and work on your curves? It would be a shame to let them fade away.'

No contest. She was starving and her fridge was utterly empty. 'Just dinner, no subtext,' she warned, just to be on the safe side after his comment about her curves, and he gave a strangled laugh.

'Sheesh, I don't work that fast,' he said with a grin. 'So, any suggestions for somewhere nice?'

Nice? Only one really great place sprang to mind, and judging by the cashmere jumper under the battered but undoubtedly expensive leather jacket he could afford it, but James and Connie were at Zacharelli's, and the last thing she needed was her boss asking questions on Monday morning. And anyway, they didn't stand a chance without a reservation and they were like gold dust.

His phone beeped and he pulled it out with a murmured apology and scrolled around for a moment. It gave her time to study him, to notice little things that she hadn't registered before, like the strength in his hands, the fact that he took care of them, the nails clipped and scrupulously clean. His hair was short, but not too short, and his jaw was stubbled, making her hand itch to feel the bristles rasp against her skin, right before she threaded her fingers through that dark, glossy hair and drew his head down to kiss his delectably decadent mouth...

'Sorry. I've turned it off now,' he told her, shifting his hips so he could slide the phone back into the pocket of his jeans. The movement drew her attention down, and she felt her mouth dry. 'So, any suggestions?' he asked.

Her body was screaming with suggestions, but she drowned it out. 'There's a nice Chinese restaurant on the front? In fact there are a few good eateries of one sort or another down there, so we should find somewhere with a table.'

'Well, let's go and check them out, then.' He stood up, held a hand out to her to help her off the stool and she took it, struck first by the old-fashioned courtesy of the gesture and then, as their skin met for the second time, by the lightning bolt of heat that slammed through her body at the brief contact.

She all but snatched her hand away, and then a moment later she felt a light touch over the small of her back as he ushered her through the crowd towards the door. She fastened her short jacket but his hand was just below it, the warmth spreading out to the furthest reaches of her body until there wasn't a single cell that wasn't tingling.

Oh, why hadn't she said no? This was *such* a mistake!

'Walk or drive? My car's just round the corner at the hotel if we need it.'

'Oh—walk. I know it's cold, but it's a nice evening for January, and it's not far.' And the confines of a car would be way too intimate and dangerous.

'OK. You'll have to lead the way. I'm in your hands.'

I wish...

She hauled in a breath and set off towards the seafront, and he fell in beside her, matching the length of his stride to hers as they strolled down through the town centre, their breath frosting on the cold night air.

'So what's Yoxburgh like to live in?' he asked casually, peering through the shop windows as if he could find the answer in their unlit depths.

'OK. Quiet, mostly, but there's a lot going on even so and there's an interesting vibe. I like it. It suits me.'

He turned back to eye her searchingly. 'You wouldn't rather be in London?'

No way. She'd lived in London all her life, worked there while she was training, and hated every second of it. 'No. You?'

'Oh, no, I hate it. I've been working there for a while now and I can't get away quick enough. I need a seaside town with good sailing like the one I grew up in.'

'You'd love it here, then. Lots of yachting types.'

He shot her a grin. 'I don't know that I'd call myself a "yachting" type, exactly. I just like messing about in boats. I was reared on *Swallows and Amazons*. Free spirits and all that. I guess I'm just trying to recapture my misspent youth.'

She laughed and shook her head. 'I bet you were a holy terror growing up.'

His mouth twitched. 'My parents would have an opinion on that but they didn't know the half of it. The most important lesson I learned in childhood was that you can break any rule you like, just so long as you don't get caught. What about you?'

What about her? She'd broken every rule going during her own disastrous childhood, but she wasn't going into all that with him, and certainly not on a first date. She forced herself to meet his eyes. 'I had my ups and downs.'

'Didn't we all?' he said with an easy laugh. 'I got sent to boarding school when I was ten.'

Which just underlined the differences between them, she thought. Not that it changed anything, because as soon as they'd finished dinner she'd make her excuses and leave, and that would be it.

She stopped outside the restaurant. 'Here we are, but it looks pretty busy.'

'The town's buzzing,' he said, sounding surprised.

'Saturday night, though. It's quieter midweek. There's the café next door if they don't have a table here—they do great pastries and really good coffee, so we could give it a try— Oh, hang on, those people are getting up. We could be in luck.'

He opened the restaurant door for her, and they were shown to the window table that had been vacated by the couple.

'That was good timing,' he said. 'I'm seriously starving and it smells amazing in here. So what would you recommend?' he asked, flicking the menu open.

'They do a good set meal for two, but it's quite a lot of food. We often stretch it to three. Here.'

She reached over and pointed it out, and he scanned it and nodded. 'Looks good. Let's go for that. I'm sure we can manage to do it justice. Do you fancy sharing a bottle of wine as we're not driving?'

Did she? Could she trust herself not to lose her common sense and do something rash?

'That would be lovely, but I'll only have one glass,' she said, and ignored the little voice that told her it was the thin end of the wedge.

'That was gorgeous. Thank you. I've eaten way too much.'

'Nah, you need to maintain your curves,' he said lightly, and looked down at her, at the wide grey eyes that wanted to be wary and didn't manage it, the slight tilt of her smile, her lips soft and moist and dangerously kissable.

Who was she?

Not a glamour model, of that he was damn sure, but beyond that he knew nothing. Did it matter? He hadn't been exactly forthcoming to her, either, but hey.

He leant over and kissed her cheek, brushing his lips against the soft, delicate skin, breathing in a lingering trace of scent that teased his senses and made him want more.

Much more.

'Thank you for joining me. I hate eating alone.'

'I'm used to it,' she said. 'My flatmate's moved out and it's eat alone or starve.'

They fell silent, in that awkward moment when they should have said goodbye and gone their separate ways, but he realised he didn't want to. Didn't want to say goodbye, didn't want to let her go, knowing he'd never see her again.

'Fancy a stroll along the seafront?'

There was a slight hesitation, and then she smiled. 'Why not?' she said, as if she'd answered her own question. 'I love the sound of the sea at night.'

'Me, too.'

They fell into step, and it seemed the most natural thing in the world to put his arm around her shoulders and draw her up against his side, but he could hear the click of her red stiletto boots against the prom with every step, and it was driving him crazy.

Red shoes, no pants...

The saying echoed in his head, taunting his imagination, and he tried to haul it back into order. They weren't really shoes anyway, he told himself sternly, more ankle boots, and her underwear was none of his business, but her hip nudged his with every step and it was all he could think about.

They'd walked past the cluster of restaurants and cafés and holiday flats to where the amusements started, but being out of season everything was shut and it was deserted, with nothing and no one to distract him from the click of her red stilettos.

The lights there were dim and spaced far apart, and between them there was a section of the prom that was hardly lit at all, only enough to make out her features as he drew her to a halt.

'Listen,' he said, and she tilted her head and listened with him to the soft suck of the waves on the shingle, rhythmic and soothing. In the distance someone laughed, and music blared momentarily as a car passed them and turned the corner, the silence wrapping itself around them again as the music receded.

'The sea's quiet tonight,' she said softly. 'Sometimes it's really stormy. I love it then. Wild and dangerous and free.'

'Mmm.' He stared down into her eyes, lifting a hand to stroke a stray wisp of hair away from her face. Her skin was soft, cool under his fingertips, and he let them drift down her cheek, settling under her chin and tilting it up towards him as he lowered his head slowly and touched his lips to hers.

She moaned softly and opened her mouth to him, giving him access to the touch of her tongue, the sharp, clean edge of her teeth, the sweet freshness and bitter chocolate of the after-dinner mint teasing his tastebuds as he shifted his head slightly and plundered the depth and heat of her mouth.

His body was already primed by the time he'd spent with her as they'd lingered laughing over their meal, tortured further by the nudge of her hip and the tap-tap-tap of those incredibly sexy little boots on the prom as they'd walked, and now it roared to life.

He drew away, lifting his head from hers, searching her face for clues as his heart pounded and his chest rose and fell with every ragged breath, but it was too dark to read her eyes. He could hear the hitch of her breath, though, feel the quiver in it as she exhaled and her breath drifted over his skin in tiny pulses.

'Stay with me tonight,' he said on impulse, and she hesitated for so long he felt the sinking disappointment in his gut; but then she smiled, a wry, sad smile as she lost some internal battle and nodded.

'Your place or mine?' she murmured, and his body gave itself a high five.

They went to his hotel.

Neutral territory? Tidier than her flat, for sure, and she wasn't ready yet to give that much of herself away. Her body was one thing. Her home—that was another. So she'd told him it was further away than it really was, which made the decision easy.

The hotel was one of those anonymous places that

could have been anywhere in the world, featureless but functional, scrupulously clean, the room dominated by the bed with its white striped bedding tucked tautly round the mattress.

It was hardly romantic, but it didn't matter.

All that mattered was them, alone together and driven by a need that had come out of nowhere and wouldn't be denied.

Their clothes hit the floor—jackets, her scarf, his sweater dragged off over his head so that his chest was right in front of her eyes and jammed her breath to a halt in her throat.

She reached out to touch it, her fingertips tracing the outline of taut, firm muscles that jerked at her touch. His hand caught her chin, gentle fingers tilting her face up to his, and he stared down into her eyes for a long moment before he stepped back out of reach.

'Undress for me.'

His voice was gruff, a muscle twitching in his jaw, and his eyes held hers, fire and ice dancing in their depths. Her heart was trying to climb out of her chest, jamming her breath, but she sucked air in somehow, coming out of her trance as the oxygen reached her brain and reality hit.

He thought she was a glamour model. How could she do this? Undress for him as if she had all the confidence of a woman who earned her living with her body? She couldn't even remember what underwear she'd flung on after her shower!

Matching? Probably not. The bra was hot pink, she knew that, because the lace was scratchy, and if she had that bra on, it was because she was getting to the bottom of her underwear drawer. Which didn't bode well for the knickers.

She peeled off her top, and his breath hissed in between his teeth. His hand moved as if to reach for her, and then stopped, hauled back into his pocket beside a tell-tale bulge that made her body weep and her legs turn to mush.

She sat down on the bed and unzipped her boots, tugging them off and then standing up again to slide down the zip on her jeans and wiggle them over her hips, catching a reassuring glimpse of her knickers. Navy lace shorts edged with pink ribbon, so sort of matching. It could have been a lot worse.

Easing her breath out slowly on a silent sigh of relief, she slid the jeans down, but they clung to her legs and there was no sexy way to get them off.

'Here. Let me.'

He crouched in front of her, the fabric bunched in his hands as he pushed the jeans down her legs, lifting her feet in turn to strip them away. His breath was hot, drifting over her legs, the tender skin of her thighs, seeping through the lace fabric just a hand's breadth from his mouth. His hands slid round and cupped her bottom, holding her still as he closed the gap, breathing out, the hot rush going straight to her core.

'There goes that fantasy,' he murmured, and her ego quailed.

'What fantasy?' she asked, just so she could flagellate herself with it in the future, but he laughed softly.

'Red shoes—'

'—no pants,' she finished, and felt her breath ease out in a sigh of relief.

'I'm sure we can fix that,' he said, his voice a low rasp, but she put her hand out to stop him as he reached for them.

'Your turn,' she said, stalling for time, and he smiled wickedly and dumped his wallet and keys and phone on the bedside table before he kicked off his shoes, peeled off his socks and shucked his jeans, kicking them away to land in a heap with hers.

There was nothing unusual or remarkable about his snug jersey shorts, but the contents...

'Keep going,' she ordered, and he quirked a brow and peeled them slowly down, letting them drop to the floor as he stood there bold and unselfconscious and gloriously naked.

How wonderful to be so sure of yourself, she thought as he pushed her down onto the bed and tipped her back, reaching out his hands to draw the dark blue lace with its pink ribbons slowly down over her hips, her legs, her feet...

'Now that's more like it,' he said, and the searing flame of his eyes stroked her with fire.

She whimpered, clenching her knees together to stop the blaze from burning her up, but he reached out a hand, pressing her knees apart, his wicked, clever fingers replacing the stroke of his eyes as his hand slid up her thigh and found its target unerringly.

The intimacy shocked and yet excited her, the tension winding tighter and tighter in her body with every touch, and then suddenly he was gone, leaving her lying there exposed and aching, screaming for release.

'Sam—?'

'Two seconds.'

She heard a slight rustle, a faint tearing sound, and then he was back. A condom, she realised. Thank God one of them was thinking straight, although he didn't need it because she was on the Pill, but she knew nothing about him—

'Shove up,' he muttered, and she wriggled into the middle of the bed as he followed her, peeling away her bra, his mouth taking its place, fastening over one breast and suckling hard as a hand found the other and cradled it in his warm palm.

His knee nudged hers apart and she yielded to him, her body aching for his, arching into him as she begged incoherently, her hesitation forgotten, pleading for something out of reach, something special, and so elusive.

'Easy,' he murmured, and then he was there, filling her, her face cradled gently in his hands as he kissed her. His mouth was hot and sweet and coaxing, his body taut and so, so clever, and the feeling inside her escalated wildly. She felt the pressure building, tried to squirm away, to stall it because suddenly to give him so much of herself seemed too great a step, making her too vulnerable to this stranger who could play her body like a violin.

He held her, though, his body claiming hers, refusing to free it, to let her escape the thing she'd yearned for and now dreaded because it would tear down her defences and leave her wide open to hurt.

'Look at me, Kate,' he demanded softly, and his eyes captured hers and held them, steady and sure, the flame burning bright as he drove her over the edge and crumbled all her defences into dust.

Then, and only then, did he close his eyes, drop his head against her shoulder and let himself go.

CHAPTER TWO

SAM PROPPED HIMSELF on one elbow and watched Kate sleeping, her rich toffee-coloured hair an unruly tangle, her limbs sprawled in exhaustion.

He knew how that felt.

Their mutual thirst was finally slaked, but on the way there he'd wrung every last gasp out of her, taken both of them to the limit of their endurance over and over again. It had been amazing, astonishing. Compelling beyond anything he'd ever felt before.

Guilt plagued him at that, but he pushed it away. It was only sex, nothing more. It wasn't disloyal, because this wasn't a relationship, just a crazy night out of nowhere. Surely to God he was allowed to have fun sometimes, to forget, just for a few hours?

A curl lay across her cheek, and he lifted it away, careful not to disturb her. Not that he thought he would. She was sleeping like the dead—

He swung his legs over the side of the bed. It was only six thirty, but the man who owned the boat was going out on the tide before nine so they'd arranged to meet at seven, but then he should be done. He could be back in town by eight, nine at the latest. Maybe she could meet him then?

Her jeans were in a heap on the floor, and her phone was lying beside them. He picked it up, and his own, went into the bathroom and called himself from her phone to get the number, then sent her a text.

Meet me for breakfast? Café by the restaurant at nine? S

He put the phones down, showered and towelled himself roughly dry, cleaned his teeth and then on the spur of the moment reloaded the new emergency toothbrush he'd found her before he pulled on his clothes and packed. He tried hard not to disturb her, but he could have slammed the door and she wouldn't have heard she was so heavily asleep. He'd ask Reception to give her a call at eight. That would give her an hour to get ready for breakfast.

He hesitated a moment, then bent, breathing in the scent of warm skin and sex as he touched his lips to her flushed, sleep-creased cheek.

She didn't move. Just as well. He was out of time.

He picked up his things, put her phone where she'd see it and let himself quietly out of the room.

A phone was ringing.

Kate struggled up out of the depths of sleep and registered her surroundings as she groped for the room phone. 'Hello?'

The recorded, electronic voice was horribly cheerful. 'This is your alarm call. The time is eight a.m.'

Alarm call? Why...?

Sam, she realised, looking round at the empty room. All his stuff was gone. He must have left for his meeting, but why hadn't he said goodbye? After all they'd shared, he'd just left without a word?

Her brain slowly coming to, she dropped the receiver back on the cradle and slumped against the pillows.

Dammit, would she never learn?

She stumbled out of bed and opened the bottle of spring water on the hospitality tray, dragged on her clothes and shoved her phone in her pocket. She was so bone tired. She was going home for a shower and then she'd fall into bed—

Her mobile rang, and she pulled it out of her pocket and stared at it in dismay. Her ward manager, which could only mean one thing. Her finger hovered over the phone, then she gave in to the inevitable guilt and answered it reluctantly.

'Hi, Jill.'

'Kate, I'm so sorry, I hate to do this to you on your day off but is there any way you can come in?'

Again? Her heart sank and she plopped down onto the bed in despair. 'Can't you get an agency nurse? I've just done seven days straight—'

'I've tried. Please, Kate? Jane's called in—she's got norovirus, too, and we're so short-staffed we're going to have to close the Emergency Department if we can't get more nursing cover. I wouldn't ask if I wasn't desperate.'

She gave in. The winter vomiting bug had swept through Yoxburgh Park Hospital in the last few weeks, which was why Petra had been called in last night, and there was no point fighting the inevitable. 'OK, I'm on my way. I just need time to shower and grab some breakfast—'

'Quick shower. I'll make you some toast when you get here. We really need you now.'

Oh, dammit. 'OK, OK, I'm coming. Give me ten minutes.'

Which meant she didn't even have time to go home

and change. It could have been worse. At least she hadn't gone out last night in a tiny dress and six-inch stilettos or she'd be doing the walk of shame.

Not that it would be the first time, she thought with a sigh, but she always kept a pair of work shoes at the hospital since the first time it had happened, and she could wear scrubs. She stripped and went back into the bathroom, and realised Sam had at least had the decency to leave her a blob of toothpaste on the new brush he'd produced for her last night out of the depths of his overnight bag. In case he ever forget to take one with him, he'd explained, proving he was way more organised than she'd ever be, but that wasn't difficult.

She cleaned her teeth with it, grateful for the burst of freshness it offered if not for his sneaky exit, then showered fast without washing her hair, wiped away the smudge of mascara under her eyes, grabbed the biscuits and water off the hospitality tray and left.

She didn't show.

He almost rang her, but stopped himself in time. She was bound to have seen the text. Maybe she just wasn't interested? Although she'd seemed pretty interested last night.

He waited until ten, dragging out his third coffee to give her time, then admitted the obvious and gave up.

It was probably just as well, he told himself, and crushed the ludicrous feeling of disappointment. He got into his car and checked his phone again. Maybe she just hadn't seen the text? But still there was nothing.

Telling himself not to be a fool, he deleted the call history and the text, threw down the phone and drove home, disappointment and regret taunting him with every mile.

* * *

It was eight that night before she finally climbed the stairs
to her flat, and one glance at it made her glad they'd gone
to his hotel.

Today was the day she'd set aside for cleaning it and
blitzing the laundry, but that had turned out to be an epic
fail. Tough. She wasn't doing it now, she was exhausted,
and it would keep. She stripped, trying not to think of
the way she'd undressed for Sam last night, trying not to
think of all the things he'd done to her, the things she'd
done to him, the way he'd made her feel.

She'd never had a night like it in her life, and it hadn't
just been about the sex, although that had been amazing.
It was him, Sam, warm and funny and gentle and clever.
He'd made her feel special. He'd made her feel *wanted.*

Until she realised he'd just been using her.

And she couldn't really have fallen for him. Not in—
what? Nine hours?

Was that all? Just nine hours? She'd wanted it to go on
for ever, but it hadn't. Like all good things, it had come
to an end all too soon, and he hadn't even had the decency to tell her.

She pulled her phone out of her pocket to put it on
charge and saw she had a message from an unknown
number.

Meet me for breakfast? Café by the restaurant at nine? S

'No-o!' She flopped back on the bed and shut her
eyes, stifling a scream of frustration. How could she
not have seen it?

Because she hadn't had time, was how. She literally
hadn't stopped, and when she had, for twenty minutes
that afternoon, she'd fallen asleep in the staffroom. She

should have rung him—sent him a text, at least, to let him know she'd had to work, but she hadn't even known he'd messaged her, never mind how he'd got her number.

By ringing himself from her phone, she realised, scanning her call log.

Damn. So he hadn't just left without trace. And all day, she'd been hating him for his cowardice.

But maybe it was as well. He didn't live here, he'd only been visiting friends, so nothing would have come of it. She didn't need to fall any further for a man she'd never see again. She would just have tortured herself that bit longer.

And anyway, she was sworn off men for life, remember? No more. Never again. Even if he hadn't just done a runner.

She hesitated, then deleted the text and the call history.

There. Sorted.

Except it didn't feel sorted. It felt wrong, leaving a hollow ache inside, but it would pass. She knew that from long and bitter experience.

Too tired to fret over it any longer, she crawled into bed and fell asleep as soon as her head hit the pillow.

An hour later she woke to a wave of nausea, a raging headache and stomach cramps, and the depressing realisation that she had the bug that had swept through the department...

It was five days before she went back to work—days in which she lost weight, grew to hate the sight of her flat and finally tackled the laundry as she waited the statutory forty-eight hours after symptoms subsided before she was allowed to return to work.

She was straight back in at the deep end, as one by one the team were hit by the virus, but after a few challenging weeks the worst of the crisis seemed to be over. It was just as well, as she hadn't really recovered her appetite and kept feeling light-headed and queasy. She staved off the light-headedness by eating endless chocolate, but she couldn't do anything about her dreams.

Too much chocolate? It had never given her any problems before, but now Sam was haunting her every night.

At first she'd been too ill to think about him, and then too busy, but it clearly wasn't as easy as all that to put him out of her mind. He was there every time she got into bed, reminding her of those few short hours she'd spent with him, making her ache with regret because she hadn't phoned him to apologise and explain.

But she hadn't, and she'd ditched his number, so regret was pointless and she was grateful when they were so busy that she was too tired even to dream about him.

And then, at the beginning of April, just over two months after her night with Sam, she went into Resus to restock and found Annie Shackleton slumped over the desk with her head in her hands.

She and the consultant often worked closely together on trauma cases and they'd become good friends, so right from the beginning she'd been privy to the blow-by-blow development of Annie's pregnancy. Because of her husband Ed's inherited Huntington's gene she'd had IVF, so Kate had been one of the first to know the wonderful news that both embryos had taken, then that both of them were boys.

But this morning Annie had gone for a routine antenatal check, and now Kate knew something was wrong.

'Hey, what's up?' she asked softly, and Annie looked at her, her eyes red-rimmed and tight with strain.

'I've got pre-eclampsia,' she said, her voice uneven, and Kate tutted softly and crouched down beside her.

'Oh, Annie, I'm so sorry, that's such tough luck. What are they doing about it?'

'I've got to stop work. Like—now.'

'Well, of course you have, but you'll be fine! You just need to rest. Are they going to admit you?'

'Not immediately, but it's going to be so hard to take it easy. Who's going to look after the girls? I can't expect my poor mother to do any more, she's been helping me since the girls were born because I was on my own, but I only work three days a week. This'll be all day, every day, because it's the Easter holidays—and because it's the holidays Ed can't take any time off, either, because of the staff with their own children to think about. The timing just couldn't be worse—'

Her voice cracked, and Kate reached out and hugged her.

'Annie, your mum will be fine with it. She's lovely, she adores the girls and they're no trouble. They'll be falling over themselves to look after you, and Ed'll be around to get them up and put them to bed, and you know he thinks of them as his own and they love him to bits. It'll be OK, Annie. Really. You and the babies have to come first and the rest will sort itself out.'

Annie nodded slowly. 'I know that, I know it'll be fine, but it's not just Mum and the girls I'm worried about. I'll be leaving the department in the lurch. Andy Gallagher's on holiday next week with his kids, and I have no idea how they're going to get a consultant-grade locum at such short notice—I was going to work till I was thirty-six weeks, and I'm only thirty-two.'

'So? They'll find someone. It's not your problem, Annie. It's James Slater's problem. He's the clinical lead, let him sort it out, and you look after yourself and the babies. Have you told him yet?'

She pushed herself to her feet. 'No, but I have to. You're right, the locum's not my problem—and even if it was, I don't have a choice. I'll go and tell him.'

'You do that. And go straight home, OK? I'll sort your locker out.' Kate straightened up, hugged her again and then watched her go, a lump in her throat. She loved working with Annie, and she'd miss her warmth and gentle humour. Not that the other doctors were difficult to work with, but—well, Annie had been a good friend to her, and it wouldn't feel the same without her, and she had a horrible feeling she wouldn't be coming back.

And she was being selfish. It wasn't about her.

She'd just finished restocking the drugs cupboard when James put his head round the corner. 'Annie's going home.'

'I know. She's worried about leaving you in the lurch.'

'Tough. She hasn't got a choice, and we'll cope. I'll cover it if necessary. She said something about you clearing out her locker for her. Can you put the things in my office, please, and I'll drop them off at their house on my way past tonight.'

'Will you be able to get a locum?'

He shrugged and ran a hand through his hair. 'Maybe. Connie's got a friend who seems to be kicking his heels at the moment, so he might agree. I'll get her to ring him and twist his arm. It might also mean he gets his blasted boat off our drive while he's here. Why he bought it I can't imagine, but hey. Who am I to judge? I just want it gone so we can get the house sold before the new baby comes.'

But Kate had stopped listening at the word 'boat'. Coincidence? Sam had gone to look at a boat. And his friends had gone to a party, on the same night that James and Connie had been at Zacharelli's for a fortieth. The same party?

But Sam wasn't a doctor—was he? He hadn't exactly said what he did for a living, apart from mentioning unmeetable targets—and they were the bane of most doctors' lives...

'How long's it been there?' she asked casually, her heart pounding.

'Oh, I don't know, a couple of months? It seems like for ever. Right, got to get on. Don't forget Annie's locker.'

'I'll do it now.'

Two months? That fitted. So was Sam a doctor? And if so, how would he feel about working alongside her?

Her heart gave a little kick of excitement as she headed for the staffroom and emptied Annie's possessions into a cardboard box.

Would they pick up where they'd left off?

She tapped on James's door and he beckoned her in, pointing to the phone in his hand and mouthing, 'Thank you.' She put the box on his desk as he ended the call and spun the chair towards her, grinning cheerfully.

'Job done. My sweet-talking wife just strong-armed him, and we have an amazingly well-qualified consultant trauma surgeon starting on Monday.' He tipped his head on one side and studied her thoughtfully. 'Just a word of warning, though, Kate. He's emotionally broken, so don't let his charisma reel you in. You'll just be setting yourself up for a fall.'

The word 'again' hung unspoken in the air between them, and she stifled the sigh. 'I'll bear it in mind,' she said with a forced smile, and just hoped to goodness it wasn't Sam because if it was, the warning might have come too late to save her.

* * *

She was off the next day, and she popped round to Ed and Annie's house on the cliff to see how Annie was doing.

'She's fine, before you ask,' Ed told her with a smile as he let her in. 'I'm pampering her to death. She hates it.'

'I bet she doesn't really. I brought her flowers to cheer her up.'

'Thank you. She'll love them. She's out in the garden with the girls because it's such a gorgeous day. Go on out. I was just making us coffee. How do you like it?'

'Can I have tea?' she said. 'White, no sugar?'

'Sure. We've got cake as well. I'll bring it out.'

She found Annie on a lushly padded swing seat under a canopy, her feet up and the girls chasing each other round the garden. Annie waved at her, and she went over and gave her a hug and handed her the flowers.

'Oh, how gorgeous, you sweetheart! They're so pretty. Thank you. I'll get Ed to put them in water. It'll give him something to do apart from clucking round me like a mother hen.'

She pulled her legs up out of the way to make room, and Kate sat down and settled Annie's swollen feet onto her lap.

'So, how are you? You look the picture of contentment.'

Annie smiled. 'I feel it. It's wonderful—and even better now I know James has found a locum who can actually do the job properly. Ed's driving me slightly nuts, but the girls have been as good as gold, and if the babies would both stop kicking me to bits I could really relax! Feel them—it's like a football team warming up. I can tell they're boys.'

Kate laughed and laid her hand over Annie's bump. 'Good grief. They're having a rare old shuffle, aren't they?'

'It gets a bit crowded in there with twins. It was the same with the girls, but I think these two are bigger. Is Ed bringing you a coffee?'

'Yes—well, tea. I can't drink coffee since I had the bug.'

'That's months ago! You're not pregnant, are you?' she teased.

She laughed. 'Don't be ridiculous. How could I be pregnant? I've sworn off men—and anyway, I'm on the Pill and it's only coffee I don't like. I think I've just had too much of it.'

Annie laughed and rolled her eyes. 'That hasn't put you off chocolate!'

'Or cake,' she said with a chuckle. 'No, it's just the bug.'

But when Ed brought the tray out then and put it down right next to her, the smell of coffee drifting towards her on the warm spring air made her gag.

Could Annie possibly be right? How likely *was* it that she'd still be feeling ill two months later? Not at all...

But she couldn't be pregnant. There was no way. It could only have been Sam, and anyway, she'd done a pregnancy test. Unless...

'Cake?' Ed asked, cutting into her thoughts. 'My grandmother made it. It's her trademark lemon drizzle and I know you'd prefer chocolate but I've never known you turn down cake of any denomination.'

'Thanks. It sounds lovely,' she said, not really paying him attention because her mind was tumbling.

Because she was on the Pill they'd thought it was OK when his condoms ran out, and it would have been, without the bug, but it had dragged on for days, too long for the morning-after pill to work, so she'd done a test and it had been negative. She hadn't given it another thought at the time, but now…

The girls went back to their playhouse and Ed took the tray inside, but she hardly noticed until Annie shook her shoulder.

'Kate? Are you OK? You look as if you've just seen a ghost.'

Or realised that her worst nightmare might actually have come true…

Annie's eyes widened as she stared at her, and she could see the moment her friend's thoughts caught up with her own. 'Oh, no. You're not, are you?'

She started to shake her head in denial, and then shrugged. 'I don't know. I don't think so. I'd put it down to the bug, but it's possible…'

'Oh, Kate. Do you want to do a pregnancy test? I've got a spare one upstairs in our en suite.'

'I've already done one, ages ago, and it was negative— and anyway, I can't just go up there to your bedroom!'

'It's fine, I'll take you up. I need to put the flowers in water and if Ed asks I'm showing you the nursery.'

So they went, dumping the flowers in a vase on the way, and she took the test Annie handed her, closed the bathroom door and bit her lip. Did she want to do this? Yes! Heavens, yes, she wanted to; she needed to know, and as fast as possible, just to put herself out of her misery.

And there it was, in black and white. Well, blue, really, she thought inconsequentially, staring at the wand as she dried her hands on autopilot.

Pregnant. It didn't tell her how pregnant, and her mind tried to sort it out. It was the beginning of April, and she'd met Sam at the end of January. So…nearly nine weeks ago, which made her eleven weeks pregnant, maybe? Her other test must have been too soon…

'Kate? Kate, are you OK?'

She opened the door, her hands shaking as she held out the wand to Annie. 'You were right,' she said, her voice sounding hollow and far away. 'Oh, God, Annie, what on earth am I going to do?'

She felt arms come round her, the firm jut of Annie's pregnant abdomen pressing against her. She could feel the babies kicking, and with a shock she realised that if she did nothing, then in a few more weeks this would be her, her body swollen by the child growing inside it.

And then what? How could she be a mother? She had no idea what a mother even *was*. Not a real mother.

Her teeth started to chatter, and Annie tutted and sat her down on the bed, putting her arm around her and rocking her. She could remember her foster mother doing that when she was sixteen, trying to soothe her when her world had been turned upside down and all feeling had drained away.

It felt the same now, the same numbness, the same emptiness and *what now?*-ness that she'd felt then.

'I can't do it, Annie. I can't do it on my own—'

'Do you know who the father is?'

She nodded. 'Yes, of course I know. Hell, Annie, I'm not that reckless, but I can't contact him. I don't have his number any more, but he won't want to know, it was just one night. Oh, God, I've been so stupid! Why…?'

'Hush, hush,' Annie crooned, rocking her gently. 'It'll be all right. You can do it. I did it on my own.'

'No, you didn't, you had your mum, and I don't have a mum—'

'But you have me. I'll help you. You won't be alone,

Kate. And you can do this, if you decide you want to. You'll be all right.'

And if she didn't want to?

If Sam really *was* the locum, she'd have to tell him, and then he'd have an opinion, want a say. He might want her to go through with the pregnancy even if she decided that she couldn't. And if the locum wasn't Sam, she'd deleted all trace of him from her phone, so she wouldn't be able to tell him, however much she might decide she wanted to.

Which meant if she kept it she *would* be all on her own to deal with it, bar a little help from Annie.

But that was fine. She'd been on her own most of her life, and she liked it like that. She'd had enough of being bullied and manipulated and lied to.

Not that Sam would necessarily do any of those things, but she wasn't inclined to give him the chance.

Even assuming Sam *was* the locum.

He was.

She knew that the moment she walked into the department two days later, at seven on Monday morning. She heard his laugh over the background noise, heard James saying something and then another laugh, and it drew closer as she turned the corner.

She ground to a halt, too late to turn and walk away, too shocked to keep on moving past because she hadn't really believed it would be him. And then he saw her and his eyes widened in surprise.

She searched his face, fell in love with it all over again and then remembered all the reasons she had to regret that she'd ever met him. One in particular...

'Ah, Kate. Let me introduce you to Sam Ryder, our

locum consultant. Sam, this is Kate Ashton, one of our best senior nurses.'

'Hello, Kate,' Sam said softly, but speech had deserted her and the ground refused to swallow her up. 'Do you two know each other?' James asked after an uncomfortable silence.

'Yes—'

'No!'

They spoke in unison, and James did a mild double-take and looked from her to Sam and back again. 'Well, which is it?'

Sam just stood there, and after a second she found her voice. 'We've met,' she qualified. 'Just once.'

Just long enough to make a baby...

A muscled clenched in his jaw, but otherwise Sam's face didn't move. No smile, no frown—nothing. Just those accusing eyes.

She felt sick. Nothing unusual. She was getting so used to it, it was the new normal.

The silence hung in the air between them, broken only by the sound of a pager bleeping. James pulled it out of his pocket and scanned the message.

'Sorry, I need to go. Sam, why don't I put you in Kate's hands for now and let her show you round? She's worked a lot with Annie so she's the expert on her role, really. I'll see you later. Come and find me when you're done with HR.'

James clapped him on the shoulder and walked off, and Sam's eyes tracked him down the corridor and then switched back to Kate. She'd forgotten how piercing they could be.

'You didn't tell me you were a nurse.'

'You didn't tell me you were a doctor.'

'At least I didn't lie.'

She felt colour tease her cheeks. 'Only by omission. That's no better.'

'There are degrees. And I didn't deny that I know you.'

'I didn't think our...'

'Fling? Liaison? One-night stand? Random—'

'Our private life was any of his business. And anyway, you don't know me. Only in the biblical sense.'

Something flickered in those flat, ice-blue eyes, something wild and untamed and a little scary. And then he looked away.

'Apparently so.'

She sucked in a breath and straightened her shoulders. At some point she'd have to tell him she was pregnant, but not here, not now, not like this, and if they were going to have this baby, at some point they *would* need to get to know each other. But, again, not now. Now she had a job to do, and she was going to have to put her feelings on the back burner and resist the urge to run away.

She pulled herself together with effort and straightened her shoulders. 'So, shall we get on with your guided tour? What have you seen?'

'His office. Nothing else, really.'

'Right. Let's start at Reception and work through the route the patients take, and then you can go up to HR. I'll give you a map of the hospital.'

And with any luck her legs wouldn't give way and dump her on the floor before they were done...

'We need to talk.'

There was a lull in the chaos that had been the day so far, and they were alone at the desk, filling in paperwork on the last case. He paused, his pen hovering over the notes.

'We do?'

He was still stinging a little from her rejection back in January, not to mention her denial to James that she knew him, and he'd spent the whole morning so far trying to quell his traitorous body, which seemed to be delighted at her sudden reappearance in his life. In fact she'd been at least half of the reason he'd taken this locum job, on the off-chance that he might run into her again, but now he had it seemed like a profoundly lousy idea, especially since they were going to be working together.

He made himself look at her, forced himself to meet her eyes instead of avoiding them as he had been.

'I wouldn't have thought we had anything to say.'

She flinched a little, but held her ground.

'There's a lot to say.'

'Like why you didn't answer my text?'

He saw her throat bob as she swallowed. 'I didn't get it—not until much later.'

'That's a lie. I saw it on your phone when I sent it so I know it arrived.'

'But *I* didn't see it on my phone. I didn't have time to check until I got home—I was called in to work that morning.'

'Sure you were.'

'Why do you have to think the worst of me? I'm not lying, and it's on record.' She bit her lip, but her eyes looked troubled, and she gave a frustrated little sigh. 'Look, Sam, I don't want to do this here. Can we meet up later? Please?'

He propped himself against the desk, hands rammed in the pockets of his scrubs so he didn't reach out to her, and studied her, trying and failing to read her expression. 'OK,' he conceded finally, massively against his better judgement—although where Kate was concerned he didn't seem to *have* any judgement. 'What time do you finish?'

'Three. You?'

'Technically five, but maybe later. We could go to a pub, I suppose,' he offered grudgingly, but she shook her head.

'No, not a pub. Where are you staying?'

'With James and Connie, but there's no way you're going there.'

She frowned. 'No, definitely not.'

'Where, then?'

She bit her lip again and he felt almost sorry for it. 'My flat?' she offered, sounding as reluctant as him. 'You could come round when you finish. Six o'clock-ish?'

He nodded, relieved that they were going somewhere private. 'OK. Give me the address. Oh, and you'd better give me your phone number again in case I'm held up.'

She nodded, and he couldn't help noticing that she looked wary. Almost—hunted?

'Kate, I get that it was a one-night stand,' he muttered, relenting a little. 'I'm cool with that, and I didn't want any more. I don't,' he added, feeling a twinge of guilt at the lie. 'But you could have answered my text.'

'And said what? Thanks for a great night, sorry I missed the chance to say goodbye when you *sneaked out of the hotel room*?'

'I hardly sneaked—'

'You could have woken me up. You could have just asked me—' She broke off and gave another impatient little sigh and pulled the phone out of her pocket. 'Tell me your number.'

She keyed it in, and his phone vibrated in his pocket. 'OK, I've got it,' he said, and put it into his contacts. 'I'll call you when I finish, give you a head's up.'

'I'll text you my address. It's the top-floor flat. Number three.'

She hesitated a moment, then turned away, leaving him puzzled and a tiny bit intrigued.

She probably wanted to set the ground rules for their relationship, he decided.

Well, that was easy. Hands off. He could do that.

He went back to work.

CHAPTER THREE

S_HE STOOD AT the bedroom window and watched a car pull up outside the house right on the dot of six, and she ran downstairs and opened the front door.

'You found me OK, then?' she said, stating the obvious, but he just gave her a quizzical smile.

'It's hardly rocket science. I've got a satnav.'

Of course he had. Her stomach in knots, she turned away without another word and led him up the narrow, winding staircase that rose to the top floor of the big Victorian townhouse. Once upon a time it had been elegant. Now it had a run-down feel to it, as if it had been a long time since anyone had truly loved it, and she wondered what Sam with his privileged upbringing would think of it. Not that it mattered.

She'd left the door at the top standing open, and he followed her in, past the cramped kitchen into the sitting room that seemed suddenly much smaller with him in it. It was shabby without the chic, but thanks to the last two hours of frantic activity it was at least clean and tidy, apart from the shelves in the alcoves, which were overflowing with books.

'Drink?' she asked, stalling for time, and he nodded.

'Yeah, thanks—I could murder a coffee.'

No chance. She waved at the sofa. 'Make yourself at home. The kettle's hot, I won't be a moment.'

She closed the kitchen door, sucked in a deep breath and tried to steady herself, to slow the heart that was lodged in her throat.

'You can do this,' she whispered, but she didn't know how, didn't know if she would ever be ready to say the words that would change their lives for ever.

He looked around, trying to get a handle on her character, but there was nothing to give her away.

No ornaments or photos, the tired furniture showing evidence of a long, hard life, but at least it was clean.

He studied the books, but all they proved was that she had eclectic taste.

Biographies, travel guides, romance, crime, historical sagas, a collection of cookery books—and a small children's book, dog-eared and tatty but presumably much loved.

What did she want to talk about?

He heard her come back in and turned, searching her face and finding no clues. She set the tray down and handed him a mug.

He glanced at it, then sniffed it experimentally. 'Is this tea?'

'Sorry, I ran out of coffee. Anyway, you've been drinking it all day and tea's better for you.'

That made him blink. 'Are you trying to mother me?' he asked, mildly astonished because she hadn't seemed like the sort of woman who'd hold back on anything if she wanted it, far less advise anyone else to, but he must have hit a sore spot because she sucked in her breath and looked away.

'Don't be ridiculous. Why would I do that?'

'Search me. Kate, what did you want to talk about?'

She met his eyes, looked away briefly and seemed to brace herself before she spoke again.

'OK. I do have coffee, but I can't cope with the smell of it at the moment.' Her eyes locked with his, defiant and yet fearful, and her next words took the wind right out of his sails.

'I'm pregnant.'

There. She'd said it.

And from the look on his face, it was the last thing Sam had been expecting to hear.

He turned away, put the mug down on the mantelpiece and gripped the shelf so hard his knuckles turned white.

'How?'

His voice was harsh, brittle, as if he was holding himself together by sheer willpower. She could understand that. She'd been doing it ever since she'd found out, and she felt as if she hadn't breathed properly for days.

'We ran out of condoms, remember? That last time.' The time she'd assured him it was safe. The irony of it wasn't lost on her.

She saw him frown in the mirror. 'But you told me it was OK. You said you were on the Pill—or is that another lie?'

'No! I am on it—or I was. But I went down with norovirus right after work and I couldn't even keep water down for days.'

'You're sure? You're not just…'

'I'm quite sure. And trust me, I'm no more thrilled about it than you are.'

'You know nothing about me or my feelings,' he

growled, lifting his head and meeting her eyes in the mirror. 'Nothing.'

'I know you don't mind breaking rules so long as you don't get caught.'

He held her eyes for a moment, then looked away. 'Not that one. I never, ever break that one. I'm fanatical about contraception.'

'Apparently not fanatical enough.'

She sighed and reached out a hand to him, then dropped it in defeat. 'Sam, we can't fight. This isn't going to go away just because we don't like it.'

He rammed a hand through his hair and turned to face her. 'Are you *absolutely sure* it's mine?'

She felt her skin blanch. 'Of course I'm sure—'

'Really? Because you fell into bed with me readily enough and you were already apparently on the Pill.'

'Which makes me just as much of a slut as you. If I remember rightly, you had condoms in your wallet just in case.'

He winced, and she nodded. 'There. Not nice, is it? But it's the truth. Neither of us knew anything about the other, and everything we thought we knew was lies. But we've made a baby, Sam,' she said, her voice starting to crack. 'I'm eleven weeks pregnant and we have to make a decision—'

His head jerked back as if she'd slapped him, and she saw him swallow. 'You want to get rid of it?'

She blanched, the words were so blunt, but her feelings were so confused, so chaotic she couldn't analyse them. 'No— I don't know. All I really want is for this never to have happened, and believe me, if I could wind the clock back it never would, but it has, and...'

'So why didn't you contact me? Why leave it to now to make a decision? It doesn't make sense.'

'I didn't know! I only found out two days ago.'

'I don't believe that. You must have noticed your cycle—'

'I don't have a cycle. I take it continuously, and I did a pregnancy test after the bug, which was negative—and anyway, I didn't have your details. I'd deleted them from my phone and I had no way of contacting you. I didn't know who you were. All I knew was your first name.'

'Are you sure? Because you didn't look surprised to see me this morning, which makes me think you knew who I was all along.'

'I didn't! I didn't have an inkling until a few days ago when James said something about you working as our locum might mean you got the boat off their drive, and I started to wonder then, but he didn't mention your name and I didn't know for sure until I saw you. How was I supposed to know? You hadn't told me you were a doctor. You hardly told me anything…'

She tailed off, finally running out of words, of breath, of any hope of an easy resolution, and just like that her emotions imploded. She felt her eyes prickle, felt the sob lodge in her chest as the fear and loneliness and desolation of her childhood rose up to swamp her.

'I can't do this, Sam,' she said, pressing her eyelids together to stem the tears but instead squeezing them out so that they trickled down her cheeks, laying her soul bare. 'I can't do it. I don't know how. I just want it all to go away…'

How could he not have seen this coming?

It was so obvious now, but it hadn't even been on his

radar when she'd said they needed to talk. Perhaps it should have been.

God, he'd been such a fool! He wished he'd had the sense to walk away, right after they'd come out of the restaurant—or sooner, before he'd started the conversation that had ended up with them making a baby, of all things—

She'd turned her back on him but she was too late. He'd seen the fear in her eyes, the tears she'd tried so hard not to shed, and he wanted to comfort her, but how, when he himself was screaming inside? What could he say that would make it better? Nothing.

Nothing at all, because nothing short of a miscarriage or termination was going to make this go away, and even then they'd both carry the scars for the rest of their lives.

'Kate—'

He couldn't go on, didn't know what to say, but he couldn't just stand there watching her shoulders shake as the sobs she couldn't hold back racked her body. His feet moved without his permission, his hands coming up to turn her into his arms, cradling her against his chest.

He felt her crumple, felt the fight go out of her as she sagged against him, and he stood there and held her and wondered what kind of a god had done this to him, to them.

To give him his dream, everything he'd always wanted, everything he and Kerry had planned, but with a woman he didn't know, didn't love, while the woman he loved lay cold in her grave—

'Come and sit down,' he said gruffly, leading her to the sofa and half sitting, half falling into it with her still in his arms while the pain exploded in his head.

He hadn't realised he could still hurt, that anything else could possibly have touched that deep, dark place inside him left by Kerry's death, but this had ripped it right open and he felt as if he was drowning in pain.

She didn't know how long they'd sat there. All she'd been aware of was the tension in him, the rigidly controlled breathing, the reflexive stroke of his thumb against her shoulder.

What was he thinking? He hadn't said anything, and she had no idea what was going on in his head. As she'd rather cruelly pointed out that morning—was that all? It seemed a lifetime ago—they only knew each other in the biblical sense. Not nearly well enough to read his mind.

She shifted, easing away from him, and his arm dropped from her shoulder as she disentangled herself and stood up, pacing to the window and staring out, arms wrapped tight around her waist, holding herself together.

At some point during the evening it had started to rain, and she watched the water dribbling down the rippled Victorian glass and wondered how to break the agonising silence that stretched between them.

'So what now?' he asked, his voice a little rough, gritty with emotion as he broke the silence for her.

Now? 'I have no idea,' she said woodenly. 'I'm still coming to terms with it. I haven't really had time to think.'

'Does anyone else know?'

'Only Annie Shackleton.'

'The woman I'm covering for?'

She nodded. 'She sort of guessed. It was the coffee thing. I usually drink gallons of it and I can't bear it now. She said it as a joke, but it turned out not to be so funny.'

Understatement of the century.

She heard him move, saw his reflection in the window as he crossed the room and stood beside and behind her. His hands were rammed in his back pockets, his posture defensive. 'So what do you want to do? You said you can't do it—was that just fear talking, or do you really mean it?'

She couldn't see his eyes, and she realised she needed to, so she turned and looked up at him and then wished she hadn't, because she could see the faint sheen of unshed tears, and there was a muscle jumping in his jaw, as if he was hanging by a thread.

She reached up a hand and touched his face, and he flinched and turned his head away. Her hand fell back to her side and she bit her lip.

'What do you want me to do?' she asked, her voice sounding hollow to her ears.

He gave a soft huff of something that wasn't quite laughter and turned back to her, his eyes dry now and oddly devoid of emotion.

'You really want to know? I want you to evaporate, never to have existed. I want that I hadn't gone into that pub, that you hadn't come in, that I hadn't talked to you, taken for dinner, taken you back to my hotel and spent the night getting *biblical* with you. But I can't have what I want. I can only have what is, and what is is that you're pregnant with my child, and like it or not—and I'm guessing neither of us do—we're going to have a baby. So I will do what I have to do. I'll stand by you, and I'll be a part of my child's life for ever, because I don't have a choice.

'I can't walk away, I can't live the rest of my life pretending this hasn't happened, and although I can't stop you having a termination if that's what you really want, I'll do everything in my power to try and convince you not to. I'll even bring it up on my own, if that's what it takes, but I will do the right thing, by you and by my child.'

Kate stared at him in astonishment. 'You'd do that? Bring the baby up on your own?'

'Of course—and so would you, if you had any decency.'

She felt panic fill her at the thought, an overwhelming dread that swamped her. She reached behind and gripped the window frame, propping herself against it for support.

'Sam, I—I couldn't. I have no idea how to look after a child. How to mother one. I don't even know what a mother *is*!' she said, her voice rising in panic. 'What if I failed? What if I did something dreadful and damaged the child for life? What if one day I realised I just couldn't do it and walked away and left her there—what then? What would happen to that child?'

'I would be there,' he said firmly. 'Always. Every day. And you wouldn't fail—'

'How do you *know* that? You can't know that. And when I do, the damage—do you know what it's like when your mother walks away? Leaves you, five years old, in the care of total strangers? Just—leaves you?'

She's talking about herself. Dear God—

'Kate...'

He reached for her, drew her shaking body into his arms, cradled her against his chest. The tight band around it loosened, easing as he held her, the contact somehow freeing him from the grip of helplessness that had taken hold of him when she'd told him he was going to be a father.

Because he wasn't helpless now. He didn't want this, but he could do it, and he *would* do it, because that was who he was. OK, he'd broken rules, but never the important ones until now, and at the end of the day he'd always known his duty and carried it out without question. And he knew his duty now.

'We'll be OK,' he told her. 'Somehow, we'll find a way. I'll look after you—'

'I don't need looking after!' she protested, pushing away from him. 'It's not me I'm worried about! It's the baby! I can't let anything bad happen to it—'

'And nor can I. So we'll look after it together—'

'How? You're only here for a few months, a year at the most, and then you'll be gone. You'll leave me—'

'I won't leave you.'

'They all say that, but they all do, in the end. Everybody leaves me—'

'But I won't. I won't leave you, Kate. I'll take you both with me, if I have to, if I can't find a job locally. We'll go somewhere you're happy to be, and we'll manage.'

She looked at him as if he was insane. 'You're talking as if we'd be married!' she said, and he felt the shapeless dread settle in a solid lump in his chest.

'Maybe we should be,' he said carefully, and to his surprise she just laughed and turned back to the window, staring out into the night.

'You're crazy,' she said, but her voice had a little shake in it and he could see the tears trickling down her cheeks.

'Maybe. Or maybe I'm just being honest. We need to be together to do this, and maybe that's the best way.'

She lifted a hand and swiped the tears away. 'You're getting ahead of yourself. You don't know me, Sam. I'm impossible to live with.'

He gave a short, mirthless chuckle. 'I've been in the army for years, Kate. Believe me, I can live with anyone.'

Anyone except Kerry, the only person I want to live with...

He slammed the door on his grief and reached out a

hand, laying it gently on her shoulder. 'Baby steps, Kate. Why don't we start by getting to know each other, hmm?'

She shrugged his hand off her shoulder. 'It's not that easy—'

'Why not? How do you know? You don't know, and nor do I. But we had fun that night, Kate. It wasn't just about the sex. We talked, and we laughed—and it felt real. It felt good.'

So good they'd ended up in bed for a night he still, even now, couldn't get out of his head. The night that had resulted in this baby.

He put his hand back on her shoulder. 'We have to try. At the very least, we have to try.'

He felt the muscles in her shoulder bunch, then relax as the fight went out of her. 'OK,' she said. 'One week. I'll give it one week, and if I don't think I can do it...'

'Then we'll talk again,' he promised, vowing that there was no way they'd get to that point. If pregnancy hadn't been on his radar earlier, it was now, and there was no way on God's earth he was going to let her do anything to harm their child. He'd just have to make it work.

But—one week? How the hell could he turn this around in a week? His stomach growled, dragging him back to the here and now, and he rammed his hands into his pockets.

'Have you eaten?'

'Eaten?' She shook her head. 'No. I'm not hungry.'

'You have to eat—'

'The baby's fine!' she snapped, spinning round and glaring at him, and he arched a brow.

'I'm not worried about the baby, I'm thinking about you. You've been working all day, the flat smells of furniture polish and bleach so I know you've been cleaning it ever since you came home, and I haven't eaten either. So—takeaway, or go and find somewhere to eat?'

She looked at the window. 'We'll get soaked.'

'No, we won't. The car's right outside and we'll go somewhere with parking.'

'Isn't Connie going to be expecting you for supper?'

'No. I told them I'd make my own arrangements.'

For an age she stood there, staring out at the rain streaming down the windowpane, and then she nodded.

'OK. But I'm paying for myself.'

He opened his mouth to argue, shut it again and held her coat for her. She took it, resisting even that gesture, and shrugged into it. 'Come on, then, if we must.'

He took her to the Chinese restaurant on the front, partly because he knew she liked it and partly because he knew it wasn't expensive and he had a feeling he'd lose if he tried to argue with her about the bill.

'This is where we started,' she said bleakly as they were shown to the same table, and he found a smile for her. It wasn't much of one, but it was a start, and frankly it felt like a miracle that he could smile at all.

'So it is,' he murmured, and took her hand, running his thumb over the back of it in a soothing sweep. 'It'll be OK, Kate,' he told her softly. 'We'll make it OK.'

He just wished he could see how.

By mutual agreement, they didn't tell anyone.

Annie knew, of course, but she didn't know who the father was, and Kate didn't tell her. It didn't seem appropriate, really, to share any more than she already had about a baby whose fate hung in the balance.

The days ticked by, but they didn't work together, not after that first day. James, she imagined, was keeping them apart because Sam was, as he'd put it, 'emotionally broken'.

How? Why?

She found herself more and more curious about that, about what had broken him so badly that the news of her pregnancy had almost reduced him to tears. Because he wasn't a crying man, she was sure of that. He'd been in the army for years, he'd said. Men in the army didn't shed tears lightly.

So—what had happened? Or who?

But it never seemed like a good time to ask something so sensitive, and so they carried on, passing in the corridors, their shifts barely coinciding, and in the evenings he came to her flat and they talked about anything but the baby and her childhood and whatever it was that had broken him, and the days ticked by.

They took it in turns to cook and she learned that he was a good cook, way more house-trained than she was, that he ate whatever was put in front of him and thanked her for cooking it—even though sometimes it was a bit hit and miss.

And he didn't touch her.

Didn't brush against her, didn't kiss her cheek or pat her shoulder or give her a hug or squeeze her hand—nothing. And sometimes, just when she thought he might be going to reach out for her, his eyes went blank and he looked away.

Until she tripped on the stairs.

It was Friday night, and for once they'd finished their shifts at the same time. He'd given her a lift home, picking up a takeaway on the way home, and as she was running up the stairs ahead of him she caught her toe on the worn carpet and fell.

'Ouch—dammit!' She sat down on the stairs, cradling her wrist, flexing it warily, and he hunkered down beside her.

'You OK?'

'Yes, I'm fine,' she said, flexing it again, but it made her gasp and she felt his warm, firm hands take her arm and feel carefully, thoroughly down the bones in her forearm to her wrist.

'Does that hurt?' he asked, but she was so mesmerised by the warmth of his touch that she could hardly feel anything else.

'No. It's OK now—just a bit hyperextended, I think. It'll be fine.'

'You need ice on it—'

'No ice.'

He picked up her bag and the post she'd dropped and scattered all over the stairs, shooed her up the last half-flight and raided the little freezer compartment in her fridge. 'Peas—they'll do. Got a sandwich bag?'

She gave up any hope of independence and pointed. 'In the drawer.'

Five minutes later she was sitting on the sofa with her arm resting on a cushion, a small bag of peas wrapped in a tea towel perched on her wrist, a loaded plate in her lap and a steaming mug of tea by her side.

'If you've put sugar in that I'll kill you,' she said mildly, and he chuckled.

'I don't think you're suffering from shock.'

She sighed. 'No. Just terminal clumsiness and stupidity.'

'Actually the carpet's worn on that tread.'

'Sam, it's been worn since I moved in three years ago. It's hardly a novelty.'

He grunted, plonked himself down beside her, adjusted the peas on her wrist and picked up his own tea.

Not coffee. In deference to her nausea, he didn't drink it if she was around, which, did he but know it, earned him a shedload of brownie points.

'Can you manage to eat that?'

'What are you going to do, feed me? Of course I can manage.'

'Just asking,' he said, sounding mock-aggrieved, and she chuckled and picked up her fork with the uninjured hand.

'Don't worry, Sam. I won't starve. It's not in my nature.'

He grunted and dug into his food, then took the plates out and came back and sat down, her letters in his hand.

'Want me to open your post for you?'

She felt herself stiffen. 'Why would you do that?' she asked, suddenly wary, and as if he realised he rolled his eyes.

'To save your wrist? I wasn't going to read it—just open it and give it to you, but that's fine, go ahead and struggle one-handed,' he said, and dumped it on her lap, but it slid to the floor at her feet.

She stared down at it lying there, feeling silly now for making a fuss. 'Sorry. I just have issues with boundaries.'

'A controlling ex?' he asked, and she laughed bitterly.

'No. Just a boy who didn't respect my privacy and went out of his way to make my life difficult.' A boy who'd hated and resented her and ruined the only decent chance at a family life she'd ever had…

He nodded, then picked the post up again and handed it to her. 'Don't worry, your boundaries are safe with me. I just didn't want you to hurt yourself.'

She handed it back—as an olive branch? Maybe. 'I'm sorry. Would you?'

And then she instantly regretted it, because the first

one out of the envelopes was her ultrasound appointment, and it was so obviously an appointment letter that he couldn't help but notice.

'My twelve-week scan,' she said, because to say nothing wasn't an option. 'I saw the midwife on Tuesday. She said it would be soon.'

There was a second of silence before he spoke. 'Can I come?'

Her hesitation was longer than his, her fear almost suffocating her because she knew once she'd had the scan it would all become so real that there would be no hiding from it. 'I don't know…'

'That's fine. Just let me know when you've worked it out. I'd like to, if I may, but I fully appreciate it's your decision.'

Did he? She had a feeling the words were choking him, but there was nothing she could do about that. She wasn't at all convinced she wanted him there. She didn't want to be there, either, but she had no choice. He, on the other hand…

'Is this just so you know how old it is, so you can rule yourself out as the father?' she asked, suddenly uncertain of his motives, but his hissed expletive set her straight.

'I thought you'd know me better than that by now?' he growled.

'No, I don't,' she said sadly, 'and you don't know me, either, but you're talking about us living together and bringing up a baby, and all the while we're dancing round each other at arm's length and avoiding any kind of contact and it just feels so cold and remote and unemotional and I just can't read you when you're keeping such a distance. I don't know who the hell you are, Sam, so how can I know if I can trust you?'

'I was just giving you space,' he said quietly, after her words had hung in the air for an age.

'Me, or you?'

'Both, maybe,' he admitted, and she searched his eyes.

'Maybe I don't want space.'

His breath hissed out in a sharp sigh.

'Kate, don't say that. It's hard enough keeping my distance as it is. That's why I've been holding you at arm's length, because I don't trust myself around you, at least not until we know where we stand. We really don't need to add the confusion of a physical relationship to this equation, it's complicated enough.'

She sighed. 'I know, and I do understand that, but it just seems so—lonely,' she said plaintively, despising her weakness but sick to death of the endless distance between them.

But then he gave a quiet sigh and buckled. 'Come here,' he said softly, and taking the letter out of her hand, he wrapped an arm around her shoulders and eased her up against his side.

She could feel the solid warmth of his body, smell the scent of his skin and a trace of the aftershave that had haunted her all week, bringing back so many memories of the night they'd met, and she wanted to burrow into him and stay there.

'This doesn't change anything,' he murmured, the sound rumbling through his chest.

'That's a shame,' she said, before she could stop herself, and she felt rather than heard the soft chuckle.

'Yeah, it is, but it's not a good idea, Kate, not with so much at stake. We need to take our time with this.'

'I thought you'd want to hustle me into bed and sweet-talk me into keeping the baby,' she said, almost disappointed, and this time the laugh was a sad huff of despair.

'You really don't think a lot of me, do you, if you think I'd sink so low that I'd use sex to manipulate your feelings?'

'Most men would.'

'I'm not most men. I'm just me, trying to do what's right for all three of us, and frankly I don't know what that is. I feel as if I'm groping my way along a narrow ledge in the dark, and it's scaring the hell out of me.'

He sounded so lost, so lonely that she lifted her hand and cupped his cheek, feeling the rasp of his stubble against her palm and longing for him to kiss her, to bring back the closeness she'd felt on that January night.

'I swear I didn't do this on purpose.'

He turned his head slightly and kissed her hand, sending shivers of need through her. 'I know you didn't. It's not your fault. It's mine. I'm the one that broke my golden rule, not you.'

'It's not all your fault—'

'Yes, it is. It's all down to me, and it's my responsibility to fix it and I don't know how right now.'

'I really did think it was safe,' she told him, hating that he was taking the blame when all the time it was just a wicked twist of fate. 'And I know this is hurting you.'

His body stiffened fractionally and although he didn't move she felt the gulf open between them again. 'Why would you think that?'

'Your reaction? I'd expected you to be angry when I told you, but you were more upset.'

'I was just shocked.'

'No, you weren't. It was more than that, much more, as if I'd hit a raw nerve. And before you started James told me to steer clear of you because you were emotionally broken.'

This time he went rigid, his body unyielding, frozen. 'Why would he say that?'

'I have no idea. That's all he said, but I have a gift for choosing the wrong men. Maybe he was just trying to protect us both, but he didn't say what from.'

He disentangled himself, getting to his feet and walking to the window, his back straight, hands rammed in his pockets as he stared out into the night, and she watched his reflection in the glass and held her breath for what felt like an age.

'He's right, I suppose,' he said eventually, his voice expressionless. 'My fiancée died two years ago, just before our wedding.'

For the first few seconds shock held her rigid, then she stumbled to her feet and crossed over to him, wrapping her arms around him and holding him tight.

'Oh, Sam, I'm so, so sorry...'

She crushed down the tears, the sobs. This wasn't her grief, it was his, and she needed to be here for him. But he didn't want her. His body was held rigid, but she didn't let go. She couldn't let go, couldn't abandon him now when it was all so raw because of her forcing him into a corner and making him drag it all back up out of the past.

'I'm sorry,' she said again, her voice a whisper in the silence, and then at last he moved, as the tension eased out of him on a ragged sigh, turning to haul her hard against his chest.

They didn't speak, just stood there holding each other as their emotions came under control again. And then he let her go, easing away a fraction, cradling her face in his hands as he stared down and searched her eyes, his own empty and desolate.

'Don't pity me, Kate,' he warned softly. 'I don't want

your pity. It's not about you. It's about me, and it's nothing to do with us, with this—situation we're in.'

She nodded, willing her tears not to overflow now, but it was hard, and she took his hands and lifted them away from her face and went into the kitchen. 'I'll make some more tea,' she said, her voice a little thickened, and she filled the kettle and started to wash up, but her wrist gave a twinge and she gasped.

'Let me do that.'

'It's fine, I can manage.'

'I'm sure you can, but you don't need to. You don't have to prove anything to me—'

'I'm not proving anything to anybody. I'm just washing up. It's hardly going to kill me—'

Her words echoed in the sudden silence, reverberating around them like a tolling bell, and then he swore and headed for the door.

She heard it slam and the sound of his footsteps running down the stairs, and still she didn't breathe. *What had she done? Why had she said that, of all things?*

The last thing she'd meant to do was hurt him with her careless words. It must be horrendous for him being stuck with her when all he wanted was—she didn't even know her name, the woman he'd lost and was still obviously grieving.

'Oh, Sam,' she said softly, and it was only after she heard the outer door close and saw his car drive away that her eyes welled with tears.

Not for herself, but for the lonely, broken man she was in danger of falling in love with, and the nameless woman he'd loved and so cruelly lost.

The wind had strengthened, and it would have made sense to have picked up his coat on the way out, but he didn't care about the cold, or the sting of the sea spray that bit into his cheeks as he strode along the darkened prom. He walked from one end to the other and back again, hands rammed in his pockets as the wind tugged at him, the sound of the sea crashing against the shore drowning out his furious tirade as he vented his anger and grief and frustration.

It was just all so *wrong*, so horribly, horribly wrong, and despite his duty, despite knowing what he had to do, it was only now that he realised the implications of what he'd said to her on Monday when she'd first told him she was pregnant.

He'd virtually promised to marry her, but how could he do it, how could he make those same vows he'd been going to make to Kerry? He couldn't stand there by the altar and wait for the wrong woman to walk down the aisle to him, her body cradling his child.

It should have been Kerry! Kerry, whom he loved with all his heart. Kerry, who should have been walking down the aisle to him...

They'd buried her in the wedding dress she'd never had the chance to wear, and he'd lifted the veil from her face and put the wedding ring on her lifeless finger before he'd kissed her goodbye, so pale, so beautiful. So dead.

He screwed his eyes up to shut out the images, but they wouldn't leave him, and now alongside them was the image of Kate's face, racked with dread and apprehension as she'd told him she was carrying his baby.

There was no place for her there with the images of Kerry, but there she was, intruding on his grief without even trying, trashing everything when he'd just got his life back on an even keel.

Or thought he had, but now he realised he'd been kidding himself; he wasn't over Kerry, hadn't dealt with her death, he'd just been running away, and he was in no way ready to take on the responsibility for another woman and a child.

Which made no difference at all, because he and Kate had both messed up, and now there was an innocent baby to consider who hadn't asked for any of this and didn't care if they were ready or not.

There was nowhere else to run to. It was time to face reality, to put the past behind him and move on.

CHAPTER FOUR

SHE WAS ALONE in the locker room the next morning when he walked in and she turned to him, racked with guilt.

'Sam, I'm sorry—'

'About last night—'

They spoke together, and he ran a hand through his hair and let out a short huff of something that could possibly have been laughter. Or despair.

'I'm sorry,' she said, before he could speak again, because the look on his face had haunted her all night. 'Sorry I said that, sorry I pushed you to tell me about her, just—I'm sorry. So sorry. I had no idea—I would never have—'

'Forget it. You didn't make it any worse, Kate, it is what it is. And I'm sorry I left like that. I shouldn't have walked out, I just needed some air.'

She nodded her understanding and then, just because she had to do something other than stand there, she opened her locker and turned back, his coat in her hand.

'You left this behind.'

'I know. I got more fresh air than I bargained for,' he said wryly, taking the coat. 'Thanks. How's your wrist?'

'Oh.' She glanced at it. She hadn't even given it a thought she'd been so distressed. 'It's fine. I'd forgotten.'

'The power of frozen peas,' he said, his mouth tilting

into the beginnings of a smile as he lobbed his sweater into the locker and turned the key, and she hauled in a shaky breath.

'Well, I'd better get on,' she said.

'Yeah, me too. I'll see you later. How about a coffee, if we can find time?'

He wanted to spend time with her? She felt her shoulders drop in relief, and she smiled at him. 'Yes, that would be good. Where are you working?'

'I think I'm in Resus.'

'Oh. So am I. James must have run out of ways of keeping us apart.'

A fleeting frown crossed his face. 'Do you seriously think he's been doing that?'

'Well, one of you has. It certainly wasn't me.'

'Nor me.' His mouth flickered in a smile. 'Ah, well, I'm sure he'll get over it. Shall we go and face the fray?'

He held the door for her, and she walked past him, close enough to smell the mint on his breath and see the tiny cut where he'd nicked his skin shaving. She wanted to reach up and kiss it better, but thought better of it and made herself keep moving.

It was busy all morning, without time to draw breath never mind take a break, and then just when they were thinking about grabbing a coffee it all kicked off again.

'Adult resus call, cardiac arrest, ETA five minutes,' a disembodied voice announced over the PA, and she went to the desk to find out more.

'Twenty-year-old male, no known history. He was playing football,' she was told. She turned towards Resus and nearly bumped into Sam.

He was standing right behind her, his face a mask, and she took his arm and moved him away from the desk.

'Are you OK?' she asked softly.

'Why wouldn't I be?'

The eyes were still blank, as if he was in lockdown, and she gave a tiny, questioning shrug. 'I don't know, you tell me.'

His eyes snapped to life. 'I'm fine. Let's just do it, please?'

There was no time to discuss it further, because the doors from the ambulance bay flew open and their patient was wheeled in, a paramedic kneeling over him doing chest compressions.

Sam was straight into it, taking over CPR from the paramedics as they wheeled the patient into Resus, listening to their report, firing the odd question, issuing instructions in a calm, clear voice as he delegated tasks to the hastily reassembled team.

James was in there too, working on another critical patient, and he lifted his head and frowned.

'Want to swap?' he asked Sam, but Sam shook his head.

'I'm fine.'

'OK. If you change your mind—'

'I won't.'

So it wasn't just her imagination. There was something wrong—something to do with his fiancée's death? Whatever, James was there in the background, so she stopped fretting and concentrated on doing her job for their patient. Frankly, he needed everyone's concentration, and even so she didn't think they'd save him, but Sam refused to stop, and so she and the rest of the team shrugged and kept going, too.

They'd been working on him for thirty minutes without success when James came over, his own patient now stabilised.

'Do you think you should call it, Sam?' he murmured, but Sam shook his head.

'No. Not giving up.'

Just that, but there was a world of pain and resolution in his terse reply, and James just nodded and took over chest compressions, letting Sam call the shots as he stayed there, ready to take over if he did crack, but he didn't.

It seemed for ever before the young man's heart finally restarted, by which time he'd been down for fifty-five minutes and they had a senior cardiologist and a team from CCU standing by to take over. Only then did Sam step back, his face drained.

James laid a hand on his shoulder.

'Good call, Sam, well done. Kate, you two go for coffee now, I'll hand over and talk to the parents,' James said softly, and she wheeled Sam out into the fresh air, waiting as he stood for a long moment, hands rammed in his pockets, hauling in air.

'OK now?' she asked when he let the air out on a long ragged sigh, and he nodded.

'Yes, I am now we've got him back. I just wasn't going to let him go without a fight.'

'No, I realised that. Come on, let's get you some coffee.'

He nodded again and walked with her round the outside of the building to the café.

'Stay here, I'll get it,' she said, and went in and ordered a coffee for him and a bottle of water for herself, added a double chocolate muffin and carried it out to him, her mind tumbling with questions she couldn't ask.

He was leaning against the side of the building, one foot propped up on the wall, arms folded, and he shrugged away from the wall and crossed over to her, taking the coffee from her. 'Sorry, I shouldn't have let you go in there. I know it makes you feel queasy.'

'Actually it was fine. It's getting better. Want to sit outside? It's peaceful but the benches might be a bit damp.'

'I'm sure we'll cope. Is that muffin for me or are you going to make me watch you eat it?'

'I had thought we'd share it,' she said, turning her head and looking up at him, and he smiled slowly, his eyes crinkling slightly at the corners, the tension receding.

'Thank you.'

'It's only half a muffin.'

'I didn't mean the muffin.'

'Oh.' *Then what...?* 'Here, this bench looks OK.' She sat down, patted the space beside her and he perched on the edge and propped his elbows on his knees, the coffee dangling from his fingertips as he stared vacantly at the floor. Seeing what?

'Want to talk about it?' she asked, when he'd sat there for several seconds without moving.

'Not really. Nothing to say.'

'You saved his life, Sam. That's not nothing.'

'I wasn't talking about Tom. And he's not out of the woods yet by a long way.'

'No, I don't suppose he is, but at least he has a chance now, thanks to you.'

They fell silent, and she watched him as he fought some inner battle and finally gave in.

'We were due to get married three weeks after I came home on leave from Afghanistan,' he said, his voice sounding rusty and unused. 'Kerry emailed me, full of all the things we had to do before the wedding, bubbling with excitement, telling me she couldn't wait to see me, but there was an army officer waiting for me when I landed.'

Kate felt her heart thud, her breath jamming in her throat as he went on.

'Her family had raised the alarm the night before because they couldn't get hold of her, and she was found dead in our flat the morning I landed. No warning, no symptoms, nothing. The post-mortem revealed an undiagnosed heart condition that had led to a cardiac arrest. And just like that, it was all gone. My whole life—all our plans for our wedding, the family we were going to start—everything, wiped out when her heart stopped beating.'

And if you'd been there, you might have saved her...

Sam took a long pull on his coffee, wiped his mouth on the back of his hand and leant back with a sigh. 'If only I'd been there, Kate,' he said softly, as if she'd spoken out loud. 'If only I'd come home a day earlier, or it had happened a day later, I might have saved her. I could have kept her going, like I kept Tom going, until her heart had restarted, but I never got the chance.'

She felt her eyes well with tears. 'Oh, Sam. No wonder you couldn't let him go,' she said softly. 'Would you ever have given up on him?'

He shrugged. 'I don't know. Maybe, when I couldn't go on any longer? When the team had deserted me, and James had dragged me off his body? I don't know. Luckily we didn't have to find out. So, are we eating that muffin or are you just going to pull it to pieces?'

She looked down at it, the paper case shredded, a big chunk of the cake broken away in her fingers. She took the chunk, handed the rest to him and swiped the crumbs away impatiently. 'Here, you eat it. I've had far too much cake recently as it is. My clothes are all getting tight.'

'Is that just from cake, or could it be the baby?'

'Maybe. I would have thought it was too soon, but—possibly.'

'When's your scan?'

'Monday. It's at eight in the morning.'

'Do you want me there?'

She turned and searched his face, wondering how he could bear to do this, how he could even look at her after what he'd told her about Kerry's death. 'Do you still want to come?'

'I do, but I thought you didn't want me there.'

'I wasn't sure last night. It seemed odd, as if you were a total stranger, but now, since you've told me about Kerry, let me in a bit, I feel as if I know more about you, about where you're coming from on this. Enough at least to know that even though you obviously wanted a family, having a baby with me isn't something that you would have signed up to in a million years, and that you deserve a say in what happens to it.'

'Is that still in the balance?'

She looked away, her heart pounding suddenly. 'I don't know. So—will you come? I'm not sure I want you in with me, but—maybe, just in case…?'

Something a little desolate flickered in his eyes, and then he nodded. 'I'll be there. I said I would, and I don't break my promises.'

He pulled his watch out of his pocket, glanced at it and swore. 'Come on, we need to get back. I've got a shed-load of paperwork to do for Tom.'

He drained his coffee, crumpled up the muffin case and lobbed it and the cup into the bin.

* * *

'Do you need to debrief?'

Sam sighed quietly and swung the chair round so he could see James. 'Why does *everyone* think I need to talk about it?'

James dropped into a chair and tilted his head on one side. 'Everyone?'

'Well—Kate, anyway.'

'Ah. Yes. Kate. How well *do* you know her?'

Well enough to make a baby.

'Hardly at all. I met her the night I stayed over to see the boat guy. I'd checked into a hotel, went for a drink, she was in the pub. We had a meal together.'

James gave him the unnervingly level stare that was his trademark, and Sam held it with effort.

'She's a nice girl,' his friend said quietly. 'She's got a ridiculously kind heart and appalling judgement, which is a lousy combo. She doesn't always make good decisions.'

No. She hadn't done that weekend, anyway, or they wouldn't be in this—no. Not mess. Situation. To call it a mess wasn't fair to the baby, and didn't really sum up the full implications. He wasn't sure 'situation' did, either, but he wasn't getting into any of that with James.

'She is a nice girl. She said you'd been keeping us apart. And that you'd told her I was broken. Cheers for that.'

James winced. 'Ah, yes. That. I was just—'

'Warning her off?'

'She's—vulnerable. And she's been hurt badly in the past. A married man, the archetypal love rat, amongst others.'

He winced. 'Did she know he was married?'

'No. She had no idea, and she was devastated. Like I

said, she's a lousy judge of character where men are concerned, and she had a troubled childhood, too. Life's been pretty crap for her, really. She's had a lot to deal with.'

'So I gathered, but haven't we all?' he said, making a mental note to delve more into her past. 'You, me, Connie. We've all lost someone we loved.'

'I guess so, but that was different. We haven't been betrayed, and, anyway, you're still grieving so a complicated person like Kate is the last thing you need.' James stood up and laid a hand on his shoulder. 'You know, you don't have to eat out every night. You're more than welcome to join us. Connie was complaining she wasn't seeing enough of you.'

He gave a soft laugh. 'Early days yet. She'll soon be sick of the sight of me. I'll be around tomorrow. I'm off all day, I thought I'd work on the boat.'

'OK. Just…'

'Just?'

'Be careful with Kate. I know you're seeing her, you can't keep anything private in a hospital no matter how discreet you are, but I don't want to see either of you get hurt.'

Too late. In just six months, God willing, he and Kate would have a baby. Too late to worry about not getting hurt. The repercussions were off the Richter scale.

'Don't worry, James,' he lied, wondering why the words didn't choke him. 'We're taking it nice and slowly.' Now the damage was done…

James grunted, patted his shoulder again and went out, and Sam went back to work.

'James warned me not to hurt you today.'

Kate blinked and turned towards him, vegetable knife in hand. 'Really?'

'Yeah. I told him what you'd said about me being broken, and—well, basically he justified it by telling me that you have crap judgement where men are concerned and you had a crap childhood and don't mess with you.'

She sighed crossly and went back to hacking up the carrots. 'He really is the soul of discretion. I don't know where he gets his nerve.'

Sam laughed and hugged her, then took the knife off her and shouldered her gently out of the way. 'He's all right. He means well. I think he's very fond of you. What are you making, by the way?'

'A stir fry—and I doubt that he's fond of me, more likely worried I'll cause trouble.' She sat down at the table and let him take over the veg prep, since he was doing such a good job of it. 'So what else did he say about me?'

The knife kept moving. 'Something about a married man—no details, just that he was the archetypal love rat.'

'Hmph. Nicely summed up. He was a locum radiologist, and he—well, let's just say he never mentioned his wife, and when I found out, he moved on to an agency nurse with bigger boobs. The only comforting thing was that at least mine are real.'

That made him laugh, as it was meant to, but he shook his head as well and gave her a wry glance over her shoulder. 'I don't know how you can joke about it. I would have happily killed him for you. And, for what it's worth, there's nothing—*nothing*—wrong with your body. Any of it.'

He looked away before she could read his expression, but his words had left her with a warm glow, and she nursed a secret smile for a moment.

'So how well does James know you?' she asked, and he shrugged and carried on slicing.

'A bit. Connie knows me better, but they were both there for me when it got really tough and I owe them.'

'How did you meet them?'

'At her first husband's funeral. He was a bomb disposal officer, and when Saffy got caught up in a controlled explosion, Joe felt really guilty, and he brought the dog to me. He shouldn't have done it, Saffy should have been shot at the scene, but we cleaned her up, Joe nursed her back to health and everyone kept shtum while he tried to get her brought home.

'And then he got caught in another blast. I was the first medic on the scene, and I watched him bleed out into the sand with not a damn thing I could do about it. His body was flown home with some injured men, and I went to his funeral. Connie was there, obviously, and so was James. He'd known them both for years, introduced them to each other, apparently. Anyway, then she came out to Camp Bastion and worked alongside me to try and make sense of the senseless waste of life. I'm not sure she managed it, or if any of us ever do, but we became friends, and Kerry and I went to their wedding, and when Kerry died they were there for me. Like I said, I owe them.'

'Gosh. No wonder they care so much about you. I haven't got any friends like that. Well, maybe Annie.'

'Shackleton?'

She nodded. 'She's been great since I found out about the baby. Really supportive, but I was there for her when she and Ed were going through a tough time. Do you know he's got the Huntington's gene?'

He frowned over his shoulder. 'Really? But she's pregnant.'

'I know, but he's only a carrier, he won't get it, and they had to have IVF to screen the embryos, which was pretty gruelling. I'm so happy for them. Ed wanted kids so much—well, that's pretty obvious since he's a paediatrician. I guess you and Kerry wanted them, too, from what you've said.'

He stopped slicing, turned towards her and leant back against the worktop, his hands rested on the edge. 'Yeah. Yeah, we did. Me, probably, more than Kerry. It was the driver behind us getting married rather than just carrying on as we were, but as it turns out, she probably wouldn't have survived pregnancy anyway with her heart condition.'

'Oh, Sam.'

She got up and went over to him, putting her arms round him and leaning into him, her head on his chest. 'I'm sorry.'

'Yeah, me, too. It's ironic that I've sort of got my way in a way I would never have imagined.' His arms came round her, and he rested his head on hers. 'I'm sorry I got you into this situation, Kate. I know it's the last thing you want, but I really mean it, I will be here for you, and one thing you can be sure of, I'm not a love rat.'

She nodded, and lifted her head to meet his eyes. They were gentle, full of regret but also sincerity, and she knew she could believe in him. She just wished she could believe in herself.

'I know that.' She kissed his cheek, stepped back and picked up the knife. 'Come on, I'm starving, let's get this food cooked.'

The next day was glorious, so he went out early for a run along the sea wall with only the gulls for company.

He didn't have to worry about Kate, because she was working the morning shift and wanted a quiet afternoon alone—to think about what the next day might bring?

Very likely. He would have done. Which meant he had no excuse not to spend the day tackling the boat as he'd said.

Not that that task wasn't long overdue. Time to have a really, really close look at what he'd bought, and while he was doing that he could try and get his head round how he felt about Kate.

Confused, mostly, although his body wasn't. He was still aching to drag her into his arms at every opportunity, and only an iron determination had stopped him from talking his way into her bed last night, but he needed distance from her until she'd made her decision. If she decided on a termination—

Dammit, he couldn't let her do that. Although he had no idea how to stop her. No right to stop her. That was the really scary thing. And yet, having seen her with patients, he knew she was soft-hearted and filled with the sort of kindness and warmth that made a perfect mother. Maybe she just didn't realise it?

He put it out of his mind and got the tools out that James had more than cheerfully lent him that morning. He was standing on a ladder stripping paint off the wooden hull and trying to assess the condition of the timber when Connie came out. She stood at the bottom of the ladder peering up at him, shielding her eyes from the sun.

'Coffee time,' she said firmly, and he turned off the blowtorch, put the scraper down and joined her on the ground in the litter of paint curls.

'It really is a heap,' she said, eyeing the boat doubtfully. 'Are you sure you can turn it around? Or were you trying to set fire to it? I take it it *is* insured?'

He sighed and dragged a grubby hand through his hair. 'I'm sorry. It was a sort of spur-of-the-moment thing and if I'd know you'd want to move I wouldn't have landed it on you.'

'To be fair to you, we didn't know at that point. You could always just sell it,' she added after a slight pause, and he tried to ignore the hopeful note in her voice. But her bump was growing by the day, and they really did want to move before their second child arrived. And much as he loved it, he had to admit the boat was an eyesore. Not to mention clogging up the drive.

'I'll get rid of it, Connie, I promise, one way or another. They might have room for it in the boatyard now it's spring. Where's Saffy?' he asked, changing the subject.

'James took her out for a walk with Joseph. Come on, I'll make you a nice strong full-fat coffee and you can keep me company while I drink my decaf one. The joys of pregnancy,' she said with a laugh over her shoulder as she led him up the steps to the veranda on the back of the cottage, and he felt a surge of guilt for keeping Kate's pregnancy secret. Not that it was his secret to tell.

'James said you had a bummer of a sticky case yesterday,' she said as she handed him his coffee.

He shrugged and blew on the coffee, taking his time. 'It had a good outcome. He's alive, at least, and under the care of the cardiology team, so he's got a fighting chance now.'

'Are you OK?'

'Yes, I'm fine. Really. Don't worry about me, Connie. I'm a big boy now.'

'I know that. Doesn't stop me worrying. It must have been a bit close to home.'

He wouldn't have taken that from anyone else, but, as he'd told Kate, they'd seen each other through hell.

'Sam?'

He gave a quiet sigh. 'You don't need to protect me, Connie. I'm fine.'

'Are you? You've been looking kind of preoccupied. And—I know you have the right to have fun, to play the field a bit to balance the books, and I'd hate you to grieve for ever, but—don't mess about with Kate, Sam, please?'

He might have known she had an agenda. No sooner did she have him captive, settled on the veranda with his feet up on the rail and a steaming mug of coffee in his hand, than she'd started. He shook his head slowly.

'Why not? We're both adults, she's alone, I'm alone, it's someone to pass the time with—'

'You could pass the time with us. We hardly ever see you.'

'Are you jealous?' he asked, knowing full well she wasn't, and she punched his shoulder lightly.

'Don't be an idiot.' She shifted so she could look him in the eye better. 'Don't hurt her, Sam—'

'Why does everyone feel the need to protect her from me?' he asked, exasperated and racked with guilt.

'Because she ricochets from one disaster to another and she'll fall for you, I know she will. You're just her type—funny, sexy—but you're broken, Sam, you know you are, and she'll end up hurt, all over again. She's a brilliant nurse, but her private life's a nightmare and I can't bear to see her hurt.'

Too late, Connie...

'I'm sure we're both grown up enough to sort out our own salvation,' he said drily, hoping it was true and that tomorrow didn't go disastrously wrong after her scan.

He heard the gate clatter, and knew he had just about five seconds to move before James came and joined in the nagging fest. 'Right, back to the boat,' he said hastily, but he was too slow. His feet hit the floor just as Saffy came racing up the veranda steps and launched herself at him.

'Get *down*, you horrible dog, you have no manners,'

he said mildly, fending her off and rubbing her head affectionately as he stood up to make his escape.

'I see you found the tools,' James said, appearing at the bottom of the steps with Joseph on his shoulders, and Sam sighed inwardly.

'Yeah. Don't worry, Connie's already had a go at me. I'm on it.'

James quirked an eyebrow, but Sam ignored it. He was well aware of the pressure he was under. It didn't need reinforcing, and he had other more important things to worry about.

'Can you do me a favour, while I think about it?' he asked James. 'I need an hour off in the morning for an appointment. Is that OK?'

'Yes, sure—unless you want to swap shifts? I'm doing two to ten today, but Connie's arranged to view a house this afternoon which I really want to see, and she's busy tomorrow, so it would suit me fine to swap.'

'Sure.' It suited him far better, because he'd be able to give his attention to Kate. 'It does mean I won't do any more to the boat this afternoon.'

'I'm sure one more day won't make a difference, Sam. And there's always tomorrow.'

He nodded, knowing full well that Kate was off all day and after the scan they'd have a lot to talk about. She'd given him a week, and it was up tomorrow evening. He had one last day to convince her she could trust him, and there was no way the boat or anything else was getting in the way of that.

CHAPTER FIVE

NOTHING FITTED.

She'd spent the last week working in scrubs, but now she needed something to wear for her scan, and that meant trousers and a top, and none of her jeans went within a mile of doing up.

Well, an inch, at least, but that was bad enough. Too much cake and chocolate, she told herself, because the other reason was still a little unreal and she wasn't ready to face it.

She found some stretchy denim jeggings and a loose top with a long cardi over it, which hid her little bump nicely, to her relief. She didn't want anyone at the hospital to guess. Not yet, not until she knew for sure that she'd go through with it.

She put a scarf on for good measure, wrapping it loosely round her neck so it hung down the front and helped with the disguise. It also covered up the little bulges where she was bursting out of her bra, and she realised she was going to have to go shopping very soon— maybe later today.

Unless…

Her hands flew down to cover the little bump that she could no longer ignore, her fingers curling protectively over it as panic swamped her.

Today was D-day. The day she'd told Sam she'd give him her decision. She'd said that she'd give him a week, and what did she know about him now that she hadn't then? What did she know that made a difference to her ability to cope with this?

More, sure, but enough to base a life together on? *Enough to trust him with her heart?*

Maybe she didn't need to. Maybe she could just trust him to care for the baby with her, to make sure that she didn't go wrong, didn't fail, didn't run away like her mother had.

And if she couldn't? When it came to the crunch, what if she couldn't do it, couldn't bond, couldn't cope? Sam had said he'd have the baby, but what if he realised that he couldn't handle it, and left? Left her, like everyone else, but this time literally holding the baby?

Would it be kinder to her baby not to be brought into a world with so much uncertainty and instability? A world like the one she'd been thrust into at the age of five?

She sucked in a breath, met her eyes in the mirror and looked away, unable even to look at herself any more she was so torn with guilt and self-loathing.

Time to go. She couldn't be late, and it was a ten-minute walk if she hurried. Damn. She shrugged on her coat, picked up her keys and ran downstairs, opening the front door just as Sam lifted his hand to ring the bell.

'You're here,' she said unnecessarily.

'Yes. I've been here ten minutes. I thought you were leaving it a bit late, so I just wanted to check you were OK.'

'I'm fine,' she said, her eyes unable to hold his. 'I'm going to walk.'

'You haven't got time, Kate. That's why I'm here, so you don't have to.'

'We can't go in together! What if we're seen?'

'What of it? What difference does it make?'

None. Everyone must know by now that they were seeing each other, but not in the antenatal department—

'Can we go in through different entrances? Just to… you know.'

He shrugged and opened the car door. 'Sure. Come on. I'll drop you off and meet you in there after I've parked the car.'

She nodded, and he held the door for her—that bone-deep politeness again that had obviously been drummed into him by a mother who hadn't run off and absconded from the task—shut it, and slid in beside her, starting the engine and pulling out without wasting a moment.

Three minutes later he pulled up outside the patient entrance, reached across and squeezed her hand.

'It'll be OK, Kate,' he murmured.

She wished she had his faith. She wanted to hang onto him but she couldn't. She had to do this bit by herself. Sucking in a deep breath, she pulled her hand away, got out of the car and headed for the entrance without a word.

She couldn't look at him.

That worried him. A lot. She'd obviously spent the whole of yesterday and all of the night fretting herself into a blind panic, and now she'd gone in without him.

He hadn't wanted that, but it was her body; he wasn't in any position to argue with her, so he let her go and tried to steady his breathing. He could feel his heart pounding, the need to be in there—to see his child for what might be the only time—overwhelming him.

His emotions were in turmoil. A child had been the last thing on his wish list since Kerry had died, but now, faced with the reality of it, the existence of a baby in his life assumed mammoth proportions and he couldn't believe how much he wanted it.

He got up, pacing to the window, hands rammed deep in his pockets to stop him from wringing them.

Please call me in. Please, please call me in—

'Mr Ryder?'

His head whipped round, and he strode towards the beckoning sonographer.

'Kate wants you to come in now.'

He nodded, went in and met her eyes. She was lying on the couch, her clothes tucked out of the way so the subtle curve of her abdomen was exposed, and that barely there bump stole his breath away.

He heard the door close behind him, and he crossed the room in a stride and took her hand, uncurling the fingers that were clenching the edge of the couch and wrapping them around his own.

She curled them tight, clinging to him, her eyes searching his.

'I can't look. Can you, please? Just to see if it's all OK?'

Her eyes were frantic, and he could feel the pulse beating in her hand—or was it his? He didn't know. They probably weren't much different.

He nodded, unable to talk, and fixed his eyes on the screen. Kate's lower abdomen was covered in gel already, as if the sonographer had started and then stopped, and as she picked up the wand and moved it over that little curve, a grainy image popped onto the screen.

A baby, very small, but instantly recognisable.

It was lying on its back, its head to the left of the screen, and he could pick out a little tip-tilted nose, the neck and spine running along the underneath of the image, with the faint lines of the ribs across the chest.

And within the chest a tiny, tiny heart, beating steadily a zillion times a minute.

His baby's heart.

How had they done this? How had some random act driven by impulse made anything as incredible, as amazing as this? It should have been an act of love, not lust, he thought with a wash of shame.

The wand moved, catching a stubby little hand waving, the teeniest fingers so clear for a moment, and he hauled in a breath and crushed Kate's hand and blinked away the sudden sting of tears.

There was something wrong.

She didn't know what, but his face was rigid, a muscle jumping in his jaw, and she felt dread flood through her.

'What? What's wrong?' she asked, her voice rising with fear, and he shook his head.

'Nothing,' he said, his voice ragged. 'There's nothing wrong. It's just amazing. Look at it, Kate. Please, look at it. It's incredible.'

I can't! I can't see it! How can I make this decision if...?

But her head turned, against her will, and she looked at the grainy screen and gasped.

'Oh—!' She reached out her hand towards the screen, her fingers tracing the line of its nose, coming to rest over the beating heart. And then the tears she couldn't stop slid from the corners of her eyes and she had to blink them away so she could see again. 'It looks so real,' she whispered.

'It is real,' he said gruffly. 'It's real, and it's ours.'

She stared at the little image, registering for the first time the full enormity of what lay ahead, the responsibility, the utter reality of the fact that a tiny, dependent child was growing in her body and she was going to have to nurture and care for it, to guide it, to protect it. To love it, as it deserved to be loved.

And as if to confirm it, the baby waved again, and kicked its legs, the little limbs flickering on the screen as they came and went.

How could she keep it out of danger if she was the biggest threat it faced, either now or in the future? And really, she knew nothing about Sam. Was he a threat as well? Too damaged by grief to take this much responsibility, no matter how good his intentions? What then? Because this wasn't Kerry's baby. Would he resent it, and her, for that?

'Right, I need to take some measurements,' the sonographer said, and talked them through it—the nuchal translucency figure which was the measurement of the fluid between the skin and the back of the baby's neck, which would help determine the likelihood of Down's, the crown to rump measurement so it could be dated— and all the time the baby waved its arms and legs and Kate fell more and more in love and further and further into an abyss of fear and self-doubt.

The sonographer smiled. 'Goodness, what a wriggler! But it's a healthy little foetus, and the nuchal translucency measurement is nice and low. And there's a good strong heartbeat—a hundred and fifty-two a minute. It's all looking good. I'd say you're twelve weeks exactly, which makes it due around the twenty-first of October? Does that fit with your dates?'

They both nodded, and she heard Sam let out a shaky breath, as if he'd not quite believed until then that it was his.

'Do you want a photo?'

'Yes, please,' they said together.

'Can we have two copies?' Sam asked, and the sonographer nodded.

'Sure. Do you want a different shot?'

'Yeah, why not?' Sam said, his voice gruff.

The second shot was a close-up, showing the baby's head and body, the miniature fingers of one hand, the fine lines of the ribs, and Kate's heart felt swamped with love.

She kissed her fingers, laid them on the screen over the baby's heart, her own breaking.

I can't bear to hurt you...

The sonographer slipped the photos into an envelope and handed it to Sam while Kate stared at the now blank screen.

'There, all done. And I'll see you in eight weeks for the anomaly scan.'

She gave Kate some paper towel to wipe the gel off her tummy, and when it was done she swung her legs over the side and stood up, tucking the little bump away out of sight.

But not out of mind.

Her child was in there, nestled apparently safely in her body, its future in her hands. But they weren't safe hands, they weren't to be trusted. They let everybody down.

I can't do this...

Sam opened the door for her, and Kate walked out of the room, her legs shaking.

So weird.

She'd gone in there a woman, and come out feeling like—a mother?

Was this what a mother felt like? Torn by fear and love and uncertainty for the future? Had her mother felt like this when she'd taken her to school and left her for ever?

'Here.'

She took the envelope Sam was holding out to her with

trembling fingers and headed for the door, needing fresh air and space to get her head around the miniature time bomb growing inside her.

Taking her arm as if he knew she needed the support, he led her to the car, opened the door and settled her in, then went round and got in beside her. 'Where to?'

Where? Somewhere a million miles away, so she didn't have to do this, didn't have to face whatever the future held.

But it wouldn't matter how far she went, she couldn't outrun it.

'Wherever. Just get me out of here, please,' she said, and closed her eyes.

She had no idea where he was taking her. She was beyond caring, beyond noticing, because all she could see was the image of the baby on the screen.

Her baby.

Their baby.

Sam opened her door, and she realised the car had stopped. He helped her out and she followed numbly, crunching over gravel. She could hear the rattle of halliards, the screech of gulls, and they walked past a big boat propped up on some kind of cradle.

The harbour, she thought numbly, and concentrated on putting one foot in front of the other as he led her up the steps onto the sea wall.

'Walk or sit?' he asked, and she shrugged, hugging her arms around herself to try and stop the shaking, but it didn't work and her legs started to give way.

'OK, sit, I think,' he said, catching her before she fell, and he led her to the steps that went down to the sand below. Her legs didn't make it, and she plopped down onto the steps, sagging against him, the emotional roller coaster of the past week and a bit catching up with her all at once, and she turned her head into his shoulder with a little moan.

The feel of his arm around her, the solidity of his body against hers, the reassuring rise and fall of his chest should have soothed her. It didn't. It just reminded her of everything that was at stake, of everything that had happened and wasn't only happening to her.

She ached for peace, but the sea was quiet today, too quiet to soothe her, its power so muted that it wasn't strong enough to override her fear. And maybe it never would be.

'I can't do it, Sam,' she whispered. 'I really can't do it.'

'*We* can, though,' he said, his voice steady and confident. 'Together, we can. And I'll be there for you, Kate, every step of the way. You won't have to do this on your own, I promise.'

His words should have been reassuring. They were meant to be, so why didn't they reassure her?

Because he didn't know her. He didn't know that everyone promised to stand by her and when the chips were down, they all left her. Left, or drove her out.

'You make it sound so easy,' she said bleakly.

'I haven't said it'll be easy. I don't imagine for a moment it'll be easy. That doesn't mean we can't do it, though, if we work together. It's just teamwork, Kate. We're both used to that. We can do it.'

He sounded so *sure*. How? How could he know it would be all right? A few hours at a time in Resus was one thing. This was a lifetime.

She pushed herself upright, shifting away from him, and became aware of another, more pressing matter.

'I need the loo—all that water they made me drink for the scan? Is there one near here?'

He laughed, got to his feet and pulled her up. 'Come on, I'll let you in. We're at James and Connie's house.'

'Oh.' She hung back, wary now. 'Is Connie here? I don't want her to see me.'

'No,' he said, to her relief. 'She's out for the day. You're quite safe, and anyway there's a bathroom in the cabin.'

'Cabin?'

'Yeah, it's in the garden—I'm living in it at the moment. Gives us all elbow room. Come on.'

He was glad Connie was out, too. He wasn't ready yet to explain all this, at least until Kate had made her decision, and he'd realised that her keeping the baby wasn't a foregone conclusion.

He opened the door of the cabin, pointed Kate in the right direction and left her to it, letting himself into the house and putting on the kettle. Technically he had basic cooking facilities in the cabin, but he didn't have any milk and he was sure they wouldn't mind, so he made her a cup of Connie's decaf tea and helped himself to a coffee from the fancy machine that James had installed.

He was watching through the kitchen window when Kate emerged from the cabin.

'I'm up here,' he said, going to the door and looking down at her from the veranda. 'I've made you tea. Sit on the bench there, I'll bring it down.'

The garden would be better than the veranda. More private if anyone wandered past, and she was hanging by a thread. Not that she was alone. So much hinged on today, and if he messed up—

He loaded a tray with their drinks and a packet of gooey cookies he'd found on the side—Connie's, probably, but she'd forgive him—and sat down beside Kate on the bench by the cabin, nursing his mug and giving her time.

She'd left her tea on the tray and was playing with a cookie, breaking bits off and staring down absently at her hands, eating the odd bit but mostly just stalling, he guessed. He let her do it. She'd talk when she was ready.

'I'm sorry,' she said after a long silence that he'd let stretch almost to the limit.

'What for?'

'Being so—cowardly?'

He turned and frowned at her. 'Cowardly? Having a baby's a big thing, Kate. It's not cowardly to be over-whelmed by it, especially not with your history. Being abandoned as a child is massive, and it's bound to shake your confidence.'

She looked away, but not before he saw the bleak sad-ness of an old grief in her eyes.

'How could she just leave me, Sam? I must have been a horrible child.'

He had no idea. Her voice was so forlorn that he wanted to kill her mother in that moment. 'Probably no more horrible than any other child,' he said matter-of-factly. 'They all have their special moments, so I don't think you can blame it on yourself. What do you know about her? Do you remember her?'

She shrugged. 'Not really. She used to read to me. I can remember that. I'd snuggle up in bed at night and she'd sit next to me with her arm round me and read. I had a favourite book and she read it to me every night—it was in my school bag that day. She must have put it there. I've still got it.'

The tatty, much loved little book he'd seen on her shelves.

'Is that all you've got of her?' he asked softly, unbearably moved by that because, for all his parents' short-comings, and they had plenty, he'd always felt secure and loved. And Kate must have done, until that day. 'Just the book?'

She nodded. 'Yes. Social services went to the flat and got my clothes, but there was no trace of her. Her things were there, but she never came back to collect them, so I was told later. She must have walked away with just the clothes she stood up in, but she simply disappeared off the radar and she's never reappeared. Well, not as far as I know. I've never really looked for her, not properly.'

'What about your father?'

She shook her head. 'No father. Social services got a copy of my birth certificate and there was nothing on that, nothing I remember her saying ever, and I don't remember there being any men around, but I was only tiny, don't forget.'

He hadn't forgotten. Not for a second. 'Are you on any social media sites? Might she have seen your name?'

She shook her head. 'No. I don't use my real name on social media, and I tend to avoid it anyway. I've been burnt.'

He nodded, unsurprised by that. 'I'm glad you're wary of it. The internet can be nasty, and dangerous. Have you tried looking for her at all?'

She nodded. 'A little. There are lots of Rosemary Ash-tons, but no one that looks like me. Not that that necessar-ily means anything, but it's all I've got, that and her name and age and my place of birth. And anyway, I'm not sure I want to see her. I don't know what she'd have to say to me that I might want to hear. It could just make it worse.'

He couldn't see how, but it wasn't his mother, it wasn't his childhood and it wasn't his business, really.

He put his hand over hers and stilled it.

'You're making crumbs,' he said gently, and took the remains of the biscuit out of her hands and put her mug in them. 'Drink up, and we'll go for a walk along the river wall. A leg stretch might clear your head.'

And his, because all he could see was the image of his baby deep within Kate's body, and the tatty little book that was all she had of the mother who'd abandoned her.

He was right, it did clear her head and make her feel better. That, and the tea and cookie, because she'd been too nervous to eat before her scan and her blood sugar must have been in her boots.

They cut across the pub car park and onto the river wall at the harbour mouth, heading behind the boatyard and up along the raised earth bank that held back the river at high tide, and as they strolled she felt the fear fall away a little.

'It's gorgeous here, isn't it?' she said, drawing the air deep into her lungs. 'The way the smell of the river mud takes over from the smell of the sea, the little boats moored out there on the water—it all looks so innocent and peaceful on a day like today with the sun shining and just a light breeze, but it can change so fast. That's what I love about the sea, all that raw power lurking under the surface.'

'Have you ever sailed?'

She laughed. 'When? I lived in London, in a succession of foster homes or children's homes. The longest I was anywhere was five years, and then it all went horribly wrong. Life as a looked-after child isn't a bed of roses, Sam.'

'No, I'm sure it isn't. I'm sorry. I wasn't really implying that. I just wondered if you'd been out in a sailing boat since you'd been here, as you love the sea so much.'

She shook her head. 'No. I don't really know any-body who sails.'

'Well, you do now. When I get the boat fixed, I'll have to take you out in her.'

'Why are they always female?' she asked curiously, strolling along beside him with his arm brushing hers, the slight jostle of it against her anchoring her somehow.

He chuckled. 'I have no idea. It stems from the Medi-terranean languages where inanimate objects have a gen-der, but boats can be a little capricious and unpredictable, so it's probably appropriate.'

'What *are* you saying?' she asked, joining in his laughter, and he slung his arm around her shoulders and hugged her up against his side, flooding her with warmth.

'Present company excepted, of course.' He looked down at her, pausing to brush a swift, light-as-a-feather kiss against her lips. 'Feeling better?'

'Mmm. A bit. It was just a bit of an emotional roll-ercoaster, really, the scan. Seeing it there, so real—I think I'd been fooling myself, really, until that moment. It hadn't really sunk in.'

'No. I know what you mean. It did make it suddenly very real, didn't it? Real, and utterly amazing. Awe-inspiring, really, the start of a life, of a new, tiny little person. And it's ours, Kate. Some of you, some of me, and yet utterly unique. That's just incredible. The most amazing thing we can ever do in our lives.'

He turned her towards him and cupped her shoulders in his hands, his eyes serious suddenly.

'It will be all right, Kate. Together, we'll make it all right.'

He bent his head, touching his lips to hers again, but slowly this time, a tender, gentle kiss that felt like a prom-ise. Then he drew her up against him and held her there, his chin resting on her head, her ear against his chest so she could hear the steady thud of his heart against his ribs, solid and reassuring.

And somewhere deep inside her, a tiny ember of hope began to flicker into life...

They turned back then, his arm still round her shoulders, his heart feeling lighter because something had happened in that moment when he'd kissed her and held her.

He couldn't define it, but he knew it was there, and it gave him a little more confidence in his ability to pull this off.

'It's just gorgeous here, isn't it?' he murmured as they strolled back up the track towards the cottage. 'The sea on one side, the marshes on the other, but it's this side that's got the best view, especially in the evening with the birds coming in to roost in the reed beds. I could sit on the veranda for hours watching it. I can't imagine why James and Connie want to leave.'

'No, nor can I. If I lived here I don't think I could bring myself to go to work, never mind move!'

He chuckled, then let out a tired sigh. 'I just have to get that blasted boat off the drive so they can sell it. And they went to look at a house yesterday, so the pressure's on a bit.'

She turned her head, following the direction of his gaze, and her eyes widened. 'That's *your* boat? Crumbs. I thought it was much smaller than that! I thought that must be someone else's.'

'Nope. That's the offending article, all twenty-nine feet of her.' They walked up beside it, standing underneath the stern high above them on the cradle, the keel propped on baulks of timber.

'Gosh. I can see what they mean. It's really—'

'An eyesore?'

She laughed softly. 'Well, you said it, but it's not going to set the house off very well, is it, when they try and market it, so what will you do? What *can* you do with it?'

He shrugged. 'Sell it? Move it? I don't know. It all depends if they've got room in the boatyard. Otherwise it'll have to go. I'm sure I can find a buyer.'

'But you really wanted it, Sam.'

'It's just a sentimental attachment to my youth, to a time before everything got too complicated. And I miss sailing.'

'So keep it.'

He gave a short huff of laughter and turned to her, taking her hands in his. 'I want to, but realistically, when the baby comes, what time will I have to work on it? I've said I'll be there for you, and I mean it, Kate. And I'm not just going to pay lip service to it, I intend to be hands-on on a daily basis.'

'If I keep it,' she said, and the bottom dropped out of his stomach.

'Kate—please. Don't do that. Even if you decide you can't cope with motherhood, please, don't do that. Let me bring the baby up. I can do it. I can get help. I'll find a way. Just—please, don't...'

She swallowed hard and looked away.

'I don't know if I could, anyway. Not now I've seen that brave little heart beating.'

'Then don't, because there's no going back. Go through with it, give it and us a chance. Please?'

She hesitated for an age while he held his breath, and then she nodded slowly.

'OK,' she said, and he exhaled sharply and dragged her into his arms, crushing her against his chest.

'Thank you,' he whispered, his voice ragged, his chest

heaving with an emotion he couldn't control, and he felt her arms slide round him and hug him back.

He held her for an age, then gradually, as his heart slowed and the world settled back onto an even keel, he released his grip and stood back, staring down into her eyes and smiling.

'Thank you,' he said again, and she bit her lips and blinked hard.

'I can't do it without you, Sam.'

'I know,' he said, his voice firming now. 'I know you can't, but you won't have to.'

'You've said that already.'

'And I meant it, and I'll say it again and again if it helps you to believe in me.'

'I believe in you. It's me I have trouble with.'

'Don't. Don't, because I believe in you. You're a good woman, Kate, and you'll be a good mother.'

'I wish I had your confidence.'

He hugged her again, pressing a kiss to her hair, holding her close. 'It'll come, you'll see.' He looked down into her eyes and smiled. 'I'm starving, and I'm sure you are. Shall we try the pub for lunch?'

'Do they do fish and chips?'

He laughed, the weight of the world suddenly off his shoulders.

'I'm almost certain they do fish and chips,' he said, and, hugging her gently, he wheeled them round and headed back towards the pub.

CHAPTER SIX

THE PUB HADN'T started serving lunch when they got there, so they sat outside in the unseasonably lovely sunshine, sipping fizzy water with ice and lemon and watching the world go by.

There were children crabbing off the little jetty by the ferry, an elderly couple sharing a pot of mussels from the hut, the odd car coming or going from the boatyard, but it was still early in the season so for the most part they were on their own.

Kate turned her face up to the sun, listened to the keening of the gulls and felt the tension inside her ease a little.

'It's so peaceful here. My flat's right in the thick of it—I can hear the ambulance sirens going, the drone of traffic, the dogs over the road barking constantly, people yelling to each other and laughing when they come out of the pubs—sometimes it's hard to get to sleep it's so noisy. And it doesn't help that it's just single glazed, with that thin old Victorian glass and rattling sash windows that let in every bit of passing breeze.'

He laughed, his eyes crinkling with wry amusement. 'You're really selling it to me,' he said drily. 'Considering I was going to suggest that I move in with you, you might need to do a better job.'

She stared at him, slightly taken aback by that coming out of nowhere. 'You want to move in?'

His brows pleated. 'Well—yes. If we're going to do this together, don't you think we should start as we mean to go on? It's not as if we need to take it slow in case it doesn't work. We *have* to make it work. We have to build trust, and learn to compromise and accommodate each other's needs. And no, it probably won't be easy, but it's going to have to happen if we want to make this work, and it's better we do it before the baby comes.'

She could feel her heart racing, fluttering against her ribs like a caged bird. 'Oh. I thought we'd do that after I have the baby.'

'Why wait? Since it's going to happen, why not just get on with it?'

Because she wasn't ready? Because she wasn't sure she could keep her emotional distance from him and preserve what was left of her sanity if he was there all the time, day and night, by her side?

'I'm not sleeping with you,' she said bluntly. 'Not until I'm sure it's working.'

He let out a soft huff of laughter. 'That again? And I haven't asked you to, Kate, but it's up to you. It's not exactly unprecedented, it's how we ended up where we are now, but if that's where it took us...'

She felt his hand cover hers, pick it up, turn it over. Felt the soft graze of stubble, the touch of his lips against her palm, and his fingers folding hers up, closing them over the kiss as if to keep it safe.

'Would it be so bad?' he asked, and she felt her pulse quicken.

Bad? Hardly. But—sensible?

She retrieved her hand, folded it in her lap with the other one to keep it out of trouble. 'No, of course not, but that doesn't make it a good idea. Not until we're sure we can make it work—and I have warned you, I'm a nightmare to live with.'

She felt him sigh. 'Maybe you're right, maybe we should take it slow. There's no hurry, after all.'

She felt the sink of disappointment, and told herself not to be ridiculous.

'I just—I don't think we should take anything for granted. I want to tread carefully, not make any more mistakes. My life's littered with them, and yes, it would be amazing if we got on and it was all dead easy and we can live together in blissful harmony, but I gave up believing in happy ever after a long time ago, Sam, and I still can't really believe we're actually going through with it.'

'No, nor can I, but I can't tell you how relieved I am that we are. I know that must have taken a lot of courage.'

She shook her head slowly. 'I was just scared, Sam. I *am* scared. I was only thinking about protecting the baby from the hell I went through as a child. I couldn't bear that on my conscience.'

A tear trickled down her cheek, and he wiped it gently away with his thumb. 'You won't have it on your conscience, Kate, because there's no way that's going to happen to our baby, I promise. It's going to have a stable home, with two parents who love it and care for it. And, yes, things will go wrong from time to time, and it will be hurt, but that's life, and life hurts. Even when it's perfect, it can hurt. It can hurt like hell. But you get up, and you dust yourself off, and you move on and find a new way forward. And that's what we have to do, starting right now. And learning how to share a home is a good first step.'

She looked at him, at those magnetic blue eyes, so

serious now, so intent, so focused on keeping her and her baby safe, and she nodded and leant in to kiss him.

It was a chaste kiss, not quite fleeting but not lingering either, and before she gave in to temptation she pulled away again and smiled wryly.

'Can we have lunch first, before you move in? I'm starving.'

After a startled second he began to laugh, and slinging his arm round her shoulders, he hugged her close. 'Yes, you crazy girl, we can have lunch first. And there's no hurry, I can stay with James and Connie as long as I want. Come on, let's go in and find a table by the window. I know you like something other than me to look at.'

It wasn't true. She could look at him all day without getting bored, but she wasn't going to tell him that. Not if their idea of a hands-off getting-to-know-each-other period was going to stand the vaguest chance of working. And as her lips were still tingling from the most innocent kiss on record, she was pretty sure the idea was doomed.

He caught James on the way in that evening.

He'd dropped Kate home because she said she needed to go shopping, and he'd spent an hour or two on the boat to keep himself busy so Connie wouldn't be tempted to waylay him with coffee when she got back, but she just smiled up at him, the baby on her hip, the dog sniffing round the bottom of the ladder in the curls of stripped-off old paint, and told him to crack on.

'Just so you know, we want that house we saw yesterday and the agent's coming tomorrow to value this one, so I'm really going to have to nag you about that heap,' she said cheerfully, and he went back to the paint stripping without bothering to tell her that there wasn't a hope in hell of him getting the boat finished and off the drive for months, let alone the sort of timeframe she had in mind.

He was still up the ladder two hours later when James pulled his car in across the back of Connie's, and he turned off the blowtorch and climbed down.

'Nice to see you hard at work, but don't stop on my account,' James said, giving the boat a jaundiced look.

He gave James a wry grin. '*Et tu, Brute?* Look, are you in later this evening? There's something I need to talk to you about.'

'Yes, of course. We want to talk to you, too. Join us for dinner?'

'No, thanks, Kate's cooking,' he said, wondering what it was they wanted to talk about. The boat, probably. Almost inevitably. 'I was thinking of later, after you've put Joseph to bed and finished eating. And I'd like to bring Kate, if that's OK.'

James opened his mouth, scanned Sam's face and shut it.

'Eight thirty? We should be done by then.'

Sam nodded, cleared up the tools and headed for the shower. He wasn't looking forward to this, but as his boss as well as a friend, James had to know what was going on. Whatever James and Connie wanted to say to him, it couldn't be as significant as his news. He just hoped they could get over it and add their support.

The shops were useless. Nobody seemed to stock maternity clothes, so she bought some underwear and a couple of long, floaty tops that might gloss over the problem for a little while at least, and went to see Annie.

She'd had yet another missed call from her during the morning while her phone had been switched off, and as she pulled onto the drive she saw her through the window, sitting in a chair with her feet up and the girls playing quietly on the floor.

She waved to them, and the girls squealed and ran to the front door, all but dragging her inside. She let them tow her into the sitting room, Chloe on one side, Grace on the other, and she smiled at Annie over their excited chatter.

'Hello, stranger,' she said softly. 'I haven't seen you for over a week. How are you?'

Kate shrugged, suddenly lost for words. There was so much she wanted to say, to ask, so much she couldn't say in front of the children, and Annie tutted and got awkwardly to her still-swollen feet.

'Are we going to have cake?' Chloe asked hopefully.

'I'm going to get us a cup of tea. If you're good and stay in here and play nicely, I might let you have some. Can you do that?'

'Yes, Mummy,' they chorused, and Annie rolled her eyes.

'Works like a charm,' she said drily. 'Come on, let's go and have five minutes' peace while the kettle boils.' And she propelled Kate out of the sitting room and into the kitchen, shutting the door firmly.

'OK, what's up? I've been worrying about you all weekend. Why didn't you ring me or answer my calls?'

'I didn't know what to say. It's been a bit momentous,' she said, knowing it was the understatement of the year. 'I had my scan,' she added, and pulled the envelope out of her bag.

Annie took it without opening it and met her eyes searchingly. 'Are you OK?'

'I think so. I'm still trying to get my head round it. Well, we both are.'

'Both?' Her eyes widened. 'Are you talking about the

father? I thought you didn't have his contact details? Did you manage to find him?'

She tried to smile. 'Yes—or rather, he found me, by accident. It turns out he's actually Connie's friend. Your locum?'

'The guy with the boat?' Annie's jaw dropped, and she recovered herself after a second and shook her head. 'Wow. So how did you meet him?'

'In a bar. He stayed an extra night to see the boat, I was supposed to meet Petra but she didn't make it, and—well, I don't know, he was just there, and…'

'Oh, Kate,' Annie sighed. 'So how is he about it?'

'Not thrilled, but actually he's been amazing, really, considering. He's talked me into keeping it, telling me I can do it, and he even said if I couldn't cope, he'd bring the baby up himself on his own.'

'Gosh. That sounds almost too good to be true.'

'That's because it is. His fiancée died two years ago, just before their wedding, and this is just so far off his radar, but he's determined that we can do it together. I just hope he's right because I honestly don't think I can do it without him, and even with him will be hard enough.'

'Wow,' Annie said again. 'Poor guy. But at least he's taken responsibility for it and you're not going to be alone.'

'No, but he wants to move in, and I'm not sure I can cope with it, Annie. What if he finds he *can't* do it? It'll be so much worse if we've been living together like a couple. We'll have so much more invested in it—not that we can have much more than sharing a child, but even so…'

'Does he have a name?'

She laughed. 'Yes, he has a name. Sam—Sam Ryder.'

'Nice name. Good, strong name. Good-looking, of course?'

Her smile was wry. 'Very. He's a proper hottie.'

Annie shook her head. 'Well, I have to say, Kate, if you had to make a mistake, he sounds like a good one. He's a doctor, he's single, he's being supportive—realistically, could you ask for more?'

She swallowed. 'Him not to be stuck with me against his will? Not to be making the best of a situation he really, really doesn't want to be in? Him to love me? He's a really, really nice man, Annie, and under any other circumstances he'd be a real catch, but I can't compete with his dead fiancée, I just can't…'

Her eyes flooded, and Annie put her arms round her and hugged her.

'Give him time. He'll get over her, and this is so new to both of you—you'll work it out.'

'Oh, Annie, I hope so.' She pulled away and sniffed. 'What about that tea? Shall I put the kettle on while you get the cake out for the girls?'

'Don't you want some?'

Kate laughed sadly. 'You know me too well, but I shouldn't, really. Nothing fits me any more as it is.'

'Don't buy any maternity clothes! I'm never going to need them again, and I'll have lots of baby clothes I can hand on as they grow out of them. Really, you don't need to get anything, Kate, unless you want to.'

'Oh, Annie, thank you,' she said, and her eyes welled again. 'I still can't really believe it's happening.'

Annie picked up the scan photo envelope and waggled it at her. 'Really?' She eased them out of the envelope and studied them for a moment, her face softening. 'They're lovely photos,' she said quietly. 'Sometimes they're just in the wrong position and they can't get a decent image, but these are perfect.'

'It waved,' she said, and nearly set herself off again,

and Annie put the photos back in the envelope, handed it to her and got out the mugs.

'Come on, you. Cup of tea, slice of Marnie's cake—chocolate this week—and then we'll go and look at my clothes. And then at some point in the not too distant future, I'd like to meet this man of yours.'

She cooked for Sam that night—nothing huge after the fish and chips they'd had in the pub, just a stir fry with noodles, but she managed not to ruin it, which felt like progress.

'I spoke to James,' he told her as she dished up. 'We're going round there at eight thirty. They're going to want to know why I'm moving out and they don't need to hear stuff on the grapevine. I thought it would be best to get it over with.'

She nodded. 'Yes, I suppose so. I told Annie today that you're the father. She was really sweet—and she wants to meet you. She's offered me lots of stuff—maternity clothes and baby things. She says I can have all the clothes as the boys grow out of them.'

'What if it's a girl?'

She smiled. 'She probably won't mind the odd blue thing.'

'I'm sure we can find some pretty pink stuff if the need arises. Do you mind what it is?'

Her hands strayed instinctively to her tummy, surprised yet again by the little bump that seemed to be growing by the hour. 'No—no, I don't think so. I just want it to be happy. It's the only thing that matters—'

He reached out and squeezed her hand. 'It will be. We'll make sure of it. This smells good,' he added, picking up his fork and digging in. 'Mmm. Tasty,' he mumbled, and she felt a ridiculous surge of pride.

'So, when are you planning on moving in?' she asked, going back to their earlier conversation.

'Whenever. I haven't got a lot of stuff. We could do it in one car load.'

'Oh. OK. What do you think they'll say?' she asked. 'About the baby, I mean.'

'James—probably not a lot. It'll be Connie that has the opinion, I would imagine. Whatever, it's our baby, Kate, not theirs, and at the end of the day it doesn't really matter what they feel about it, but I like to think they'll be supportive.'

Kate wasn't so sure, and her heart was pounding a little as they pulled up outside on the dot of eight thirty.

'OK?' Sam asked her, pausing on the veranda before knocking, and she nodded.

She wasn't, but it had to be done. 'OK,' she lied, and tried to smile, but she was too nervous and if it wasn't for the fact that they were Sam's friends, she would have legged it.

'It'll be fine,' he said softly, stroking his knuckles over her cheek in a gentle gesture of reassurance.

'I doubt it.' She heard scratching at the door and the handle rattle, and his hand fell away as James opened the door, his hand firmly in Saffy's collar.

'Come on in. Connie's in the sitting room. Kate, are you all right with the dog or shall I shut her away?'

'No, I'm fine with her,' she said, fondling Saffy's ears, and she was rewarded by a thrashing tail and a cheerful, lolling tongue that reminded her of her foster parents' dogs. They'd been a refuge for her when things had turned sour, and she'd missed them ever since.

She followed Sam through the kitchen and round through a wide opening into a lovely, cosy room, with a pair of sofas facing each other across an old leather trunk that doubled as a coffee table and, beyond them, framed by a huge bay window, was a spectacular view of the sea.

The light was fading now, a pale band on the distant horizon all that was left of the day, and Connie switched on the table lamps as they went in, banishing the dusk and flooding the room with warmth.

'Hello, Kate, how are you? I haven't seen you for ages. Are you OK?' she asked, and Kate nodded, wishing the ground could open up and swallow her. These were her colleagues, people she'd worked with, people who'd seen her at her best and worst.

And this, she thought grimly, was definitely her worst. She pasted a smile firmly on her face and mentally battened down the hatches. 'I'm fine. How are you?'

'Blooming. I love being pregnant,' Connie said, her happy smile just underlining the difference in their circumstances. 'Can I get you a drink? Glass of wine? Cup of coffee?'

What could she say to that that wouldn't give the game away? Not that Sam wasn't just about to, but even so...

'Actually, have you got any sparkling water?'

'Yes, sure. Sam?'

'I'll have coffee, Connie, please.'

She went into the kitchen, leaving Sam crouched down rubbing Saffy's tummy, and Kate stood in the bay window watching the rapidly fading light and wondering what it would be like to live in a house like this. She'd never been in it before, but it was love at first sight, and she couldn't imagine how James and Connie could even consider leaving it.

'So, what was it you wanted to talk to me about?' Sam asked as Connie and James came out of the kitchen.

'Oh, no, you first,' Connie said, putting the tray of

drinks down on the old trunk, and Kate's heart gave a thump.

James waved at a sofa. 'Kate, Sam, sit down, make yourselves at home.'

There wasn't really a prayer of that, but as she didn't have much alternative she perched on the nearest sofa. Connie plonked herself down on the other sofa next to James, with the result that she and Sam ended up facing them across the trunk. It felt as if they were being interviewed, and she was glad when Saffy came and leant against her legs so she could stroke her to give her hands something to do apart from shake.

'So, come on then, what is it?' Connie prompted, and beside her Kate felt Sam haul in a deep breath before pulling one of the scan photos out of his jacket pocket and dropping it on the trunk in front of them.

'We're having a baby,' he said quietly, and Kate held her breath in the stunned silence that followed.

To her surprise Connie's eyes filled with tears as she picked up the photo and stared at it. 'How? You haven't had time...'

'It doesn't take long, and I would imagine you know *how,* so I won't elaborate,' Sam said drily. 'We met in January, the night I stayed on to see the boat.'

'Well, I know that, but I hadn't realised you'd...'

She trailed off, and he nodded. 'And that's it, really. There isn't a lot more I can add.'

Connie let her breath out on a shaky sigh and put the photo down. 'Oh, Sam. Are you OK?' she asked, her voice gentle, as if she knew he wasn't.

'We're working on it,' he said quietly, and Connie glanced across at Kate.

Until then her focus had been on Sam, all her concern for him, but that was natural. He was her friend, and he'd been through hell recently. She and Connie weren't much more than acquaintances, so she didn't expect any sympathy, but now Connie's eyes were on her and she realised she'd been wrong about that.

'Kate?' she asked softly.

Kate shrugged. 'You know me, Connie, one disaster after another,' she said lightly, trying to get the quiver out of her voice. 'I mess everything up. It seems to be my job in life to ruin other people's, never mind my own—'

'No!' Sam's voice was firm. 'It was an accident, Kate, and at the end of the day it was my fault, not yours, so don't go taking all the blame.'

'But it *was* my fault! If I'd taken the morning-after pill—'

'You were sick, it would've been too late, and anyway, you shouldn't have needed to—'

'Whoa,' James said, chipping in for the first time. 'You two really are having a guilt fest, aren't you?'

Sam sucked in a breath and let it out in a rush. 'Sorry, we're a bit fraught. It's been a tough day for both of us at the end of a difficult week, but we just wanted you to know the situation.'

Sam's hand found hers, enclosing it in a reassuring grip, and she leant against him, grateful for his solid warmth in the turbulent sea of emotions that filled the room. As if to reinforce the comfort, she felt Saffy lick her hand, and she stroked the warm, silky head that lay across her knees.

'Will you be really all right?' Connie asked. 'It's so soon—you don't even know each other. What are you going to do?'

'We're keeping it,' he said calmly, although Kate was sure he was anything but calm. 'Together. I'm going to move into Kate's flat, and we'll work it out as we go along.'

Kate felt Connie's eyes on her and looked up to see concern flare in them, but who it was for she couldn't tell. Any one of the three involved, the baby included, would have been a suitable candidate.

'Kate?'

She tried to smile, but it was a pretty poor effort so she gave up and shrugged. 'We have to start somewhere. Now is as good a time as any. We've only got six months before the baby comes, and we need to—how was it you put it?' she asked, turning to Sam. 'Find a new way forward? Especially Sam.'

'No,' he said firmly. 'This is just as hard for you, if not harder. It's a no-brainer for me to keep the baby. It's taking much more courage for you to do it.'

That was news to her. She'd felt it was him who was struggling the most, him who was finding it so hard because of his grief, because of Kerry. She was just plain terrified and convinced it was doomed to failure like every other relationship, but he seemed to have understood the depth of her fears, and just that simple fact suddenly made it all seem so much easier.

'So—you're really going to live in the flat?' Connie asked. 'Up all those stairs with a baby and a buggy and all the shopping? You live on the top floor, don't you, Kate?'

'Yes, but it's fine—'

'It'll be fine for now, but we'll sort out something a bit more permanent when we know where I'm going to be working next,' Sam said, and she felt a little stab of unease.

She knew her flat wasn't great, but it was her home, and although at times it was lonely, it was hers, nobody could tell her what to do in it, and suddenly that all felt threatened. Especially the possibility of moving away from all her friends…

'Actually, you may not have to go anywhere,' James said, stopping her thoughts in their tracks. 'I've got a feeling Annie won't come back after her maternity leave, and if the job comes up, we'll need to replace her. Would a part-time consultancy be enough for you?'

Sam shrugged thoughtfully. 'Maybe, if the contract was right. It would give me time to bond with the baby, and to be near our friends would be a massive bonus for both of us.'

'The job's not set in stone,' James warned him. 'But we already need more consultant cover than we have at the moment, so I might be able to do something anyway. Would that tempt you enough?'

It would, he realised. It did.

He turned to Kate, searching her face. 'How would you feel about that?'

'Staying here, near my friends?' Her face seemed to light up from within, and he felt a pang of guilt that he'd even contemplated taking her away from them. 'It would be amazing. I really don't want to leave—'

'It's not a firm job offer,' James reminded them. 'Not yet, anyway, and you'd have to be interviewed, of course, but getting people of your calibre is extremely hard so there's a definite possibility I could talk the board into offering you a full-time senior consultant's post, especially if Annie does leave. Just bear it in mind.'

He nodded, his heart suddenly beating a little faster, the prospect more appealing than he could possibly have imagined. To be here, near his own friends, near the sea...

'Leaving that on one side for a moment, it's high time we said congratulations about the baby. I know it won't be easy, but you're both determined enough to make this work. I hope you'll be very happy together.'

Sam swallowed hard, trying desperately not to think of the last time he'd heard those words—his engagement to Kerry.

'Thanks,' he said gruffly. 'We'll give it our best shot.'

He put his arm round Kate, hugged her to his side and dropped a kiss on her cheek. She smiled, curled her fingers over his jaw and kissed him back, and her warmth flowed into him, easing the sadness.

Maybe it will work, he thought. Maybe...

'So, having got that out of the way, what was it you two wanted to talk to me about?'

James gave a slightly awkward laugh, and met Connie's eyes.

'You, or me?'

'It's the boat, Sam,' Connie said tentatively.

He sighed. 'I thought as much.'

'I know it's not a good time to hassle you,' James cut in, taking over, 'but we need to move fast on this, if we want the house we saw yesterday. They've had other offers, lower ones, but we're not in a strong position unless we've got a buyer, and we don't need anything that's going to put someone off, and we're very afraid the boat will.'

Sam nodded slowly. 'Look, I'll talk to the guy in the boatyard about moving it. How long have I got?'

James sighed. 'Someone wants to view it tomorrow. They haven't even seen the details, but the agent sounded them out and they seem keen. And we know you can't move it by then, but if we could at least tell them it was going...?'

'Or you could always buy the house yourself, Sam,' Connie said with a laugh. 'That would solve it at a stroke.'

There was a stunned silence, and he turned and looked at Kate. 'Fancy living here?'

He saw her jaw sag slightly.

'I think Connie's joking,' she said, before he could talk himself into it. 'And anyway, you haven't got a job yet.'

'I *was* joking,' Connie chipped in. 'Seriously, I don't expect you to buy the house, Sam. That would be crazy!'

He gave a wry smile and sat back. 'Yeah, you're probably right,' he murmured, and mentally put the idea on the back burner. 'So, tell us all about this new house that you want.'

CHAPTER SEVEN

THEY LEFT A short while later, but not before Connie got in a parting shot.

'Let us know how you get on with the boatyard,' she said, a weeny bit pointedly, but Sam just grinned at her.

'You're a nag, do you know that?'

As he slid behind the wheel and started the engine, he glanced across at Kate and said, 'So how *would* you feel about living there?'

She felt her heart lurch. 'Really? It would be amazing, but it's never going to happen so I don't really want to think about it.'

'What if it could happen?'

She turned so she could see him better, but the interior light was out by then and the night closed in around them as he drove off, so her only clue was his voice.

And that was giving nothing away.

'How? Where are you going to find the money? Because I haven't got any—well, not that would make any difference.'

'I've got a house. Kerry and I bought it, but we never lived in it. We were going to move in after the wedding, but—whatever, it was furnished, ready to go, so I just contacted a letting agent. I'm sure he could sell it for me.'

'You can't do that!' she said, shocked that he would

even consider it when it had so much meaning for him, but he just shrugged.

'Why not? I've never set foot in it. It means nothing to me, I only ever saw it on plan, but the tenants have wanted to buy it since the word go, and it's risen hugely in value. I could sell it to them.'

His voice was still emotionless, so she could only presume that it really did mean nothing to him. Either that or he was better than she thought at hiding his feelings.

'You still don't have a permanent job, though, so you don't even know how long you'll be in Yoxburgh.'

'No, but I'm here for a year, Annie's told James that much, and I don't suppose their house would be hard to sell, not with that view. And he was dangling the carrot of a pretty decent job firmly in front of my nose. He wouldn't do that if he didn't think it was possible. So—should I see if the tenants still want it?'

Kate let out a long, slow breath. 'Sam, it's a huge thing to do, to give up your house like that—'

'No. It's not huge, Kate, it's just a house, and I don't even have a mortgage on it. The life insurance covered it, so it was paid off in full. It's just an investment, nothing more.'

She wasn't convinced, but then nothing about their relationship was without drawbacks or compromise on both sides.

'Don't you think we should find out if we can actually live together without killing each other before you do anything radical?' she asked, trying hard to be sensible in the face of his overconfidence and her own self-doubts, but he just laughed softly and reached out a hand and found hers.

'We'll be fine,' he said, threading his fingers through

hers and giving them a little squeeze, and she felt a little of his confidence seep into her along with the warmth.

He pulled up outside her house, and she took off her seat belt and turned to him, searching his face in the dim light from the streetlamps.

'Fancy a coffee?'

He hesitated, then shook his head, the engine still running. 'No, better not, we've both got an early start.'

She nodded, then leant across and touched her lips to his.

'I'll see you tomorrow, then,' she said, moving away, but before she could go far his hand reached out and eased her back towards him. He met her halfway, his lips grazing hers, questioning, tasting, sipping, until on a slow, soft outbreath he moved in closer, deepening the kiss, exploring her mouth until she whimpered.

The needy sound was enough to make him go still and pull away, to her regret, but he didn't go far—just enough to rest his forehead against hers and let out a ragged sigh.

'Sorry, I didn't mean to do that. You'd better go in while I'll still let you,' he said gruffly after a long pause, and she nodded, pulled away reluctantly and opened the door.

'Goodnight, Sam. I'll see you tomorrow.'

'Yeah. Sleep well.'

'And you.' She shut the car door, ran up to her flat and waved to him from the window. He lifted a hand, then drove away, and she rested her head against the cool glass and swallowed hard.

OK, so maybe they wouldn't kill each other if they lived together, but hands off? Not a chance. Not while her body was burning up from that brief but thorough kiss, and she had a feeling he wasn't doing any better.

* * *

He contacted the letting agent in the morning, then rang the boatyard—just in case.

'Any joy?'

'Do you usually eavesdrop on people's conversations?' he asked mildly, and James just chuckled.

'You're talking on the phone in the middle of the ED in a very unnerving quiet spell, and you're worried about me eavesdropping?'

He slid his phone back into his pocket and ignored that. 'In answer to your first question, not yet. They certainly can't move the boat today, but I'm serious about the house.'

James frowned in surprise. 'Really? I thought you were just being silly.'

'No. I'd love it. It's got everything we need. Why wouldn't I want it?'

'I don't know. Come on, let's move this into my office and we can have a proper conversation about it.'

They'd taken two steps when the red phone rang, and James rolled his eyes.

'I thought it was too quiet. We'll catch up later.'

The trauma call went out on the loudspeakers as he was talking.

'Adult trauma call, five minutes. Paediatric trauma call, five minutes. Adult trauma call, ten minutes.'

James pulled out his phone. 'I've got to make a quick call and then I'll meet you in Resus. Can you pull together a couple of teams?'

'Sure.' He turned on his heel and nearly ran into Kate. He hadn't seen her all morning, she'd been in Minors, but the kiss was fresh in his mind and he'd had to force himself to focus.

'Are you free?'

'Yes. Do you want me?'

He gave a wry, frustrated chuckle. 'Can we talk about that after we've taken the trauma call?'

She coloured slightly, bit her lips and tried not to laugh. 'I'll take that as a yes, then,' she said, and he picked up the information from the desk and followed her into Resus where the teams were already waiting.

'OK, we've got two adults and a baby all from the same car,' he told them. 'Dad's still being cut out, mum and baby will be here in a minute. I'll do the primary surveys while we wait for James, and we'll go from there. Is someone coming down from Paeds?'

'Not sure. Ed Shackleton's gone off,' someone said, 'so they're trying to find his registrar.'

'OK. Right, we're on. Let's go and meet them.'

The paramedics wheeled the mother in, the screaming baby strapped safely in an infant carrier.

'Mother and five month old infant, vehicle in collision with a van which swerved across the road out of control. We've secured the spine, but she's complaining of abdominal pain and there's evidence of seat belt injuries. BP one-thirty over eighty, pulse one-twenty, GCS fifteen at the scene. The baby's stable but we haven't taken her out of the carrier. Father on his way in with leg injuries.'

Sam nodded, and then turned to Kate. 'Can you get her on a monitor, please, and we need to get some pictures of that spine. I just want to make sure the baby's OK.'

He checked it quickly, one ear on Kate's reassuring voice as she talked to the mother. She was on a spinal board with a neck brace and she was coherent, but he needed to check her over, too, and the baby seemed fine and was moving normally and the cry was one of distress rather than pain.

'OK, little one, let's see how Mum is, shall we?' he

murmured, and went over to her bed, leaving the baby still in her carrier in the care of a nurse until Ed's registrar came down.

Agitated, was the simple answer. 'I need to be with Evie!' she said, trying to get off the trolley, but Kate restrained her gently.

'She's in good hands, Jenny, and so are you. This is Sam. He's one of our consultants and he's going to be looking after you so let's get you checked over quickly and we'll do our best to get you back with her.'

'Hi, Jenny,' Sam chipped in, running his eyes over her carefully after scanning the monitor. 'Evie's fine, from what I can see, but I need to have a look at you now. Can you tell me where you hurt?'

'Uh—my shoulder? My hip—where the seat belt was. And sort of under my ribs?'

'OK, can we cut these clothes off, please, so I can get a proper look, and can we have portable X-rays, please?'

Kate cut them away and he palpated her carefully, but even so she gasped as he touched the area over her liver, and he looked up at Kate.

'Can we do a FAST scan and get a line in, please?' he said softly. 'I just want to check for free fluids. And we'd better get four units of O-neg down here and cross-match for four more. She might have an encapsulated bleed, or it could just be bruising from the seat belt or maybe a fractured rib.'

'I'm on it,' Kate said, and Sam took charge of the ultrasound while she dealt with the bloods.

They moved quickly, and by the time her husband was wheeled in, Sam had established that she had a broken rib, but there was no free fluid, the monitor was tracking a steady blood pressure and her spine and pelvis were uninjured, so Kate could remove the brace.

But in the meantime the baby was still crying, and Sam looked up at Kate and made a decision he hoped he wouldn't regret.

'Can you help me with the baby? I don't know where Paeds are, but I want to get her out and check her over properly.'

She nodded and bent over the mother. 'Jenny, we're just going to look at Evie again. We'll do it right here, next to you, OK, so you can see her?'

Jenny nodded, and he undid the straps on the baby carrier and slid his hands round under the baby. 'You take her head, and we'll lift her on your count,' he said, and they laid her gently down on the bed so he could examine her.

'I want to roll her to check her back. Can you try and keep her head still and in line, please, while we do it? That's lovely.'

She held the baby rock-steady, talking soothingly all the time as he felt carefully for anything untoward, but there was nothing and as he rolled her back and refastened her nappy, Evie lifted her arms and wailed pathetically.

'Can I?' Kate pleaded, and he nodded.

'She's fine. Go for it.'

He watched her stoop and lift the little girl tenderly into her arms, and had to swallow a lump in his throat.

'There, there, sweet thing, it's all right,' she crooned, 'you're OK. Come on, now—there, that's better.' She was rocking gently from foot to foot, cradling little Evie against her shoulder as if she'd done it a million times before, and the baby's wails faded to hiccupping little sobs as she snuggled into the comfort of Kate's shoulder.

He eased his breath out on a sigh and met her eyes.

'There you go,' he said, his voice a little gruff. 'You're a natural. She just needed a little cuddle.'

Kate bent her head and pressed her lips gently to the baby's soft, downy curls and smiled at him, and he felt something he hadn't known was tight release inside his chest.

An hour later all three of them were out of Resus, the father to Theatre, the little girl to Paediatric ICU for monitoring, her mother in a wheelchair by her side after a clear CT scan, and Sam flashed Kate a smile that made her heart beat faster.

'Good job. Thank you,' he said, and she felt a little rush of warmth.

'You're welcome. Have we got time for a coffee?'

'I hope so. I haven't had lunch yet, either, and it's nearly two. Grab a sandwich together?'

She nodded, and they headed for the canteen, just as Sam's phone buzzed.

'Ah, text from the letting agent. The tenants still want the house.' He shot her a quick glance. 'I am serious, Kate,' he said softly. 'I do want this, but only if you do, too.'

She felt the usual rush of conflicting emotions—hope, excitement even, and the dreaded 'what-ifs'.

What if we can't live together? What if he can't stand the sight of me by the time the baby's born? What if something goes wrong with the pregnancy and I lose it—?

She gave a little gasp, her hand flying to her tiny bump, and Sam stopped.

'What? What is it?'

She shook her head. 'Nothing. I was just thinking— Sam, if you buy the house and I lose the baby—'

'You won't lose it.'

'You can't say that! I might! It happens. And then what?'

He let go of her elbow and turned back towards the canteen. 'You won't,' he said again, as if he was trying to convince himself.

'You sound like King Canute. Fight the battles you can win, Sam. That isn't one of them. If it happens, it happens, and then you'll have another house you won't want to live in.'

'It's still a good house,' he said, when they'd paid for their drinks and sandwiches, and she let out a little sigh and headed for the benches outside.

'Yes. Yes, it is still a good house. It's a lovely house, you're right, and you wouldn't have any trouble selling it on.'

'Have you ever looked round it?'

'No. That was the first time I'd been inside. I'm not really friends with them, Sam, but I don't need to see any more to know it's wonderful.'

'Why don't I ask James if you can have a look round tonight?'

'Because they've got someone else viewing it,' she reminded him.

'Even better, it'll be tidy. And talk of the devil,' he said with a grin as James came over to them. 'We want to look at the house tonight.'

James perched on the arm of the bench and shook his head slowly. 'Sam, I can't promise you a job yet—'

'You don't need to. I've got one for a year—'

'No. You've got one until Annie comes back. If anything goes wrong she's still entitled to her full maternity leave, but she might not want to take it. And safe pregnancy isn't a certainty.'

'You two are full of gloom and doom today. Kate was just talking about that with our baby.'

Our baby.

The words seem to trip off his tongue so easily, and she found them so hard to say. So hard to believe, to comprehend the full implications of those two little words, but her arms had felt so empty when she handed Evie over to the paediatric team and she could only imagine how Jenny had felt while she'd lain there helpless with Evie crying.

Her phone jiggled in her pocket, and she pulled it out and felt her heart sink. 'They must have heard us talking. Annie's been admitted. Her blood pressure went up and they're doing her C-section today. Oh, lord, I hope she's all right. That must be where Ed was. I wondered.'

'How many weeks is she now?' Sam asked.

'Thirty-four? Not enough.'

'That should be OK, though.'

'Whatever, I'm crossing my fingers, just in case,' Kate said, tapping in a reply. 'Poor Annie. She so badly wanted to get to thirty-five weeks, if not more, but when I saw her yesterday she seemed tired.'

'Not as tired as she's going to be,' James said with a wry laugh. 'I couldn't believe how tired we were with just *one* baby. Right, back to work. Keep us posted.'

It was hard to concentrate for the rest of her shift, and by the time she went off at four she was really twitchy.

She'd been checking her phone all afternoon, and she was halfway home when it pinged and she pulled it out of her pocket to see a text from Ed, a picture of a smiling Annie cradling two tiny, perfect babies in her arms. She turned round, went back to the hospital, showed it to Sam and James and burst into tears.

'Hey, come on, they're all OK, that's good news,' Sam said, hugging her, and she nodded furiously and sniffed.

'I know, but they lost a baby before they got married and it's just so lovely for them...'

She welled up again, and Sam put his arm round her shoulders and hugged her again, then tilted her chin up so she met his eyes. 'Go and see her,' he said.

'She won't want me. She'll be tired, and the girls will want to see her, and her mum, and Ed's grandmother—she won't want me.'

'Of course she will. Just pop up—five minutes, that's all, not even that. Just to give her a hug. It'll mean a lot.'

Trust Sam to understand. Apart from when he was trying unsuccessfully to stick to their hands-off rule, he was a very tactile person, and so was Annie. She nodded and headed for Maternity.

Annie was alone when she got there, and for a second Kate thought she was asleep, but then she stirred and opened her eyes and her face lit up. 'Kate—you came! Did you get Ed's text?'

'I did—they look gorgeous,' she said, stooping to hug her and blinking back tears. 'You must be so happy. Are you all right?'

'I'm fine—still numb at the moment so everything's peachy! The babies are in SCBU for the night, just to make sure everything's OK, but they're looking great, really strong and feisty, and I'm feeling better already now I know the babies are OK.'

She caught hold of Kate's hand. 'Sit down, talk to me.'

'No, you need to rest. You don't need me here, I just came to hug you.'

'Oh, please stay!' she protested. 'I feel tired but my mind's whirling and I'm too wired to sleep, so some nice friendly company would be lovely. You can tell me more about Sam.'

'OK, if you're sure?' She perched on the edge of the

chair, still holding Annie's hand, and told her about Sam wanting to buy James and Connie's house. 'I've told him he's crazy, because he hasn't even got a proper job—'

'He can have my job,' Annie said instantly.

'He's got your job,' she pointed out, but Annie shook her head.

'No—permanently. I'm not coming back.'

Kate felt her eyes widen. 'Seriously? You're not coming back at all?'

Annie shook her head again.

'I missed so much of the girls when they were tiny because I had to work, and I really, really want to be there for them all this time, so I'm going to stop. I'll be a fulltime mum for the first time ever, and I can't wait. Tell James. I'll let him know officially later, but he ought to know, especially as it affects you and Sam.'

Kate nodded. It could mean that they'd stay in Yoxburgh near their friends—living in James and Connie's house? She didn't get that lucky...

'Sure. I'll tell him later, we're seeing them this evening,' she said. 'And I'm really pleased for you, because I know how worried you were about relying on your mother so much, but—oh, I am going to miss working with you.'

'No, you won't! You'll have your own baby,' Annie reminded her gently. 'And you'll be able to come and see me whenever you want.'

'I'll have to go back to work, though,' she said. 'I can't expect Sam to support me. It's only the baby he's interested in.'

Annie eyed her thoughtfully. 'Are you sure about that? Maybe it's the package—the whole deal.'

'What—playing happy families? I don't think so. There's still plenty of chemistry between us, but that's not enough on its own, and I'm not going to get my hopes up. If we can just share the house and the baby without killing each other, I'll be more than happy.'

Annie laughed softly, and rested her head back on the pillow. 'Silly girl. You'll be fine. You'll see...'

Her eyes drifted shut, and after a moment Kate slipped her hand carefully out of Annie's and left her sleeping. She saw Ed on the way out, standing over a crib in SCBU, and he beamed at her and came to the door, his grin nearly splitting his face in two.

'Congratulations, Daddy,' she said with a smile, and he gave a choked laugh and hugged her hard.

'Thank you. I never thought this would ever happen to me, Kate, and it's just amazing.'

'I'm so pleased for you,' she said, blinking back tears and trying to find a smile. 'So how are they?'

'Incredible. Want to see them?'

She shook her head. 'No. Well, yes, of course I do, I'd love to, but I'd better let Annie show them to me. She's sleeping now, so I left her. Say goodbye to her for me, and well done, both of you.'

She kissed his cheek and left him to his new family, trying really hard not to be jealous of their obvious happiness. And at least Sam was standing by her and the baby and they seemed to be getting on OK. That, frankly, was more than she could have hoped for.

The agent's valuation was neither higher nor lower than Sam had been expecting because he'd had no idea what the house would be worth, but it fell within his budget which was all that mattered, and he told James so.

'So, can I bring Kate round this evening to look at it?' he asked again, and James shrugged.

'Sure. The others are coming at seven thirty. Do you want to come before or after?'

'Before. I don't want you getting all random on me and accepting their offer before you have a chance to hear mine.'

James laughed. 'As if. Come round as soon as you finish. Connie'll be busy with Joseph, but I'm sure she won't mind if you just wander round and make yourselves at home.'

He sent Kate a text, and she rang him straight back.

'Fabulous,' she said, sounding unusually cheerful. 'Pick me up from mine as soon as you're done.'

'Ten minutes?'

'Perfect. I've got some news for you, too. Bye.'

'News?'

The phone went dead, and he slid it back into his pocket and frowned.

News? News about what? Unless...

He finished off the paperwork on his last patient, handed over to the registrar and headed straight for her flat.

She was sitting outside on the low garden wall, and she jumped up the moment she saw him approach and got straight into the car.

'Annie's leaving,' she said without preamble. 'She's got to tell James officially, but she's not coming back to work ever.'

'Wow. Is it still under wraps?'

She shook her head, but then pulled a face. 'Well, sort of. She wants me to tell James, but until she's done it officially I suppose it shouldn't be broadcast. So it looks as though you might have a job.'

'If James can rig the interview panel,' he said, showing the first slight glimmer of doubt she'd seen from him, but she just laughed.

'You'll get it. Our ED has been notoriously difficult to find staff for, maybe because James has such high standards, maybe because they just don't want to work in what they perceive as a provincial centre, but trust me, if James thinks you're qualified, you're in. Well, barring flood, fire, civil commotion and acts of God— isn't that what they say in insurance documents as the get-out clause?'

He laughed. 'Something like that,' he said, and then he leant across and kissed her, taking her breath away.

'So, what do you think of it? Is it big enough? Could you live here?'

They'd worked their way up through the house and were standing in James and Connie's bedroom on the top floor, looking out of the huge east-facing roof lights, and all she could see was the sea and sky.

'Big enough? Are you crazy? It's got four bedrooms, a fabulous living space, stunning sea views, a garden—it's even got an en suite! I've never had any of those things in my life, Sam! Could I live here? Absolutely. Can you afford it?'

'Yes.'

Just that, no hesitation.

She turned and stared out of the window again, watching the light playing on the surface of the waves, listening to the sound of the sea breaking on the shingle, and she wanted to cry.

Instead she closed her eyes, counted to ten and turned back to him.

'Then buy it, if you want it, if you think it's the right thing to do. It's not really up to me, it's your money, and you'll have to firm the job up with James, but I can't tell you what to do.'

'But—in principle? Does it tick all the boxes on your wish list?'

She just laughed. 'Sam, my wish list is a roof over my head, security, central heating and preferably no noisy neighbours partying all night. Trust me, I'm not hard to please.'

He drew in a long, slow breath and let it out again, then gave her a wry smile. 'Kerry had a wish list as long as your arm. She knew exactly what she wanted, how she wanted it, what colours, what materials—'

'I'm not Kerry,' she said softly, and he frowned slightly.

'No. No, you're not, are you?' he said thoughtfully, as if he'd just discovered something new and rather interesting, and then he nodded and gestured towards the stairs.

'Better go and tell them, then, hadn't we?' he said, and she wasn't sure but she had a feeling she might just have earned some brownie points...

'We want it.'

James nodded slowly. 'OK, but timing's crucial, Sam, and I can't get you a definite job offer yet. Annie has to make it official, and then we have to go through all the hoops—not that that'll be a problem unless you blot your copybook between now and then.'

'I have no plans to do that,' he said with a smile, 'and if the job doesn't materialise, it'll be a sound investment anyway. And the tenants definitely want my house. They'll move fast.'

James nodded again. 'OK. What about the price?'

'I'm not going to make you a cheeky offer, if that's

what you mean,' he said with a laugh. 'We'll give you the asking price, and if it should go to a bidding war—'

'It won't. If you're sure you can deliver and it means we get our new house, then it's yours.'

His.

'Wow,' he said softly. Little more than a week ago, he'd had nothing to look forward to. Now, suddenly, everything was falling into place in the most unlikely way, and it felt like the sun had come out from behind the blackest cloud.

He was speechless for a second, then he felt his face crack into a smile he had no hope of suppressing. 'That's amazing,' he said, and shook hands with James, then hugged him just for good measure. 'Thank you.'

'Don't thank me. I want your money,' James said with a grin, and Sam laughed and turned to Kate.

'Woo-hoo! We're going to have a house!' he said, the smile still plastered all over his face, and he picked her up in his arms and hugged her.

'Put me down,' she said with a breathless laugh, and he lowered her slowly to the floor, her body in contact with his from head to toe, and then just because he couldn't help himself any longer, he bent his head, cupped her face in his hands and kissed her.

'Are we celebrating something?' Connie asked, coming into the room behind him, and he let go of Kate and hugged Connie, too.

'Absolutely. You're talking to the next owners of your house.'

'Really? Are you sure? It's not just because of the boat, is it? Because we can work round that, Sam. Or because we need a quick sale? For God's sake don't be noble.'

He stared at her in disbelief, and then laughed, the joy bubbling up in him like fine champagne.

'No, Connie. There's no way I'm that noble. Not by a country mile. I want this house—*we* want this house—not because the boat's a pain or you want to move, but because we love it, pure and simple, don't we?'

He looked at Kate, and she smiled at him. 'Yes, we do,' she said softly, and Connie grinned.

'Right, well, in that case, James, get on the phone and cancel the viewing tonight, and then crack open the Prosecco. I think it's time we had a party!'

CHAPTER EIGHT

SHE HARDLY DRANK any Prosecco, and nor did Connie, but it didn't stop them celebrating.

Not that the celebration was really about her, she knew that, but the spin-off was that she might, if it all worked out, end up living in the sort of house that she'd never even dared to fantasise about.

But only if she and Sam could live together, and the worry about that was still niggling at her. Only one way to find out, though, and that was to get on with it, so when James offered Sam another glass and he hesitated, she chipped in.

'I could always drive, if I'm insured?'

Sam frowned thoughtfully at her. 'Yes, it's insured for anyone over twenty-five with a clean licence, but that won't help me get back here tonight, though.'

'So stay at mine,' she said, and met his searching eyes.

He held hers for a breathless moment, then turned to James and held his glass out.

'In that case—'

She felt her heart thud as he turned back, met her eyes again and raised the filled glass a fraction, in a silent toast.

Or a promise?

* * *

She unlocked the door at the top of the stairs, pushed it open and walked into the kitchen on legs that weren't quite steady.

'Do you want coffee?' she asked over her shoulder, only to find he was right behind her.

'Not really. Shall I make up the spare bed?'

'Only if you want to,' she replied, her heart in her mouth, and held her breath for his answer.

She felt the soft brush of air against her cheek, the touch of his hand on her shoulder turning her slowly towards him, saw the pulse beating at the base of his throat before he tilted her head up to meet his eyes.

How could ice smoulder?

'You know what I want,' he said quietly, his eyes locked on hers, searching for her answer, 'but I need you to be sure.'

She swallowed, hesitating for a fraction of a second before she lifted her hand up and laid it against his jaw, feeling the slight graze of stubble against her palm, the heat of his breath as she trailed her thumb over his lips.

His eyes held hers, the fire in them burning all the way down through her body and setting it alight with need.

'I'm sure,' she murmured, moving her hand and drawing his head down to meet her lips, and his breath hitched as his eyes closed and he eased her hard up against him, one hand cradling her head, the other cupping her bottom and lifting her closer as the fire in her raged out of control.

She pressed her hands against his chest and pushed him gently away. 'Not here,' she said breathlessly. 'My room.'

How could it be so good?

He shifted to his side and trailed his free hand slowly

down over her throat, across her shoulder, down her arm, across her hip, coming to rest over the gentle curve where his child lay sheltered.

'Hello, baby,' he murmured, stroking his hand lightly over it, and then he shifted his attention higher, back to Kate, studying her intently. 'Your body's changing,' he said softly, his hand moving on, gliding back up to cradle the soft fullness of the breast nearest to him, the nipple darkened from rose to dusk by her hormones. He brushed his thumb over it and it peaked obligingly, making him smile.

'Why did you tell me you were a glamour model?' he asked idly, his thumb still toying with her nipple.

She gave a tiny shrug. 'I don't know. I was sick of men either fantasising about me in uniform or telling me their health issues, I suppose. And it wasn't an outright lie. I have done it.'

His hand stilled. 'Really? When? Why?'

'For money. I was eighteen, I was about to start my nursing course and I was broke. I didn't want a massive student loan and a friend was doing it, and she persuaded me to go with her.'

'And?' he asked, sensing that there was more, and she sighed.

'And it paid well, but I hated it. I hated having to put my body on show, but I needed the money. And then this guy—well, let's just say he wanted what he thought was on offer. So I stopped doing it and focused on my studies.'

He sensed a world of unspoken words, and his gut tightened. 'Did he hurt you?'

She shook her head. 'No. Not my body.'

'Just your spirit.'

'My pride? My dignity? My sense of self-worth? Not

that it wasn't already in the gutter.' She closed her eyes, and he leant in and kissed her gently.

'I'm sorry.'

They opened again. 'Don't be. It was a steep but valuable learning curve.'

'Sounds like the rest of your life.' He cupped her cheek, turning her head towards him and kissing her again before rolling onto his back and drawing her gently into his arms.

'Tell me about it,' he murmured as she settled against him. 'Your life. What happened, where you lived, who opened your post—who made you think you ruin everybody's lives.'

She gave a short, sad huff of laughter. 'Have you got all night?'

'If that's what it takes.'

So she told him, hesitantly at first, then as he felt the tension go out of her, more fluidly, moving through her mother's desertion to the foster parents who fought about her and drove her out.

'I heard them fighting, him yelling, "That bloody girl's ruined everything!", and so I ran away.'

'How old were you then?' he asked, appalled.

'Eight? I'd been there over two years, and all I can remember is them fighting the whole time, and then he said all that and left, slamming the door so hard I thought it was going to break, so I got my things and I ran away.'

'So what happened then?'

'Another failed foster placement, and then social services put me into a home because it was my fault, apparently, because I was disruptive, so I was there until I was nearly eleven and hated every minute of it. And then they found me some new foster parents, a professional couple with a younger child, which was so much better. She'd been a nurse, he was a teacher, and they were wonderful people, but after a while their son started to resent me, and when the son hit puberty...'

She broke off, pressing her lips together, and he hugged her gently, unsure of what was coming, sure he wouldn't like it.

'Go on.'

'He didn't respect my boundaries. He used to walk into my bedroom when I was dressing and sit on the bed and watch me and refuse to get out. One day I caught him in my underwear drawer. Another day I found him reading my diary—'

'Which is why you didn't want me to open your post for you?'

She nodded. 'I told him to leave me alone, to keep out of my room, but he wouldn't, and every time they heard us shouting he blamed me, so I told them what he was doing and they gave him hell and grounded him, but that just made him worse.'

'How?'

'Oh, you know kids. There's no end to the subtle cruelties they can inflict when there's nobody looking, but that wasn't enough for him. He wanted more, and he wanted me out, so he waited until we were alone in the house one day, and then he tried to rape me.'

Sam swore, softly and viciously, and his arms tightened reflexively around her. 'What did you do? Did you report him?'

'What was the point? He would just have lied, like he always lied, so I did the only thing I could do. I ran away, which was exactly what he wanted.'

'Where did you go?'

'The park. I hid from the park keepers, but there were some really dodgy people there, a lot of drugs, deals going down, and I didn't feel safe. His parents had given me a mobile and I didn't answer it, but in the end I was so scared I rang them and they got the police to open the gates and let me out.'

'Jeez, Kate. What did the police do?'

'Nothing. I told them I'd got shut in there by accident and they believed me, but my foster parents didn't, and they were worried sick.'

'I'll bet they were. And the boy?' he asked. 'What happened to him?'

He felt her shrug. 'He wouldn't tell them what had happened and nor would I, I just said I couldn't stay there anymore, so social services found me a place to live while I finished my A-levels, and they kept an eye on me. My foster father gave me private tuition because he knew how important my future was to me, and my foster mother helped me with my entry for nursing, so without them I wouldn't be where I am today, but I didn't feel truly free of him until I was at uni.'

She ground to a halt, and he rested his head against hers and sighed quietly. 'Oh, Kate. I'm so sorry. No wonder you've got issues. And I thought my life was tough because I got sent to boarding school.'

'I don't suppose it was so very different to being in care.'

He gave a hollow laugh. 'I don't know. Probably not, really, except I imagine you were mostly with underprivileged kids who had an excuse, and I was with spoilt little rich kids who just expected Mummy and Daddy to buy them out of trouble and didn't give a damn who they hurt. I expect the end result was much the same.'

'Kids are kids, Sam. They can be amazing, and they can be unspeakably cruel. But you learn how to keep out of the way, and you move on and try not to make the same mistakes over and over again, but it doesn't always work and you never really forget. It's always there, lurking in the background, waiting for an unguarded moment, which is why I don't talk about it.'

Her hand came up and cupped his cheek, her face tilting up to his as she turned his head so she could kiss him. 'Make love to me, Sam,' she whispered. 'Make me forget it all.'

How could he refuse? That first night, he'd used her to help him forget his grief, so he knew that it worked, if only for a while. He could do the same for her.

He threaded his fingers through her hair, cradled her head and kissed her back until there was nothing left in the world but him and her, and the fire raging between them burned away the pain.

They were nearly late for work, not least because they'd woken late and shared the shower to save time, which had nearly derailed them completely.

'Later,' he promised, towelling himself roughly dry as he left the bathroom, and she bit her lip to stop the smile, dragged the knots out of her hair, cleaned her teeth and ran to the bedroom, to find him dressed in the clean clothes he'd grabbed from the cabin the night before on their way home.

He was the only tidy thing in the bedroom, and she scooped up a pile of washing, threw it out of the way, found some clean underwear and clothes and followed him downstairs to the car with ten minutes to go before their shifts started.

'Cutting it fine,' James said drily as they walked in, and she saw Sam's lips twitch, which just gave her the giggles.

'Hussy,' he muttered. 'You'll give us away.'

'And the whisker-burn won't? And anyway, do you really think there's anyone in the hospital now who doesn't know we're an item? Dream on.'

'Well, we'd better give them something to talk about, then,' he said, setting the smile free, and pulling her to a halt he dropped a kiss on her startled lips and walked away, whistling softly to himself.

'Whoa. He is smokin' hot!' Petra said, coming up behind her and gazing after Sam.

'Petra! I haven't seen you for ages. How was your holiday? Did you have a good time?'

'Not as good as you, apparently,' Petra said, her eyes still on Sam. 'We need to go out tonight, and you can tell me all.'

She gave a slightly crazed laugh, and shook her head. 'I can't go out tonight, I'm busy, and anyway, I wouldn't know where to start. Well, I would. January.'

'He's the hot guy?' Petra squealed, and Kate flipped her mouth shut with a finger and wondered why she'd told her friend so much.

'Shh. Actually, it's all a bit more than that. We're—' She didn't know quite where to take that one, so backtracked hastily. 'Look, I'll tell you another time, but there is one thing. We're having a baby.'

Petra's mouth fell open again. 'Oh, my... Kate, are you OK? What are you going to do? Are you getting rid of it?'

'No! And keep your voice down,' she hissed. 'Nobody knows, and it hasn't been easy. His fiancée died two years ago.'

Petra's eyes widened, and she grabbed Kate's hand. 'Honey, are you OK? Seriously? Because that sounds like a whole cartload of baggage. If I was you I'd run for the hills.'

Yes, you would, she thought, and a few days ago she

would have done, too, but now nothing was further from her mind and she wondered what on earth she and Petra had really had in common, apart from both being single.

'I'm fine,' she said, then glanced at the clock and yelped. 'Seriously, I have to get to work. I'm not even in scrubs and I'm ten minutes late. I'll see you later.'

'Promise?'

'I promise. I'll call you, if nothing else.'

She fled, changed at the speed of light and reached the doors of Resus at the same time as the patient who was being wheeled in.

Sam was there waiting, and he frowned questioningly and mouthed, 'Are you all right?'

She was, she realised. Very all right. She smiled back, nodded and took her place in the team.

Annie sent her a text during the morning, and she skipped her lunch break with Sam and ran up to Maternity and found her in SCBU with a baby in her arms.

She beckoned her in, and Kate gowned up and went over to her, giving her a careful hug.

'Hi, I got your text. So who's this? He's gorgeous.'

'Theo. Here, sit down and give him a cuddle.'

'Are you sure? He's so tiny—I don't think I've ever held a baby this small before.'

'Ah, well, you'd better start practising. Here you go.'

And there she was, with another baby in her arms, but so tiny this time, so precious, so fragile, and she felt a surge of protectiveness and fear in equal measure.

'Oh, Annie,' she breathed, staring at him as if he was the most amazing thing she'd ever seen, and right then he opened his eyes and stared up at her, and she blinked.

'Oh, he's so like Ed!'

'I know. It's hilarious. He's so tiny, but he's Ed to a T.'

'And the other one?'

'He's like me. We've called him Freddie, for my father,' she said, a tender, bittersweet smile on her face. 'He would have loved them all so much...'

'Oh, Annie,' she said again, and then laughed at herself. 'I'm sounding like a stuck record,' she said a little unevenly, and looked down at Theo again, at the tiny face the image of his father's, and she wondered if her baby would be like Sam. She hoped so. 'I can't believe this is going to happen to me,' she said softly, and Annie reached out a hand and squeezed her shoulder.

'Get used to it. It's amazing.'

'It's terrifying.'

'Well, that, too, but you soon get used to it.' She searched Kate's eyes. 'So how are things with Sam? Did you like the house?'

'I loved the house,' she said. 'There was nothing not to love about it. And—Sam stayed with me last night. He's moving in later, properly.'

'Oh, Kate, that's wonderful!'

'Well, I hope so. It is at the moment, I just hope it lasts. Wish us luck.'

'You don't need luck, you need guts and determination and compassion, and you've got all that in spades. You'll be fine, Kate. You wait and see.'

Theo started to cry then, so Annie held her arms out and winced, and Kate felt a pang of guilt as she handed the baby over.

'I haven't even asked how you are,' she said lamely, and Annie gave a wry laugh.

'Oh, I'm a bit sore, but so, so happy.'

'Worth it, then?'

'Oh, yes.' She gave a contented, happy laugh and

looked back down at the baby in her arms, her face softened by love. 'Every single moment.'

Sam moved in properly that night, and while he packed up the cabin and discussed solicitors and timescales with James and Connie, she loaded the washing machine, blitzed the bedroom and scrubbed the bathroom within an inch of its life.

By the time he got back with all his things, the bed was made up with fresh linen, and she'd cleared space for him in the wardrobe in the spare bedroom, consigning the other half to charity shop bags.

And her spare set of keys were on his pillow in her room.

He picked them up, hefted them in his hand and smiled. 'Thank you.'

'Don't thank me. It's only so I don't have to run downstairs and let you in all the time,' she teased, and he chucked them back on the bed, pulled her into his arms and kissed her, then looked around and blinked.

'Good grief, you've been busy.'

'I needed to be, it was a slum.'

'Not quite.'

'Verging on it. I've made you space in the wardrobe next door for shirts and stuff, and there's a drawer in there for your underwear.'

He nodded. 'Thanks. Have you eaten?'

She shook her head. 'No, not really. I was waiting for you, but I've grazed on a ton of chocolate. You?'

'Connie fed me a sandwich, but that's all and it was ages ago. Want me to cook while you put your feet up?'

'No. I've got some stuff in the freezer. Why don't I do it while you unpack?' she said, touched that he'd offered, and she was almost done when he came up behind her, put his arms around her and rested his chin on her shoulder.

'So what are we having?' he asked, nuzzling her ear.

She laughed. 'Well, I thought it was chilli, so I cooked some rice, but turns out it's Bolognese sauce.'

She felt his chuckle through her shoulders. 'I'm sure it won't kill us,' he said, and for a second the words echoed in the air around them before he straightened up and moved away, his warmth replaced by a chilling draught that came from nowhere.

'I'll get the plates,' he said, and she stood at the sink draining and rinsing the rice and wondering if Kerry's ghost would overshadow them for ever.

They ate their meal in a polite silence, hardly exchanging a word, and when it was finished he thanked her, cleared the table and ran the water to wash up.

'I can do that—'

'No. Go and put your feet up. You've done enough today.'

He should have turned and smiled at her, softened it, but he couldn't meet her wounded gaze, and as he heard her leave the room, he plunged his hands into the hot water, leant over the sink and closed his eyes.

Just when it was all going so well, he thought, and swallowed a block of emotion that threatened to choke him. The grief he recognised, but guilt, too—guilt for betraying Kerry by moving on so readily with Kate, guilt for short-changing Kate because a part of his heart would always be with Kerry, guilt for fathering a child in such unpromising circumstances—the list of his emotional crimes was endless, and he had an overwhelming urge to curl up in the corner and cry, but he'd done enough of that.

More than enough. It was time to man up and deal with reality.

He finished the washing up, wiped down the kitchen, cleared and polished the sink—Kerry there again, being fastidious beyond reason—and stuck his head round the door.

'Can I get you a drink?'

She shook her head. She'd turned away from him so he couldn't see her face, but he knew with a sickening certainty that she'd been crying.

He went over to her, crouched down in front of her and turned her face towards him, tsking softly at the clumped lashes and the dribble of mascara sliding down her cheek.

'I'm sorry,' he said heavily.

'Don't be. It's too soon for you, I know that.'

Her voice was cracking, and he shifted to the seat beside her and drew her into his arms with a sigh.

'It's two years, Kate, I should be over it, but sometimes it just creeps up on me and takes me by surprise. One of those unguarded moments you were talking about last night, I guess, but it's not a part of us, of what we have.'

'Yes, it is, because I'm just a constant reminder of what you've lost. I'm just there, in your face, getting in the way of your memories, being the wrong person in the wrong place at the wrong time, and I can't do it, Sam. I can't compete with her for your affection—'

'You don't have to! This is nothing to do with her, and you're not the wrong person, Kate, you're just you.'

'And that's supposed to be a good thing?'

He let out a sigh. 'Yes. Yes, it is, for us. I wasn't trying to replace her—I wasn't trying to do anything when I met you except forget, just for a little while. I certainly didn't expect this to happen, but it has, and, no, it's not the same, but that doesn't make it bad or unworkable. It just takes getting used to, and that's going to take time, but we'll get there.'

She nodded, snuggling closer, sniffing a little until he handed her a tissue.

'Here. Blow your nose. I'll get you tea.'

He brought it in, but she didn't linger after she'd finished it, just took her mug back to the kitchen when the programme she was watching ended, and told him she was going to turn in.

'Don't feel you have to rush, I just fancy an early night,' she said, and went into the bedroom and pushed the door to.

He stared at it for an age, then dropped his head back and let out a long, quiet sigh. She hadn't shut it completely. He supposed that was a signal that he was still welcome in her bed, but maybe just not yet.

He'd give it a while, he decided, and then go and join her, but he wouldn't expect a rapturous welcome—unlike last night, when she'd opened her heart to him and told him the story of her sad and fractured childhood. Well, the walls were up again now, without a doubt, and he had to respect her boundaries.

He turned off the television, washed up their mugs and went quietly into the bedroom, undressing and slipping into bed beside her without disturbing her.

'Night, Kate,' he murmured, but there was silence, so he punched the pillow, turned away from her and closed his eyes.

No good. She wasn't asleep. He could tell because her breathing was too even, too measured, too—conscious?

He rolled onto his back and turned his head towards her. 'Kate?'

In the dim light from the streetlamp outside he saw the soft sheen of tears on her cheek, and with another wave of guilt and regret he rolled towards her, pulled her into his arms and kissed her tears away.

'Don't shut me out, Kate,' he murmured. 'I'm sorry I hurt you—'

'You didn't hurt me. I just can't be her—'

'You don't have to be her. Just be you. There's nothing wrong with you.' He kissed her again, trailing his lips over her cheek, her nose, her eyes, then down again to her mouth, taking it in a long, slow, tender kiss that made her sigh.

He felt the tension go out of her, her arms creep round him, and he gave a quiet sigh of relief, shifted her further into his arms and held her as she settled into sleep.

CHAPTER NINE

IT WAS DIFFERENT after that.

They'd stopped being so wary around each other, having to weigh every word, and they settled into a comfortable routine. She'd thought it would be difficult, that she'd find it hard to have him there all the time, day and night, but it grew easier with every passing day.

They told some of the people at work, of course, and got mixed reactions, but she'd expected that and she knew some of them would be waiting for her to mess up, but she was determined not to, and she kept her head down and avoided the doom-mongers, and gradually it slid down the gossip charts.

They'd been sharing the flat over a week when they heard that Tom, the young man who'd had the cardiac arrest, was out of danger, and Sam went up to see him and brought her back a celebratory coffee from the canteen.

'How is he?' she asked, conscious of the fact that Sam had found his case especially hard, but he was genuinely happy.

'He's great. He's got a long way to go, but he'll get there. I'm just so relieved for him. Oh, by the way, the house paperwork came through in the post this morning after you left. We need to sign the contract and get it back.'

'Wow. That was quick!'

'It had to be. Right, I'd better get on.'

He dropped a kiss on her lips, lingered just a moment too long and then winked as he walked away, and her heart gave a happy little jiggle.

They exchanged contracts on the house within the four weeks James had stipulated, and then he started to make lists of things they'd need.

Lists of furniture, lists of curtains, lists for the kitchen, for the nursery—it was only the nursery that really interested her, and for the first time she expressed a preference.

'I want white. White everything. It's easier.'

'I thought babies were supposed to have bright, stimulating colours?'

'Not in their bedrooms,' she said, although she didn't actually know that for a fact, but she knew if she was in a room filled with colour it was harder to settle to sleep, whereas a white room with soft grey and putty accents lowered her stress levels and soothed her instantly. 'And anyway,' she added, 'I don't want to get anything yet. Not so soon.'

'We can still look. Let's go shopping,' he said, turning off his tablet with its endless images and pulling her to her feet.

'What—now?' she said, hanging back, because she still didn't really feel it was her house, and she didn't want to make a massive emotional investment in it. In her mind it was something he and Kerry had done, and she just felt it would be an utter minefield.

'Yes, now. It's Saturday morning, the shops are open, we can go and wander round them and choose what you like.'

'Sam, I really don't mind—'

'Of course you do. I know you're being noble because you think it's my house, but it's not, it's our house, and I want you to like it and help me make it a home, so stop being so noncommittal and tell me what you like or we won't have a stick of furniture to sit on.'

Was she being noble or noncommittal? Or was it that she wanted so badly for it to feel like home that it was terrifying her?

'Sam, I'm not like Kerry, these things really don't matter to me,' she said, and he frowned and let go of her hand and sat down again.

'I know you're not like her. I'm well aware of that. If I was with Kerry doing this, I'd be trailing round behind her ticking her lists and agreeing just for the sake of peace. I don't think it even occurred to her to ask me what I wanted. She was just like a kid in a sweetshop.'

She stared at him in astonishment. 'Gosh,' she said softly, after an age. 'Where did that come from?'

He shrugged. 'It's the truth. It didn't stop me loving her, it's just how she was. She was sweet, kind, funny, generous, but she didn't have a spontaneous bone in her body. She was meticulously organised, fanatically tidy, she planned everything down to the last detail—nothing was allowed to happen by chance. And I still feel guilty that I didn't take any interest, that I was glad I was out of the country when she was planning the wedding, because she would have driven me mad with the endless trivia. But you're not her, and nor am I, and I really have no idea where to start, so your help would be very much appreciated.'

He fell silent, and she let out a long, soft sigh and wrapped her arms around him. 'Oh, Sam. I'm sorry. I didn't know that. Of course I'll come shopping with you.'

* * *

It turned out that she did have opinions, and it surprised her.

'How about this?' Sam would ask, and she'd frown and he'd laugh and walk on. 'This?' Frown, laugh, walk on.

They left that shop, because in fact neither of them liked anything they had in stock, and went to the next one and tried again.

'Oh, this is better,' she said instantly as they walked in, and he smiled.

'I'm glad we agree. So—sofas?'

'I like this one.' She sat down, leant back and shook her head and got up. 'You can't slouch in it.'

'Well, that's a must. Let's find a slouchy one,' he said, and threading his fingers through hers he led her round the displays until they found one with the right degree of slouchiness.

He sat down at one end, and she sat at the other, swivelled her legs round and put her feet in his lap.

'Perfect,' she said with a grin, and he chuckled.

'I agree. I think we should have a pair, like James and Connie. What about the fabric?'

'I like this leather,' she said. 'It's nice—sort of battered and not intimidating. And you can wipe leather. Babies are very messy, from my limited experience. They tend to leak a bit.'

He stifled a laugh and hailed an assistant who'd been hovering discreetly in the background.

'How long will they take to come?' Sam asked. 'Because we need this quickly. We're moving in a couple of weeks.'

'Well, you're in luck, then, if you like this, because our sale starts tomorrow, and all our display stock is going to be marked down. Otherwise it'll be six weeks.'

'So we could have this one sooner?'

'Yes. And if you wanted a pair, we have another one in the window.'

'Perfect,' Sam said. 'Do you do beds?'

Of course they did, and to Kate's relief they'd all be discounted, too. They'd almost agreed on a painted wooden bed when they went round the corner and he spotted a different one.

'How about this for the master bedroom?' he said, pointing at a huge mahogany sleigh bed, and she nodded slowly.

'That's lovely. It looks welcoming.'

'After a long, hard shift, bed is *always* welcoming,' he said drily, and lay down on it. 'Oh, yes. Try the mattress,' he coaxed, patting the other side, and she lay down, feeling like an idiot, and then totally forgot to care how she looked, because it was bliss.

'That's amazing,' she said softly. 'It's like lying on a cloud. How much is it?'

He laughed and told her you couldn't put a price on a comfortable bed, which by extension meant it was shockingly expensive, and then reminded her it would be in the sale.

'Well, it's your money,' she said, getting up reluctantly. 'Don't forget we'll need something for the spare bedroom, as well, before you blow the entire budget on this one.'

'Don't worry about the budget. Now, is it big enough, or do we need a super-king? By the time the kids are in it, too...'

Kids? *Kids?* She was still getting her head around the one they were having, and he was planning *more*?

'I think you're getting ahead of yourself,' she said quietly, and the smile on his face disappeared in an instant.

'Yeah. Sorry. Anyway, the super-king might not go up the stairs.'

He cleared his throat and moved away from her, from the blissful but contentious bed, from the idea of a huge, happy family bouncing around in it, and after confirming the details with the assistant, he shot her a glance.

'Coffee?'

She nodded, ready to sit down on something she didn't have to have an opinion on, and they went into the store's café. He sent her to find a seat, and came over with coffees and a huge slab of chocolate fudge cake.

'What's that?'

'A peace offering.'

She looked up at him, at his sombre eyes, his mouth set in a tight line of regret, and she shook her head.

'Oh, Sam. It's OK. It's just that I'm still coming to terms with having *this* baby, and with the idea of living with you, and frankly that's hard enough to get my head round.'

'Yeah. Baby steps. I'm sorry.' He sat down, handed her one of the two forks and smiled wryly. 'Can we share?'

She smiled back at him. 'Since you ask so nicely.'

'Hmph.' He scooped off a chunk and inhaled it, and she laughed.

'Shopping getting to you?'

'Absolutely,' he groaned. 'I don't know how women have the stamina for it.'

'Me, neither. Maybe it helps if it's someone else's money, but I've never been in that position so I wouldn't know.'

'You are now.'

She shook her head. 'No. This stuff is for your house—'

'Our house. I'm putting it in joint names.'

She felt the blood drain from her face, then surge back

up. 'Sam—no! Why? That's not fair! It's your money, from the house you bought with Kerry. You can't give it away!'

He stared at her, obviously shocked. 'It's not like it was ever our home, Kate. I told you that.'

'But it should have been your home,' she said, her eyes filling for a woman who never got to live in it, never got to realise her dream, and Sam gave a soft groan and covered her hand with his.

'Kate—let's not do this here.'

'Why not? We're getting in so deep, Sam, and you're just being noble and doing the decent thing and you're not ready—'

'It's not about being ready, Kate, it's about reality, and what's happening to us, whether we're ready or not. The baby won't wait, and it needs a home.'

'Then put it in the baby's name,' she said desperately.

He sighed and shook his head slowly. 'Do you really hate Kerry that much?'

'What? No, of course I don't, but it was her dream home—'

'Not mine, though. It was sensible, manageable for her on her own while I was away, and close to her parents so that if anything happened to me she'd have their support. It was me who was supposed to die, not her, which was why I just let her do what she wanted with it, but I could never have been truly happy there. It was too far from the sea, too hemmed in by other houses, too—hell, I don't know, too suburban. I don't think we would have stayed there that long. It just wasn't me.'

'And this one is,' she said slowly, knowing it was true.

'It is. It's so perfect for me I can't believe I'm going to live in it. I've always loved it, since the first moment

I saw it, and if it makes you feel any better, no, Kerry never saw it.'

He fell silent while she assimilated all of that, and the thing that came to the top of the pile was his bald statement that he was the one who was supposed to die.

'You've got survivor guilt,' she said softly, and he nodded.

'Yes. Yes, I suppose I have, in a way. She was in a safe place, while I was out in the field with bombs going off all around me, snipers trying to pick me off when we flew in to rescue someone who'd been ambushed by an IED—it was a miracle I didn't get hurt, but I got away without a scratch, and she...'

He broke off, stirred his coffee absently and then looked up and met her eyes.

'Look, I know it's tough for you, but I don't want it to be. None of that is anything to do with you, it's all in the past. We're buying the house now, it needs furniture, it's going to be our home. It's a new start, Kate. A new start I desperately need. Please, don't make it harder for either of us than it already is.'

She felt her eyes welling, blinked away the tears and nodded. 'Of course. I'm sorry. Let's just have our coffee and get on with it, shall we? We've still got a lot to do.'

Kate crawled up the stairs, plopped onto the sofa and put her feet up.

'I'm never going shopping again,' she groaned, and Sam laughed, bent over the back of the sofa and dropped a kiss on her head.

'Well, at least it's done now, or most of it. I can't believe the trivia, though—so many decisions about nothing that matters.'

She turned her head round and peered at him over

the back of the sofa as he went into the kitchen. 'So you agree with me, then, that it doesn't matter?'

He laughed. 'I didn't say that. It's just that when you have to make decisions about what kind of cutlery, which glasses, crockery, tea towels, for heaven's sake—it's just endless!'

She followed him into the kitchen, trying not to laugh. 'So were you just passing the buck, then, making me choose so you didn't have to commit?'

'Damn. You rumbled me.'

He chuckled and pulled her in for a hug, and she rested her head on his chest and sighed. 'Oh, Sam. Are we really going to be OK?'

'Yes. Now go and sit down, and I'll make you tea and try and work out what we've got to eat. Or we could order a takeaway?'

'What, make another decision?' she said, and they both started to laugh, clinging to each other and laughing until their sides ached, and then he stared down at her, still in his arms, and bent his head and kissed her.

It wasn't passionate, it didn't linger, it was just—'healing' was the only word she could come up with, building a bridge over the rivers of grief and doubt and insecurity that ran between them, and she realised she felt safe.

Safe with Sam, with life, but also with her future, because for the first time ever, she had one that she might just be able to rely on.

The days ticked by, and before they knew it the twenty-week anomaly scan for the baby was coming up, and so was the move.

They had less than two weeks before the sale was due to be completed, so the furniture delivery was due for the Friday after that, giving them the weekend to unpack everything and settle in before they were back at work on the Monday.

And in the meantime, he thought, watching Kate across the ED, he needed to make a new will and get Kate named as the beneficiary on his forces and NHS pensions. Just in case, because, as he knew only too well, life didn't come with any guarantees.

He added that to his ever-growing 'to-do' list, and gave a wry smile. Kerry would have laughed her socks off at the very thought, but then her 'to-do' list used to start with 'Wake up'. He wondered what she would have made of the spontaneous loose cannon that was Kate, and decided she would have liked her, even though she probably wouldn't have understood her at all.

He was beginning to, and he was discovering a thoughtful, sensitive, compassionate woman with a huge heart and enormous courage. Not to mention a wicked sense of humour and the ability to charm the devil incarnate into submitting to a procedure that was definitely not on his wish list. And on that subject...

He capped his pen, tucked the list into the pocket of his scrubs and went to help her talk Mr Lucas round.

'He's a nightmare,' she said with a sigh after Mr Lucas had finally allowed them to dress his ulcer. 'He's probably the worst of our frequent flyers. He never takes care of himself, he treats us like his personal doctors' surgery and complains bitterly about everything we do for him. I swear, I could kill him sometimes.'

Sam chuckled and gave her a discreet hug. 'You're wonderful with him. Goodness knows why, he doesn't deserve it.'

'Oh, he's just lonely and his life's a mess. I can understand that, even if it does annoy me. How's your to-do list?'

'Growing,' he said wryly. 'Kerry would have laughed at me.'

She gave a soft chuckle at his expression, the rueful self-mockery echoed in his words, realising with a slight shock that they were talking quite naturally about Kerry, as if she was finally taking her rightful place in the dynamics of their relationship.

'She must have felt about you the way you feel about me, then, because you're way more organised than I'll ever be,' she told him honestly.

'Not at work,' he said, shaking his head. 'At work, you're like a streamlined machine. You don't overlook anything, and even when we're ridiculously busy, you still find time to be kind to the patients and make them feel comfortable and safe. That's a real gift, Kate, and you have it in spades.'

She felt her eyes fill at the sudden unexpected compliment, and blinked and turned away. 'Thank you,' she said softly, and then cleared her throat. 'Right, who's next?'

So this was it.

His own home at last, emptied now of James and Connie's possessions, echoing hollowly as he walked around it, his fingers trailing over the walls, the banisters, the doorframes, coming to rest on the handle of the roof light in the master bedroom.

He tugged it gently and it pivoted open, and he leant out, drew the sea air into his lungs and sighed.

His own home, at last, he thought, and wandered through to the en suite bathroom, throwing open the roof light in there and taking in the spectacular view over the marshes behind the house, lonely, desolate and inhospitable, but teeming with nesting wetland birds at this time of year.

'Hello, house,' he said softly, and turned, looking straight through and out at the sea once more. He could feel it tugging him, the urge to fix up the boat and get out on the sea almost overwhelming, but he had a lot to do before that was even on the bottom of his agenda.

With a sigh he closed the windows and ran back downstairs. He had to get Kate. Her shift should have finished now and she'd want to see it, too, but he'd had a selfish urge to see it alone first. He felt a twinge of guilt for not waiting, but he'd needed it, this quiet time alone with the house to make its acquaintance. Heaven knows the peace won't last long, he thought, with the baby coming in just a few more months.

He paused on the veranda and closed his eyes briefly, sending up a silent prayer to whoever might be listening that it would all work out, that the hell and confusion of the past two years could be laid to rest and he and Kate and the baby could make the family he hadn't even realised he needed so much, here in this beautiful and welcoming home.

Then he locked the house, ran down the veranda steps and went to fetch Kate.

'Have you got the keys?'

He nodded and held a bunch out to her. 'That's your set, and we've got two spare sets in case we need them. Are you ready to go?'

'Definitely. Have you been down there yet?'

He hesitated, and she knew instantly that he had, that he didn't want to tell her in case she was somehow disappointed that he hadn't waited for her, but that it had been important for him in some way.

Laying a ghost to rest? She could only hope so.

'Sam, it's fine. I totally get it. Come on, let's go and look together.'

They walked up the veranda steps and he unlocked the door, pushed it open and let her go in first. She stepped over the threshold, crushing a tiny flicker of disappointment that he hadn't carried her over it, but this wasn't a love nest, it was a house that would hopefully turn into a home for their family, and so she walked through the kitchen and into the large open living room with the huge bay window framing the sea.

'OK?'

She turned to him, nodded and slipped her hand into his. 'It's beautiful. I love it.'

'Good. So do I. Let's go and have a look upstairs.'

They wandered round for ages, spotting things they hadn't seen before, like the clever storage in the bathroom, the little train frieze around Joseph's old bedroom, the colourful mural on the wall behind where his cot had been.

'I guess all this will have to go,' he said, and her hands fell automatically to caress her bump.

'Probably. It seems a shame, but if it's a girl she might not be into trains.'

'It might be a boy.'

'Do you mind what it is?'

He shook his head. 'No, not at all. I don't care about anything except that it's healthy.'

'What if there's something wrong with it?' she asked.

'We'll deal with it. It might not be easy, but we'll find a way. What about you? Do you care what it is?'

She shook her head. 'Not really. I think I'd like a girl, just because I know more about them than I do about boys, but I'm like you, I just want it to be all right.'

He laid his hands over hers, then froze. 'Was that a kick?'

She nodded, pulling her hand out from under his so he could feel it better, and he let out a soft huff of wonder.

'That's amazing. How long have you been able to feel it?'

'A week or so? I wasn't sure at first, but it's been having a good old wriggle today.'

He laughed, then wrapped his arms around her and held her close, and she rested her head on his shoulder and sighed.

'Are you OK?' he murmured.

'Mmm. Just happy.'

'Me, too.' He eased her away, looking down intently into her eyes, and then he slid his hands down her arms and took both her hands in his.

'Marry me, Kate. Please? Let's be a proper family?'

She blinked, then took a tiny step back, mentally as well as physically. 'Why? Why do you want to marry me, Sam? Why can't you just accept what we have?'

'Because I want more? Because I'm old-fashioned and I believe a child's parents should be married?'

She shook her head. 'No. That's not a reason to get married. Plenty of parents aren't—and plenty of those who are get divorced.'

'I know. And I know it's no guarantee of happiness, but you'd be better protected in law if we're married.'

'That's not a good enough reason, Sam. People should only get married because they *love* each other. I'm not going to marry you when I don't think either of us is ready for it. I'll move in with you, I'll live here with you and our baby, but I can't marry you just to make it tidy.'

He dragged his hands down over his face, let out a heavy sigh and shook his head.

'No. I'm sorry. You're right. Maybe I wanted to do it for the wrong reasons, to undo our mistakes.'

'You can't, Sam. Nobody can do that. And right now, neither of us is ready for this step—not yet, at least. And we've got so many other things to think about—moving in here, the scan, getting ready for the baby—it's all too much at once. Give us time—please? Let's see how it goes?'

He nodded, but the happiness she'd seen in his eyes was gone, wiped away by her refusal, and as he turned away she pressed her lips together and blinked away the stinging tears.

CHAPTER TEN

THE FURNITURE CAME on Friday morning, as planned, and immediately it started to look like a home.

He'd taken the day off to supervise, and it had paid off because everything had been put in its intended place, everything unwrapped and the packaging taken away, and he'd even had time to make the beds. All that remained was finding a home for the kitchen things, and that was Kate's province.

She was working, but the moment she finished she drove down and joined him, and her face when she walked in made all the angst and effort worthwhile.

'Oh, Sam—it looks amazing!' She ran her fingers over the back of a sofa and scanned the room. 'I love that table. I'm so glad we chose it and not the other one.'

'I thought you didn't care? I thought it didn't matter?' he teased, and she laughed and hugged him.

'It does matter, of course it matters. If it's not yours, you just accept it, but if it's yours, there's no point in it being wrong for the sake of a bit of effort.'

He chuckled. 'Well, you've changed your tune. Come on, come and see the bedrooms.'

He took her by the hand and led her upstairs, and they paused by the door to the nursery at the foot of the attic stairs.

'It looks so empty,' she said, her hand curving over their baby instinctively as if she feared for it.

Did she? She'd refused to buy anything for it until after the scan, so was she still wondering what would happen if she lost it? God forbid, he thought, but if she did, the nursery would hang over them as a constant reminder of all they'd lost.

'Why don't I redecorate it?' he suggested quickly. 'Paint it white, like you said?'

'Or maybe a pale grey? It faces east, it'll be very light.'

'I'll do it white first. I reckon it'll take a couple of coats at least to cover the mural. Then you can decide.' He took her shoulders and pointed her towards the attic stairs, patting her on the bottom. 'Come on, come and see our room.'

He followed her up, and she pushed open the door at the top and gasped.

'Oh, Sam, it looks fabulous! I thought the bed would be huge in here, but it's perfect!'

She ran her hand over the bedding—pure white hotel stripe zillion thread count Egyptian cotton, over a goose down duvet, because as he'd said you couldn't put a price on a comfortable bed—and sighed.

'It's gorgeous. The whole house—it's gorgeous. You must be so happy with it.'

Not as happy as he would have been if she'd agreed to marry him, but if she wasn't ready—

'Yes. Yes, I am happy with it,' he said firmly. 'I think it'll suit us very well. Come on, I'm starving, I haven't stopped all day. Let's go to the pub and have dinner, and then go back to yours. We can move in tomorrow.'

In fact it took two days, mostly because he wouldn't let her do any of the carrying, and there was a limit to how much even he could carry down the stairs on his own at once.

Anyway, she had enough to do, because it was ages since all the furniture had been pulled out and the flat needed a serious deep clean, so they emptied her possessions out of one room at a time, and while he ran up and down, she blitzed the nooks and crannies that hadn't seen the light of day for yonks.

'How can you have so many clothes?' he asked on the third pass, and she could see him wondering if there could possibly be enough wardrobe space.

So it was Sunday afternoon by the time everything was moved and her flat was ready to be handed back to the landlord.

'All done?'

She nodded. 'I'll just have one last check. I'll see you downstairs.'

She walked through the rooms alone, saying goodbye to her old life. The end of an era, she thought—and the beginning, hopefully, of a better one? Certainly different.

The rooms were all clean now, but they were tatty, in desperate need of new furnishings, and the contrast between it and Sam's house was shocking.

And yet it had been her sanctuary, a place where she could retreat to lick her wounds, and she was sad and a little afraid to let it go.

She closed the door for the last time, turned and tripped on the torn stair carpet, grabbing the banisters to save herself.

'Kate?'

She heard him run up the stairs three at a time, stopping in front of her, hands on her shoulders.

'Are you all right? What happened?'

'I'm fine. I tripped, that's all.'

He sighed sharply. 'That wretched carpet—it's a miracle you haven't killed yourself on these stairs. Come on, let's go.'

She followed him down, out of the front door, closing it with a solid *thunk* behind her.

Time to move on...

Her twenty-week anomaly scan was on Wednesday evening, three days after they'd moved in, and everything was fine. She hadn't realised how tense she'd been, how worried, and now all she felt was the most enormous sense of relief.

'Do you want to know what it is?' the sonographer asked, and she shrugged.

'Sam?'

'I'm not sure. I'll let you decide.'

'I can't decide!' she wailed, half laughing, and the sonographer smiled.

'I tell you what. Why don't I write it down and put it in an envelope? And then you can think about it.'

'OK,' she said slowly, still massively undecided, so Sam took over.

'Give it to me,' he said with a smile, taking the decision out of her hands and tucking the envelope in his pocket. 'Then she won't be able to open it without convincing me she really wants to.'

They left the hospital and drove home—odd, how she was beginning to call it that in her head, even though she still maintained it was his house.

They picked up fish and chips on the way, and ate them out of the paper, sitting on the veranda watching the sun set over the marshes and listening to the keening of the gulls and the clatter of the rigging on Sam's boat.

'I must get on with it,' he said, staring at it thoughtfully. 'I should be able to get it in the water before the end of the summer. That's what it needs, to be in the water. Wooden boats shrink when you take them out, and then they leak, but it shouldn't by the time I've finished.'

'What about the inside?'

'Oh, it's fine. It needs a good clean and a polish, but the interior was refitted a few years ago and it's more than adequate. I'll take you out in it.'

'While I'm pregnant?' she said, feeling a little frisson of alarm, but he just grinned at her.

'It's got an engine, sweetheart. It's not like a little sailing dinghy, it won't capsize.'

'Good,' she said, and handed him the rest of her chips. 'So, what about this baby? Do we want to know?'

'Do you? Or do you want a surprise? That's what you said before.'

'I know, but…'

'Sleep on it. It doesn't really matter, one way or the other. It is what it is, but at least we know that everything's all right.'

She nodded and thought about it for a moment. 'I feel that, if we know, it might seem more real, as if it's a person and not just a wiggly bump. We could stop call it "it".'

'Up to you,' he said, holding up his hands and passing the buck firmly back to her. 'I can't make that decision for you, Kate. It has to be your choice.'

She took a deep breath. 'Let's open it.'

'Sure? There's no going back.'

'I'm sure.'

He handed her the envelope, and she opened it with trembling fingers and pulled out the slip of paper.

'Turn it over.'

'I can't—'

He held her hand, and together they turned the paper over.

'It's a girl! Oh, Sam, it's a girl, we're going to have a daughter!' she said, and burst into tears.

His arm came round her, holding her against his side, and she swiped away the tears, stroking her bump tenderly.

'I can't believe it's a girl…'

'It's what you wanted.'

'I know. Oh, Sam. She feels so real now.'

He hugged her again, then bent his head and kissed her. 'You'll have to choose a name.'

'No, we will. She's our baby, Sam,' she said, taking his hand and resting it over the baby. 'We'll choose her name together.'

His hand moved, caressing their child, caressing her, and she tilted her head and searched his eyes.

'Do you mind that it's not a boy?'

'No, of course not!' he said softly. 'It really doesn't matter to me so long as you're happy. That's all I want.'

He did. She could see it in his eyes, and it changed everything. She lifted her hand and laid it gently against his cheek.

'Let's get married,' she said impulsively, and his eyes widened.

'I thought you weren't ready?'

'I thought I wasn't, but I think I was just worrying about the scan, and at the time it was all I could think about, that and the move. I was just overwhelmed, but— now, somehow, it seems right.'

'Oh, Kate—'

He lowered his head and kissed her tenderly, and she

could feel he was shaking. 'Are you sure?' he murmured, lifting his head and searching her eyes.

'Yes. I'm absolutely sure.'

'Then let's do it, and soon, before the baby comes.'

She nodded slowly, snuggling in against his side. 'Can we have a simple wedding? I don't really want a lot of fuss. It's not as if I've got any family, just a few friends.'

'Me, too. Well, other than my parents and my brother. A small, simple wedding sounds perfect,' he said, and she remembered his comment about Kerry and the endless trivia, and was glad she'd said what she had. She didn't want their wedding spoilt by comparisons, even if the other one had never happened.

'Even if it's going to be small, I suppose we'll need to choose a venue,' she said doubtfully, and he just smiled, a slow, sexy smile that made her heart race.

'Can we talk about that later? Right now, I really fancy an early night, and we've got the perfect venue for that right here.'

He led her up to the attic, to the huge mahogany bed, the bedding almost luminous in the moonlight. He didn't turn the lights on. He didn't need to. He could see everything he needed to without them.

He undressed her slowly, his hands tracing the changes brought about by her advancing pregnancy—the fullness of her breasts, the smooth, firm curve below them where their daughter lay safe and snug, awaiting her time.

He matched the curve with his hands, fingers outstretched, and felt a subtle shift beneath them, a tiny kick against his palm. It made him smile.

'Shut your eyes, little girl, you're not old enough for this,' he murmured, and stripped off his clothes, turning back to Kate to draw her into his arms. The warmth of her skin, silky soft, smooth under his hands, the firmness of her belly, the soft fullness of her breasts—they intoxicated him, making him feel drugged with happiness, swept away by the beauty and the honesty of her body.

He lowered his head and kissed her, and felt her catch fire, her hands searching his body, urgency replacing reverence as he laid her down in the huge and wonderful bed they'd chosen together.

And soon it would become their marriage bed.

He couldn't remember ever feeling this happy, this complete in all his life. It was his last coherent thought before the wildfire raging inside him engulfed them both.

'Can we get married here?'

They were sitting on the veranda, drinking coffee from the wonderful built-in machine James had had installed and had grieved about leaving behind, and nibbling pastries for breakfast.

It felt wonderfully decadent, almost honeymoon-like, but they had plans to make soon if she didn't want to be so far into her pregnancy that she waddled down the aisle.

'I don't think it's legal.'

'No, probably not. Can we do the ceremony paperwork somewhere else and then come back here for the party?'

'Then we can't leave, and I might want to get you on your own.'

'Oh, might you?' she said, laughing softly and batting his hands away as he explored her body yet again.

'Yes, I might. I might want to do it now.'

'Behave. You've got to go to work in a minute. Can we have a sensible conversation about this?'

'We've had that conversation. I think we should have the party elsewhere, so we can escape—and anyway, the

weather might be wet, you can't be sure. Is there anywhere here with a smallish function room we could hire?'

'Zacharelli's?' she suggested. 'Although it's probably
hideously expensive.'

'Let's find out,' he said, and glanced at his watch.
'Oh, damn, I have to go, I'm supposed to be there in ten
minutes. You could try ringing them. See what dates
they've got.'

He dropped his feet to the floor, kissed her goodbye
and grabbed his car keys. 'I'll see you later.'

'OK. See you.'

She watched him drive away, feeling warm and fuzzy
inside, and sat back, letting the fresh June morning air fill
her lungs for a few more minutes before she cleared away
their breakfast things and went and wrote, of all things
calculated to make Sam laugh his head off, a to-do list.

'So, I've got some dates for Zacharelli's,' she said when
she caught up with Sam in the ED later. 'They haven't got
any Saturdays except one in four weeks because they've
had a cancellation. Is that too soon?'

'Probably not. We need to sort it with the registrar.
I'm due a break, I'll ring them. Can you give me the
exact date?'

She handed him her notes, and he raised his eyebrows
and stifled a smile. 'Is this a to-do list?' he asked carefully, and she closed her eyes and tried to look offended.

'You are so rude.'

His lips twitched. 'Surely not. OK, leave it with me.
Did you get any prices?'

'They're emailing me.'

'OK. So once we've got it confirmed, we need to tell
people. Do you want to draw up your guest list?'

'It'll take me all of two minutes.'

'How about your foster parents?' he suggested, his voice gentle.

She shrugged. 'I don't know. I owe them so much, but it's sort of difficult.'

'I know. Think about it, though, and maybe at least tell them.'

She nodded slowly, then glanced at the clock. 'I'd better get on. I'm due in Minors. I'll let you know what I find out.'

He dropped a kiss on her lips, winked at her and sauntered off, and James, coming round the corner at that moment, raised an eyebrow at her.

'Tut-tut, public displays of affection in the workplace,' he murmured, but she could see he was smiling.

'How's the house?' she asked.

'Chaotic. Congratulations, by the way. Sam tells me you're getting married.'

'Yes. I can't quite believe it, really. How's Connie?'

'Getting bigger. Only ten weeks to go now. Why don't you both come over and see the house and have a drink with us this evening?'

'Oh. OK. I'll have to check with Sam—'

'I'll do that, I'll see him in a minute. Are you in Minors? There's a man in there I'm not happy about. Ryan Jarrold. He's got abdominal pain, but nothing showed on the ultrasound so we're waiting for a CT. Can you keep an eye on him and page me if you're concerned? I'll be back in a bit to check on him. And hustle CT.'

'Sure. Will do.'

It turned out that he was right to be worried, because five minutes after she arrived at Ryan's bedside, he broke out in a cold, clammy sweat and was rushed into Resus.

'He said he's been feeling rough for a couple of weeks,'

she told James. 'Especially if he's hungry or after he's eaten a big meal.'

'Could be a bleeding ulcer. Right, let's get some fluids into him stat and see what we can find out.'

It was a perforated duodenal ulcer that, left neglected, had given him peritonitis and a massive intra-abdominal bleed, so the surgeon had told James later that afternoon, but they'd managed to save him.

'He was a lucky man,' James said. 'If that had happened at home, he might not have made it, and if Kate hadn't spotted the change in him so fast, we could still have lost him.'

'It was pretty obvious,' she said, but it still made her feel good to know she'd been appreciated.

They were standing in the garden of James and Connie's house, the sea at their backs and a renovation opportunity in front of them, and Kate was massively glad they hadn't taken on anything drastic like that.

'And I thought my boat was bad,' Sam said, eyeing it warily.

'It'll be fine. We can take it bit by bit,' Connie said placidly. 'At least it's clean now and we can live in it and work out what to do. Anyway, enough. Tell us about your wedding! It's much more interesting. When's it going to be?'

'Four weeks on Saturday,' Sam said. 'We're getting married at the Register Office at five, and then going down to Zacharelli's for the party. We've booked the function room, and I think we're going to have a buffet and an open bar.'

'Yowch. Do you trust your friends that much?' James said with a laugh, and Sam chuckled.

'It'll be fine. I'll make sure they're not too well stocked.'

'So, what are you going to wear?' Connie asked, looking at Kate. 'You'll need a wedding dress.'

Sam frowned slightly. 'I thought you didn't want a lot of fuss?'

'I don't—'

'Oh, come on, she's got to wear something, Sam! It doesn't have to be a meringue with foaming acres of tulle, but she'll still need a dress.'

Kate was hardly listening, because something about Sam's face was making her uneasy. Because of Kerry's wedding dress? She could hardly ask him, though, especially then and there, so she filed it for later.

'I doubt if it'll be a traditional one,' she said to reassure him. 'I'll be six months pregnant by then.'

'There are loads of pregnant brides these days,' Connie said, flapping her hand. 'They make some fabulous dresses.'

But Sam was still looking uneasy, and she changed the subject.

'Talking of babies, will you be upset if we paint the nursery?' she asked Connie.

'Of course not! He'd outgrown it anyway. Do you know what you're having?'

'A girl.'

'Oh, that's lovely! So are we!'

'Well, it balances Annie's two boys,' she said with a laugh, and the conversation moved on and Sam seemed to relax again, but she still had an uneasy feeling, and she tackled him about it when they got home.

'Talk to me about the wedding dress,' she said gently as he was getting into bed.

He froze for a second, then turned off the light and lay down on his back, staring at the ceiling. She rolled towards him.

'Sam?

'It's nothing.'

'No, it's not nothing. Tell me.'

'She never got to wear it,' he said, after a pause that seemed to stretch out into the hereafter. 'It was hanging in the wardrobe in the flat, and I gave it to the funeral directors. She was wearing it when we buried her.'

'Oh, Sam.' She wriggled closer, resting her head on his shoulder and her hand over his heart. 'I'm sorry. I won't wear a dress.'

'No. You can wear whatever you want to, Kate. It doesn't matter. Just—maybe not lace.'

His eyes were closed, squeezed shut, and in the light of the moon she could see the thin, silver trail of a tear running down into his hair.

She wiped it away and kissed him, and he turned towards her and made love to her with a desperation that broke her heart.

The next four weeks flew by.

Annie and the babies came home from hospital, and she and Sam went over there for a barbeque so they could meet him properly. Ed of course had already met Sam at work, but they started talking boats and that was that, so she and Annie talked babies and discussed the wedding.

'I don't think I want my foster parents to come,' she confessed. 'It's a part of my life I want to forget.'

'Maybe your wedding's not the right time,' Annie said sagely. 'Why not leave it till afterwards, and contact them then.'

She nodded. 'Yes. Yes, that makes sense. You will be able to come, won't you?'

Annie laughed. 'Just try and keep me away. Do you

want to stay here the night before? You can get ready here—and you can keep the dress here, when you get it.'

She didn't want to talk about the dress, not with Sam in earshot, so she just nodded and thanked her, and let it go.

CHAPTER ELEVEN

The day of the wedding dawned bright and clear and sunny.

A good omen? She wasn't sure. There was a tightness in her chest, an unnamed fear that wouldn't go away, and it stayed with her all day.

She'd stayed at Annie and Ed's because she was traditional enough to want to do it properly, and she'd spent the morning having a lovely facial that should have been relaxing, and her nails were painted in readiness, and then that afternoon the hairdresser had come to Annie's to put her hair up, but it didn't feel right.

Nothing felt right.

Not the hair, not the nails—certainly not the dress that she'd agonised over so much.

She'd gone shopping for it alone, because it was such a difficult issue what with Sam's feelings being so intricately involved in the subject, and it certainly wasn't lace, but it was still unmistakeably a wedding dress.

She stood at the bedroom window in Annie's house, staring out across the clifftop at the sea and thinking about Sam. Was he staring at it, too, down in their house by the harbour? What was he thinking about this, the wedding day that never should have been, or about the wedding that had never happened?

Annie tapped on her bedroom door. 'Can I come in?'

She opened the door, and Annie took one look at her face and hugged her.

'Oh, Kate, sweetheart, what's the matter? I thought you were happy?'

'I was, but now… I don't think I can do this. I don't think he's ready, Annie.'

'Nonsense. If he wasn't, he would never have asked you.'

'Yes, he would. He asked me on the day he found out I was pregnant, only the second time I'd ever met him. He's just being noble, doing the right thing, ticking the right box. He says he's old-fashioned and thinks a baby's parents should be married. I said no the first time he asked me, and the second, just a few weeks ago, and then when we found out it was a girl, and it all seemed real, I just said let's get married, but it was only a few days later, and maybe it really was too soon. Nothing had really changed, and when we talked about the dress—'

'What about it?' Annie prompted, so she told her what Sam had said about Kerry, and Annie sighed softly and hugged her.

'Darling girl, that doesn't mean he doesn't love you, just that he loved her, too, and it was desperately sad, what happened to him. It doesn't stop him loving you.'

'But he doesn't! He's had endless opportunities to tell me that he does, and he hasn't. Not once. And I can't bear to marry him when he doesn't love me,' she said, and the sob that was jammed in her throat broke free and she sank down onto the floor and cried her heart out.

Sam was standing in their bedroom gazing blindly out to sea and wondering how he'd got to be so lucky when his phone rang.

He stared at it, a feeling of foreboding creeping into him and chilling him to the bone. 'Hello?'

'Sam, it's Annie. You need to come.'

Fear coursed through him. 'Why? What's happened? Is she all right?'

'She's fine,' Annie said quickly, and he hauled in a breath. 'She's fine, but—Sam, she needs to see you, to talk to you. She's having a wobble about the wedding.'

'What? OK, OK, I'll come. Just—don't let her go anywhere.'

He ran downstairs, grabbed his car keys, locked the door as an afterthought and drove the two minutes up the road to Annie and Ed's in a minute flat, abandoning the car on the drive.

Ed opened the door and let him in. 'They're upstairs in the front bedroom on the right. Take a deep breath.'

He paused, catching his breath, trying to slow his heart but it was still racing, the dread clinging to him like a mantle.

'Why?' he breathed, and Ed laid a hand on his shoulder.

'I think she just needs your reassurance.'

He nodded, hauled in another breath and forced himself to walk slowly up the stairs. Annie was on the landing, standing by the open bedroom door, and she patted his shoulder and left him to it.

Kate was sitting on the floor in a puddle of pale grey silk, and the sight of her nearly broke his heart.

He reached out his hands and pulled her gently to her feet. Her eyes were puffy from crying, and she had a wad of crumpled, soggy tissues in one hand. He took them from her, steered her to the bed and sat down beside her, her hands held firmly in his.

'Kate, whatever's the matter, sweetheart? Talk to me—tell me what's wrong.'

Where did she start?

'I can't do it,' she said, blinking away tears and trying her hardest not to cry. 'I can't marry you, Sam. You're just doing it to be noble, because you're that sort of man, kind and decent and honourable, and you think this is all your fault, but I can't let you do it, because it won't work, and when it all goes wrong and you leave me—'

'I won't. I've told you that and I don't renege on my promises.'

'But you can't know that. What if it gets unbearable? Or is it that you're so dead inside that you don't really care what happens because you can't feel it anyway?'

Emotions flickered over his face so fast she couldn't read them, but she recognised enough to know it might be true.

She eased her hands away from him and stood up, walking over to the window and clinging to the frame for support. 'Sam, I can't. I can't marry you when I know you don't love me, can't marry you just to ease your guilty conscience. I don't want to be your consolation prize, someone there for you to distract you from your grief while you go through the motions, while all the time you're secretly wishing I was Kerry.'

She turned and met his shocked eyes.

'I'm sorry I'm not her, I'm sorry it's not her here in her lovely lace dress, having your baby, planning a future with you in your lovely new house, but I'm not her, I'm me, and I can't marry you just so that you can play happy families and pretend to yourself that it's all OK. Even I know I'm worth more than that.'

'But—Kate...'

'Kate nothing, Sam,' she said heavily. 'I'm not going to enter into a loveless marriage. I've seen enough of them in my life, and I don't intend to be part of one. I'm sorry—'

'It's not loveless. Not on my part, at least.'

He got up and walked over to her, taking her hands again, staring down at her with eyes so sincere she almost believed him. 'I didn't expect this. When you told me you were pregnant, all I could think about was doing the right thing. You were right about that. But in the last few weeks, somehow—I don't understand how, because I never thought it would ever happen to me again, but I've grown to love you. I think I started to love you when you decided to keep the baby, because it was such a hard decision for you, a really difficult and courageous choice to make, and I had to ask you to trust me when you really didn't know me, and yet you did it. You put your future in my hands, and in doing so you gave me a future, too, something to look forward to where there'd been nothing.

'Do you know, I woke up this morning feeling happy, with everything I'd ever wanted? Marrying a beautiful woman who I love, who's carrying my child, a job in a fabulous place, a stunning house overlooking the sea we both love—the only fly in the ointment is that you don't love me. I always knew you were going for the safe option out of fear and a need for security, and I can't blame you, not with your childhood, but I can work with that and hope that, given time, you'll come to love me, too, as much as I love you.'

She stared at him, wanting so much to believe it, unable to dare. 'No. You love Kerry, Sam,' she said sadly. 'You can't let her go.'

'I can. I have. Yes, Kerry will always be a part of my past, and she'll always hold a part of my heart, because

I did love her, and I can't just turn that off, but it doesn't hurt any more in the way it did. I'm still sad for her that her life was cut so cruelly short, but you're my life now.

'I love you, Katherine Ashton, and I love our baby, too. I'll love you both to the end of my days, whether you marry me or not. That won't change. But I won't force you to do something you're unhappy about, and if you really feel that you don't love me, and my love isn't enough to make this work for you—'

'Why haven't you told me? If you love me, why haven't you told me?'

He gave a sad little laugh. 'I only really realised it today. I was going to tell you right before we got married. It was stupid of me. I should have told you before, I should have rung you. I'm sorry. But you haven't told me, either, and maybe that's why I was holding back.'

'Oh, Sam—of course I love you, but I was afraid to say so. I didn't want to give too much of myself away because I thought you weren't ready to hear it, and I was trying to save myself from any more hurt—'

His arms closed round her, crushing her against his chest.

'Silly girl,' he said raggedly, and his chest heaved with emotion as he held her there and told her, again and again, that he loved her.

And finally she believed him.

She eased away, trying to smile at him through her tears. 'Well, if we're going to do this we'd better hurry,' she said, and he pulled her back into his arms for one last, quick hug before he let her go.

'You need to sort out your makeup,' he said with a wry grin, and she ran over to the mirror and wailed, dabbing at her tear-stained face.

'I look a wreck!'

'You look beautiful. Just a little streaky.'

He smiled at her in the mirror, and she smiled back, dabbing at her cheeks.

'Give me two seconds.'

It took a little more than that, mostly because her hands were shaking, but then she turned to him and smiled unsteadily.

'There. How do I look? Will I do?'

He pressed his lips together hard, and swallowed.

'You look lovely,' he said gruffly. 'Absolutely beautiful. I'm so proud of you.'

His voice cracked, and she put her arms around him and hugged him. 'Oh, Sam. Are you OK?'

He nodded, looked down at her and smiled tenderly.

'Never better. I love you,' he said again, just in case she hadn't quite got it yet, and then, taking her by the hand, he led her out of the house.

The wedding was wonderful.

Quiet, of course, with so few guests, but they were the people who mattered. James and Connie, Ed and Annie, Sam's parents and his brother, a few old friends—and her foster parents, who she'd finally contacted just a few days before, because of all the people in her past, they were the only ones she loved and who loved her.

They'd hugged her and cried, and Sam had to find a box of tissues to mop them all up, and then they moved to Zaccharelli's for the party. She was standing outside on the balcony overlooking the sea when Sam came up behind her and slid his arms around her, resting his hands on the baby.

'OK?'

'Definitely. You?'

'Mmm. Only one thing could make it better.' He turned her into his arms. 'The car's here. Ready to go home?'

'Absolutely.'

They ran the gauntlet of the confetti, scrambled into the car and snuggled up in the back for the short journey to the house.

He helped her out, tipped the driver and led her up the veranda steps, then he unlocked the door, swept her up into his arms and kissed her.

'Sam!' she squealed, wrapping her arms firmly round his neck for safety. 'What are you doing?'

'What I should have done weeks ago,' he said, and he carried her over the threshold, setting her carefully back on her feet in the hall.

'Welcome home, Mrs Ryder,' he said gruffly, and she went up on tiptoe and kissed him.

'Thank you,' she whispered. 'Thank you for everything. I never thought I could ever be this happy. I love you, Sam. I love you so much.'

'I love you, too.' He kissed her back, slowly and thoroughly, then lifted his head and gazed down into her eyes. 'Do you think you can manage to walk upstairs to bed?' he murmured with a mischievous smile, and she laughed and took his hand and went with him up to the attic.

He turned on the lamps, revealing their beautiful bed strewn with rose petals, and emotion choked her.

'You old romantic,' she said unevenly, touched almost to tears, and he drew her into his arms and kissed her again.

'I thought you'd like it. I wanted to make you happy, today of all days.'

'You did. You do. Every day of my life. Now stop stalling and make love to me, Mr Ryder.'

He chuckled softly. 'It'll be a pleasure.'

EPILOGUE

'I CAN'T BELIEVE you've sold her.'

Sam stood at the top of the veranda steps, and watched as the boat, carefully loaded onto a trailer, was towed slowly away, and he realised that all he felt was pride in the restoration work he'd done over the summer, and relief that it was over.

'She's served her purpose,' he said softly, moving to sit beside her in the glorious October sunshine. 'If it hadn't been for her, I wouldn't have met you that night, and we wouldn't be sitting here now.'

'Are you sure?'

He took his eyes off the boat and turned to face her. 'Yeah. Why would we?'

'Because James and Connie asked you to come, as a favour?'

He smiled thoughtfully. 'I've wondered about that. I think I probably would have come, so I would have met you.'

'But James warned us both off, so maybe it wouldn't have gone any further.'

Sam chuckled. 'Seriously? I struggled to keep my hands off you while we were trying to make some fundamental and life-changing decisions, so I'm pretty sure we would have had an affair, at least.'

'But I wouldn't have got pregnant. It was the perfect storm—if you hadn't broken your golden rule, and I hadn't had the bug, it wouldn't have happened, and there would have been nothing tying us together, nothing to hold you here in Yoxburgh.'

'Nothing except love,' he said softly, wrapping his arm around her and resting his head against hers. 'And that might have happened anyway, but we did have the perfect storm, and we have a beautiful, perfect little baby who we really need to find a name for.'

Kate's eyes went back to the boat. 'How about Isadora?'

'Isadora?' His eyes traced the name he'd lovingly repainted on her stern. 'Why?'

She smiled fondly, her eyes misting. 'We owe her everything,' she said, 'and anyway, it's a beautiful name.'

'Isadora,' he said, tasting it, and then he nodded. 'Yes. Yes, it is. I like it. How about a middle name?'

Kate hesitated. 'I thought—maybe Rose? For my mother? I don't know why she left me or what happened to her, and I probably never will, but I know that she loved me, I remember that, and now that I'm a mother, I know it must have been the hardest thing in the world to do, to let me go into school that day knowing she'd never see me again.'

'Maybe you would have been in danger? Maybe she was in some kind of trouble.'

'I think she must have been, and it's only now, when I realise just what love is, that I can forgive her because I know what a sacrifice she made for me.'

Sam hugged her closer and pressed a kiss to her hair. 'I think it would be lovely to call the baby Rose.'

'Not for her first name, but just there, so I remember her.'

He felt his eyes fill, and blinked.

'Isadora Rose. It's beautiful.'

He looked down at her, lying asleep in her mother's arms, her mouth a perfect rosebud, and he leant over and feathered his lips against her downy head, then settled back, his arm around his wife, and watched as the boat disappeared from their lives, her job done.

* * * * *

If you enjoyed this story,
check out these other great reads
from Caroline Anderson

RISK OF A LIFETIME
THE SECRET IN HIS HEART
BEST FRIEND TO WIFE AND MOTHER
SNOWED IN WITH THE BILLIONAIRE

All available now!

A MUMMY
FOR HIS BABY

BY
MOLLY EVANS

This is a work of fiction. Names, characters, places, locations and
incidents are purely fictional and bear no relationship to any real
life individuals, living or dead, or to any actual places, business
establishments, locations, events or incidents. Any resemblance is
entirely coincidental.

Published in Great Britain 2017
By Mills & Boon, an imprint of HarperCollins*Publishers*
1 London Bridge Street, London, SE1 9GF

ISBN: 978-0-263-92629-3

Dear Reader,

Thank you very much for reading my latest book! This is a very special one as it is set in my home town. Some changes have been made to suit the story, but the essence of the area is still true.

Readers and friends from here have been asking to have our little home town as a setting for one of my stories and so I finally did it. Some of the characters are named after childhood friends, and my mother even has a character named after her. The town I grew up in is in rural western Pennsylvania, where there are more cows than people, no sidewalks, and it's miles from the nearest store. As a child, much of my time was spent in the woods, at the lake, or catching fireflies on long summer evenings. During the winters I spent many an hour reading books, which fostered my love of a good story and the desire to write my own.

I have many fond memories of growing up in this community, and I wanted to share them with my readers. If you are so moved, drop me an email at mollyevansromance@gmail.com and let me know what you're up to, what you might like to see in a future story, or tell me a story of your own. After all, all good books start with a good story.

Regards,

Molly Evans

CHAPTER ONE

WHAT HAD POSSESSED Aurora Hunt to return to this little town, she didn't know. She should have figured out on her own how to survive, how to find a new job, how to create a new life. Somehow. But after being beaten down by life during several unforeseeable events she'd given up, given in, and gone home to her childhood home in western Pennsylvania to lick her wounds. Wounds that scarred her on the inside as well as the outside.

Nothing in this vast wilderness settled in the heart of the Appalachian Mountains had changed much in two hundred years. The car models were newer, farmers plowed different fields, and there were more houses built on what had once been pasture. At the heart of it, its people, their culture, hadn't changed—had refused to change—and that was why she'd left in the first place. In order to grow, things had to change, and she'd wanted to do all of that where there were more opportunities than in this remote village.

But due to a nearly catastrophic car wreck, she was back to square one. In one second, one dramatic turn of the wheel, her life had taken a path she'd never expected and she'd been forced to move in with her mother.

For now.

This situation was only temporary. Until she regained

her strength and figured out what she was going to do with her life. A few weeks, tops. Living with her mother on a permanent basis was *not* an option.

Getting out of her car wasn't as easy as getting into it. Nearly every movement she made was difficult, but she was grateful for the pain. At least it meant she was still alive, still moving forward. Nothing was what it had used to be. Nothing.

Today she was calling on an old friend to help put her life back together, one aching bone at a time.

The sign for the local medical clinic was a red arrow, pointing to a door. Until a few months ago there had been no medical clinic in Brush Valley. The closest one had been miles away. So it was understandable that this building didn't quite look like it was a thriving business just yet.

It looked like the building had once belonged to an animal doctor instead of a people doctor. Faded paint indicated dogs to the left, cats to the right. She didn't know which one to take, but since she was more of a dog person she entered through the left door. Fortunately both doors opened into the lobby of the clinic, which was nearly deserted.

"Good morning, can I help you?" A woman in an advanced stage of pregnancy smiled and offered her a clipboard to sign in.

"Yes. I have an appointment."

"Okay, great." She looked at Aurora's name, then frowned. "Are you related to *Sally* Hunt?"

"Yes, she's my mother."

"Oh, then you must have grown up here!" She held out her hand. "I'm Cathy Carter. I think I went to school just after you."

"Oh…great to meet you."

Though Aurora didn't recall everyone who had gone to school around the time she had, the woman did look vaguely familiar, with her big brown eyes and long brown hair.

"I'm sure you don't remember me." She patted her belly. "I looked much different back then."

That made Aurora laugh. "Didn't we all? Nice to see you again."

"Have a seat and he'll be with you in a few minutes. Just one patient ahead of you." Cathy nodded to a young woman with a sniffling infant, pacing the small waiting room.

"No problem."

"Angie, why don't you bring Zachary back and we'll have a look at him now?" Laboriously, Cathy rose from the chair and followed the mom and baby into the first exam room.

Aurora felt sorry for the woman, who looked like she was carrying a watermelon beneath her clothing. But although Cathy looked uncomfortable, she also looked happy, and there was something to be said about that.

While Aurora waited she paced the length of the waiting room as sitting caused her too much pain. As she moved back and forth, trying to keep her joints moving, she noticed a bulletin board, with notices for parents, and a table full of retirement magazines. There was a section of toys for little kids, but nothing for anyone else. It was a sparse attempt to keep those who were waiting entertained. These days, with all the electronic devices and people being plugged in, the corner looked lacking, without at least one charger available.

"Aurora?" Cathy called her to the desk. "I can take you back and get you in a patient room, take your vitals, while Beau—I mean Dr. Gutterman—looks at his other patient."

"Oh, you can call him Beau. I know when we're behind the desk we all go on a first-name basis."

"That's right. You're a nurse, too, aren't you?"

"Well, yes." At least she *had* been. She didn't want to say that she wasn't a nurse any longer. Just because she was in between jobs at the moment. "I'm not working right now—but I guess once a nurse, always a nurse, right?"

"Yes, we're kind of like the Marines that way."

Cathy led the way and indicated a nice patient room. After a quick check, she left Aurora waiting for Beau.

"Leave the door open, please. I get a little claustrophobic."

"Oh, sure. He'll be right here." Cathy pressed a hand to her back as a twinge of pain crossed her face.

"Are you okay?"

"Yes. It's just pushing on my back more and more the last few days."

"Oh, boy. When are you due?" That low back pain was an ominous sign. Labor could commence at any moment.

"A few more weeks—but I'm feeling like I want to pop right now." Cathy paused in the doorway and looked like she was about to pass out. "I've been having Braxton Hicks for days."

Feeling that nurse's instinct kick in, Aurora quickly moved to Cathy's side and began to assess the woman. Maternity wasn't her specialty, but she could see the swelling in the woman's hands and face, the flushed cheeks and the fine sheen of sweat on her face and neck.

"Cathy, I'm not so sure they were false contractions. I think you'd better sit down."

"I do, too."

Without releasing her grip on Cathy's arm, Aurora dragged one of the wheeled chairs in the room close, right behind the pregnant woman's legs. "Here's a chair."

"Oh, boy." Cathy dropped into the chair, then clutched her abdomen and leaned forward with a groan. "I think I'm going into labor right now."

She blew out a breath and her face reddened further.

"Oh. Oh, *no*! My water just broke."

The amniotic fluid housing the baby and adding cushioning splattered onto the floor. This was going to go hard and fast.

"Let me call for Beau."

Aurora left the room for a second to dash across the hall and rap on the patient room door.

"Dr. Gutterman—there's an issue out here!"

Beau jerked the door open with a scowl, then a surprised look raised his brows and a grin lit up his face. "Aurora! What are you—?"

"Cathy's going into labor. *Now*." Trying not to panic, Aurora released the doorknob.

"Oh! I knew she was close, but not that close." Beau turned back to his patient's mother. "I'm sorry, Angie. I'll call in a prescription for Zach as soon as I can. Give me a call if he's not better in a few days."

Dispensing with any more pleasantries or greetings, Aurora grabbed his arm and dragged him into the hallway. "I mean *right* now."

"Oh! I see."

Beau headed into the other patient room. He looked at his nurse, struggling against pain in the office chair.

"Oh, boy. I haven't delivered a baby in a long time." He offered a quick glance to Aurora, his eyes wide. "Are you *sure* she's going to have it right now?"

"Yes," Aurora said as Cathy screamed again.

"We'd better call 911."

"Do it—but you may be delivering a baby before they get here. This looks precipitous."

Though Aurora had done several rotations in Delivery, she hadn't attended a birth in some time—and this one was looking like it was going to be a doozy.

"No! I don't want to have it here. I can't!" Cathy huffed her breath in and out, her doe eyes wide in fear as she looked at Aurora for help. "We have *plans*."

"Honey, those plans are about to go up in smoke," Aurora said. "Where's your husband?"

"Home."

"You'd better call him," Aurora said, and watched as Beau called the emergency services to send an ambulance as soon as possible. Out in the country, nothing was "stat", or "fast," as they were miles from everywhere.

"Okay. Okay..." Cathy took a deep breath and leaned back in the chair as the pain obviously eased. She held the phone to her ear. As she looked at Aurora for reassurance another frown crossed her face and she took a deep breath. "Honey? The baby's coming!"

Aurora took the phone before Cathy crushed it to pieces in her hand. "Your wife is at the clinic and she's in labor. You'd better get here quickly if you want to see your baby being born."

Then she hung up. He'd either get there or he wouldn't. Aurora's first priority was to see this woman and her baby safe.

"Cathy, we've got to get you ready to have this baby."

"What about the ambulance?" She rose from the chair with Beau and Aurora's help, leaning heavily on both of them.

"You know as well as I do that it'll take them half an

hour to get here, and you're going to have this baby long before that."

Beau ripped off his lab coat and rolled up his sleeves, then scrubbed his hands and arms vigorously at the sink, jumping into the mode necessary to save both his nurse and her baby.

He knew heroes weren't born. They were made. In situations like this.

"Aurora—good to see you, my friend, but it looks like we're going to be welcoming a baby in the next few minutes. Are you up to it?"

"Absolutely." There was nothing, not even the pain in her back, that would interfere with her ability to save a life or two today.

"Great. Let's get her on the exam table and see what's going on."

His jaw was tense, and he didn't look at Aurora as he scrubbed. When his child had been born his wife had died. That was all she knew. The shock of this unforeseen delivery was obviously stirring that memory. Was he struggling to push it aside? Until now she hadn't thought of that, and her heart ached for him. Those memories had to be incredibly painful for him, but he was mustering through and doing what was needed in the moment.

"Oh, no. *Oh, no.*" Cathy bent at the waist and clutched her abdomen, nearly crushing Aurora's fingers. *"Agh!"*

"Beau, I don't think the table is going to work. It's not designed for this. How about we put some blankets and sterile sheets on the floor and let her squat, like she seems to want to?"

"Okay. Good idea." Beau grabbed blankets and two sterile packages.

Together she and Beau turned the room into an impromptu delivery suite. This was so over the top of what she'd expected to be doing today, but knowing there were no other options, and that Beau had her back, she had his—she knew they could do it together.

"Do you have a surgical kit around in case we need it?" Chewing her lip for a second, Aurora didn't want to think about the possibility of having to do an emergency C-section, but planning for the worst and hoping for the best had always worked for her.

"Yes—there." Beau pointed to another cupboard over the sink. "It's a general kit. Everything we need should be in it."

"Breathe, Cathy. Just breathe." Aurora tried to keep her voice calm and not let the woman know about the anxiety pulsing through her body. "I'm going to reach around you and remove your shoes and leggings."

"Okay." Cathy nodded. "It's easing now." She took in a few deep breaths, sweat pouring off of her. "Beau, you aren't going to fire me because I had my baby in your office, are you?"

Beau barked out a laugh and gave her a comforting pat on the shoulder, the light in his eyes not as dark as it had been a few moments ago. "No. Although I do have to say it's going to go down as one of the most interesting days I've ever had."

"That's *g-o-o-o-o-d*!" Another contraction hit, nearly dropping Cathy to her knees.

"Let's get you down before you fall." Aurora tucked a hand on Cathy's waist and eased her to her knees, then sat her back so that Beau could check and see if the baby was crowning.

A door slammed in the front office.

"We have company."

"Cathy? *Cathy!* Where are you?" Hurried footsteps got closer to the room.

"We're in the back, Ron!" Beau yelled toward the door.

"Oh, my God. You *are* in labor. It wasn't a joke." Ron, clearly Cathy's husband, stood in the doorway, panting from his exertion, his eyes wide as he took in the scene. "I can't believe it."

"No jokes today. Wash your hands over there," Aurora pointed to the sink. "This is going to go fast."

"She's definitely crowning," Beau said after he had a quick look.

"He. It's a he. I know it." Cathy began to pant again. "Oh, here he comes! I have to push again—get me up!"

Cathy struggled to a sitting position, then Beau and Ron helped her to her knees. With one hand she held onto her husband, with the other she clutched the edge of the patient table.

"Go with it, Cathy. Wait until you can't wait any longer and then push."

"I'm pushing *now*!" Her statement ended in a scream, a gasp, then another push.

"He's almost here," Beau said from his position on the floor nearby. He placed a sterile cloth beneath the baby's head and supported it. "Pant. I need to check the cord."

Cathy cast tear-filled eyes at her husband, who looked like he'd been hit by a truck. "Honey? We're having a baby today!"

"I… I can see that." He looked down at his wife and pressed a kiss to her cheek. "Wasn't quite what I was expecting, though."

"Me, either. Oh! Pushing again."

"Go ahead. One more ought to do it."

With a great groan, Cathy pushed the vernix-covered baby into Beau's waiting hands.

"Ron? Can you help me sit her back?" Pain was slicing through Aurora's back and she couldn't do it alone.

"Yes."

Together they eased Cathy into a reclining position, supported by her husband's chest. Exhausted, Cathy drew in cleansing breaths and closed her eyes.

"We have to do a few things, then you can hold your baby."

Beau's voice, choked with emotion, drew her attention. He focused, he did the job, but she could see the pain in his face. Tears pricked Aurora's eyes at the miracle of birth that had happened so unexpectedly right in front of her, but she shoved them back. Now wasn't the time to think of the family that she'd wanted and never been able to have. Might never have. Beau was struggling with his own issues and had set them aside. So could she.

"You were right, Cathy. It's a boy. He's perfect."

Beau provided the news, the tension in the room eased, and Aurora was able to take a deep breath, too.

"All parts are there, and exactly where they belong."

He finished wiping the baby's face, then Aurora used a suction bulb to clean out his mouth and nose and placed him in his mother's arms.

"I can't believe this! We delivered a baby today." Beau gave a laugh and shook his head, some of the emotion leaving his face and his shoulders relaxing.

"I can't either," Cathy said, with tears flowing down her face as she looked at her baby, then leaned into her husband's neck.

"How did this happen?" Ron asked. "I thought you weren't due for two more weeks."

"Well, your son had other plans."

"I can certainly see that." He let out a shaky breath and with one trembling finger touched his son's hand. "I just can't believe this." He held out his hand. "I'm shaking. Nothing *ever* gets to me, but I'm shaking like a leaf."

"Well, this circumstance is very different than anything else you've ever experienced, isn't it?"

It wasn't every day that a new dad had to come screeching into the parking lot of his wife's place of work to see his baby being born.

"You're right about that." He blew out a breath and shook his head, letting out a tremulous laugh. "You are *definitely* right about that."

The front door opened again, to admit the ambulance crew with their stretcher and equipment.

"Did we miss the party?" A leggy brunette paramedic stuck her head into the room, offering a cheery grin, but her observant dark eyes were looking for anything that was out of place.

"You sure did. It was a doozy, too." Aurora shook her head, still in shock at the day's events.

"Aurora…?" the paramedic said, and frowned as if she were trying to figure something out. "Is that really you? I haven't seen you in years! It's *Missy*!"

The woman who had gone to high school with Aurora held her arms out and embraced her.

"Missy—hi! Yeah. It's me." She gave a nervous laugh. This was turning into quite a day of friends from her past showing up unexpectedly. "It was a trip I hadn't really planned. But here I am. It's great to see you."

"You, too. Everyone okay?" Missy asked. Those eyes of a trained observer looked around the room again, focusing on the mom and baby.

"I think so—but they're going to need a trip to the hospital for a full exam." Beau stripped his gloves off and tossed them on the growing pile of trash.

"You got it. Sirens or no sirens?" Missy gave a smile and a wink.

"No sirens today." Beau shook his head and gave an amazed laugh. "Wow!"

Cathy reached out to Beau and he stepped forward and clasped her hand. "Beau. I hate to ask this right now, but can I have my maternity leave starting today?"

Everyone laughed at the absurd request.

"Of course you can. It's not a problem. But I'll miss you, and I just hope I don't destroy the place while you're gone."

"You won't. You'll be fine."

"Six weeks, right?"

"Yes. I'll let you know if it needs to be longer." She cast a loving eye on her husband and her baby as tears filled her eyes. "This has been such an amazing event, I'm not sure I'm going to want to come back."

"Don't talk like that." Beau squeezed her fingers again and shook Ron's hand. "Just keep me updated and let me know when you're ready to come back." He snorted. "*If* you are."

"I will. I promise."

"Ready now?" Missy asked.

"Ready." Cathy sighed and clutched the baby securely in both arms.

After mother and baby had been packed onto the stretcher and were headed to the hospital Aurora and Beau faced each other, alone for the first time since the event had begun. For a few seconds they stared at each other, unblinking, then Aurora laughed.

The tension-reliever caught her by surprise, and she clasped her hands to her face. "*Beau!* We delivered a *baby*!"

"I know—I was here." A grin split his face and he held

his arms wide. "Now that all the excitement is over, let's have a proper greeting. Come here."

"I don't think I can walk after that. My legs are shaking."

But she had enough strength to close the gap, and Beau met her halfway.

"You held it together during a crisis—the sign of a true professional, right? That's the most important part." He closed his long arms around her and squeezed.

CHAPTER TWO

THE SURGE OF adrenaline and attraction that pulsed through her was completely unexpected in the embrace of an old friend she hadn't seen in ten years.

Her heart did a little flip at the sight of his long, sun-bleached blond hair that had a tendency to fall into his eyes, and the strength in that jaw she hadn't remembered being so masculine. Memories of the past, of her secret crush on him, surged forward, and she hesitated a second, trying to breathe through the onslaught of unanticipated emotions suddenly swirling within her.

Wow. She certainly hadn't expected *this* reaction.

Though she'd sworn off men after her recent painful break-up, her hormones obviously hadn't taken the same oath.

Clearing her throat, she reined in those wandering senses of hers that appreciated a fine-looking man. Now wasn't the time to be ogling anyone—let alone a good friend—no matter how broad those shoulders were.

She returned the embrace, trying not to gasp in pain. The strength of his arms, the pressure of his hug closed in on her, lighting up the injuries in her back like an electrical grid. A groan of discomfort escaped her throat.

"Did I hurt you?" He pulled back, his green eyes assessing, concern evident, and ran his gaze over her face, trying to determine what had happened.

"I'm sorry. I'm in quite a lot of pain right now—which is why I'm here to see you in the first place."

Back to her original goal: to be pain and medication-free, to get her life back in order. Starting now.

"Pain? You hid it well during this whole thing." He released her and gave her one gentle pat on the shoulder.

"Probably an adrenaline surge got me through."

He lifted one hand and indicated that she walk ahead of him into the nearby patient room. "You're my last patient of the day, so we can take our time—have a look at you and do some catching up." The dark brows over his green eyes lowered, pinning her with a direct look. "Tell me what's going on."

"I'll give you the short version. Car wreck. Lots of back pain. I want to get off the pain medications."

The last few months had been beyond brutal. A severe car crash had ripped her life and her relationship apart. Every time she told the story the pain surfaced—the emotional pain she'd gone through as well as the physical pain which was the reason for her visit today.

She handed him a folder with copies of her medical records. "The long version is in here. If you don't mind, read it later. Right now I just want to see if you can help me with the pain."

That was short, sweet and to the point. Rehashing her past wasn't going to help her today. Telling him about the fight with her boyfriend—the reason for her car accident—was going to have to wait. The end of their relationship had come soon after the crash, due to her physical scars, and had destroyed her.

"That doesn't sound very good." He harrumphed and placed the manila folder aside and focused on her. "I'll take a look at that later, for sure. Right now I want to look at *you*."

"Thanks, Beau. I'm sorry, but I *hate* this pain. Every time I move something hurts, and then if I stay still too long I get stiff."

The pain receded slightly as she walked along beside him, but the memory of it lingered.

"I can't win."

Tears pricked her eyes, but she pushed them back. Tears hadn't been tolerated by her father, so she'd learned to suppress her emotions. Even now she had difficulty sharing them.

"You certainly can win—but winning may look a little different than you thought. You were in a serious crash. Getting through an experience like that takes time." They entered the patient room. "Did you go through any physical therapy?"

"Yes. Two months of inpatient rehab. They said they did everything they could, but there's got to be something else."

Tears filled her eyes—tears she'd thought she'd finished shedding. Desperation circled her heart and squeezed hard. The pressure in her chest of the emotional pain focused there was like talons, digging in and not letting go.

"Though you did go through some rehabilitation, there's still work to be done. Rehab facilities often focus on one modality, not on being open to other adjunctive aspects of care that can help people just as much as the traditional ways."

"Really?" That statement perked her up. Somehow, deep in her gut, she knew there *had* to be alternative treatments, but she just didn't know what.

"You came to the right place."

The look in his eyes caused a surge of warmth through her. Hope pulsed in her chest. With the help of this man— her friend—she knew she was going to get through this tough time.

He peered at her with those intense green eyes that perfectly fit his streaked blond hair. He wouldn't look out of place with a surfboard tucked under one arm and hanging out on the beach. Except there wasn't a beach for three hundred miles.

"I'm so glad. You don't know what a relief it is to hear that."

Struggling with her emotions, she swallowed twice before she could speak again.

"It was awful. Having doctors telling me I'd never walk again, accept it. I think their sympathies ran out at the same time my insurance benefits did."

She clutched her hands together to stop their trembling. The memory of the accident had faded somewhat, but she still felt the aftereffects.

"I'm trying not to think too much about that part of it. I'm moving forward, working on my physical abilities, but the pain is so intense at times I can hardly move."

"You are one tough lady, Aurora—but you always have been."

Beau pressed his hand against hers, this time offering comfort with a simple touch, and she appreciated the gesture.

"I can see you're in pain. I'm a D.O.—Doctor of Osteopathy—and I perform manipulations of the body in addition to running the straight-up medical practice. That's probably a little different than you're used to."

"Yes, it is, but I'll consider anything that will get me where I want to be."

"Where *is* that? What's your goal?" The smile he gave

lifted one side of his mouth, making him look like he had a secret.

"I want to be pain-free, off the medications, and back to my old self again. There has to be a way other than just taking more pills or different pills."

What a relief, a joy, a gift it would be to have her old life back. Or at least to have her body back so she could take the rest of her life where she wanted it to go.

Right now she didn't even know where that was. Working in a hospital again might not ever be possible due to her injury. Her job was on hold, her apartment had been packed up and put in storage… She looked at her friend, hoping he could really give her the help she needed when no one else had been able to.

"There's always another way—no matter what the issue is." Beau went on to describe several natural methods of pain control. "Massage would work. Yoga would be helpful, gentle, and it would provide the flexibility you need."

"Yoga? I never thought of that." She sighed as relief started to form in her mind. "I have to be back in action as soon as possible or my mother is going to drive me nuts."

That was something Beau couldn't do anything about. Her relationship and her problems with her mother were long term and would probably never change.

"How so?" He opened up a computer program, typing as they talked.

"I moved into her house with the intention of staying just a few days, until I can really figure out what I'm going to do. Unfortunately she's determined to be my nurse, psychotherapist and nutritionist instead of my mother."

Yeah, it was all or nothing with her. Always had been.

Always would be. At her mother's age, there would be no changing her.

Yet another reason she'd left home at such an early age. While growing up Aurora had felt like she'd been hatched or adopted. She hadn't felt as if she belonged to her family. They'd had very distinct ideas on what she should be and what she should do with her life that hadn't matched at all with what *she'd* wanted. *Her* needs, her wants, her dreams, had been squashed by her family.

The only solution she'd been able to come to had been to leave. To get away. Forge a life for herself elsewhere. So she'd broken out and left the state to fulfill her career goals at a large university hospital in Virginia.

At least she'd gotten that part right. A husband and family of her own had been more elusive.

Being in charge of her life was something that she would never change. But those ideas of building a life with someone, having a family, had begun to surface— then had crashed into oblivion after the breakup with her boyfriend and the car wreck. Eventually she'd figured out that he wasn't a long-term kind of guy. Wasn't in it for the long haul and didn't have the fortitude to be the man she needed.

The first time he'd seen her scars he'd recoiled. That had been the end for both of them. All the plans she'd made for her future had come crashing down and she'd come home to Brush Valley to lick her wounds, heal, and recover from the accident and the breakup.

Here she was. Home again. Starting over. A new Aurora, reinventing her life.

Beau looked at her for a moment, contemplating. "I'm sure your mother was scared when you were hurt, right? She's probably not over the shock of it, so you'll have to cut her a break a while longer."

That thought *had* occurred to Aurora, and she dropped her eyes away from the intensity of him, the truth in his words. "I know, and I appreciate her efforts, but if I hang around the house all the time she'll feel compelled to wait on me. It won't be good for either of us."

Beau lifted his hands and looked around, as if suddenly struck by a bold new idea. "Well, as you know, I'm suddenly without a nurse and I need one immediately. I would *love* to have you help out as much as you can. If you'd be interested in working with me, that is?"

"What? Really?"

She hadn't thought of working while she was in Brush Valley, let alone working with Beau. She hadn't let her mind wander in that direction, but now it seemed like a great idea.

Her heart thrummed in anticipation, her throat constricted for a few seconds, and then her eyes widened. "I couldn't work full-time yet, but I can answer phones, make patient appointments and work the triage line for you."

The stress would be way less than working in the hospital, so she might be able to swing it. Could this be the answer she needed?

"What triage line?" Beau gave a sideways smile, lifting one corner of his mouth. "I bought the building a year ago…right before Chloe was born. A lot has happened since then, and I haven't gotten everything in place." He shook his head, but there was a smile there. "Maybe you can help me get caught up."

"That would be fantastic! I could start any time. Like tomorrow."

The idea of working with Beau, helping to get his business going and refilling her bank account were both very appealing.

"This would solve so many of my problems—just like that." She snapped her fingers.

"For me, too. Agency nurses are hard to find this far out in the country, and I hadn't even thought of looking for one yet because Cathy still had a couple weeks before she was due." He snorted and shook his head, his eyes wide in self-deprecation. "Underestimated *that* one, big-time. But, if you're serious, can you really start tomorrow?"

"Absolutely." Joy lifted her mood immeasurably. "My temporary disability payments run out in a week, so working for you will be the perfect answer until I can figure out a more permanent solution."

"Deal. You're hired." He looked away for a second, then back at her. "Do you want to return to Virginia and your job there? Or are you considering something else? You've been missed around here. By everyone."

The look he gave her was pointed, and guilt filled the empty space in her gut. The people around here had once been her friends, her family, and she'd left them behind in order to have a life for herself elsewhere. Now...? Who knew what the future held, but returning here permanently hadn't crossed her mind.

A sigh tumbled out of her throat. "I just don't know. With hospital work there's always a lot of lifting and pulling and tugging of patients or beds or equipment." Her shoulders drooped as saying the words aloud made them more real. "I couldn't physically do the job right now, which is really disappointing."

"All the years you spent training and gaining experience feel like they're going down the drain?"

Somehow, he'd hit it right on the head.

"Yes. Maybe it's not true, but at this moment it sure feels like it."

Sadness, grief for her loss, overwhelmed her for a second. She'd left this small town to create a life for herself, and now that life had been changed dramatically the first thing she'd done was head home—back to Brush Valley, where she knew she could recover. Could she leave again so quickly? It felt like a betrayal to think of leaving again and it made her very uncomfortable.

"So, be objective for a few minutes. What would you tell a patient if they were in your position?"

"I don't want to play this game, Beau." Being vulnerable was hard for her. Being vulnerable in front of Beau was even worse.

"That's because you know I'm right. What I'm trying to do is get you to think outside of your pain. Come on—humor me. What would you tell a patient? If it helps, consider this a job interview question."

Huffing out a sigh, Aurora closed her eyes for a moment, thinking, then opened them and looked at Beau. "I would tell a patient that this is a moment in time, and not to make any big decisions while still recovering, to relax about it."

"Perfect!" He patted her on the knee. "Now you know exactly what I was going to advise *you*."

He twitched his brows once at her and a smile found its way to her lips.

"Fine. You're right. I'll hold off on making any big decisions. At least for now. I'll work with you and we'll see how it goes, how my back does, and what other opportunities arise for my future—what I want to do, where I want to live."

Saying it like that, all in a rush, sounded reasonable, but it was so hard to accept. Time marched on while she stood still. At least it seemed that way.

Maybe all she needed was a little more time, and Beau

was right about that. Being driven, focusing on accomplishing her goals in life, had gotten her places. Having her goals and her life stalled due to injury was *not* the way she wanted to live. Doing nothing was incredibly frustrating.

"Good idea. Speaking of living situations, you mentioned your mom...? Think you'll be okay there?"

Having lived alone for years, she valued her private space. "Although I love my mom, I can't stay with her for long. Do you know of anyone with a room for rent? It doesn't have to be much."

"As a matter of fact there's a small apartment upstairs you can use for free. It's not fancy, but it would give you some privacy, and it's a short commute down the stairs to work."

He winked and some of the tension in her eased.

"I was going to rent it out eventually. For now, consider it one of the perks of working for me."

"Oh, Beau. That would be fantastic." Could this day get any better? "I would *love* that. And as my finances improve, I can pay some rent."

This was the first time in ages she'd felt so excited about anything. Allowing hope to find a place in her heart had been an exercise in disappointment over the last months. Maybe now, maybe here, the time had come to take it out for a stroll.

"You'll get turned around in no time. For now, I'm not going to worry about it. It doesn't cost me anything for you to live there." He waved away her protest. "What are friends for, anyway?"

"I can't thank you enough. Just know that as soon as I can I'll pay you back. I don't want to owe you any more than I have to."

"You're a qualified pediatrics nurse, if I remember correctly—right?"

"Yes, but currently a semi-disabled one."

That fact irritated her. Depending on others for jobs and apartments wasn't the way she wanted to live her life. She'd made her own way in life since she'd graduated college.

"Semi-disabled *temporarily*." He held up her file, then set it aside. "What's contained in that file isn't all of who you are. Remember, it's a bump in the road and we'll get you over it—or around it—one way or another. For now consider the apartment as part of your pay." He picked up the file again and read a few lines. "According to your doctors you've made excellent progress."

A snort of derision escaped her throat. "According to *them*, but it's not enough for *me*. It won't be until I get my life back."

A grin split his face, lighting up his eyes and adding a sparkle to them she'd hadn't yet seen today.

"Knowing you, you won't be satisfied until you're swinging from the rafters in your dad's barn."

That made her laugh—a genuine feeling that surfaced from deep within her, eliciting memories that hadn't seen the light of day for years. The pleasure bubbled up from her chest and burst out of her. This expression of joy was unfamiliar. The last few months had been brutal. A good laugh was definitely called for today.

She wiped her eyes with the heels of her hands and took in a tremulous breath. "I guess you're right. Those were good times, weren't they?"

"They sure were."

A haunted look flashed through his eyes. She'd seen fatigue in the lines of his face, how he rubbed his eyes when he thought no one was looking, and the look of pain when he'd handed the newborn baby to Cathy. Although she knew that his wife had died, she didn't know all of the circumstances.

"You said the office is new, but I guess I didn't realize how new your practice really is."

Changing the topic away from things that were too personal for both of them seemed like a good idea. Now that she'd be working with him there would be plenty of time to get reacquainted. Right now she needed pain relief.

"After working for someone else in a large city clinic I figured out pretty quickly that it wasn't for me. So I broke out on my own, bought the building and got it ready for business." He winked and gave that charming grin of his. "I like to run the ship, not swab the decks. At this point in my life building my own business the way I want it seems like the way to go."

The tension in the air that had been rising between them evaporated. They were back to an easy back and forth banter which eased her mind as well as some of the knots in her back.

"That doesn't surprise me." She looked around. "This seems more like you than working at a large clinic. I think you're better suited to a rural setting, where you know your patients, than having huge numbers of patients run through your office every day." She shrugged. "Not you. At least in my opinion."

"Yes, you're exactly right. I'm just getting going here, but I have high expectations. People have told me for years that Brush Valley needs a health clinic, so now we have one."

Though he was saying the right words, there didn't seem to be much passion in him—for them or for his new business venture.

"It's a good thing. Maybe it will inspire more people to start businesses, too."

"Then why do you look like hell?"

"That's one thing I love about you, Aurora—you shoot straight and tell it like it is." He gave a chuckle, but the laughter didn't extend all the way to his eyes. "I appreciate it that you didn't tell me I look worse than that."

"You look like you haven't slept in a year." There was something going on with him—more than just running a new business.

"You're almost right."

He shoved a hand through his hair and his eyes darkened for a moment. The fun-loving Beau she'd known had had some hard times recently.

"Seriously?" She blinked, startled by the answer. "That's a long time to go without a good night's sleep."

He nodded, his face grim. "It's been a rough year." He rubbed a hand over his face.

"Is it something you want to talk about?" She leaned forward, then cringed when her back tightened at the movement.

"You know that I have a child? A daughter... Chloe."

"Oh, I see. If *she* doesn't sleep, you don't either?" She smiled. That explained a lot. In her pediatrics experience she'd heard that story many times from parents.

"Yes, well... Julie...my wife...died right after Chloe was born, so it's always been just the two of us." He dropped his gaze and cleared his throat, then picked up Aurora's file from the desk again.

"Beau, I'm so sorry. Do you have someone to help you?"

Surely he wasn't trying to cope with everything all by himself. Everyone needed help—especially in a situation like this. Grief for him cramped her heart. He had to be in such pain. No wonder he wasn't sleeping.

Instead of answering her question, he looked away and cleared his throat. "How about for now we focus on you? We can talk about the disaster of my personal life another time."

"Okay. Sure." Now she reached out and placed her hand over his. As she did so the simple movement stirred a hot, burning sensation from her wrist to her hip. "Oh! Ow." She cringed, unable to hide the grimace on her face.

"You really *do* need some body work done, don't you?"

"Body work?" Her eyes went wide, then she frowned. "What does *that* mean?"

"Manipulation and massage."

"Then let's get to it."

"Let's get you into the treatment room and I'll see what I can do."

CHAPTER THREE

WHEN AURORA LEFT the clinic an hour later she was walking straight for the first time in months and she could take a deep breath of the fresh Pennsylvania air without pain. Awesome. All because of Beau.

For the first time since the crash she had hope. Beau had given that back to her.

After making the drive to her mother's house, Aurora stepped through the door to the fragrance of her mother's cooking. Instantly she was transported back to when her mother had given her cooking lessons as a child, when she'd had to stand up on a stool to reach the counter and the stove. Those were lessons she'd hated at the time, but she used them almost every day now. *Go figure.*

"Mom? Where are you?"

"In the kitchen."

Walking through the living room to the kitchen, Aurora began to feel the stiffness that Beau had warned her about. She wanted to lean back on an ice pack, the way he'd recommended, and read on the couch for a while. Reading had saved her life as a kid, during the long Pennsylvania winters, and she hadn't done nearly enough of it in the last few years. Today seemed like a good time to catch up a little, but first there was the task of telling her mother she was moving out.

"What are you making? It smells great." Steam wafted up from every pot on the stove and a blast of heat caught her in the face.

"Making beef stew for dinner. It's better if it simmers all day." Sally looked at her daughter. "You didn't forget that, did you?"

"No, I remember." Her stomach growled in response to the fragrance. "Guess I need to eat something *now*, though."

Opening a drawer, Aurora pulled a zipper bag out of the box that her mother always kept there. She moved to the refrigerator and filled the bag with ice cubes.

"How was your appointment with the doctor? Does he think he can get you straightened out?"

"Yes. Beau thinks he can get me fixed up and off the pain medications." Now she was going to try ice on the hip he'd adjusted and go with an anti-inflammatory instead of the narcotic-based medicine.

"Beau? Do you mean Dr. Gutterman?" Her mother tossed a small glare over her shoulder and stirred some mysterious spice concoction into the brew. "You shouldn't call him by his first name. It's disrespectful."

"I went to school with Beau. I've known him a long time. I can't call him Dr. Gutterman now. That would be weird."

She tried it out inside her head and it sounded like the name of some old doctor, ready to retire. So *not* the Beau she knew, who was young and vibrant and sexy as hell.

"Well, *I'm* going to call him Dr. Gutterman. It's good to have a hometown boy bringing some business to the area. We need more medical people around here." Sally inspected Aurora through fogged-up glasses and gave her a pointed stare.

Perfect introduction.

"That's good, because he offered me a job." "Offered" was a loose interpretation of their mutual arrangement. *Desperately needed* was more like it.

"What?" The expression on her mother's face looked as if she said she'd just gotten a job at an exotic dance club, not a respectable healthcare business. "You can't be working yet! You're still recovering."

"Mom, it's been over two months since the accident. When I got out of the rehab facility we agreed I would come here *temporarily*. I can't sit around doing nothing or I'll go mad." She patted her mother on the shoulder. "It'll be all right. It's part-time, and I'm not going to do more than I can handle. That was my agreement with Beau."

That assurance would comfort her mother and buy her some time. Her mother was a controller, and wanted things done her way, which was part of the reason Aurora had left town at such an early age.

"You won't believe this, but his nurse went into labor just after I got there and we delivered the baby together."

"You're kidding!" That got her mother's attention, and she gaped at Aurora. "Everyone's okay?"

"Yes—but that's why he needs a nurse right now, and I start tomorrow."

"Tomorrow? So soon?"

Concern showed in her mother's eyes, and though she hated to disappoint her Aurora knew she had to live her life—not the one her mother had planned for her. Although her mother loved having her around, she had no objective boundaries. It was all or nothing. And Aurora wasn't about to be turned into an invalid lying on the couch while her mother spoon-fed broth into her mouth.

"Yes. Tomorrow. Which brings me to another point. Beau has a small apartment over the office that I'm going to move into."

There—she'd said it. Short. Sweet. Firm. No question about it.

"What? You just *got* here." This time her mother faced her fully, major disappointment on her face. "I had so many plans for us."

"I know you did. But right now what I need is to work, get my career back, and not let the accident take away any more of my life than it already has." She looked into her mother's concerned eyes. "We can still do some of those things you have planned, but I *have* to work. It's what I'm good at, and I need that right now."

Boundaries. It was all about boundaries with her mother.

At that her mother pressed her lips together for a moment as she surveyed her daughter. "You always were too independent."

"For me, there is no such thing, Mom. I'm as independent as I need to be." She shrugged, but remembered Beau's words about taking it easy on her mother. "Everything will be fine. Don't worry."

"I suppose you're going to move tonight, aren't you?"

Pulling away from Aurora, Sally stirred her stew and pouted. Yep, nothing had changed.

"It's best if I move in right away. Most of my things are still in the car or on the porch, so it will be easier this way."

"Easier for whom?" her mother asked, but didn't really require an answer.

"Mom, I'm only going down the road a few miles. We'll still have plenty of time to do things together. I really need to work. You *know* that."

"I guess." She sniffed. "If you can find time to spend with your poor old mother."

Guilt trip. There was always the guilt trip.

"I'll make time—I promise. But first I have to get

settled into the apartment and the job. It's not like I'm
going back to Virginia right away."

She might never be able to go back to her old life. Perhaps there really *wasn't* a life to go back to there, and she
just hadn't realized it.

The car crash seemed to have been a defining moment in her life.

There had been life before the crash. There would be
life after the crash. Each of those times was vastly different and she didn't know which way to go. Forward or
backward. Or was any direction still forward?

"Well, get your stuff organized and I'll put some of
this stew into a container—and some of the bread I made.
You can have some home cooking in your new place."

Though her mother didn't like the idea, she appeared
to be accepting it. Maybe she was listening to Aurora
after all.

"I'd like that. Thank you." Having a bit of home in a
new apartment would be a great way to settle in.

"Okay, but I'm going to hold you to it," her mother
said, and pointed at her with the wooden spoon, giving a
mock glare. "I'm going to find out when the Amish festival is in Smicksburg and we're going."

"That sounds like a great time. I haven't been there
in years."

Funny… She'd used to hate driving around to different
festivals and displays, museums and other events that had
interested her mother, but now she was actually looking
forward to it. Late summer and early fall was the time of
year for celebrations, harvest gatherings and other festivals in Pennsylvania. There was always something new
and interesting to be seen.

But all of it would have to wait until she'd turned
her life around.

* * *

Two hours later a sharp pain knifed its way through Aurora's hips, but she mustered on and dragged the last of her belongings into the small apartment over the medical clinic.

Beau had arrived with the keys earlier, but had had to rush off to an out-of-hours emergency call. Now, as he returned, he tutted at her.

"Hey, you aren't supposed to be lifting this kind of stuff." Beau took the last box from her, carried it up the stairs and backed through the door. "You'll undo all the adjustments I just did on you."

"I know. I know. I'm sorry." She had to admit that her back was screaming with pain, but she just had to get this done, then she could rest. And ice. Ice was a magical treatment she was just beginning to discover. Thanks to Beau.

"You say that, but you're doing it anyway, right?"

Beau gave her that sideways smile of his. Somehow it chastised and encouraged at the same time.

"You are correct about that. Nurses are terrible patients." She pointed to the plaid couch up against one wall and Beau sat the box on it. "While I had some momentum going I wanted to push through, then it'll be over with, and I can relax."

Without another word Beau placed his hands on her shoulders and turned her to face him. His hands were warm, his touch gentle. Resisting him was impossible and all those unrequited feelings of long ago surfaced as her eyes met his.

What she wouldn't have given to have been in this position ten years ago. Before they'd both been too hurt by life and love. But that was then and this was now. There was no way for them to go back to the innocence they'd once had as kids. Now she was too broken even to try. At least at the moment she felt that way.

"Promise me one thing," he said.

"Okay. What's that?" A deep breath filled her lungs, helped her push away the longings he'd momentarily stirred in her.

"That you'll call me for any heavy stuff you need either to be carried or moved."

"I'll try. I promise." With a nod, she pulled back from him, curiously aroused by his touch and the gentle tones of his voice. Having someone offering to do something nice for her was almost foreign.

Looking back, she could see that her last relationship had been doomed from the get-go, and now she wasn't certain what had really attracted her to the man in the first place. Chad had been a controller, and demanding— which was not the kind of man she wanted in her life. Too much like her father.

But maybe that was what had appealed to her before she'd realized it. Drawn to the familiar rather than someone new, someone different. Seeing Beau in such contrast made her wonder about her mental state, having put up with that relationship for so long.

"I'm going to hold you to that. Your injuries are overcomeable, but you do need to be babied for a while after every manipulation."

"I see."

She huffed out a breath and changed the subject to one more comfortable to her.

"Speaking of babies—how's Cathy and her baby? Have you talked to her since she got to the hospital?"

"Yes. I just spoke to her a few minutes ago and they're doing great."

The grin that split Beau's face was contagious.

"That's awesome. I still can't believe that happened right in front of us."

"I know—but better here than at home alone or something." Beau opened a box and started to unpack it, then stopped. "Oh, sorry. Do you *want* me to help you?"

"Oh, sure. That's just bedding. You can toss it on the bed. I can make it later."

"No, that's another back-bending chore. I'll help you with it."

Beau shook out the sheets and together they made up the queen-sized bed that took up the majority of the space in the efficiency apartment.

"Did you tell your mom you were moving out?"

"Yes." Aurora nodded. "It wasn't as bad as I thought it was going to be, but still uncomfortable. I hate confrontation of any sort."

"Yes, but it's necessary sometimes."

"Not according to my mother. If I just went along with all the things she's planned for my life, everything would be just fine." Aurora tossed up one hand for emphasis.

"Except you'd be unhappy."

"Yeah. She kind of forgot about that part."

There was real sympathy in his words, in his expression, and she knew he understood. Had always understood her, even when they were kids.

"She had visions of us being gal pals, or roommates or something."

"Oh. That's kinda weird." Beau's brows crinkled.

Aurora tucked the corner of a sheet in. "Since my dad died last year she's been left without a mission in life, I think."

"How so?"

"Well, she's been a caretaker all her life, and without

Dad needing her all the time she doesn't have enough to keep her occupied."

"Sounds like she needs a project."

Aurora barked out a laugh and it felt good. For the first time in a long time, it felt good. "She does—as long as it isn't me."

The bed was finished in short order, and Aurora's stomach rumbled.

"It's getting to be that time, isn't it?" Beau patted his stomach. "I could eat something myself."

"That's good, because my mom sent along a huge jar of beef stew she made today." Aurora pointed to the jar on the counter. "And homemade bread. If you'd like some I'll be happy to share."

"Awesome. I never turn down free food. Especially homemade." He pulled his phone from his pocket. "Let me check on Chloe first. She's still at the sitter's." After a short conversation, he nodded. "Good to go."

"I'd love to meet her some time."

"Oh, I'm sure you will. I have her in the office sometimes."

"Great. Babies are such fun."

"Says someone who hasn't had a child yet."

"Are you telling me I have a skewed perspective?" With a grin, she parked her hands on her hips.

"Yes."

The grin was returned, and she could see some of the pain of this morning had eased. This banter was fun.

"I dare you to make that statement again after you've been up three nights straight with a teething infant."

"Oh, no, thanks. Not accepting that challenge."

In minutes they had poured the still steaming stew into bowls, buttered bread, and sliced some cheese to go with it.

"Sorry, I don't have any wine. It doesn't go with my medications."

"Oh, that's okay. I'm not much of a drinker."

He scooped some of the stew into his mouth and closed his eyes.

"Oh, my God, that's good. She could open her own restaurant and just serve this. She'd make a fortune." His brows shot up. "Hey, maybe you could talk her into opening her own diner or something? Then she'd be too busy to run your life."

"I like the way you think." Aurora laughed again and relaxed a little more.

Watching him enjoy the stew—a simple meal in her new place—stirred good feelings.

Forbidden feelings—especially after that comment about having her own baby. That had been her lifelong dream, to have a family, but it wasn't meant to be apparently.

Recalling how Beau's wife had tragically died after giving birth reminded her that having a family wasn't without risk. And as she sat there in the small apartment, across from Beau, she wondered if the risks were worth it.

There was only one way to find out.

CHAPTER FOUR

MAYBE COMING HOME *hadn't* been such a bad idea after all. Though returning to her childhood home had been a temporary plan, she liked how it felt right now. Cathy would be off for at least six weeks, so she had that long to think about things and maybe come up with another plan.

"What are you thinking about?" Beau set his spoon down and placed his hand over hers on the table. "You look so intense, so sad."

"I was just thinking how far we've come since high school."

She squeezed his hand and enjoyed the warmth of it in hers. Of course they'd touched. Many times. But now, in the closeness of the little apartment, things seemed different somehow. More grown up. More intimate than she'd imagined.

"You're right." He nodded and kept hold of her hand. "We've come a long way for sure. Sometimes I look back at who I was then and can't believe I was such a self-centered, immature jerk."

"Oh, Beau!" She leaned back in her chair with a laugh. "You were *not*." No way. At least not the way she remembered it.

"Seriously?" Doubt shone in his eyes. "You don't know half the things I did back then. I thought I was such hot stuff, that I could have any girl I wanted. Cheer-leaders. Homecoming queens. Any girl I set my eyes on." He shook his head and drew his mouth to the side. "I was an idiot. All ego. No brains. Not like you."

"I certainly wasn't all brains—and you weren't all ego." Amusement shot through her. "Maybe a little. If you were so bad I could never have been your friend, you know." She lifted one shoulder.

"Really?" Beau's brows shot upward. "How do you figure that, Miss Academic Student of the Year?"

"Oh, that was a silly thing. A fluke, really. I was so shy and introverted in high school I could barely talk to guys, let alone be friends with one." A light pink colored her neck. "Or ever think of going out with a jock."

She leaned closer, conspiratorially.

"I did have a secret crush on you, though. You were totally into the hot babes, and never looked at *me* like that, so I got over it." Or so she'd thought. Until now. Until she'd looked into those green eyes again.

"You... *What*? Now *that's* a surprise." He crossed his arms over his chest and a curious expression showed on his face. His brows came together and an intensity showed in his eyes, as if she'd just told him some deep, dark secret. "You thought I was out of reach, yet you picked me to be friends with? That's odd."

"No, actually..." she said with a laugh, and pointed at him with her spoon. "*You* picked *me*. Don't you remember?"

"No. Refresh my memory."

"In Mrs. Dixon's typing class." A memory and a laugh bubbled up inside her as she recalled him trying to squeeze his bulk behind the small desk the computers had been set on.

"No way. I don't remember that. All I remember is

struggling to get my fingers on the keyboard and not totally screw things up."

"Yes—you said if I helped you with typing you'd get me into all the football games the rest of the season for free."

"I did?"

Surprise showed clearly on his face. He didn't remember.

That tidbit disappointed her. He obviously hadn't had the same sort of feelings for her that she'd had for him. This reinforced that she'd been right to keep her feelings to herself. Pining after him would only have brought her heartache.

"Yes, you did."

"I don't remember it that way at all."

"No? Well, that's exactly how it was."

That particular memory was clearly etched in her mind. How embarrassed she'd been when he'd talked to her—then how thrilled she'd been that he'd talked to her! All for naught, as it turned out.

"Nothing is *exactly* anything—let alone memories so old. I think you're yanking my chain." He narrowed his eyes playfully at her, trying to discern the truth.

"You're right, Beau. Nothing is ever exact or perfect, the way we thought it would be when we were kids."

She had to admit that. Nothing in *her* life had been that way. Not ever. And it was one of the reasons she'd left town so soon after nursing school. She'd wanted— *needed*—something in her life to be perfect, and she'd known she'd never get it here. At the time, that was how her mind had worked. Now she wasn't so sure there was a perfect *anything* out there.

At the time she'd thought her happiness had lain out there. Somewhere. Somewhere else. Somewhere new, different, exotic. Someplace where she knew she'd fit in.

Where no one knew her past or had preconceived notions of what she should be. No one would try to make her fit into a mold they'd developed for her. Where she could live and be herself, with no one to please *except* herself.

Beau leaned back and patted his abdomen again. "Nothing's perfect except for this stew. *I'd* be tempted to stay with your mother just for her cooking."

With his words the tension in her eased and she relaxed.

"I know. She *is* a great cook, but it doesn't come without strings."

Yet another reason she'd had to leave her mother's home as soon as she could. But despite all her faults Aurora loved her mother, and had to accept her as she was—not continue to wish she were different. Another part of her childhood that she had to let go of.

"That's too bad, 'cause she's a really great cook."

One corner of Aurora's mouth lifted. "And then there's her bread." Another thing Aurora had to admit was a huge bonus of hanging out with her mother. She loved to bake and was excellent at it. "She tried to teach me, but I only made lead bread so I gave up."

"It's amazing."

"Incredible."

"Which is unfortunate."

"Why?" A confused frown crossed Aurora's face.

"Well, if she was a good cook and a bad baker, then I could justify a strike against her. If she was bad at both, that would be two strikes."

"I see. So since she's good at both, then it's two points in her favor?"

Fortunately, Beau hadn't lost his sense of humor. It had kept him from going crazy with grief after his wife's death. It made him see things a little differently, but he liked it that way. It had helped him turn himself around after the worst time in his life. It had helped him begin to view life in a different way.

"You got it. You catch on quick."

He winked, and a little squiggle of pleasure shot through him as she held his gaze just a little bit longer. That was interesting. She'd had a crush on him and he'd never noticed? He was an idiot. At least he had been back then. Now he could appreciate what a great woman Aurora had become.

"You have a strange scoring system." She laughed and shook her head.

The outer corners of her eyes crinkled up and the laugh came from her chest, not her throat, and was a genuine expression. That made him feel good. That he'd made her laugh when the past few months had been filled with anything but joy for either of them.

"Well, it works for me. I have to say that."

After they'd finished, he took the dishes to the sink. Aurora rose with obvious stiffness in her back.

"Just put them in the sink. I'll deal with them later."

Beau could hear the fatigue in her voice, and her eyes were dark with pain. "Come here."

She approached, and he turned her to face away from him, her back against his chest.

"What? What are you doing?"

"Just relax. I'm going to do another gentle treatment on you. A fine tuning."

"Er...*now*?" Surprise lifted her voice into a question.

"Yes, now." He pushed her long hair off her shoulder and to the front. "Cross your arms over your chest. I'm going to hug you from behind."

"How is a backward hug going to help?"

"Shh. Trust me. Take a breath and relax."

Although she performed the movements as he'd directed, when she lifted her arms and put them on top of his, and he embraced her from behind, something in him changed.

He struggled to tamp down the attraction he felt for her in that moment. She'd been there in his formative years and he trusted her. He had always trusted her. Now he needed to be strong for her—not some affection-starved, struggling single father who needed feminine companionship.

Getting a grip on his hormones, he secured her against his chest, wishing for just a second or two that things could be different between them. They'd been friends. They'd always be friends. He wouldn't change that for a quick escape between the sheets. Aurora was more important to him than that. Way more.

"Now, just relax. Lean back against me and let me hold your weight."

"I don't know if I can. I'm so tense."

Her chest rose and fell quickly with her breathing. With one hand he eased her head back to rest against his left shoulder.

"Close your eyes and listen to my voice. Take a breath in. Let it out slowly."

Beau rocked her gently back and forth while he tuned in to the feel of her body against his, waiting for the moment she relaxed. Her head nestled perfectly against his shoulder and felt so very right. The way her back and hips lined up against his chest was an exact fit.

All she had to do was turn her face toward him and it would be in the perfect position for him to place his lips against hers, to breathe in her scent and take this embrace to a whole new level. He hadn't held a woman in a long time and now, holding Aurora this way, he realized how much he'd missed having a woman in his life.

How much he missed Julie.

Choking down the emotions swirling in him, he swallowed hard. Distracting himself right now was as important as distracting her.

Eventually she relaxed her head against his shoulder and the tension in her back eased.

The moment he felt it shift he lifted her by the arms and gave her a quick shake.

"Oh!" She cried out at the sudden jerking movement, but he hadn't hurt her—just surprised her. "Oh, wow. I feel different already."

"Don't tense up. Just stay with me. Rock with me."

He set her feet on the floor, but didn't release her. He kept her snuggled against his chest, taking a second or two to savor the feel of her body against his even if it was wrong.

"It's hard not to brace myself. I've been so locked up for months that feeling the release, the relief, is kind of strange at the moment."

One of her hands patted his arm as he held her. The gentle motion of her touch on his skin stirred him and he had to tamp down his reaction again.

"I know. You'll have to get used to feeling good again and then *that* will be your norm."

Slowly, reluctantly, he released her, and she took a moment to turn inward and check her body. He could see that she liked the feeling of relief.

"Like I said, soon you'll be swinging from the rafters in your dad's barn."

"Beau…" She reached one hand out and put it on his chest. The light in her eyes, the beauty of her, was almost irresistible.

"You're welcome."

He swallowed hard, trying to resist the attraction that had swooped down to surprise him. After the wonderful relationship he'd had with Julie he'd not expected to be attracted to another woman. At least not so soon. Shaking himself mentally, he berated himself for going down that path. Now wasn't the time. A year hadn't passed yet and he was still mourning Julie, still in love with her—wasn't he? Or had the time come for him to move on?

"I don't know how to thank you for helping me."

"Every day it's going to get better and better."

Irritated with himself, he moved away before he was tempted to cup his hands around her face and draw her closer, to kiss those full ruby lips and breathe in her scent. Aurora was his friend, and now his employee. This wasn't the time to take his libido out for a stroll.

"You can pay me back by helping me get the office going and organized."

That was the goal. That was what he needed to be focused on—not on having thoughts about Aurora that would only get him into trouble.

"Oh, for sure."

When Beau released her she was amazed. Not only could she stand up straight for the first time in ages, but the pain was almost gone. And she had Beau to thank for it.

"Thank you so much."

Cupping her hands under his arms and hugging him to her, she pressed her chest against his. He was strong, and muscled, and not as lean as he'd been in high school—but, then again, neither of them were. When his arms encircled her she had that feeling she'd always been looking for—that feeling of coming home, of belonging, of being needed and wanted, of being able to lean on someone.

She abruptly pulled back. That was *not* the direction her thoughts should be taking her.

Although it had been just a flash of emotion, the feeling was powerful, and she had to pull back before she did something she'd regret. Her future wasn't here in Brush Valley. She wasn't going to be in Pennsylvania for long. Just a few more weeks. Maybe a month or two, tops. Indulging in an affair with an old friend just wasn't going to benefit either of them. Their lives were entangled, but only as friends, and she didn't want to destroy that by giving in to a momentary flash of physical need.

They weren't children any longer. She had a grown woman's needs and desires. A man like Beau would certainly have his own needs, too. Opening *that* pandora's box with him would be something she could never take back. She would never be able to shut the lid on those old feelings if she let them out. Back then they'd been just kids, trying to figure out who they were. Now they were different. Grown up. The consequences were much greater—especially now that he had a child. Hurting him or being hurt wasn't something she wanted. He was still in recovery after the loss of his wife, and losing their friendship would only end in more loss for them both.

"You're welcome."

When she looked up at him the look in his eyes was curious, as if he'd felt something too and didn't know what to say about it. Then he looked away, cleared his throat, and the moment was gone. She breathed a sigh of relief. This was *not* the time to crack the lid on that box.

"So, tomorrow I'll start on that messy desk of yours and get it organized."

Distraction. Lots and lots of distraction. That was the key to keeping those feelings of hers subdued.

"That will be great."

An alert beeped on his phone.

"Oh, that'll be Ginny. Chloe must be ready to go home." He double-checked the message and nodded. "See you in the morning, then?"

"You got it."

As he turned she wanted to say something, say anything, but she didn't know quite how to put it into words.

"Beau?"

"Yeah?"

He paused and looked at her. Really looked at her. As if he saw her, saw *into* her, knew what she was going to say even before the words formed in her mind. Her last boyfriend had always seemed like he was looking through her, was looking for the next woman to capture his attention. But not Beau, not now. Not in this moment.

"I... I just remembered something my mother mentioned. Brush Valley Day is coming in a few weeks."

At the last second she changed her mind, not wanting to say anything that would interfere in her new job, or the dynamic of their friendship. That had to come first. No matter what.

"I remember seeing that somewhere. You'd like that day off? No problem."

"No. I mean, yes. What I'm trying to get to is that it might be an opportunity to do some community outreach—set up a blood pressure clinic, give flu shots, stuff like that."

She hoped he'd like the idea. Even though it was off the top of her head, it was pretty good.

"You're brilliant—do you know that?" He took three steps toward her, clutched her by the shoulders and planted a hard kiss on her cheek. "That's a perfect idea, and I never even thought about it."

"Fall is festival time. Might as well take advantage of

it when it's in our backyard, right?" The heat of a blush bubbled up inside her—pride at having an idea that hadn't immediately been shot down by someone who thought it was stupid or outrageous. "I think it could work nicely."

"Absolutely. We can have a sign-up sheet that will offer follow-up appointments and get people in to see the office. Really show off what we offer here."

Excitement glowed in his eyes.

"We can hand out fliers or appointment cards for people to take home with them—or magnets for their refrigerators with first aid information on them."

The energy pulsing around him was contagious.

"Are you sure you're a nurse? 'Cause those sound like excellent marketing ideas." Beau shook his head and looked at her in admiration.

"I do like marketing. Not like for used cars, though. Just finding ways to get services to people who need them."

"Well, you're hired."

"I think you already did that."

"Right."

He snapped his fingers and pointed at her with a grin. The joy that had been bubbling in her system now gushed over.

"Tomorrow at lunch we'll order something in and make a plan. Write up your ideas tonight, and we'll go from there."

"Great. See you in the morning."

He walked over to the door and Aurora followed him.

When he turned back, he paused with his hand on the doorknob. "It's great to see you again, and I can't tell you how happy I am to be working with you."

"Me too, Beau. Me too."

"Goodnight."

As Aurora closed the door she listened as his footsteps echoed down the wooden stairs. A grin split her face, and she felt like she'd just walked a date to the door.

"Oh, dear. I may be in serious trouble."

CHAPTER FIVE

BEAU PICKED UP Chloe and drove home, but his thoughts were still in that apartment over his office. Aurora had really gotten him thinking about so many things—like how to promote his office, his services, how he could be a better and long-term part of the community.

Things he'd never thought about before. Things he probably shouldn't be thinking about now. Like how good it had felt to hold her in his arms, to laugh with her, to feel whole and human again after losing his wife.

He'd been in survival mode after Julie's death. Learning how to raise a baby alone as well as opening a business had taken up all of his available brain cells. Those had been dark, dark days, but now he was able to see the possibilities for his future as a father, as a doctor. Maybe someday as a partner in a relationship again.

He glanced in the rearview mirror at his sleeping daughter. "She's right, baby girl. We have to be part of the community—not just live here like we don't belong in it."

That meant changes were on the way. Big changes. And he was finally ready for them. At least in the office and his business life. His personal life was still something that was going to get left behind for a while. Looking at the curly-haired replica of Julie sitting in the back seat, he felt his chest burn, emotion pulsing.

Was he ready to open himself up to anything outside of the little world he'd built with just him and Chloe? Could he ever have another relationship like he'd had with Julie? Was he even ready to consider dipping into the dating pool again? With a child, it was so much harder, with so many more things to consider.

He sighed, not knowing the answer to any of those questions. He wasn't sure he was ready, but then again, was anyone ever totally sure they were ready? For anything?

A noise from the baby in the back drew his attention. Didn't Chloe deserve to have a mother in her life? Not just a daddy who ran in too many directions? This little angel, the love of his life, deserved everything, and it was up to him to provide it. Somehow.

The empty house offered no warm greeting, no glowing lights to let him know someone was there waiting for him. He gathered Chloe and headed into the quiet, solemn house as a cloud of heaviness lay over his shoulders and pressed down on him. He hung his backpack on a peg beside the door, placed Chloe in her basinet, and opened the fridge out of habit, even though he'd already eaten with Aurora.

He noticed the meager supplies inside. Hadn't he started a list of groceries? He'd so not appreciated how well Julie had kept their life organized until he'd had to do it all himself.

This wasn't the life he'd imagined for himself just a few years ago. Not at all.

He'd expected to come home to his happy wife and snuggly baby, for them to go on outings together, to get bundled up and play in the snow, to have picnics at the lake and relax in the shade of a willow tree. That had been his dream, what he'd envisioned having with Julie, but it had all come crashing down around his shoulders late in her pregnancy, when she'd collapsed in his arms.

Beau sighed, not wanting to go back and visit that horrible memory tonight. Tonight all he wanted to do was relax and put his feet up, but his emotions, his memories, had other plans.

He grabbed a beer and twisted the top off, but there was laundry and dishes to do, and the dog needed to be let out for a run.

Fortunately his property sat on five acres of mostly wooded land, and Daisy could take a run without the neighbors being bothered by her roaming. He never feared that she wouldn't come back. She was the other constant in his life. The loyalty of this wonderful animal had gotten him through some terrible days. Knowing she needed him too, mattered.

After a futile hour of household chores and dealing with a fussy infant Beau tried to feed Chloe what she normally ate. But tonight nothing was working. The little miss was *not* happy.

Maybe she was teething. Maybe she had an upset stomach. Maybe she needed something he hadn't even thought of.

Babies were generally pretty easy to diagnose. Food. Sleep. Diapers. After those were checked off, then it was anyone's guess. Perhaps tonight she was missing her mother the way he was. Could she even have a memory of her mother?

The heat and weight of Daisy's head resting on his leg attracted his attention.

"What can I do for you, girl?"

He spoke gently to the chocolate Labrador who had seen him through the thick and thin of the last year. She adjusted her head to a more comfortable position and cast golden eyes filled with adoring patience and eternal understanding up at him. She didn't give him any real answers, but an idea did come to him as he stared at her.

"Let's go for a ride. Maybe Chloe will fall asleep in the car."

At the mention of the word *car* and the jangle of keys Daisy whipped her tail around in eager anticipation. She even drooled on his leg. Obviously she needed more attention than he was giving her, too.

"Come on, girl. Let's get out of here for a while."

Within minutes he'd gathered his daughter and stowed her in her car seat. Daisy, a wagging mess of excitement, stood on the other side of the back seat, sticking her head out the window, sniffing the early evening air to her heart's content.

They drove for an hour, until the sun sank below the horizon. Beau didn't know where he was going, but on these narrow highways and back roads he didn't care. He could drive all over this township and never get lost. He'd delivered newspapers as a kid on his bike, then in a beat-up SUV. He knew every rutted lane and pothole-filled road.

Memories of those easy days filled him with nostalgia, and some of the tension in his shoulders eased. Now that Aurora was back a little bit more of his life was complete. He'd missed her and their friendship. Their lives had gone in different directions after school, but she'd been the kind of friend he'd been able to count on when he'd needed one—and, man, did he need one now.

Absentmindedly, he drove past the clinic on his way back home. It was just force of habit, he told himself, to check on his business one last time before the end of the day and make sure nothing was amiss, that he'd locked everything up tight. It wasn't an excuse to see Aurora again.

As he slowed the vehicle, tires crunching in the gravel parking lot, he looked at the apartment window overhead. A dim light glowed behind the curtains.

Was Aurora still up? Was she reading before bed the way he knew she always had? In high school she'd always had a book in her hand, so it wouldn't surprise him if she was reading one now.

So many feelings swirled around in him, confused him. He didn't know what to do. Looking in the rearview mirror at Chloe's sleeping face, he blew out a sigh of relief. *Finally.*

Having such a tiny person depend on him so completely was something he was still getting used to. Though she was only nine months old, she was changing every day. Some new issue, new problem or new growth-related thing he had to learn about raising a baby came up constantly. Although he was a physician, trained in pediatrics, being a father brought a completely different perspective. When it was your own kid that was sick, or hurt, or troubled, the game changed.

His phone rang and he jumped, then answered it even though it was an unfamiliar out-of-state number. "Dr. Gutterman."

"What are you doing out there?"

Aurora's soft voice posed the question, and he grinned, then looked up through the windshield as she looked down at him.

"I'm not stalking you, if that's what you think." He waved.

"Well, why not?" She waved back.

That made him laugh. She'd always made him laugh, and it felt good inside his chest now. Some of the heaviness that had been following him tonight lifted. After months of grieving over the unexpected death of his wife, this lighthearted feeling was foreign, but he welcomed it. Needed it.

"I guess I could start…since I know where you live."

"And work. Don't forget that."

"I won't."

Having her beside him in the office was going to be so amazing.

"Seriously, what are you doing down there?"

Looking up at the window, Beau could see her there, with the curtain pulled back. She looked like a widow of old, standing in her window watching for her man to return from the sea. But he was no sailor, she was no widow, and there was no sea.

"I took Chloe for a drive because she was so fussy. We ended up here to check on the building, because I didn't remember locking up, and I didn't know where to go from here."

"Don't you want to go home yet?"

He paused. Was he that transparent? Then he sighed. "No. Not really. So here we are."

"Why don't you bring her up? We can fix a bed for her here and see if she'll rest."

"It's late. I don't want to bother you."

Though he said the right words, to give her a way out, he didn't really want to go home. It wasn't home any longer—just a place he lived. He wanted her company. Was it wrong?

"It's not that late, and if I didn't want to do it I wouldn't offer."

"I have a dog, too." He cringed.

Her soft laugh flitted into his ear and the tightness in

his chest eased some more. "Well, bring the whole family and we'll be just fine."

"You're awesome."

Carefully he collected Chloe, who still slept and cuddled against his shoulder, then let Daisy out. When he turned toward the outside staircase Aurora stood there, bathed in the light from the kitchen. Surrounded by a golden halo, she looked like an angel. Maybe right now she was.

He didn't know how he was going to repay this woman for her kindness, her generosity and her friendship, but somehow he was going to. Giving her a job and an apartment wasn't enough.

"So, this is Chloe?" Aurora kept her voice to a whisper.

"This is my baby girl."

Beau turned around to give Aurora a look at her beautiful face. As she was only nine months old she hadn't evolved her own looks, but he thought she looked like Julie.

"Put her on the bed. See if she'll settle down and sleep there." On the way past, she reached out and patted the little girl on the back. "She's beautiful, Beau. Just beautiful."

"Looks like her mother, fortunately. I think so, anyway. My mother says she looks like me. Isn't that what mothers always say?"

"Babies tend to favor their fathers in the first six months."

"Really? I wonder why that is?" That made him frown. He hadn't heard that before.

"Probably some evolutionary thing that helps fathers bond with their children." She shrugged, and pulled the covers back on the bed.

He placed Chloe face down, away from the pillows, covered her with her blanket and tucked in the little ratty stuffed dog she loved.

"God, I hope she sleeps." He rubbed his face with his hands and stifled a yawn. "I'm so tired I could sleep standing up."

"Why don't you forget about everything on your shoulders right now and lie down? The bed's big enough for the three of us, I think."

Beau's eyes popped wide in surprise. "I hadn't planned on staying the night. I don't want to inconvenience you on your first night here."

"Look. It's not quite ten o'clock. I usually read for a while." Aurora glanced down at the sleeping child. "We're all wiped out. Let's just call it a night, okay?"

"Frankly, Aurora, I'm too tired to try to convince you otherwise." He removed his boots and stretched out on the bed beside his sleeping daughter. "I don't know how to thank you."

He closed his eyes, sighed, and flung an arm over his face. The peace that he needed, that he sought every night at his empty house, was here in this little apartment. It immediately surrounded him, flinging off the dead weight of grief clinging to his shoulders and bringing relief he'd not known possible.

"Just get some sleep. That's all the thanks I need."

"Thank you."

Morning brought a streak of sun shining through the window onto Beau's face. He lay on his side, facing the wall, and blinked as his memory failed to alert him to his immediate surroundings. They looked familiar, but strange at the same time.

Night had dropped on him like a brick building going

down, and he'd slept like the dead for a change. Taking a deep breath in and looking around, he saw the boxes he'd carried in for Aurora last night, still sitting where he'd left them, and realized he'd fallen asleep at her place.

That was why it looked and seemed so familiar. He'd lived here for a few weeks with Chloe after Julie's death, while he got his office space converted from ready for animals to ready for people. That way he'd had a place to stay, it was nearby, and it had allowed him to grieve for Julie without being confronted by her clothing in their closet, her make-up in their bathroom, or the lingering fragrance of her perfume in the air. Facing the truth of her absence in their home was more than he'd been able to bear at the time.

He sat and looked over his shoulder. Pressure filled his chest at the sight.

Chloe slept like an angel, cuddled up against Aurora's chest, and Aurora's hand rested protectively on her back. Even in sleep they were both angels, for entirely different reasons. One had saved his soul, and the other was going to save his business.

Some of his movements must have awakened Aurora because she took a breath and stirred. Her baby blues fluttered open, and she looked over at him with a sexy sleepiness he'd never imagined seeing in her eyes. At that moment he could just imagine waking up with her in his arms, taking his time to rouse her with kisses and caresses, sharing the morning with skin against skin.

When she looked into his eyes, still half asleep, and smiled, he realized his body was trying to take him down a road he didn't want to go. At least not yet. He needed a shower. A cold one. *Fast.*

"Morning," he whispered, and turned away. He didn't

need to see any more of Aurora if he was going to get through this morning without embarrassing himself.

"Good morning." Aurora stirred again and rose, extricating herself from Chloe without disturbing her.

"Looks like you've done that before," he said, impressed with skills it had taken him many months to acquire. Being a dad, learning everything he'd had to learn, had not been easy. At least not to him. Women, though, seemed to have some instinct about it. Probably why the human race had survived.

"Lots of practice."

"Really? How?"

"Babysitting as a teenager, then being a pediatric nurse. I've had lots of practice getting babies to go to sleep and stay that way."

"When she was a newborn I spent *hours* trying to get her to sleep for fifteen minutes. Maybe you can teach me a few of those tricks as I obviously still need them."

He shook his head and pushed his hair out of his face, thinking again that he either needed to get a haircut or start wearing a man bun. *Not happening.*

"Happy to."

She stretched and pulled an extra-long sweatshirt over her head, which covered her from her neck to mid-thigh, and stuck her feet into fuzzy black slippers. Though it wasn't the lingerie of a fashion model, the look was certainly endearing and totally Aurora.

A rhythmic slapping on the floor caught his attention and he saw Daisy by the door, looking up at him with a message in her eyes.

"Time to go out, girl?" The slapping got faster and she sat up, eagerness written all over her face, if that were possible. "Okay. Let's go."

He turned to Aurora.

"I'm going to take her out, then I'll be back."

"Okay." She glanced at the sleeping infant, sucking on her lip. "She'll be fine."

With a nod, Beau opened the door and the dog rushed out, bounced down the stairs, then raced over to a patch of grass and squatted.

"Good girl."

For a few minutes he took her out to the fenced pasture that had been used to hold livestock at the veterinary practice. What Beau liked about the location of the clinic was that it was surrounded by green fields and acres of forest after that—not parking lots and rows of buildings. City living was not for him. Not after going to college there and then working at a clinic. This was home. Country living would always be home for him.

No other business could build too close, and there was plenty of parking, plenty of room for growth. There was even enough room to build a house back by the edge of the woods, so he could combine his business and his home in one property.

Thoughts of the house he'd shared with his wife brought no joy, no sense of peace or of belonging. Now, it was just a place to put his belongings, not a place to which he had much attachment. When the business got going he was definitely going to put a house at the edge of the woods and sell the other house.

Daisy returned shortly, after a romp around the grass, wet with morning dew. "Find any rabbits, girl?" At the mention of rabbits, her ears perked up. "We'd better go back inside, before you find something you really want to chase."

They reentered the apartment to the smell of coffee brewing and something mysterious sizzling on the stove.

"Hope you're hungry."

"I wasn't hungry until I smelled that." He leaned closer to the sizzling skillet and inhaled. "Oh, *my*. What is it? It smells heavenly."

Aurora gave him a smile and stirred. "In my family, we call it *stuff*."

"Why? Doesn't it deserve a better name than that?"

"Well, there's all kinds of *stuff* in it. I guess it was easier." She shrugged and continued to stir. "My grandmother made it, and it was passed down from someone else in the family before her. We used to make it before family events, or when the guys would go hunting, things like that."

A soft look covered her face as she stirred the ingredients in the skillet.

"What are you thinking right now?"

There had been an unguarded moment when she'd talked of her family. Though there had been some trouble with her and her family, he knew she loved her parents.

"Oh, it's nothing. It's just…" She shrugged and gave a head-tilt. "It just reminds me of good times when I was growing up. Cousins. Holidays." She gave him a glance, then returned to stirring. "The age of innocence, you know? The days before you knew what life was really like."

"Life can suck sometimes. But other times…" A lump formed in his throat as he looked at the baby on the bed. "It's more precious than you could ever imagine."

She met his gaze then, looking deep into him, trying to see if he'd told her the truth. It was the truth as much as he knew.

Stepping closer, he took one of her hands in his and gave it a squeeze. "Somehow, deep down, there is hope and joy that pushes away the pain and sorrow. We have to wait sometimes for that to happen. The older I get, the more I realize that timing is everything."

He'd seen it. He knew it. He just had to hold on to it through the tough times. Maybe that time for him—for them—was now. Together.

"Sometimes we wait a long time to be in the right place at the right time to get what we want...what we need."

Aurora gave him a watery smile and held his gaze. "I hope you're right, Beau."

"I know I am." He placed his hand on her shoulder for a quick squeeze. "I also know I'm ready for some of that *stuff*." He patted his stomach, which had begun to gnaw a hole in his abdomen. "Is it ready yet? I'm starved."

Aurora laughed, and sniffed back that hint of tears he'd seen in her eyes and heard in her voice.

"Okay. Stuff coming right up."

In just a minute she'd dished up a plate full of it, set it and a cup of coffee in front of him—and he'd never been happier with a simple meal, in a tiny apartment, early on a late summer morning.

After the first bite, he closed his eyes. "Oh, my God. This is fabulous. It definitely needs a better name."

A pleased smile appeared on her face and in her eyes. As he watched she even seemed to stand a little taller, too.

"Is your pain any better this morning?"

Her eyes popped wide. "Oh, wow. I almost forgot about it!" She leaned to the left, then to the right. "I can't believe that."

"You don't have to put yourself *in* pain to realize you've been *out* of pain, you know." He'd seen many patients do that.

"I didn't realize I was doing that."

She moved her back to the left and right a little more, then laughed in pure joy and it was good to hear.

"I want to dance now." She did a little wobbly pirouette, then grabbed onto the counter for stability. "Whoa. I'm a bad ballet dancer, but this is so awesome, Beau." She grabbed hold of his forearm. "*Awesome!* This is the first night I've slept without pain in months. *Months!* You have no idea how fantastic this is."

"No, I don't—but I like how fantastic it looks on you." Had he just said that out loud? "I mean, it's great that you're feeling so good and it shows."

Clearing his throat, he hoped she hadn't heard that.

"I don't suppose this will last, will it?"

The vulnerability, the fear and need in her eyes as she stood so close to him, was about all it was going to take for him to pull her into his arms and kiss her. Those boundaries they'd had as kids were gone. He was a man fully grown, and she was no longer the off-limits virgin on a pedestal he'd thought her to be back then. She was beautiful, and ripe, and he wanted her.

Heat and lust, experience and desire pulsed between them. He felt it. So did she.

Focusing on the moment, he pushed away those other thoughts that would only lead to trouble for both of them. "It *will* last, Aurora. As long as you continue to strengthen, and stretch, and do the work you need to do, it will last. The work will be life-long, though."

"Well…" She looked away again and took a step back from him, reached for her coffee with a trembling hand. "It's like any new habit or new thing you do, right? You have to work at it until it's second nature."

"Right."

He was glad she'd moved back. Each of them was vulnerable in different ways, and to put those two together would be a powder keg of heat and sex he didn't think either of them was ready for just yet.

"You'll be fine." He glanced at Chloe, who still slept, one finger in her mouth. "If you don't mind, I'm going to go downstairs and shower while she's asleep. I've got spare clothes in the car, so I'll grab those."

"No problem. But what about Daisy? She needs some food, too."

At the mention of her name, that long tail of hers began to thump on the floor.

"Right. Well, I guess I'll pack up the whole gang and—"

"No—wait. What I'm trying to say is…why don't you go home and shower, change, and bring back Daisy's food? She can stay here, then be with us at the clinic so she's not lonely at home all by herself."

"Bring her to the clinic? Seriously?"

But other healthcare businesses had mascots or resident animals, and Daisy was as well-behaved as any of them…

"Why didn't I think of that?" He looked down at his beloved canine. "She's certainly got the temperament for it."

"Go. I'll hang out with the gang while you go have a peaceful shower for once."

"Aurora, you've no idea what you've done."

The relief that flooded through him was monumental. He hadn't had a moment of peace—not really—since Chloe was born. There had been so much to do and not enough time to do it. Things like leisurely showers had been cut to the bone.

"What?" Her eyes widened with worry. "What did I do?"

"You're about to make yourself indispensable to me." He was not kidding.

"I'm sorry. I'm not meaning to. If that's a problem I can stop, and you can do it all yourself."

Though the words were not what he wanted to hear, he could see the teasing light in her eyes and the grin about to burst across her face.

"No. No, thank you." That humor of hers was infectious. "I'll take indispensable any time."

With a last glance at Chloe, he headed out the door, with a lightness to his footsteps and in his heart that had been absent just yesterday.

In an hour he was back and ready to go. Daisy was fed and walked again. Chloe ate some of the "stuff" that Aurora had made, and he was about to take her to Ginny's house for the day.

For the first time in a long while all was right in his world.

CHAPTER SIX

WHEN BEAU LEFT with Daisy, to take Chloe to the sitter, Aurora took a deep breath and blew it out, trying to blow away the feelings swirling inside her. Having company on her first night in the new place had been good, but it had made her think of things best left alone. Surges of her teenage dreams, of having a family of her own, had emerged. Thoughts of being married, having her own children. Things she thought she'd put away long ago.

She was certain her mind was playing tricks on her, and she *hadn't* seen that flash of interest in Beau's eyes— that he *hadn't* been drawing closer to her more than once.

Perhaps it was because she'd been stuck in the rehab center for two months and she was lonely, or needed to reconnect with her friends. There were so many other reasons why she'd begun to think of Beau in a way she hadn't for a long, long time. Not simply that he'd wanted her. Confidence in her womanhood, her sexuality, had been destroyed by her ex. Beau was the first man to look at her like he was interested, like he found her attractive, and that was heady stuff. Her ego stood a little straighter.

Be that as it may, at the moment she could barely take care of herself, so she needed to cut it out right now. Focus only on why she was here in Brush Valley, on the fact that she was only here *temporarily*.

Everything about her life was temporary.

Everything about Beau's life was permanent.

Having some sort of unfulfillable fantasy about a man and a baby being plopped down into the middle of her life and rescuing her from herself was just ludicrous.

She'd worked hard to get out of Pennsylvania, to make a life for herself elsewhere. Letting a few weeks and some idealistic fantasy about her and Beau ruin all of that wasn't going to happen. This was not her life.

She took a few breaths and blew them out. Again.

When she arrived at the clinic she realized she didn't have a key to get in, but knew Beau would be back shortly.

"Add that to the list of things I need to do. Get a key to the clinic."

Pushing aside those fanciful thoughts of having a relationship with Beau, she focused on the here and now.

A car arrived with two people in it, and Beau pulled in right behind them, with Daisy hanging out the back window. She barked once when she saw Aurora, which made her laugh, and the tone of her heart changed in an instant. Life was good right now, and Aurora relaxed. The day was beautiful, with the sun warm and shining, a light breeze lifted her hair and teased her cheek. Even though this time was temporary, there was no reason she couldn't enjoy it.

Beau let Daisy out of the SUV and looked at her with a grin lighting up his face. "It's a good day when people are waiting at the door to get in."

"It is." Aurora had to agree with that. "I think I should have a key, in case you're late or something—don't you?"

"Absolutely." He led the way with Daisy to the clinic door and opened it. "Come on in, folks. Give us a few minutes to get organized, then we'll see you right away."

"It's okay. You go ahead. It'll probably take me that long just to get in the door." The woman getting out of the car waved them ahead as her caregiver retrieved a walking frame.

Within a few minutes Beau had opened the doors, turned on the lights and grabbed Daisy's bed from the car. She followed him, sniffed it, then turned around in a circle three times and settled into a tight ball beside Aurora at the desk.

"Sign in, please, and we'll get you back to see the doctor shortly."

"It's okay, dear. Take your time. I'm in no hurry." The elder woman walked stiffly with her walker, and the young caregiver in attendance. "We'll wait over here."

"Thank you... Mrs. Kinsey." Aurora read the name, then looked at the woman, trying to place her. "Mrs. *Janet* Kinsey?"

The woman didn't stop, but nodded. "Yep. That's me."

"You were the high school librarian, weren't you?"

"For forty-five years." She negotiated her way to the chair and turned around to peer at Aurora through thick glasses.

"I graduated there a few years ago. I'm Aurora Hunt."

"I remember you now. Always a bright smile, if I remember correctly."

At that, Aurora couldn't help but grin. Another fond memory was bubbling up inside her. All the wonderful times she'd spent in the library, feeding her reading addiction. "That's what you remember about me?"

"Was I wrong?" Mrs. Kinsey turned to her attendant. "It's that smile I've never forgotten."

"Me either, Mrs. Kinsey."

Beau appeared at the desk and surprised Aurora.

Though he spoke to the elderly woman, his gaze was on her.

"That smile is etched in *my* memory, too."

With that, he stepped over to the woman and offered his assistance.

"Let's get you back and have a look at you."

"Oh, thank you, Beau."

She abandoned her walker for the arm of a strong, handsome man. Nothing wrong with her decision-making processes.

"You're a dear, too." She patted his arm and held on to him.

Aurora took her vital signs. "Your blood pressure is up, Mrs. Kinsey. Are you taking your medication?" She referred to the patient's medication list on the computer chart.

"Yes, but I ran out on Saturday and didn't realize 'til then."

"We'll get you squared away." Aurora put the equipment down.

"I know it's none of my business, but I was wondering…are you and Beau dating?"

"Dating? Oh, no. His nurse went on maternity leave yesterday. We're just friends and co-workers. I'm helping him get the clinic organized."

The older woman snorted, and cast a look of disbelief at her caregiver. "That's what Mr. Kinsey and I said when we were working together and people asked. *Just friends.*" She slapped her thigh and barked out a laugh. "'Til I got pregnant—then it was all over, with a quick wedding at the JP."

"Oh, really. There's nothing like that going on between us, Mrs. Kinsey."

The heat of a blush worked its way up Aurora's neck.

That was always a dead giveaway when she was emotional. Just because she'd had carnal thoughts about Beau it didn't make them true, so technically she wasn't lying.

"Guess we'll see how true that is if I see an announcement in the paper someday."

"An announcement about what? Tuning in to the gossip of the day, are you?"

Beau smiled and gave his best doctor face to his patient.

"Oh, I'm just giving Aurora a hard time."

"I'm going to head out to the front. I think I heard someone." Aurora made a beeline for the door.

"Awfully flighty for a nurse, don't you think?" Mrs. Kinsey asked Beau.

"She's just fine. Today's her first day, so I think we'll have to give her a break."

"She's a fine girl. Make someone a good wife, too." The woman gave him a pointed look over her glasses.

"You seem to be pretty focused on getting one or both of us hitched."

"Yes, well…" She sniffed and looked away for a second. "I'm itching for some grandchildren, but my kids aren't cooperating, so I guess I'm taking my frustration out on anyone I can." She patted Beau on the arm. "Sorry about that."

"I'm certain you're right about Aurora. I just hope she doesn't leave me to go on maternity leave the way my last nurse did."

"You need yourself a good woman, Beau. It's been enough time now. You'll never forget Julie, but moving forward is important, and that little baby of yours needs a mama." She patted his hand, offering sympathy in a simple gesture.

"Thank you, Mrs. Kinsey. I appreciate your concern. But how about we talk about *you* today?"

How was he going to steer the conversation away from this direction?

"I don't think talking about me and Aurora will get your blood pressure back where it belongs."

"You can divert the conversation, but the facts remain the same." With that, she huffed out a sigh of resignation.

"No doubt. Now, what's bothering you today?"

Though Beau didn't let on to his patient that she'd struck a nerve with him, he was irritated that people thought they could tell him what he needed to do with his life. That was the one giant problem with living in a small town. Everybody knew everybody's business, and if they didn't they thought they should. Right now all he needed to do was get his clinic to the next level and take care of his daughter and his dog. That was all. Not have his intriguing thoughts about Aurora reinforced.

He listened to her chatter on about this and that, general aches and pains, all attributed to the aging process of a seventy-year-old and maybe a bad pair of shoes.

"Give me that bag of dirt," she said to her caregiver, who handed her a zipper bag of a white powdery substance, which she held out in front of Beau.

"What's that?" It looked like powdered sugar—or an illicit substance he didn't want to know about.

"Diatomaceous earth. Ever heard of it?" She held the bag up in front of her.

"It keeps bugs out of your kitchen, doesn't it?" He had a vague memory of hearing about it in his biology class or something, but that was it.

"This is food-grade diatomaceous earth, and I want to take it. Any problems with that? A friend of mine takes it and tells me all her joints have stopped aching. I want mine to stop, too."

"Got plans for dancing at the Legion Hall?"

"Don't you put it past me, young man." She gave a sly smile, and Beau barked out a laugh.

"I certainly won't."

"Since Mr. Kinsey died a few years ago I've been known to shake a leg now and then. I just don't want to break a hip while I'm at it, you know?"

"I'll have to check into this a bit further and run it against your medications in our computer program, but at this point I don't see that it will interfere."

"Good—'cause I'm already taking it. At my age, I can't wait around on things."

"Maybe that's why your blood pressure is up, then?" He posed the question.

"Nah. I ran out of my prescription and the pharmacy wouldn't fill it until I came in and you approved it. Sheri's such a stickler for the rules. So approve it. Then I can get on with my life before I have a stroke."

"Mrs. Kinsey, why weren't you this funny when I was in high school?" Beau felt an inappropriate chuckle bubble within him.

"Oh, I was—but back then staff weren't supposed to show they had a sense of humor. Made for some pretty dull classes, I have to say."

"Well, I'm glad you're not holding back now."

He finished the appointment and escorted her and her caregiver out to the front.

"Do you need a follow-up appointment, Mrs. Kinsey?" Aurora asked as they approached the desk, which was amazingly clean for the first time in months. How had she done that so quickly?

"No. She's good," Beau said. "Mrs. Kinsey, I'll call you with the information on any medication interactions."

"Good. If I'm not there leave a message, 'cause I'll probably be out looking for a new dancing dress. There's a sale on this week."

Beau didn't know whether she was serious or not and looked at Aurora, who widened her eyes and shook her head. It was anybody's guess.

"At least she's not driving, right?" Aurora said after the woman and her attendant had left the building.

"No kidding. I don't remember her being so funny when we were in school."

"She wasn't. Seriously."

"But how about this desk? What did you do? Just shove everything into the trash and make it look like you cleaned?"

"No, that's something that *you* would do—not me." She placed her hands on her hips and gave him a serious look.

"Oh, *touché*." But he had to admit she was probably right. He tended to clean with a backhoe.

"I did come up with something I'd like to go over with you."

"Oh, sure—what is it?"

"How about you pull up a chair beside me and we can look at this together? It's for the Brush Valley Day celebration."

"Oh, right." He dragged a chair close to her and settled in to look at the piece of paper in front of them. "Hit me with it. What's your mad plan?"

"My mad plan is to have a booth there all day and reach out to people coming and going. We can offer a blood pressure clinic and be on the lookout for people who are at risk who might need a follow-up. It's also time for flu shots. At the other end of the table we can have that going. Both are ways to get people to stop for a minute and get something for free, which they love, and a quick check that takes less than five minutes. We can have them fill out a form for our information, and we can give *them* some information, too."

With her excitement, her eyes became animated and filled with light, while her hands gestured over the most important points. It was an endearing sight.

"Get something. Give something. Makes sense."

"Exactly. We give them something—the BP check or the shot—and they give us the chance to introduce ourselves to them, tell them about the clinic and make contact with potential new patients."

"Think that will work?"

At this point he had no idea. He didn't like wasting time or resources, but this felt right. Felt good. In this area he had little to no experience, so he was going to have to trust Aurora's instincts.

"Well, sure. Why not? A lot of the people we know are aging. Besides, who wants to go to a town eleven miles away or more through the mountains just to have a flu shot or a checkup when you can get it in your own backyard?" She took a breath, warming to her topic. "Especially in the winter. The roads are treacherous a lot of the time, and people simply won't go when the roads are bad."

"Good point."

He knew his mother hated to drive when the roads were bad, so he had firsthand experience with that. There was no bus or taxi service out here. If you couldn't drive, you were stuck.

"There are all kinds of unhealthy things going on at

the fair, but it brings people in—especially the barbecue chicken at the firemen's booth."

"That's my all-time favorite and it's caused me years of indigestion." Just the memory of it made his mouth water.

"I know—me too. I love the contrast of the firemen using their fire to teach safety to kids and at the same time to cook chicken as their fundraiser."

Beau sat back and thought about her ideas as he looked at the paper and the unreadable notes she'd scribbled all over the notepad.

"I think this is a fabulous idea. Too bad it's too late for us to get into the county fair."

"I can call them and see if there's space—or maybe we could set up shop in the tent with the firemen. They have a spot already, right?"

"They do. Okay. Give them a call and see what you can come up with."

Minute by minute his admiration for her was growing.

"Okay. We've got a lull now for a bit, so I'll do that. What was that you were talking to Mrs. Kinsey about? Something interacting with her medications?"

Those blue eyes of hers looked directly at him and for a second, his heart paused and his mouth went dry. How could an innocent look cause such a reaction in him? Had he been suffering from a lack of female companionship for so long that a look could turn him inside out? He didn't think so and he frowned, turning away from that idea. He was made of sterner stuff than that. He had to resist.

"Oh, yeah. I'll do that now. She was wondering about diatomaceous earth. Ever heard of it?"

A change of topic was a good idea right now. It would keep his mind off what he would do to Aurora if he could.

"No, can't say as I have. What is it?"

"It's an insecticide—"

"*Eww.* And she's taken some?" Horror filled Aurora's eyes.

"No. She wants to take some *food-grade* DE for her aches and pains."

"Wow." She made a face that showed she was interested, but equally puzzled. "Think I'll have to look it up. I have aches and pains too, and as long as I'm not poisoning myself I'd give it a shot."

"Oh, really? My manipulations aren't enough for you?"

Mock horror filled his eyes, and he placed a hand on his heart, as if she'd seriously wounded him there.

"It's not that." A light blush crept from her neck up over her cheeks.

"Then what is it?"

He was teasing her, and thoroughly enjoying the light blush that filled her cheeks. She used to blush a lot in school, and he'd gone out of his way to do or say things that would embarrass her. Now he felt a stirring in his heart that hadn't been there since Julie had died and part of him had died with her.

Maybe that part of him wasn't dead after all...just wounded. Deeply. That was curious and interesting and scary at the same time.

Mrs. Kinsey's words came back to him. It was time. He'd mourned Julie and would never forget her, or how deeply they had loved each other. Was it really time to move on? How was a man to know after a relationship like that? He'd never love that way again. That much he knew. But some part of him was waking up, wanting to connect again.

Aurora had just come back to town. She was here

temporarily. He couldn't start depending on her, or start liking having her around so much, or he was going to get his heart broken all over again. He had to think this through with more than one certain body part. Chloe was his number one priority. He couldn't let Aurora into her life and then watch her walk away. *He* could deal with the pain, but he wouldn't put his child through that.

With a frown, he pushed back and stood. "Never mind. Give the county fair people a call and see if we can get in anywhere."

"Beau? What is it?" She placed a gentle hand on his arm to stop him from walking away. "We were having a good time, then you switched gears and shut down. Did I say something I shouldn't have?"

Those big blue eyes of hers looked up at him like he'd just stabbed her through the heart. He had to remember she had baggage, too. It wasn't just him. Yet that was even more reason not to think of her as anything else except temporary and a friend who was helping him out for a while. So many reasons they shouldn't be together.

"No. Nothing." He looked away and shoved his hands into his pockets. How was he going to explain this to her?

She stood and faced him, her eyes wary but determined. "Now, that's just not true. We both know it. If you're uncomfortable about something it's best to talk about it—not pretend it's not going on or ignore it." She curved one hand behind her ear, the way she did when she was nervous.

"No, you haven't done anything. It's just that—"

The door opened, and they froze.

"Is this the right place?" A middle-aged man entered and took off his coat. "I can't decide if I'm a dog or a cat today."

At his words the moment between Aurora and Beau was shattered. It was all business again.

"Of course this is the right place." Aurora greeted the man with an overly bright smile. "What can we do for you today?"

Beau waited as she had the man sign in and give her his insurance information. After that Beau led the man back to the patient exam room and focused on the problem in front of him—not on making new ones with Aurora.

Keeping herself busy with filing and organizing took up the majority of Aurora's morning. Although she hadn't quite lied to Beau, she had misrepresented what she'd done in order to clear the desk. She wasn't *that* efficient. What she'd done was put all the piles of paperwork, lab results, faxes and miscellaneous other stuff into two boxes that now sat on the floor at her feet, out of view of the patients. This gave an immediate view of cleanliness and organization—a professional atmosphere a patient would feel comfortable in.

After that she'd cleaned the surface of the desk, so she had a clutter-free, dust-free surface to work on. Clutter, she understood. Dirt, she had a personal problem with.

Now that everything was clean she began to go through the papers, sorting them into piles: letters that needed to have copies mailed to patients, information that might need a phone call for follow-up, before being scanned into the electronic medical records. All things that made a good first impression on new patients.

After an hour of sitting in the chair, the pain began in her hips and she stood. With her hands on her hips she arched her back, looking at the ceiling. This was a stretch she'd learned in physical therapy.

"Looks like you'll be good as new if you keep up the exercises—and no more lifting things you shouldn't," Beau said to his patient as they came through the clinic door.

"I know. I'm finally going to have to admit I'm not as young as I used to be."

The patient walked out with Beau.

"That's true. But here's your chance to delegate authority, Vern. You're the *owner* of the company. You don't have to tote every beam or bag of cement yourself. Get some of those young guys to do the heavy lifting."

"Good point, Beau."

Vern walked a little straighter as he left the office, and saluted Aurora on the way out.

"Are most of your patients here for adjustments?" she asked as she worked on another stretch.

"Maybe about fifty percent. There's a chiropractor in Indiana, but he's usually swamped, so I get his leftovers." A shrug lifted his shoulders. "Works for me for now."

"Wow. Maybe that's something you should put on your advertising, too. After studying your appointment calendar, it looks like you can usually get people in the same day. That would be a major selling point for people who need an adjustment quickly. Like Vern, there. He just walked in and you were able to see him. Maybe we could set aside one or two appointments every day for emergency adjustments."

"That's a great idea. Are you *sure* you aren't a marketer disguised as a nurse?"

"Oh, no." She laughed, and stretched her back to one side then the other. "I guess I could be called an opportunist. When there's an opportunity that presents itself, I jump on it."

"Very observant."

He stepped closer to her and her senses went on high alert. After their last conversation had fizzled, she wasn't sure what to expect as he neared.

"*I'm* being very observant right now," he said.

"What are you seeing?"

She was seeing him very close, and observing that the hairs on her arms were going up, alerted like she was in a dangerous situation. Only this situation was dangerous to her senses.

"I'm seeing that you need a break. Your back is bothering you, isn't it?"

"Yes…but it's okay."

"No, it's not. You had your hands on your hips in a classic sore back posture. Take a break. That paperwork isn't going anywhere."

"There are lab reports that need to be looked at." Proving her worth to him was extremely important to her. "I don't want you to replace me already because I'm slacking on the job."

"That's just not possible. I'll look at them." Beau glanced down at Daisy, who cast her eyes in adoration up to him. "Maybe you can take Daisy out back for a walk along the edge of the pasture. She hasn't been out since we got here."

"Oh, good plan."

She looked down at the dog on its bed and her heart cramped a little. Beau had had his perfect world and then it had been shattered.

"Do dogs grieve, I wonder?"

"What?"

"Oh, God. I said that out loud, didn't I?" How humiliating.

"Yes, you did. What made you think about that right now?"

A puzzled expression covered his face. Then it was closed, and she hoped she hadn't offended him.

"I was just thinking of you and how your world was broken up when your wife died and I wondered if Daisy misses her, too."

The ache in her chest was twofold. One for him and one for his daughter, who had never known her mother at all. Tragedy was everywhere, and never closer to home than at this moment.

"Well. Yes." He cleared his throat and looked away, obviously uncomfortable with the topic. "I think dogs *do* grieve. Daisy wouldn't eat for a week, and she slept on Julie's side of the bed until she realized Julie wasn't coming home again." He sighed. "After that, she slept on the floor beside me. Hasn't gotten back up onto the bed since."

"Beau…"

She held her arms out to him as tears filled her eyes. It was still painful—that was obvious—and she hadn't meant to bring up anything to open the wound for him. But sometimes that was what friends did, they helped each other to heal. They dug at the hard stuff until it was all out in the light.

"I'm so sorry."

Beau wrapped his arms around her and they held on to each other for a few minutes. No words were spoken. None were needed in order for them to communicate. She felt the trembling in his body and it was echoed in her own. The pain he was in was *real*.

Daisy nudged at their legs with her nose and pushed with her head until Aurora pulled back with a watery laugh. "I see. You need to go out, don't you, girl?"

"Thanks. I needed a hug and didn't even know it."

"We all do, Beau. It's up to our friends to point it out now and then."

She stepped back before that haunted look in his eyes overwhelmed her and she took a step past her boundaries that she'd regret. They were friends, and if she gave in to the impulse to be more, their friendship, and their work relationship would be changed forever. She didn't want that. She didn't need it right now. She needed him as a friend, and she needed this job more than anything. That was all it had to be for her, or she wouldn't be able to carry on working here.

She snapped her fingers at Daisy. "Let's go, girl. I think we both need a walk."

But before she could open the door Beau caught her by the arm, pulled her back toward him.

"Wait. Just a second."

"What?"

The second her blue eyes met his, Beau felt something cramp in his chest. The pace of his heart was usually strong and even, but now he felt like a kid with a crush. He didn't know what it was, but he knew he couldn't let her walk out the door without saying something to her.

It was just a walk. Just taking the dog out. Only a few minutes away from him. But something pulled at him. A connection. That was what he needed—a connection. Heat burned in his chest in a way that he hadn't felt for a long time, and he wasn't comfortable with it now, but he was powerless to resist it.

"Um…" What was wrong with him?

"Beau? Are you okay?"

Concern filled her eyes as she looked at him. Though she still held her body stiffly. It was probably because she'd become used to holding herself that way. She leaned toward him and her eyes showed her interest.

What would happen if she reached out to him the way he wanted to reach out to her?

CHAPTER SEVEN

"I'M OKAY. I just…just wanted to tell you how much I appreciate you being here with me, helping me. Us." He glanced down at Daisy. "Helping us get our lives back together."

Why was it so hard to admit that? That he needed help. That he needed *her*.

That made her smile, and his heart fell into place. Despite all of his precautions, his vow to be self-protective, that smile of hers was sending him over the edge.

"It's okay, Beau. You're helping me, too."

"A mutually beneficial arrangement, then—right?"

The smile she flashed at him created a thrumming in his chest where the heat had just been.

"Right. Guess we'd better go before she gets impatient." She opened it and the dog dashed through it. "We'll be right back. You're on phone duty!"

A short while later the two of them returned. Daisy dashed through the door and leaped up into his arms like she'd done when she was a puppy. Now, with seventy pounds of grown dog flying through the air, he wasn't ready for it. At the last second he made a grab for her, and they both landed on the floor amidst kisses and licks and happy dog slobber all over his face.

He laughed. He tried to capture her collar and drag

her off him, but the dog wasn't going to be deterred. She stood on his chest and then lay down on him, so happy to see him, although she'd been gone only a few minutes.

Another laugh erupted from his gut, and then another. Before he knew it tears of laughter and joy that he hadn't shed for a long time fell from his eyes and down his cheeks. He pulled Daisy against him and caught his breath. She whined once, then settled against him on the floor.

Aurora's hand touched his shoulder, and her touch, her energy, her compassion all reached out to him. He took her hand in his. Lying on the floor with Daisy and Aurora, he didn't feel silly, but for some reason he just felt loved.

"Are you okay?"

The tone of her voice was different. Quietly questioning. She wanted to engage him, he knew, but didn't want to pry into his emotions. She was such a compassionate woman, and totally perfect as his office nurse. Somehow, lying there on the floor, being suffocated by his dog, Aurora's beautiful caramel blonde hair all tousled, he decided he needed to figure out a way to keep Aurora with him.

Permanently.

"I'm good. I haven't felt this good in a long time."

His breath wheezed in and out of his throat. Daisy seemed to have pushed out all the heavy stuff that he'd kept locked inside and each new breath he took pushed out stagnant air and brought more life into him.

"We used to do this when she was a puppy. She must have had a memory strike her, or something, 'cause she hasn't done that in ages." He cupped Aurora's hand in one of his and massaged Daisy's ear with the other. "This is the kind of greeting everyone should have. From someone who loves them unconditionally—don't you think?"

"Absolutely." She sniffed. "There hasn't been much of that in my life, Beau. Seems like the people who loved me only loved me for the things I did for them, not because I was a cool person or anything." She rubbed Daisy's back. "Maybe I need a dog, too."

"That's so wrong." He turned his head to look at her, though she was upside down. "You *are* a cool person, and you deserve so much more than that."

Hesitating for just a second, he brought her hand to his lips and kissed it. That was as far as he could go right now. Though he wanted to reach out to her, there were so many reasons he shouldn't. So much was at stake for both of them.

"Now you're really going to make me cry." She wiped her face with the back of her hand just as the bell over the front door rang, admitting another patient.

Abandoning her human pillow, Daisy trotted over to the door to see what was going on. Fearful that she might jump up and injure a patient, Beau opened his mouth to call her. Before he could do that Aurora snapped her fingers once and ordered the dog to sit—which Daisy quickly did, then offered a paw.

A squeal of delight shattered the peaceful air as Beau picked himself up off the floor. He held a hand out to Aurora and assisted her to a standing position.

"Down. *Down!*"

An impatient little girl of about four years old, with wild blonde curls, struggled from the grip of her father.

He looked at Beau and Aurora while holding on to the struggling child. "Is it okay?"

"Oh, yes. Daisy's good with children."

"Good, 'cause this kid loves dogs." The dad grinned

and shook his head. "Every single stuffed animal she has is a dog."

The father set her down and the girl immediately fell to the floor in front of Daisy, as if worshiping her, then hugged the dog's sturdy neck. Daisy just sat, as if she knew what to do, as if she knew this was her purpose in life—to be hugged by kids and to love them.

Beau offered the sign-in sheet to the man. "You new around here? You don't look familiar."

"I am—but she's not. My wife, Dana, usually brings her in, but today it's my job." He ruffled his daughter's hair with affection. "Needs a booster shot of some sort. Dana said you'd have it in the records in case I forgot—which I did."

"No problem." Beau took a quick look at the sheet for the name and handed the clipboard back to Aurora. "I'll grab her chart."

After the shot was administered, and the requisite ear-piercing scream had lifted the hair on his arms, Beau led them back to the front desk.

"Daisy gives good hugs if you need another one." He crouched down to talk to the little girl with big, tearful eyes. "Nurse Aurora might have a lollipop for you, too."

After a few seconds of consideration, apparently deciding between crying or hugging the dog, she nodded and hurried over to Daisy for another hug.

Aurora gave the treat to her dad. "You might want to keep it, or it's going to have dog hair on it."

"I'll do that." He tucked the lollipop in his shirt pocket. "Come on, Misty. Say goodbye to Daisy."

"Aw…" she said and shook her head, setting her curls to bouncing. "But I *like* Daisy." Casting a pair of soulful blue eyes on her father, Misty tried her best to linger a while with the dog.

"I know. But Daisy will be here next time you visit." He looked at Beau. "Right, Doc?"

"For sure." He turned to Aurora. "Decision made. Daisy is the official mascot for the clinic."

"Good decision," she said, and then her gaze skittered away from him.

He'd noticed she hadn't sat down since coming back into the clinic.

"I'm thinking I need to go upstairs and lie down for a while…if you can handle the clinic for an hour or two?"

"Your back? Or something else?"

Though he'd just kissed her hand, he really wanted to kiss her lips, and she probably knew it. He hoped she wasn't uncomfortable with him now. That was something he didn't need, hadn't intended, and certainly didn't want. But he still wanted to do it.

"Yes. It's the chair, I think. Sitting for so long puts too much pressure on my back in the wrong places."

"Got it. Maybe we can put some sort of support into it for you."

"That would be nice—but don't go to any fuss, Beau. This is a pain I'm going to have to learn to live with, I think."

The change in her face was obvious. The bright, sunny features that had been there moments ago now held disappointment.

"Go. We'll be fine."

Daisy followed her to the doorway, then looked back at him, as if trying to tell him he needed to do something, but he let her go. She needed the peace right now and, frankly, so did he.

He snapped his fingers the way Aurora had, and Daisy returned to sit at his feet. He dropped into the desk chair and quickly scanned the schedule. There was an empty hour, with no one coming in. If no one dropped by he could get the task he had in mind done in no time.

He opened an internet browser and clicked on the local office supply warehouse to see what they had in stock.

He had a sudden need to upgrade his office chairs.

Aurora could delay only so long before she had to go back down to the clinic. After having lunch and lying down for a bit she felt the spasm in her back ease, as if someone had pulled on the end of a bow to unravel it. Now she felt great, and had no excuse not to see Beau.

If she were being honest with herself she had to admit that there had been a moment between them—a special moment—when Beau had looked at her in a way he'd never done before, and she'd responded in a way she'd never done before, either. But there were so many reasons not to give in to her desires, not to let herself feel things for Beau. This new situation, this new phase of her life, could all go down the drain in a heartbeat if things didn't work out between them.

Could she risk their friendship, risk her new job and stability, for something that wasn't a sure thing? Right now, she couldn't. There was *never* a sure thing when it came to relationships.

Plastering a smile on her face, she opened the back door to the clinic and found Beau on the floor, his legs splayed out at awkward angles. Alarm cut right through her, and her heart raced erratically. But Daisy lay quietly beside him, not bothered, so Aurora paused a second.

Beside Beau was a box. A very large box with a picture of a chair on the side.

"What…?" She took a few steps forward. "Beau? What are you doing?"

"Can you hand me that screwdriver? It said flathead,

but it's a Phillips. I don't know who writes the instructions for this stuff, but they need a new job."

He pointed to the twelve-inch tool with its hefty black and yellow handle. Stooping down, she handed it to him.

"As you can see, I'm putting together a chair."

"But why?"

He looked at her and blinked, as if she'd said something crazy. "Because you need one."

"Oh, Beau. You didn't have to do that."

No one had ever done anything like that for her, and a little flutter of warmth shot through her heart, tearing down those flimsy little barriers she'd just put up.

"Sure I did. The other one was giving your back trouble, so this is an easy fix. Your back's happy, you're happy. You're happy, I'm happy."

"Simple as that?"

"Simple as that."

Beau turned the screw a few more times. "Done." He rolled over and jumped to his feet. "Here. Take it for a spin."

A ridiculous bubble of pleasure pulsed inside her chest. "Well, okay. If you insist."

"I insist."

He put one hand on the chair to steady it, and with a sweeping gesture of his other hand offered it to her. With a giggle she sat, and Beau pushed her over to the desk.

"How's it feel?"

Aurora wiggled her hips, trying to decide how the chair fit her.

With excitement in her eyes, she looked up at him. "It's great."

"Awesome."

He spun her around in a circle and then put his hands on the arms of the chair to stop it. Her face was only inches from his, and the second he looked down at her mouth that familiar zing shot through her system.

God, she wanted his hands on her, his mouth on hers, his skin against hers. His head slowly lowered, his lips aiming to claim hers. Could she kiss him? Should she kiss him? She wanted to. But what about their friendship, his daughter, her temporary life here…?

Aurora shook her head, the heady fog clearing somewhat. There was too much at stake. She took a deep breath. "I know we're not teenagers, Beau. But this thing that's happening between us is so new—"

He stooped, so she didn't have to look up at him and crane her neck. "I know. For me, too. We've never looked at each other this way before. It's crazy. It's exciting. It's scary."

He blew out a sigh and placed one hand over hers, but didn't back away from this conversation that was difficult for both of them.

"But if we don't reach out, take a step that's scary, we'll never know, will we?"

Unable to stop herself, she placed her right hand on his cheek and looked into his eyes. "You've been through some tough times…you have a child and a business now. Your life's complicated." She looked down, uncertain how to say what she wanted to say to him. "I'm so ruined, I don't know if I can find my way back. You shouldn't—"

"Don't tell me what I should and shouldn't feel." After placing his hand beneath her chin, he raised her face to his and waited until she looked at him. "You're not ruined, Aurora. You've hit a pothole in the road. That's all. And I'm… I don't know what I am…but right now I really want to kiss you."

He leaned in, and this time she met him halfway.

She paused for a second, savoring the feelings swirling

inside, trying to decide whether this was a good idea or not, but curiosity and need won over any caution whispering in her ears.

When his lips touched hers she opened up to him and met his tongue with her own. The soft, silky glide stirred feelings in the pit of her stomach, in her feminine flesh, that hadn't stirred in entirely too long. He held her face as if she were precious, and fragile, and important, and beautiful.

Tears sprang to her eyes. She pulled back, her breathing coming fast, her heart thrumming in her chest.

"I didn't mean to make you cry. Was it that bad?" A sideways smile lifted Beau's mouth.

"No, you goof. In fact it was quite the opposite. You made me feel things I haven't in a long time."

"That's good, then—right?" He eased back down to kneel in front of her.

"I don't know, Beau. This is so strange and wonderful all at once, and I've no experience with it."

None at all. There were so many reasons not to go down this road with Beau. Had they already gone too far?

"Me, either. We're both on new and unfamiliar ground. All we can do is see if we're a good match, other than as friends, and go from there."

"There's so much about me you don't know."

That worried her. She'd changed so much from the old days. So had he.

With a gentle hand he pushed her hair back from her face. "There's a lot of me that you don't know either, and I'd like you to." He closed his eyes and cleared his throat. "I'd like to tell you about my wife sometime, too."

"I'd like that." With hands that trembled a bit she cupped his face, brought him closer for a light, tender kiss. He didn't try to take it any further than that. "But for now we have a business to run, and you've got a baby to go get in a few minutes."

"You're right." He stepped back, still watching her, considering. "We'll need to revisit this conversation another time, but tomorrow how about you tell me some more of your ideas for Brush Valley Day? I think you're really onto something there."

"I will. I have a notebook full of stuff."

He kept backing toward the door, watching her until he'd backed into the wall and stumbled before gaining his feet.

Without taking his gaze from her, he reached behind him for the door. "I'll see you tomorrow."

"Tomorrow, then."

She sighed, her heart pulsing with a new warmth as he left.

"Wow. Just *wow*."

Grabbing her keys and her purse, she turned off the lights in the main room just as the door opened.

"I'm sorry, but we're— Beau! What are you doing? Did you forget something?"

"Uh, yeah." He emitted a sharp whistle. "Kinda forgot my dog."

Daisy trotted out from beneath the desk and went to Beau.

"Oh, dear. Glad you remembered her."

"Yes. I was a little distracted there for a few minutes."

"Glad you're better now."

That little hum in her chest hummed a little faster, a little warmer and a little louder, and the warning bells faded away into the distance.

This was a new and very interesting development in their relationship.

The tremor in her hands still hadn't receded when she

reached for the phone after Beau left. The time had come for her to call in reinforcements.

Tammie had been her friend forever. They'd been pals since first grade. No matter when she called Tammie, they could have a conversation like they'd seen each other yesterday. That was a sign of true friendship.

"Hey, girlfriend!"

Tammie answered the phone with her usual exuberance. The blue-eyed redhead always had a big smile and a quick joke whenever Aurora needed it.

"Hey."

After chatting for a minute, Aurora finally admitted her reason for calling.

"I have a problem, and I need to talk. Do you have time to listen and offer some advice?"

"Oh, absolutely. Is this an I-need-popcorn kind of chat, or an I-need-booze-and-ice cream talk?"

"I'm thinking it's somewhere in the middle." It wasn't that bad, but it wasn't that good either. "Can you meet me at the coffee shop?"

"Sure. Be there in twenty minutes…"

After settling in at the coffee shop with their choice of beverages, Tammie got the conversation rolling.

"Okay, shoot. What's going on? You sounded stressed out on the phone."

Aurora blew out a breath, took another one, and then filled her friend in on the dilemma of Beau and their mutual attraction.

"I don't want to start something if I'm only going to leave here and go back to Virginia, but I don't want to go back to Virginia if I've started something here!"

How convoluted was *that*? Of course hearing the words out loud made things sound way worse than in her head.

"You sound very confused about it."

Tammie always got to the heart of a situation quickly. That was what made her a great friend and an awesome therapist.

"I am. I can't believe it. I'm usually the levelheaded one and you're the wild child."

"Oh, really?" Tammie's delicate brows rose at that statement.

"Yes, really. Like you don't remember."

Aurora relaxed as she reminded her friend of how many times she'd come home intoxicated or taken a horseback ride through town at midnight. Naked.

"I guess you're right. But in all of my adventures what I gained was perspective."

"It's that perspective I need now."

Seriously. There was no one else she could go to.

"Go for it."

Tammie gave the simple advice and sipped her green tea.

"What do you mean?" Had she heard correctly? "Go for it? With Beau?"

"I mean *go for it*. Everything. There's no sense in going back to Virginia when you'll be wondering if you gave up the chance of a lifetime here. You'll regret it if you don't at least try, right?" Tammie adjusted her position. "For me, I don't want to be on my deathbed and say, *'I wish I had...'* How about you?"

"No. No, I don't." Aurora paused and thought a minute. "That's one way to look at it. But is it too late already? I mean, will Julie be a ghost between us forever? Will he think about her every time he looks at Chloe?" Hesitation swirled in her abdomen. "Another way to look at the situation is, what if we go for it, it goes badly, and we lose our friendship? That would make me so sad."

Tammie placed her warm hand over Aurora's. "You could both win, too. If you stay without at least giving it a shot you'll both be frustrated, which can ruin a relationship in a whole other way."

"That's yet another way to look at it." She slapped her hands on the sides of her head and closed her eyes. "God! This is so hard. What do I *do*?"

"Take a breath. Relax and let it go. It's only hard if you try to control it. If you let things unfold naturally it's much better. If you think about things too much—and you *do*—you'll end up with a big, fat headache."

"Yeah. My special brand of self-torture."

She leaned back in the chair and stared at her friend as if the answers would come flooding out her mouth.

"You really need to relax. Why don't you take one of my yoga classes? It helps a lot."

"Beau mentioned yoga for my back, but it might help me with everything else, too."

"It's mind-body-spirit therapy. Can't get any more comprehensive than that." Tammie gave a sharp nod. "Might help you get off the pain medications, too."

Decision made.

"I can use all of that. Still at the community center, right?"

The place had been built after Aurora had left for Virginia. In the center of the little town, it was a gathering place for many people and many reasons.

"Right. Check the website for class times. I can't keep track of all the days and times in my head." She waved a hand, dismissing the idea.

"Thanks, Tam. I appreciate you listening."

Over the years she'd had other girlfriends, but none like her old friend from home. The thought occurred to her that if she remained in Brush Valley she could see Tammie more often, too. That would be a wonderful thing.

"So, what are you going to do?" Tammie watched Aurora with interest. "I can keep a secret."

"I don't know, but I'm not going to give up…on any of it…just because it's difficult."

"There you go. You came up with your own answer. When you let go of security, of things that are familiar, that's where growth occurs. Sometimes answers."

"So, you're an old sage now?"

Those wise words coming from Tammie, who seemed not to have a care in the world, had surprised Aurora.

"No. My yoga teacher is. I learned that from her." Tammie sighed. "I hated that advice when I first heard it, but now I know it's the truth. You just have to find a way to let go of the old and embrace the new. Drop what no longer serves you."

"Great. Right now I don't know what's old and what's new, and if I let go of anything I'm just hoping there's a net when I fall."

Tammie leaned forward, her eyes intense and looking wise beyond her years. "You have to trust that you don't *need* a net. That's the key."

"How do I *know* that?" Panic flashed through her at the thought of not having a new stronghold before leaving the old one.

"There's only one way to find out, right?"

"By letting go? *Completely?* But it's so scary. I hate being scared."

Right now her heart was going on a marathon race in her chest.

"Life *is* scary, my friend."

"I thought you were supposed to be giving me support and telling me lies, saying that everything is going to be okay."

"Everything *is* going to be okay. It just may not be in the way you imagine it right now. That's no lie."

"I still have a life to get back to in Virginia."

Didn't she? Wasn't that where she belonged?

"Isn't that what I worked so hard to find? If I stay here, doesn't that mean I've given up on my dreams?"

"Says who?" Tammie leaned back in her chair, cradling her cup of green tea. "What makes you think your life is in Virginia any longer?"

"Are you *serious*?" Aurora's eyes popped wide. "I had a job in Virginia, I had a life there until a car crash took it all away from me. I want that life back." A cramp tugged at her heart. "Don't I…?"

"Listen to yourself. You *had* those things. *Had*. Perhaps the universe is telling you that you need a different life now, and it took the crash to kick you out of what you *thought* you needed." Tammie nodded. "You learned what you needed to learn there, and now it's time to move on."

"That crash almost killed me." The words were a whisper coming from her soul and tears clouded her vision. "I can't give up, Tammie. I *can't*."

"It's not giving up. It's redefining what you want out of life. There's no shame in that. Some lessons are harder than others. Sometimes we don't listen to the signs until something this traumatic happens. This was a wake-up call and you need to listen."

"How do I know I'm not making a royal mistake by not returning to my old life?"

"You *can't* return to your old life."

"What?" Startled, Aurora widened her eyes.

"It's gone—and I'm wondering if that old Aurora, so determined to not need anyone, is gone too."

Before Aurora could protest, Tammie held up a hand.

"Think about it. Think about what you really want in life. Do you want marriage, a family, friends and a community, or do you want independence, to have work be your life?"

"Can't be both, can it?" Aurora's shoulders dropped. Those were straight, honest words and it was a concept she hadn't considered before.

"Not usually. We can't have it all. We have to pick the things that work the best and leave the rest behind." She shrugged and her silk shawl slid from her shoulder. "Besides, do you *really* want it all? Having it all comes with a lot of responsibilities."

"I suppose so."

Her friends in Virginia had come from a variety of places, but the one thing they'd all had in common was that they were driven. Was that *her* anymore? Did she want a simpler life now?

An image of Chloe popped into her mind. She was such a beautiful baby, with her green eyes and blonde hair so like her father's, and Aurora already wanted to be around her more. Maybe one day have a child of her own.

"Just think about it—see how things go. Maybe write down the pros and cons of each. Seeing it on paper might help."

"I'll try it."

Tammie half closed her eyelids and appeared to be listening to something other than Aurora's voice. Maybe she was listening to the universe.

"Tammie?"

"Yes, sorry." She leaned forward across the table and took both of Aurora's hands in hers. "You go get 'em. Listen to your instincts and your heart. They can't both be wrong at the same time, right? Call if you need me."

"Are you going to be around this weekend?"

Without answering right away, Tammie tilted her head to the side and gave an enigmatic smile. She could be a redheaded Mona Lisa.

"Uncertain. I have a date with an artist in Pittsburgh on Friday. The weekend could go anywhere after that."

"You go, girl!"

Aurora laughed and some of the tension lifted. They chatted for a while longer over another cup, parting ways with a hug and an agreement to meet the next week.

After talking to Tammie she felt better. Sharing her burden, her fears and anxieties had helped. Reconnecting with an old friend had helped, too. Not trying to keep everything tied up inside made her feel lighter in the chest.

The drive back to her little apartment took her past the road leading to her mother's house, but she kept going. Right now there wasn't enough time to have a visit. Maybe tomorrow she would stop. With her mother, there was never a short phone call or a short visit.

CHAPTER EIGHT

SEVERAL BUSY WEEKS passed at the clinic, with a flurry of people coming in for school checkups, and sports physicals, and a variety of the ailments that were the lifeblood of Beau's office. The appointments calendar was getting fuller every day, making Beau very happy. And working with Aurora was the icing on the cake.

"Seems like word is getting out about the clinic. It must be the perfect location. People drive by and realize it's here."

That was proof, as far as he was concerned, of the good choice he'd made in location.

Aurora chewed her lip and a worried look came into her eyes. "I may have dropped some informational fliers at the community center."

"*May* have? You don't know?"

Hmm...

"Well, yes... I do know." She cringed.

"So, did you or didn't you?"

"I did. I'm sorry. I signed up for Tammie's yoga class and thought while I was there I'd see if they had room to promote local businesses, and they did."

"That's great." He definitely approved of the way her mind worked.

"And the library and the post office, too."

"Seriously?" Dumbfounded, he stared at her.

"That's where people around here can be found. And in the fire hall, too. *Ooh!* I hadn't thought of that one. Let me put it on my list."

She opened a drawer of the desk and pulled out a large yellow notepad, flipped through several pages of notes and scribbled another one at the end.

"That's your list of ideas?"

Beau was impressed. He thought she'd have a few notes jotted down on a sticky pad—not an entire notebook filled with ideas.

"It's a manifesto."

"Yes. I'm sorry." She clutched it to her chest, eyes filled with worry. "Is it too much? Have I overstepped?"

"I don't know yet." He held out his hand. "Let's have a look at it."

Hesitating for a second, Aurora placed it in his hands. "Why don't you sit down and I can explain it to you? You might not understand my scribbling."

"Okay." He grabbed the old desk chair and scooted it close to her. "Tell me about your ideas."

Aurora leaned closer to him and her fragrance washed over him. It was a subtle mix of spice, maybe sandalwood, that stirred his senses, and the words on the pages blurred. He stopped trying to focus on the pad and just listened to the excitement in her voice, let her fragrance wash through his mind.

Her ideas rolled in his brain, and he was intrigued by the way her mind worked, how she had come up with a marketing plan for opportunities he'd never even thought of.

"So that's it." She closed the pad and her eagerness showed in her eyes.

"That's it? That's *all* you've got?"

He was teasing her, and enjoyed the flustered look on her face.

"Well, I haven't had much time to focus on it lately, but—"

"Relax, Aurora. I'm just giving you a hard time. You've done more in a few weeks than I could have done in months." A bubble of pleasure churned inside him. "I *knew* working with you was going to be awesome."

Every day there was something new, something interesting. Some new burst of life that made him want to enjoy, to live fully again. Yet guilt surfaced right after, to dull the edges and pull him backward.

The bubble he'd been living in burst.

"What's wrong? I can see it on your face." She took a big breath. "Are you having second thoughts? About a lot of things?"

Without answering, he stood and walked a few steps away. Her nearness, her fragrance, the easy way they worked together shook him to a depth he didn't think he was ready for.

"No. It's nothing."

"Stop it." She stood and faced him, anger snapping in her eyes, in the posture she took as she faced him. "Right now."

"Aurora, I don't think this is the time—"

"Yes, it is. Right here. Right now. If you can't face moving on, that's fine. If you're having feelings for me that you're having difficulty with, that's fine too. But don't shut me out—because it's not my fault, and yet you're punishing me. You have been for weeks. Ever since…"

Their kiss.

For a few seconds he stared at her. There was truth in her face, in her eyes, and he knew it. There were questions. There would always be questions. But if he didn't at least try to take a step forward, he'd never get anywhere.

"You're right." He blew out a breath. "Admitting that is hard for me, Aurora. Very hard. But you're exactly right. You don't deserve to take the brunt of my pain."

"We all have pain, Beau. But if you share it, even a little bit, it doesn't hurt as much, you know."

An encouraging smile lifted her lips, but a bruised uncertainty still filled her eyes and that he couldn't take. *He* was responsible for putting it there.

"I'm sorry." He pulled her against him. "I know I'm all over the place with this, but I'm coming to depend on you so much, so quickly, it's frightening."

"I'm with you—but we have to be able to communicate about things, whatever comes up. I don't want to wonder what you're thinking or what I've done wrong."

"I understand what you're saying. But sometimes the best thing seems to be to keep quiet, when that's really not the best thing at all."

"So from here on out let's really try—"

At that moment the shrieking sound of car tires skidding on pavement tore their attention away. They clung to each other for a few seconds, both cringing, waiting to see if there would be a crash.

There was.

The impact of the crash shook the building like an earthquake. They all jumped, including Daisy, who cowered beneath the desk.

"Oh, boy. That didn't sound good." Beau grabbed her hand. "Come on."

Together they dashed out the door.

Beau wasn't a trauma doctor, but he and Aurora were the best bet as first responders. A small car had missed the sharp turn in front of the clinic and crashed head-on into a utility pole right beside the building. No wonder the impact had shaken the whole place.

"Oh, my God. Beau!"

Aurora squeezed his hand, then raced around the other side of the car, looking in through the broken window.

"Three people."

"I'll try to get the driver's door open. Can you turn off the ignition? I can't reach it from here."

"Yes."

Since the passenger window was broken, she was able to turn off the ignition, hopefully preventing any sort of electrical fire in the engine.

"I'll call 911 now."

She pulled her phone out and made the call for emergency assistance. Out in this area of the county most rescue services were volunteers, so help wasn't mere minutes away as in larger cities. Out here people depended on their neighbors, friends and Good Samaritans to help out in emergencies.

Beau focused on the handle of the driver's door. It was an old car, and he pushed the handle down and tugged. The metal was twisted and crunched. There was no way he was getting anyone out through this door without heavy machinery.

The driver moaned and raised a hand to his head. A teenager, with two friends in the car, he'd probably been talking, and distracted, and hadn't realized the curve was so sharp.

"Aurora? Go grab a few blankets or sheets. I want to cover the driver so I can push the glass out."

"Got it. This one's still out, has a bump on the head, but that's all I can see right now. The girl in the back is unconscious, too."

She gave him her quick assessment, then ran back into the clinic.

Tugging on the door again brought no better results than his previous attempt, but he couldn't just stand there and do nothing. He'd had to stand by and watch his wife die while he did nothing. That was *not* going to happen here. Here he could help, he could rescue, and he could save lives.

A car horn beeped and a large pickup truck made a quick turn into the parking lot and stopped beside them.

"Hey, looks like you need some help." One of his old classmates, Robby Black, hurried over. "Did it just happen?"

"Yes. I can't get the door open." In an example of frustration, he yanked on the door again, but it still didn't move.

"I got a crowbar in the truck…" Robby made the offer as he stared at the mangled car.

"Get it."

There was no time to waste.

Aurora rushed from the building, her arms full of linens and an emergency kit, just as Robby arrived with the pry bar.

"Aurora, cover them the best you can with the sheets. If the glass goes flying it will protect them."

"Got it."

While Aurora set about her task, Beau and Robby set the end of the steel rod in the buckled edge of the driver's door.

"On three."

Together they used their combined strength to try and pry the door open, but it wasn't budging.

"Again."

They tried again, but their effort was still futile. The door was not going to move.

"Why don't you try the back door? Maybe it's not as bad."

Aurora made the suggestion and the men moved the tool to the back door—and popped it open on the first try.

"Awesome…"

The young female was rousing from her slumped position.

"At least she's buckled in."

Together Beau and Robby extricated the girl and placed her on a blanket on the ground, away from the vehicle.

"Aurora, stay with her and keep her head in alignment while we try to get the front passenger door open."

More people had stopped their cars, seeing the increased activity.

Two people Beau knew from the pharmacy hurried over. "Can we help out?"

"Yes. Relieve Aurora so she can come over here with us."

"Got it."

In a few minutes Aurora returned to his side. "What do you need me to do?"

As the physician, he was in charge of the scene until rescue services arrived and everyone looked to him for direction—even Aurora.

"We're going to try to get this door open and take them out this way. Can you get into the backseat and hold onto his head, keep him still while we work on the door?"

"Yes."

Aurora climbed into the backseat on the passenger side and placed her hands on the sides of the passenger's head, holding it steady.

"Ready here."

"One, two, three—go."

The door popped open with just two forceful applications of the crowbar.

"We need to get him out, but I want to immobilize his neck."

"Do you have any collars in the clinic?" Aurora asked.

"No. None." He'd never thought he'd need those kinds of supplies.

"How about some towels and tape? We can use them to make a soft collar."

"Brilliant. You stay here and I'll go get them."

"I can go."

"You're already in position."

"Beau, it's my back…"

A twinge of pain crossed her face. Though she'd tried to hide it, he was glad she'd spoken up before letting it get too far.

"I'll relieve you."

He placed his hands on the young man's head, over top of Aurora's, and she slid her hands out from under his. Looking over the seat at her, he saw her meet his gaze with determination shining. She was so good at this. *So* good. The woman could do anything.

"I've got him now. Go."

With the help of the little band of people who had stopped by they were able to safely extricate all three youths from the car, and then the ambulance crew and paramedics arrived, just behind the fire truck.

"What do we have going on here?" Randy Overdorff, the chief of the fire group, bailed off the truck even before it had come to a halt.

"Looks like they took the turn too fast. Three in the

car, all with injuries, all three with loss of consciousness. Two have awakened."

Beau gave the assessment as he watched Aurora placing an IV in the third victim.

"Got it," Randy said, then gave a slow whistle as his brows shot up. "How did you get them out of that mess without hydraulics?"

"Crowbar," Beau said.

"And muscle," Robby added, and flexed both of his arms like a champion wrestler.

"Good going. We'll call for another ambulance from Armagh and they can take one in. We'll get the first two."

Randy spoke into a handheld radio, calling for backup from the small town of Armagh, just four miles away. Armagh was like Brush Valley. A wide spot in the road where people had settled, opened a few businesses and called it home.

The next two hours passed in a flurry of activity as the three teenagers were taken to hospital, the scene investigation was completed, and a tow truck hauled the car away. Beau took a few seconds to text Ginny that he'd be late picking up Chloe.

"Someone's going to have to call the utility company about the pole."

Looking exhausted, Aurora sat on a landscaping rock beside the door of the clinic. Until now, he hadn't noticed how pale and drawn she was. This event had taken its toll on her and he hadn't noticed.

"Already on it," Randy said. "They'll be out in the morning to work on repairs. Meantime, looks like you're closed until that can be done."

The fire chief stood beside Beau with a clipboard full of notes.

"Oh, boy. Does that include the apartment?" Aurora asked.

"Afraid so." Beau looked up at the apartment window. "Hadn't thought of that."

"I guess I could go stay with my mother—or light a few candles." She took a deep breath in, resolving herself to the issue. "I'll be fine."

"I'll leave you to it, then." Randy saluted.

"Thanks, Chief."

Though he spoke to the man climbing onto the fire truck, Beau kept his gaze on Aurora. The longer he watched her, the angrier he got. He'd been so focused he'd completely forgotten about her medical condition, and she'd said nothing. *Nothing*. Not until she was in great pain.

"Aurora?" He approached her, his steps stiff and rigid. He couldn't seem to make himself relax.

"Hi, there." She looked up at him from her position on the rock, and couldn't hide the wince the movement caused. "What a day. Sure ended with a bang, didn't it?"

"We need to talk. Let's go inside."

"What? What's wrong? What did I do?"

Dammit. His temper was getting the better of him, and he didn't mean to take it out on Aurora. *Again*. He took a breath and huffed it out, trying to ease the anger boiling inside of him. He held a hand out to her, to assist her up from the rock.

"Let's just go inside. Please."

Hesitating for a second, she placed her hand in his and allowed him to help her to her feet. Though it was getting dark, they had enough light to have a private conversation. Once they were inside, the wide-eyed look of shock on her face gave him pause. He took a deep breath and blew it out before he spoke. Irritated, he ran a hand through his hair and shoved it back from his face. He still hadn't gotten a damned haircut.

"What's wrong? What did I do?" she repeated. Wide-eyed, she faced him.

"Nothing, it was me. I'm sorry I didn't take care of you out there. You're in pain and I didn't realize. I should have had someone relieve you." He strode to her, got as close as he could and placed his hands on her shoulders and squeezed. "Aurora, you're important. You're *very* important. And I don't want you putting yourself in pain unnecessarily."

"Beau."

She tipped her head to look up at him and those dewy blue eyes of hers got to him, stripped him of all propriety and good sense.

"To be perfectly honest I didn't feel anything until I sat in the car to stabilize that kid's neck—then it hit me." She gave a small laugh and patted one hand on his chest, trying to soothe away his irritation. "I think adrenaline gave me such a rush I didn't know it was getting bad 'til then."

"I think it's having the same effect on me, too." In a totally different way.

His concern, masked as anger, dissipated as he held her close. As he looked down at that tempting mouth of hers. As desire filled him.

"What are you talking about?"

"This."

He pressed his mouth to hers and kissed her. Cupping his hands around her face, he pulled her closer against him and breathed in her scent, touched her skin, eased her in so they were pressed against each other. Tension filled him. This was so good, but so wrong at the same time. He'd leaped over and toppled all the boundaries they'd set.

She was his friend, his employee, and his patient. There were so many reasons he shouldn't be touching her, kissing her, needing her right now. But he ignored all of them as he explored the sweetness of her mouth.

Shaking with need and fear, he pulled back. "I'm sorry, Aurora. I…"

"Shh."

She placed her fingers over his lips and he kissed them. God, she was so beautiful, and so wonderful and he wanted her with everything he had in him. But there were so many reasons not to.

"But—"

"I understand. Completely." Leaning forward, she pressed a small kiss on his mouth, then pulled away. "We have things to do right now—like you going for Chloe, like me getting my pain medicine out and closing up the office for the night." She gave a quick frown. "I may have to stay at my mother's place tonight."

A frown wrinkled his brow at the mention of her pain medicine. "Hold off on the meds for a bit—and your mother. I have a hot tub at my house. Since the office will be closed tomorrow, why don't you come over tonight? We'll put some ice on your back, some heat in the spa, then see if you still need the medication."

"Are you sure?"

"Absolutely."

Relaxing a little, he tried to focus on calming down, on treating Aurora's pain, and controlling the desire thrumming through his system. Months had passed since he'd felt this rampant surge of life rippling through him. The thoughts running through his mind kept telling him no, but the feelings in his heart and his soul told him to let go of the past and move forward. With Aurora.

"I'd like that. I'd like to spend some time with you and Chloe. Just hang out and relax."

"Tonight will be perfect. Just perfect."

Shaking his head, he stepped back and took a breath, not realizing he'd been holding it. Stepping to the now immaculate desk, he found a pen and scribbled on a notepad, then tore the paper off and gave it to Aurora.

"Here's my address. I'll go get Chloe, and grab a pizza from Sanso's Deli. Come over in an hour or so and bring your swimsuit."

"Okay. I'll see you in a bit."

Before Beau could change his mind, or turn around and kiss the daylights out of her, he headed out the door. The parking lot was still torn up, gravel and dirt strewn everywhere. That would have to get taken care of next week. Yet another task that belonged to a small business owner.

At the moment it didn't bother him. What bothered him more was his desire to pull Aurora into his arms and never let go of her.

An hour later, car lights moving across his yard indicated that Aurora had arrived. A flutter of excitement lifted his heart to a faster rate.

Neither of them was ready for a serious relationship, right? Or were they? They were both scared, but one of them had to take the leap of faith.

Chloe squealed in delight at something Daisy had done and it drew his attention. One side of his mouth curved up as he watched his daughter tug on Daisy's ear.

Didn't Chloe deserve a mother? Didn't *he* deserve a wife, a partner and friend? For both of them to love, and hold, and laugh? To live together?

Daisy alerted him to Aurora's presence with her excited romp to the door and a pointed look at him.

"Okay, okay. I'm coming."

That twitch in his pulse returned, and he couldn't prevent the smile on his face. He pulled the door open and the smile on his face froze as he took in Aurora's face. Pale and drawn earlier, her appearance hadn't changed any. She was still in pain.

"Get in here. We've got to get some ice on you right away."

"It's okay. I'm okay."

The stiff movements of her body told him otherwise.

"That's obviously not true." He took the tote bag from her hands. "Sit on the couch beside Chloe and I'll get the ice packs. The pizza can wait."

"Okay." Aurora made her way to the couch and eased onto it.

Babbling and gurgling, Chloe crawled over to Aurora's legs and pulled herself up.

Aurora held her hands out for Chloe to take hold of and she stood on her feet and squealed. "Oh, Beau. Look at this."

He arrived moments later with his hands full of ice packs.

"She's been trying to pull herself up, but hadn't made it that far yet. Pretty soon she'll be walking." Beau sat. "Lean forward." He placed ice packs in strategic areas. "Now lean back."

"Oh, that is *cold*!" She closed her eyes and shivered once. "But I know it's going to ease the burn."

"Yes, it will. We'll hang out here and eat pizza, then get in the tub later."

Beau brought the pizza box over to the coffee table with two bottles of beer.

After sitting for half an hour on the ice, Aurora visibly relaxed. Seeing her hanging out on his couch with his baby on her lap and his dog at her feet tugged at his heart. If things stayed this way, his life would be complete.

This was all he needed—right here in this room.

At that moment he knew he'd fallen for her. The last few weeks had been wonderful, but tonight sealed the deal in his heart.

Chloe had maneuvered herself to face Aurora and now rested her head against Aurora's left arm. The two snuggled together and a soft humming reached his ears.

"That's a beautiful sight." Beau could hardly speak as he watched them together.

"What?"

Aurora looked at him and he felt the full brunt of his emotions in that moment. There were no more questions for him. This was what he needed in his life. Somehow he was going to convince her of it, too.

"The two of you. My beauties." With his right hand, he pushed the hair back over Aurora's shoulder. "Are you okay with her on your lap?"

"Yes." Aurora hugged the little girl against her. "I love having her so close. She's a wonderful baby. You've done such a good job raising her, Beau."

"It's not been easy, and I've had a lot of help." This image of the two of them would remain etched in his mind forever. "I love her so much it hurts, sometimes."

"That's the way it should be, right?"

Unable to stop himself, he leaned closer and pressed his lips against Aurora's for a kiss. "Yes. It should be." He whispered the words from his heart.

After a second's hesitation, she raised her face and parted her lips to his.

The feel of her lips, her tongue against his, was just luscious and it stirred him deeply. "Aurora…"

Chloe took that moment to push at him and he looked down at her.

"Am I squishing you, baby girl?"

He leaned back, but his gaze clung to Aurora's aroused blue gaze. Standing quickly, he took Chloe in his hands and tossed her a few inches into the air. The movement had the desired outcome, and as she squealed with delight the tension between he and Aurora eased.

"I'm ready for the tub now—how about you?"

"Yes."

He tucked Chloe against his side. With the other hand he helped Aurora up from the couch. He led the way down the hall to the guest bathroom.

"You can change in here." He cleared his throat, trying not to imagine her naked and emerging in a tiny red bikini.

Instead, she emerged in an oversized shirt that ended at her knees. "I didn't have a suit, so I figured this would work."

"Absolutely. Can't tell you how disappointed I am, though. I remember that hot red number you used to wear in high school."

"Oh, *you*!" A light blush colored her face, but at least it was some color. "Always the kidder."

"I'm not joking. Not at all."

"Seriously? What's life without a little temptation?" The sparkling light in her eyes caught him off guard.

Timing was everything, and they'd been circling around each other for weeks. Maybe tonight was the night they closed the gap.

"Come this way. You can get soaking, and I'll go change."

He led Aurora to his back patio, where the spa steamed in the evening air.

Aurora stopped, her gaze fastened on the rolling hills of the Appalachian Mountains. "What a stunning view."

"You should see it in October. That's when it's really amazing. The leaves turn incredible colors, and you can sit here and take it all in."

At that, she turned her gaze to him. "I'd... I'd like that Beau. I'd like to sit here...with you...this fall and watch this view."

Intrigued, he moved closer and looked down into her warm and curious eyes. "Then you'll have to stay longer. You'll have to make your time here more than temporary. Are you willing to do that? To give up your life in Virginia? To trade that...for this?"

Leaning in, he pressed another kiss to her mouth.

She gave a nervous lick of her lips and curved her hair around one ear. "I've been thinking about that lately. A lot." After dropping her gaze, she brought it back to his. "And you."

"Well, I think we should talk more about that—but for now, let's get you in."

He took her hand, assisted her over the edge of the padded shelf and waited until she'd swung those long legs into the churning water.

"Oh..." She closed her eyes and squeezed his hand hard. "That's *so* good, Beau. I think I'm in heaven."

Slowly she adjusted to the temperature and eased down onto one of the seats. Another moan of satisfaction escaped her throat as she settled in.

Beau changed into his swim trunks. When he was alone he went naked, but tonight a suit was in order if he intended to maintain his dignity. He dressed Chloe in the suit his mother had bought for her, picked up her floaty ring and settled her against his side, then grabbed two bottles of beer before heading outside.

"Oh, *squee*!" Aurora grinned. "There's the little girl—in a pink swimsuit, too."

Beau made a face. "Grandma thought she needed one—even at this age when she's still wearing a diaper."

"I agree. It's never too early to start having some style."

Chloe squirmed and hooted in delight when she realized where they were going, and Beau nearly lost her, and the beer, but managed to hold on to both.

CHAPTER NINE

"LET ME HELP." Aurora took the bottles from him, and he focused on climbing in with his wiggly daughter safely tucked against him.

"She loves the spa. To her it's a giant bathtub, and we usually have floaty toys swimming around with us." Beau reached into a plastic basket full of toys and tossed a few in, to Chloe's delight.

"I agree with her. This is fabulous." She opened the beer bottles and handed him one. "Thanks. This is really great. I can feel my back relaxing already."

"That's good. Working so physically today—in and out of the car, running in and out of the clinic over a gravel parking lot." He shook his head at his oversight and single-mindedness. "I should have thought of the effect it would have on you. I'm sorry."

"It just reinforces that I'm not cut out for physical work any longer, and it's not your fault. It's the car crash. Everything comes back to that damned car crash."

She shook her head and a haunted look filled her eyes, as if she were going deep inward, seeing things that he couldn't.

For a few moments they sat in companionable silence, except for the bubbling of the jets and the night birds settling into the trees around the house. Crickets began their nightly song and one lone cicada buzzed from high up in a tree. Chloe slapped the water with her hand and squealed in delight.

"It's so peaceful here. I imagine you just love it." Aurora grabbed one of the toys and sent it over toward Chloe, who splashed in excitement.

"I do. I just…well, it was Julie's dream home."

"Do you want to tell me about her? We're settled in for a soak and a beer. Why not?"

The smile she offered was soothing, compassionate. So very Aurora.

For a nanosecond he *didn't* want to talk about Julie, about his life with her, but here in his arms, squirming and talking nonsense, was the product of his love for Julie. How could he not acknowledge that?

Tree frogs chorused as he gathered his thoughts and absentmindedly he reached for a yellow duck floating just out of arm's reach and handed it to Chloe. She shoved its bill into her mouth and chewed on it.

"Well, the short version is we met in college, fell madly in love, waited until I was out of school to start a family, and when we did she died."

"I'm so sorry, Beau. If it's too painful, I understand."

"I'm okay." He looked at Chloe and determination filled him. He took a deep breath and blew it out, letting go of the pain, of the unfulfilled dreams he'd had. "Some women have bad pregnancies from the beginning, but Julie's was wonderful until she collapsed in her ninth month. The doctors said it was an AVM."

Saying the words out loud still sounded like it had happened to someone else.

"I don't know what that is."

"Arteriovenous malformation. There's a malformation, a growing together, of an artery and a vein in the brain. It usually isn't bothersome until the extra blood supply of a pregnancy puts added pressure on the weak area. And then..." He didn't have to explain.

"Oh, my God." Aurora closed her eyes, anticipation clearly showing on her face. As a nurse, she could follow the implications and come to the correct deadly conclusion.

"As you guessed, it ruptured, and she suffered a catastrophic brain injury. Fortunately we were sitting in the doctor's office when it happened, and she was taken to hospital right away. If it had happened at home I'd have lost them both, and I don't really want to think about that again."

Pulling Chloe closer, he pressed a kiss to her chubby little cheek. Telling the story was difficult, but somehow sharing it with Aurora took some of the sting out of it.

"With Julie's parents, I made the decision to have Chloe delivered by C-section...and then we let her go."

He pressed his lips together as emotions tried to bubble up. The image of removing that life support was something that would never leave him, but now the pain of it wasn't so real.

Without a word, Aurora held her hand out to him. After a second's hesitation he took it, and looked into her watery eyes.

"I'm so sorry, but thank you for telling me. I know it wasn't easy. None of it. But it sounds like you did the right thing—the only thing that could be done."

"Yes. I know. Intellectually, there's no issue. It's just the wondering...if things had gone differently...blah, blah, blah."

"That's always the hardest part, I think. Of anything. The *what if.* I had the same sort of thoughts about my car crash. If only I'd gone another route that day, would

I be fine now?" She met his gaze. "But then I wouldn't be here. With you. And Chloe."

"Yes, well… Grief is something we all go through in life, but that doesn't make it easier. Some days are just fine and other days are not."

Chloe yawned and drew his attention to her sleepy eyes.

"But for now I'd better get this little one out, give her a proper bath, then put her to bed."

"Would it be okay if I stayed in a little while longer? It really is helping." She moved her shoulders back and forth and twisted each one with ease.

"Certainly." He squeezed her hand and released it. "That wasn't a subtle invitation for you to leave."

"If you're sure?" There were questions in her eyes.

"I'm sure."

As he turned away, he didn't know whether he had any answers.

Aurora listened to the sounds of a happy baby splashing in the bathtub and Beau's voice as he played with her. The sounds stirred something in her heart she'd thought she'd left behind. The desire for a family of her own. Having been independent and on her own for so many years, she'd tucked that fantasy away. Now, being with Beau and Chloe had opened the door to shine some light on it.

Closing her eyes, she let herself go back, remember. Remember what she'd used to want. What she'd put aside for her career. Marriage. Children. A happy home. The warmth in her heart had nothing to do with the heat of the water she was simmering in. She raised her hands.

Definitely pruned. Time to get out of the tub. Unfortunately Beau wasn't there to offer assistance, and she wasn't willing to risk falling out of the tub. The rim was too high for her to ease herself down without jumping. She sat on the edge, lifting most of her body out and cooling off, waiting until Beau returned.

In minutes she heard him in the living room and called out to him. "Beau? Can you help me get out?"

"Just a minute. I'll put Chloe down."

She heard his footsteps approaching a few minutes later.

"Okay, you need a—" Beau stopped and stared at her. His eyes looked over her body. What she hadn't counted on, with being covered up by the long shirt, was that it was going to be plastered to her body when she got out.

Beau swallowed and took a step closer to her, his gaze dropping from her face down over her breasts, firmly outlined by the wet shirt. Her nipples stood out prominently and ached to have him touch them. Moments ago she'd been relaxed and lulled by the hot water, but now her breathing came in short, quick gasps, her heart fluttered, and a reckless feeling stirred in her feminine region.

"Beau?"

"Don't move," he whispered, and stepped closer.

He'd changed into a pair of sweat pants and an old shirt, and looked as sexy as she'd ever seen him with his bare feet sticking out. Placing his hands on her knees, he parted them gently and moved between them. "There's no good reason why I should do this, other than I really want to, and many reasons why I shouldn't."

His breathing was as fast as hers, and in the dim light she could see the desire filling his face, in his posture, in everything.

"Do what?" she dared to ask. She wanted to know. *Now.*

"This." He leaned over, took one of her nipples in his mouth and sucked.

Aurora gasped at the sensation of his hot mouth closing over her chilled, taut flesh. She clutched his shoulders and hung on.

"Oh!"

Beau's tongue and mouth caressed and tortured her nipple, stirring feelings she'd thought were long gone. Now she realized they'd only been dormant, waiting for the right moment to surface. Tenderly, he slid his arms around her, moved to her other nipple and closed his mouth over it, tearing down any resistance she might have thought of.

Neither of them had been prepared for a relationship—hadn't thought of it until circumstances had brought them together. Now she knew this was what she wanted, and it seemed like Tammie was right. The universe had led her here…right into his arms.

A soft moan escaped Aurora's throat as he stirred her body to perfection. Moving upward, spreading kisses, Beau reached her mouth. He cupped her head in his hands and kissed her thoroughly, parting her lips and taking her deep as his tongue sought hers. This was so wonderful—to be wanted, and kissed, and touched, and held in Beau's arms.

He pulled back and rested his forehead against hers, his rapid breath matching hers. "Aurora, I want so badly to take you to bed right now, but if it's too soon, and you're not ready, or—"

"I'm ready."

The words sprang out of her mouth, but emerged from her soul. This was the moment she'd been waiting for and hadn't even known it.

"I'm ready." With hands that trembled, she cupped his head in her hands. "Kiss me again."

With those words, Beau groaned and complied, teasing her lips with his, rubbing his nose against hers, then parting her lips with his tongue. The night creatures around them lent a natural music that stirred her desire to be with Beau—now. Everything was perfect.

He pulled back and looked down at her body. He frowned.

"What?" She looked down and couldn't see anything wrong.

"You simply can't wear that shirt inside. It's all wet. And dripping."

"I see." Aurora liked this sexy, playful side of Beau. "What do you suppose we should do about that?"

"It needs to go, for sure."

He clasped the hem of it, which was hanging around her knees, and pulled it up over her head. She shivered once, the cool air chilling her, raising goosebumps on her skin. It was a strange sensation, having the air teasing her body and Beau's gaze stirring it further.

"I think we'd better get you inside and dried off."

"If you'll help me get down from here."

A zing of fear hit her. How would he react to her scars? The pulse pounded in her throat and she swallowed. There was only one way to know—one way to move forward. If they were going to have any chance at a relationship she had to bare herself to him, scars and all.

"I can arrange something."

He returned to his former position between her knees and clasped her hips, bringing them against his. He lifted her against him and let her slide down the length of his body. The soft cloth of his sweats didn't hide the hard arousal within. She ached to touch him, to feel his skin sliding against hers and join their bodies together.

Once they entered the house and closed the door to the patio everything changed. The intensity of Beau was almost overwhelming as his hands clasped her by the hips and brought her against him.

Any sane thought went out the window as Aurora allowed herself to breathe in his scent, to savor the sensations he created in her, knowing he was feeling the same.

"This is so good…so wonderful to touch you, to have you against me." Aurora tunneled her hands beneath his shirt and drew it upward.

He flung it to the floor. "I just don't want to hurt you."

That made her pull back a little from him to look into green eyes that were filled with need for her. "Hurt me?"

"Your back." He stroked her face and pressed a kiss to her nose, breathed in her scent again.

"I have an idea about that," she said. "Why don't you lead the way?"

She grabbed her purse from the kitchen counter and followed him. In just a few seconds they entered his bedroom, and he led her to a large four-poster. The sheets were warm against her skin, and together they tangled themselves up in the covers and each other.

Aurora leaned into Beau, and then lay him back, draped over the top of his chest. "This is my idea…"

"I see."

Kisses and breaths mingled as they learned each other's bodies for the first time. A stroke here, a lingering kiss there, licking, sucking, touching, tasting, all bringing them closer to each other.

Aurora was ready, and moisture filled her feminine sheath. She tugged on his pants and he swiftly removed them, leaving nothing but skin between them.

"Lie back," she said, and moved over on top of him, straddling his hips. She clutched his erection in her hand and feminine power pulsed deep within her. This was the moment she'd been waiting for.

"I don't have a—"

"I do."

"Really?" Beau's eyebrows twitched upward and a Cheshire cat smile covered his face.

"Really."

She dug a condom from her purse and tore the cellophane package open with her teeth. Keeping her eyes on his, she removed the condom, then slid it down over his erection. Watching his eyes close at the pleasure of her touch thrilled her. This was so beautiful. So *right*.

Rising up further on her knees, she lowered herself onto him. Though she hadn't made love in a long time, her body was ready. As they joined together for the first time new and beautiful sensations overwhelmed her as her body accommodated his.

"Oh…" A moan stirred from her throat as she took him in all the way.

Beau's hands clasped her hips and he began to rock her in rhythm to the movements of his own hips. "You feel incredible, Aurora. *Incredible*." One hand strayed upward to caress her breast and stir her nipple.

Drawing herself upright, she placed her hands beside his knees and allowed herself to take in sensation after sensation, to feel the power of him inside her, to be a woman fully for the first time in way too long.

Beau slid his hands up her thighs, his fingers lightly grazing her skin and sending a thrill through her. He delved one thumb into her folds, searching for the center of her pleasure zone, and teased it softly.

Her breath caught in her throat as his hips, his touch, his body sent her over the edge and she shattered, clutching the bedding in her hands and crying out her pleasure. Wave after wave pulsed through her.

Sensing a change in Beau's breathing, she lifted her

head and focused on him. She moved his hands to her hips to help her keep the pace that would satisfy him, bring him to his peak. Digging his fingers into her hips he rocked her and plunged into her sheath. Faster and harder. Then he clutched her tightly as he found his release.

She draped her torso forward, allowing her chest to touch his, then released her weight with a sigh.

"This was beautiful, Beau."

"Absolutely."

Her words and the sound of her voice drew him in and pushed him away at the same time. Being with another woman, loving another woman, was hard. He'd never dreamed life would turn out this way. He'd never dreamed he'd lose himself in the arms of a woman again and that that woman would be Aurora.

"Where are you?" she asked, drawing his attention to her mouth again.

"Lost in space, I guess."

She placed a hand on his face and moved in for a long, slow kiss. "What are we going to do about this, Beau?"

"About what? Us?" He eased his hands up her back, drawing his hands across her smooth, silky skin until an irregularity stopped him. "What's this?"

"A scar. I had a chest tube for a few days after the crash. It's ugly. Don't look at it."

"It saved your life." Just as she was saving *his* right now. "About your question… I don't know what we're going to do. I just know I don't want you to leave."

That made her drop her gaze away from his again. "Do you mean tonight, or what?"

"I mean I don't want you to leave Brush Valley." With one hand, he curved her hair behind her ear and cupped her face. "It's only been a few weeks, but we've connected in a way I never imagined, and I don't want to let go of that any time soon."

"Me, either. It's too soon for either of us to be making promises, though, don't you think?" Closing her eyes for a second, she savored the sensation of his hand, warm against her face.

"I know. I don't want either of us to make any promises we can't keep or will feel guilty about if things change." He raised his face to hers and encouraged her to press another kiss to his lips. "I want a chance with you, Aurora. That's all. I just want to give *us* a chance. Be my partner, be a mother to Chloe? Are you willing to do that? Are you willing to stay, to work with me in the office and see if we can make it work?"

The intensity of him was overwhelming. "I know we can make it work in the office. It's the other stuff, the personal stuff, I'm not sure about."

"Is it because of Chloe?"

He had to ask. Not every woman was prepared to take on a child *and* a new relationship.

The shock on her face was his answer.

"*No! Absolutely not. She's a delight, and I would be happy to be part of her life." She sighed and pulled away, then sat up on the edge of the bed. "But what if *we* don't work out? It's not fair to Chloe to think I'm going to be around and then for me not to be here."

"There are no guarantees in life." He snorted out a bitter laugh. "*My* life is certainly evidence of that."

"I'm not asking for a guarantee, Beau."

"Yes, you are. You aren't saying it in so many words, but that's what it is—and I don't know. I just don't know." He tugged on his sweats and a shirt while she wrapped the sheet around herself. "This is not the conversation I envisioned us having after making love the first time."

"Me, either." One side of her mouth lifted in a half-hearted smile. "How about we go back a few minutes and agree to see how things go? I'd like that."

She moved closer to him and placed a hand on his chest. The heat of it moved through him, warming his heart.

"I'd like that, too."

Wrapping his arms around her shoulders, he brought her up against him for a few minutes and just held on as emotions threatened to swamp him.

What if she was right? What if their relationship didn't work out? Then what? Was it really fair to Chloe to present her with a new mother, then watch her walk away?

The next day dawned bright and shiny. Aurora was slow to get moving, enjoying the peace of the quiet morning, the chirping of birds in the field beside the office as they foraged for seeds and insects trapped by the morning dew.

She turned on the light switch, but nothing happened. The power was still out.

Though Beau had asked her to stay the night with him, she'd declined. She wasn't ready for that yet, and she didn't think he was either. It was too much, too fast. Making love had been wonderful, but now she wondered if that had been a mistake, too.

Were they just two lonely, damaged people who'd sought a moment of comfort in each other's arms? It had been known to happen. Were they really a relationship in the making?

Her phone rang, ending her peaceful moment.

"Hello?"

"It's your mother."

"Hi, Mom. What's up? Everything okay?"

"Sure. Can't I call my daughter without there being a crisis?"

Aurora wondered, and suppressed a snort of amusement. "Well, when I was living in Virginia you only called when someone died or there was a disaster."

"Yes, well, today's different. I wanted to see if you wanted to go to Smicksburg with me today." There was hope and eagerness in her mother's voice. "If you don't have anything else planned, I mean."

"No. I don't have any plans."

Nothing that couldn't wait anyway, like laundry and bills. With no power in the apartment, she wasn't going to do much else. "Sounds like fun."

"Good. I'll pick you up in thirty minutes, then."

"Make it an hour. I'm just waking up." She needed to do her exercises and get something to eat.

"Oh, I suppose… I'll pack us some lunch and it'll be a fun day."

"Great. See you soon."

Aurora threw the covers off and got moving. As she packed her purse with necessary supplies she hesitated over whether to take her pain medications with her, but she grabbed the bottle and tossed them in. She locked up and waited for her mother in front of the building.

The parking lot had been really torn up by the car crash last evening. It was definitely going to need some professional work done, not just a few shovels full of dirt.

Pulling out her phone, she made a call to a friend to see if he could help out. Just as she finished the call she spied her mother's little SUV.

"Thanks, Tim. I'll talk to you later."

"Right on time," her mother said as she got into the car. "I don't like to wait on anyone, you know."

"I know. So let's get going and have a great day."

This could be an opportunity to repair her relationship with her mother, which had always been a bit tense.

"Who were you talking to?"

"Tim. An old high school buddy. I wanted to see if he could bring his grader and smooth out the parking lot for Beau."

"He's the owner. Shouldn't *he* be doing that?"

"Oh, sure he could, but as his office nurse I can make a call and get it done for him. He's got Chloe all day today, and if I can take one thing off his plate then I'm happy to do it."

"You *are*?" Sally nodded.

"What's that supposed to mean?" Aurora cast a suspicious glance at her mother.

"Nothing." There was an upward inflection to her voice, solidifying Aurora's suspicions.

"Mom, with you there's never 'nothing.'" There was always something behind any comment her mother made.

"Oh, I was just thinking that since you're so involved in the office, and Beau, you might think about staying for a while." The last sentence was all said in a rush.

This was it. *This* was the reason for the "spontaneous" trip. Even though Aurora had promised to go on a day trip with her mother, there was definitely a mission behind this one today. Her mother was pumping her for information.

Before answering, Aurora took a breath and centered herself, as she'd learned to do in rehab. "It's hard to say at this point, Mom." Facts—just facts at this point. "Beau has a nurse who has simply gone on maternity leave. We don't know if she's coming back or not."

"Doesn't he have room for more than one nurse? Seems like business is booming."

"At this point, no—but that could change in the future."

"Every time I drive by someone's always coming in or going out. So it's getting busier, right? That's good."

"Yes, it is getting busier, and we have some plans for promotion—like at Brush Valley Day and at the fair."

"Wonderful. Maybe there will be enough business to keep you here full-time, then."

"That's a whole lot of speculation right now. For today, how about we just forget about work, plans, the future, and just have a nice day together? The leaves will be starting to turn, so we'll have to plan another trip for that, too."

After a moment's hesitation her mother agreed. Though Aurora sensed her mother wanted to push her point and drag this conversation on.

"Okay," she said finally. "Today is just about us having a good time." She cast a quick sideways glance at Aurora. "And eating. We can't forget that part."

A warmth filled her chest, and Aurora laughed. Maybe there was hope for healing the relationship with her mother after all. "Definitely not—especially if you're the one who's cooking."

They spent the day together, wandering through the Amish village, shopping, talking and thoroughly enjoying themselves. But with all the walking, getting in and out of the SUV, the bumpy roads and sitting for too long, Aurora's pain soon sprang up from her hips, spreading like wildfire through a dry forest with nothing to stop it.

By the time her mother dropped her at the office seven hours later she didn't think she would be able to make it up the stairs. Though she'd taken one of her pain medications an hour ago, it hadn't helped.

Dammit. Things had been going so well. Until now.

With hands that trembled, she called Beau.

"Aurora?"

The sound of his voice saying her name in her ear was immediately reassuring. He would help her. No matter what happened between them, she knew she could count on him.

"Beau." Tears filled her eyes as she let herself go, let herself need someone—need Beau. "I need you. Can you meet me at the office?"

"Yes. What's wrong? Are you okay?"

There was immediate focus in his voice, which reassured her further.

"I need you to come as soon as you can."

In the background she heard rustling, and Chloe's happy baby sounds. Though she hated to disturb him, there was no help for it. She couldn't drive to meet him.

"I'll be there in fifteen minutes. Hang on, darling. I'll be there. Don't worry."

"Thank you," she whispered into the disconnected line.

She unlocked the office, dropped her purse and the bags with her purchases just inside the door. She flipped on the light switch and the lights responded. Power had been restored while she was gone.

Within fifteen minutes she heard the crunching of tires on the gravel and knew relief was just moments away. The door opened and Daisy bounded in, rushing over to greet her, then Beau, looking casual and handsome with his arms full of baby girl. The concern on his face made her wish she hadn't put it there.

CHAPTER TEN

"I KNOW YOU'RE in pain. What happened?"

He set Chloe's bouncy chair on the floor and placed her in it. Though he paid attention to what he was doing, he spoke to Aurora. When Chloe was strapped in, he turned to her, and his expression changed from concern to empathy as he read her posture and her face. He knew. He knew just what she needed.

Opening his arms wide, he walked toward her and placed those strong arms around her, holding her for just a moment.

The tears she'd been holding back could no longer be contained. This was where she needed to be—here, in this man's arms. "I'm so sorry to drag you to the office on a Saturday, but my back is on fire."

"You were fine last night." He pulled back to look at her face and used his thumbs to wipe away the trails of tears on her cheeks. "What did you do? Go rock climbing today or something?"

That made her laugh, and a smile won its way onto her face. "No. I took a long car ride with Mom to Smicksburg, walked all over creation, up and down stairs, in and out of the car. Now I'm paying the price. I don't think I can even get upstairs to the apartment right now."

He glanced down at his daughter, happily bouncing in

her chair, trying to make her way toward Daisy. "She'll be okay for a while. How about I see what I can do to get you straightened out again?"

"Thanks, Beau. I knew I could count on you."

"Always, sweet. *Always*."

Thirty minutes later Beau had massaged and made several adjustments to Aurora's back and the relief was significant.

"I think this is a reminder for you to be more careful, and that you're not ready to go gallivanting across the country—even if it is with your mother."

"You mean it's a *lesson*."

It felt akin to being sent to the principal's office, but that ended when Beau placed a finger under her chin and raised her face to his.

"No, I don't like that term. Too punitive. An 'opportunity for growth'—that's what I like to call these little life experiences." His brows twitched at that.

"You're kidding, right?"

"No, I'm not. I've been through enough pain to last me the rest of my life. I'm not giving in to it. I'm not letting it get me. I am just acknowledging I may have to adjust my game plan now and then."

"You're so positive, Beau! How can you be positive after the devastating blows life has handed you?"

"It ain't easy, my sweet." He stepped a little closer to her and drew her against his chest, holding her as if she were a fragile thing. "But if life hadn't delivered those blows I wouldn't be holding you in my arms right now, would I? The same is true for you. Maybe we had to go through the tough times alone in order to find each other now."

That silenced her. The pain of it. The truth of it. Without the car crash and ensuing difficulties she wouldn't be here right now with him, falling in love with him in a way she'd never thought possible. And she *was* falling for him—she couldn't deny it.

"How are we going to deal with this? I mean—"

"I know you're a planner. Every nurse I know is. But right now there's no plan, no schedule of events. We live in the moment."

"Then—"

"We just see. We wait, see how things go, and in the meantime we enjoy ourselves." He kissed her temple, then her cheek, his breath warm on her skin. "Thoroughly."

Warmth spread from her lower abdomen outward and settled in her chest. Never mind falling—she was so in love with Beau already. When he said stuff like that to her it didn't help her resolve not to give in to the feelings in her heart.

"I see." A frown crossed her face as she remembered something she'd been going to do tonight. "Rats. I was going to take Tammie's yoga class this evening, but I don't think I could drive to town."

"How about I drive you? Chloe and I can hang around while you stretch. Then I can ice it afterward."

"Again with the ice?" A smile tried to work its way across her face and her heart lightened a bit. Spending time with Beau and Chloe was never a bad time.

"No hot tub for you tonight."

"I'm not getting into a giant bowl of ice water either." That was *not* happening.

A chuckle escaped his throat. "No. Just ice packs will be fine."

"Okay, then. I accept your offer to drive me to class." Another thought occurred to her. "People will see us going in together and make assumptions. Are you ready for that?"

In small towns like this, any sort of activity—no matter how innocent—was subject to speculation and gossip. Stopping the fire after it was a raging inferno was impossible.

"I'm good." He nodded and seemed not bothered. "I know the truth. So do you. That's all that's important—if *you're* okay with being seen with us."

A slight frown crossed his face. She almost didn't see it, but it was evident he did have some concerns, too.

"Oh, absolutely! I didn't mean to imply anything like that." She placed a hand on his arm, offering him reassurance. "I just wanted to give you the opt-out in case you were…you know, bugged by it."

"Hardly."

Unhappy baby squeals caught their attention.

"Let's go see what kind of mischief the little miss has gotten herself into."

They entered the waiting room and found Chloe had bounced herself into a corner. After scooping her up and planting sloppy kisses on her neck, making her squeal in delight, Beau tucked her against his side, ushered Daisy out and locked the office behind them.

Then he stopped dead in his tracks, his mouth hanging open, shock etched on his face. He looked at Aurora.

"What happened out here?"

"What do you mean? It looks fine to me." Aurora looked around at the parking lot. The perfectly groomed parking lot that only hours before had been torn up from one end to the other.

"The gravel. It's all where it's supposed to be."

"Oh! I almost forgot. I called Tim Verner to see if he could bring one of his graders and go over the lot. I hope that was okay?" She chewed her lower lip, hesitating. Had she overstepped her boundaries as the office nurse?

Beau looked at her and shook his head. "*Okay?* Are you kidding me? It's *fabulous*! Just look at this place. It looks better than new."

The warmth that had been circulating in her chest pulsed hot and deep within her. Pleasure and joy at his response thrilled her. "Oh, good."

"There's only one problem I can see right now."

His eyes widened, and he gave her a look she wasn't able to quite figure out.

"What's that?" Everything looked fine to her.

"I'm probably going to be doing free back adjustments for Verner for the next year to make up for it."

"He wouldn't do that, would he?" She hadn't thought of that.

"No, I'm teasing." He finished buckling Chloe into her seat then turned to Aurora. "I probably shouldn't do that, but it's so much fun to see that pink color in your face. Reminds me of the old days, when anything I said to you made you blush."

"Just *stop*, you."

She gave a playful push against his arm, but he caught her hand before she could pull it away. He reeled her in and brought her close against him.

"Never." His eyes darkened as he looked down at her mouth, seconds before he pressed his lips to hers.

Heart fluttering, Aurora lifted her face to his and reveled in the simplicity of the kiss and felt herself falling over the edge of that cliff she'd sworn never to approach again with such careless abandon as she had in the past. Here she was, teetering on the edge, and no longer caring if she fell as long as she was falling into Beau's arms.

"Let's get you to class, so you're not late." Beau squeezed her arms and pulled away.

"It's okay. It's Tammie teaching it. She won't get upset."

"In my experience I've learned it's best never to annoy a redheaded woman. Knowing Tammie as well as I do, I think it's doubly important."

"Good point. Let's go."

After a short ride to the community center, they walked in together to the great room where many activities took place. Several people acknowledged them, and she recognized others she hadn't seen for years. From school, from church, and from various other times in her life.

Turning back to Beau, she gave a nod, choking back the sudden nameless emotion trying to squeeze her throat shut. "See you after the class."

"Okay. Have fun—just don't overdo it."

"I won't." She watched as he took Chloe into the children's playroom and closed the door, then grabbed a yoga mat and joined the others.

"Nice to see you could make it, Aurora." Tammie was sitting on a mat at the front of a class of about ten ladies of varying ages.

"Yes. Sorry I'm a few minutes late, but I needed a lift."

"Hmm… Yes…" Tammie nodded at where Beau could be seen through the window of the children's room. "A handsome man always gives *me* a lift, too."

She winked as the other women chuckled at her small joke.

"Okay. Let's take a deep breath in and blow it out, then another one…and hold."

Once the class began in earnest Aurora focused, tried to follow the instructions and let the soothing sound of her friend's voice help her let go of the tension and the knots in her back.

Beau's words about living in the moment helped, and

she pushed away all the stress of the day and the last few months with each breath she took.

Beau watched, trying not to look like he was watching, as the class moved through varying positions. He tried to tell himself he was just keeping an eye on Aurora. He was concerned about her back, about her safety. Watching her was only reassuring him that she was okay, given the condition she had been in earlier today.

Yeah, right.

His tongue was all but hanging out and it was all he could do not to stare. Hard.

The sight of her stretching, the moves she made and the focus on her face took his feelings for her to a new level. Well beyond what he'd thought he'd feel again for a woman. The new pulse in his chest, the recent smile on his face and, frankly, the aching throb in his groin. All new. All wonderful. All because of Aurora.

He was living again.

This was what they could be doing every week—working in their community and being a family. Together. Though guilt still took refuge in his heart, its stronghold had been breached since Aurora had landed in his life. Again.

Chloe stood on her feet, balancing against a little table, and squealed at him, then took a few stumbling steps toward him.

"You're trying to walk, baby?"

A grin shot across his face and his heart thrummed as he watched his baby girl try to take her first step. All wobbly legs and flailing arms, she hooted with excitement.

"I wish Aurora could see you right now."

A cramp in his heart killed the smile.

I wish Julie could see you right now.

His phone rang, jerking him out of his musings, and his heart almost stopped as he read the number.

"Hello, Darlene."

He closed his eyes, bracing himself to talk to his mother-in-law. The sound of her voice was so close to Julie's that he'd had a difficult time talking to her in the days after Julie's death. Each time she called it got easier, but right now it was like some demon had dragged him back in time.

"Beau. Sorry to bother you, but I was wondering when you could bring Chloe over for a visit. We haven't seen her for a few weeks, and I miss that little darling."

"Of course. You know you can see her any time."

They made arrangements for the following afternoon, for Chloe to spend several hours with her grandparents. He wanted her to know them, and know her mother through them, though it was still hard for all of them.

Puzzled at the bitter feelings suddenly swirling inside him, he took a breath and blew it out, like Tammie was teaching in the class. Maybe he should sign up for one, too.

Minutes later the ladies rose from their mats, bundled them up and left the room. He gathered Chloe and met Aurora in the great room again, well aware that a number of people observed his actions.

"How was it?" he asked Aurora as she approached.

"Wonderful. Thanks for—"

Chloe interrupted by leaning toward Aurora and holding her arms out.

"Looks like she wants to go to you." Beau adjusted his position, to pull her back, but she insisted, crying out and wiggling to get her way.

"Oh!" Aurora held her hands out to the baby. "You

want to come have a visit with me, do you?" Chloe rewarded her with a delighted squeal. "Well, there's a happy girl now."

"Indeed." Beau released Chloe to Aurora's arms and for the first time in months felt the release of the strain of being a single parent. "Looks good on you."

"Yes… What?" Aurora's eyes popped wide, and she gaped at Beau.

"You look like you should have a baby in your arms." He shrugged and she closed her mouth. "I'm just saying you look comfortable with her, and she likes you. She doesn't ask just *anyone* to hold her."

"I see that." Aurora adjusted the baby more comfortably on her hip as they left the building, knowing full well they were being watched.

"Does it bother you?"

"A little." After they'd left the building she looked up at him. "I'm finding I'm less bothered than I thought."

"Good. Then it's okay if I do this." Before he thought better of it he leaned over and kissed her on the mouth, leisurely, exploring her mouth, until Chloe had had enough and bashed him in the nose with her fist.

"What was that for?" Aurora asked, her eyes soft and searching his for answers.

"Because you're wonderful, and I thought you should know it."

He cleared his throat. Was this the right time to say it? Was this the right time to say *anything*? What about his desire to live in the moment, not to plan too far ahead? Out the window when he kissed her.

"Oh. Thanks. You're wonderful, too."

Beau finally got a clue as he watched her reposition the baby again. "Here. Let me take her. Holding her is not good for your back."

He took Chloe from Aurora's arms and tossed her a little into the air, eliciting an excited scream from her.

"Beau, be careful."

"It's okay. I'm not going to drop her." He tucked Chloe against his side and then pulled Aurora close to his other side.

This is the way it's supposed to be, he thought. *This is what I want, and somehow, some way, I need to help Aurora see it, too.*

The last few weeks before Brush Valley Day had been a bustle of activity. Though she and Beau had spent a lot of time together at the office, their private time together had been limited. Neither one of them had pushed to repeat the intimacy of their one night together, sensing the need each of them had for space, time to think and make decisions. Beau had said to see how things went and they were. Cautiously.

As Aurora left her apartment the day before Brush Valley Day a hint of crisp fall air teased her face and tugged a strand of hair across her face. Fall was her favorite time of the year. Summers in Pennsylvania were hot and muggy, winters were too cold, and her feet didn't thaw out until spring.

Fall was peace. It made sense. The energy in the air was filled with comfort. Things were the way they were supposed to be. The intense energy and flurry of summer wound down. Leaves turned vibrant, earthy tones in this valley in the heart of the Appalachian Mountain range. No matter where she turned, beauty surrounded her.

Standing for a few moments on the stairs, she looked around, taking in the staggering beauty of the early morning. She stood there and looked at the rolling hills surrounding her. A dark-winged crow warbled a morning greeting to her. Overhead, a flock of geese in classic V formation made their way from their northern summer climes to their wintering grounds far to the south.

A hint of tears filled her eyes as the beauty of nature surrounded her, filling her with a bittersweet pain. She could take in this scene every day if she chose to. All she had to do was reach out to Beau, let go of her past, and take his hand to build a new future with him.

She snorted. That was *all*?

Carrying on with her morning duties as she did every day, Aurora opened the door, turned on the lights, cranked up the cooling system and fired up the coffee pot. She'd have to talk to Beau about offering coffee to patients and their families, hot chocolate for the kids, when the practice got busier.

Just as she was going through the mail from yesterday, she stopped.

Was she planning on being there when things got busier? That thought paused her heart for a few seconds. She hadn't planned on it originally. Now…?

She could easily envision herself working with Beau, helping to grow the practice, spending weekends with him and Chloe, watching her grow too.

Tears filled her eyes at the thought that everything she'd ever wanted was within her reach. A relationship. A marriage. A family. All of it. Right there.

Dismissing her tears, and her thoughts of a fantasy long past, she took a breath and tried to put it aside.

It's only fall that's making me this way. It's the change of seasons. Always gets to me.

Reaching for her notebook, which was getting fuller every day, she wrote it down. Maybe Cathy would want to institute having refreshments when she came back. Her maternity leave was going to be ending soon. Aurora added that to her list of things to do. Call Cathy to see when she was going to return to work.

Call Cathy to see when Aurora's life was going to change again. Call Cathy to see when she had to move, find a new job, leave everything she'd grown to love.

The tears she'd thought she'd set aside managed to push themselves to the front again, insistent that she deal with them. Right now.

As she sat down the unmistakable click of Daisy's nails neared the desk. Her insides began to tremble, feeling the excitement of seeing Beau first thing every morning.

The phone rang, and out of reflex training Aurora answered it. "Brush Valley Medical Clinic. May I help you?"

Lunch arrived with a new patient, just before they were ready to take a break.

"Can I help you?" Aurora looked up, then grinned. "Wait. I know you, don't I?"

The man's face was familiar, but at the same time not. Narrowing her eyes, she studied him.

"You sure do, if you're Aurora Hunt."

The man was about her age, and had a few sun-kissed wrinkles on his face. He was dressed in work jeans and dirty work boots, looking like he'd just come in from a barn. He removed the cowboy hat and peered closer at her.

"Recognize the eyes?"

"Tim?" Aurora moved out from behind the desk. "Tim Verner, you ole cowboy. Thank you so much for sorting the car park. How the heck *are* you?"

She hugged the man who had gone to school with her and Beau.

"I've had better days." He gave her a one-armed hug that was halfhearted at best. Not like his usual boisterous self that she remembered.

"Is that what brings you in?" She indicated his dangling left arm.

"I tripped on a stray board and fell over."

"What did you hit?"

Knowing him, it could be anything from a stack of hay to an old engine hanging from the ceiling in his barn.

"Actually, I caught myself, but when I stood up again I had this going on." He raised his left hand for her to see and there was a rusty nail sticking out of it.

"Geez. *Tim!*" She took hold of his wrist and held it out away from her, like it was a dead rat. "Why didn't you say so in the first place?"

She drew him toward the back. There was no time to waste in this situation. If they didn't act now he could die from infection, tetanus, or even lose the hand.

"Beau! I need you—*now!*"

"That's what I like to hear." Beau put a smile on his face to greet his patient, but when he saw Aurora holding Tim's arm up he froze for a second, then shot into emergency mode. "Holy hell, Tim!"

"That's what I said, too." Tim cleared his throat. "Among other things."

"Get in here." Beau directed him to the first patient room. "Aurora, get the hand trauma kit. It's in the cupboard over the sink."

"We *have* a hand trauma kit?" she asked, confused but impressed by his thinking.

"We do. Brush Valley is an agricultural community. From the day I opened the doors a farmer has come in every week with some sort of hand injury. I just came up with a kit to make it easy."

"Got it." She dashed out and returned in a few seconds with the appropriate item.

"Got any whiskey in there?" Tim asked with hope in his eyes. "Hurts like hell."

For the first time, Aurora noticed that under that farmer's tan of his he was pale.

"Sorry. Not a good idea now." Beau shook his head as he opened the tray and removed the sterile coverings.

"I know—but *damn*." He shook his head and clenched his teeth.

"Let me get a look at it first. Then I can give you something for the pain."

Tim nodded and clenched his teeth.

Beau put on a pair of specialty magnifying glasses in order to see deeply into the wound, then peeled back the dirty and bloody handkerchief wrapped around the hand.

"How did you do this?" Beau asked without looking up.

"Tripped. Caught myself on an old board with a rusty nail sticking out of it."

"When was your last tetanus shot?" Aurora asked.

"Hell if I know. I know you're supposed to get them boosters every couple years or so, right?" He looked to Aurora for clarification.

"Ten years, but every five if someone has increased risk. Like you." She raised a brow at him, letting him know he was one of *those* people.

"I guess…" He looked away.

"Don't worry, Tim, you're not the only one around town who's not caught up on his shots." She looked at Beau. "Ooh. I just thought of something. Maybe we can add that to our roster at Brush Valley Day."

"What?"

"Seeing if people are up to date on their shots, like

tetanus. Adults need shots too—not just babies. In addition to the flu shots and pneumonia. *Oh!* We're going to have to order more serum."

"Good idea. Put it on the list." He sounded distracted as he focused on the injury. "I'm going to need some Lidocaine and a twenty-two gauge needle."

"Needle? What for?" Tim's jaw dropped a second. "A needle? *Really?*"

"I have to pull the nail out and it's gonna hurt, so I want to numb the area."

"No. Just yank it outta there." Tim reached for the nail.

"No!" Aurora and Beau yelled at the same time.

Tim paused. "Why not? Can't hurt any worse coming out than it did going in."

"We don't want to damage any more flesh, nerves or tendons. It has to be done carefully. Ideally by a hand surgeon."

"I see."

"I'll get the Lido." Aurora left the room, and Beau watched her go.

"She gonna stay this time?" Tim asked.

"What?" Beau was having a hard time shifting gears today.

"Aurora. She gonna stay this time around? Seems like she needs a place to stay put instead of living down there in Virginia. She say anything about whether she's gonna stay?"

"She's just helping me while my nurse is out on maternity leave." Beau pressed his lips together as he said the words. Still not liking the idea.

"You should try to get her to stay. We can use good people like her around here."

"That's exactly what I thought," Beau said aloud, and

looked over the glasses at Tim. A snort escaped Beau's nose before he could stop it. "Exactly what I *told* her, too."

"Thought what and told who what?" Aurora asked as she returned to the room.

"Nothing…" Beau and Tim chorused at the same time, trying very hard to not look guilty.

Aurora snorted and gave them both the stink eye, the way she had back in high school. "Like I'm gonna believe *that* anytime soon."

She handed a syringe to Beau.

"Here's the Lido. I'll go round up some tetanus booster."

"Oh, man," Tim said, concern in his eyes and a frown on his brow.

"What?" she asked, and gave Tim a look.

It was all Beau could do not to laugh at the look on Tim's face. He looked like he was heading to the executioner.

"Am I gonna have to drop my drawers for that one?"

"Only if you really want to, Tim. But I'd rather not be traumatized. I can give it in your arm."

Without another word she left the room.

CHAPTER ELEVEN

TIM GRINNED AT BEAU. "Feisty now, isn't she?"

"You have *no* idea."

Tim eased forward a little bit, his bright blue eyes eager for some gossip. "Tell me. I'm gonna be here a while, so tell me."

"No way, Tim." Beau reached for sterile saline to cleanse the wound and distract Tim from the direction he wanted to take the conversation. "This might hurt."

"Oh—*oh!*" Tim sat straight up and hissed a breath out between clenched teeth.

Aurora returned and rolled up Tim's sleeve. "Hold still." She jabbed the needle into his arm and injected tetanus vaccine while he was occupied with Beau.

"Damn, you two. You're double-teaming me."

"It's easier that way." Aurora rubbed the injection site on Tim's arm. "It'll be sore for a few days, but after that you'll be good as new."

"Dangit. Now *both* arms hurt."

"Tim." Beau looked at the man and removed the specialty glasses. "I'm going to have to send you to the ER after all. This is beyond me. I don't want to take a chance on damaging anything."

"No," Tim said and shook his head adamantly, his eyes

no longer glittering with amusement. "I'm not going to town for this. If you can't do it I'll do it myself."

Before Aurora or Beau could react Tim had grabbed the nail and yanked it out of his hand.

"Holy hell, that hurts!" he said, and dropped the nail. His face was three shades of pale and he looked like he was going to faint.

Aurora and Beau jumped into action and pressed sterile gauze to the gaping hole in the middle of his hand. But there was little blood.

"Let me see what you've done this time." Beau put the glasses on again. "I'll be damned…" Beau said, and eased the gauze back from Tim's hand. "Only you, Tim. Only *you* could do this."

"What'd I do now?"

"Only you can trip over your own feet, fall on a nail and miss every vessel and tendon in your hand." He shook his head.

"I did? Then why's it still hurting so much?"

"You still have a hole in your hand. With a few stitches and a visit to a hand doctor you'll be in good shape in a few weeks."

"Weeks?" Tim shook his head again. "No way. I gotta be back on the job in an hour. Keith dropped me off and went to get us some lunch at Greg's Diner. He'll be back in an hour."

"You're going to have to knock off for the day. Sorry."

"Nope. Ain't gonna do it. Just wrap it up." He pressed his lips firmly together.

"Tim, don't be a horse's—" Beau started, but was interrupted by Aurora.

"Let me interject a little sanity, a little perspective, into your life here, Tim."

Calm as Beau had ever seen her, Aurora placed a hand

on Tim's shoulder and gave him a smile that he'd bet she'd often turned on doctors and medical students who were just about to do something monumentally stupid.

"Go for it."

This he had to see. Beau sat back and gave her the floor.

"You have a lot of people who depend on you, right?"

"See? You *do* understand. That's why I need to get back to work."

"So, I just have one question for you. What if your hand gets infected, rots and falls off? Your family—the people who depend on you—will not be happy when your business falls apart because you can't work with only one hand. The other will have been amputated because of pure stupidity. They'll have to sign up for unemployment and government assistance. *Then* what are you going to do?"

"Uh…technically, that's two questions…"

Aurora gave him a narrow-eyed look and planted her hands on her hips.

"The answer you're looking for is: *You're right, Aurora. I'm not going to do that.*" She squeezed his shoulder for emphasis. "Repeat after me."

Tim hung his head. "Okay. I'll take the day off and go see the damned hand doctor." He looked at Beau with a glare.

"Hey, don't look at me."

"She's *your* nurse."

"She's her own woman, though. Always has been." Beau looked at Aurora and a half smile crossed his face.

"Told you she was feistier than she used to be."

Tim said it as if it was a bad thing, but Beau could see her spirit rising every day.

"Let's get this show on the road so you can get to

Truitt's Pharmacy for your antibiotics, and Keith can take you home." Aurora handed a printed prescription to Beau. "I wrote up the medications for you—antibiotics and some pain medicine."

"Can you put a sturdy dressing on him?"

Beau took the piece of paper from Aurora. His hand touched hers and lingered. Her gaze flashed to him, then she looked away.

"Oh, sure…" She cleared her throat and reached for a pair of gloves. "I'll put a dressing on you, Tim, but you'll have to come in tomorrow for me to change it. I'm sure Beau's going to want to see you again, too."

"Okay."

"Don't look so glum, Tim. You need a break. Fact is, I ran into your wife at Greg's Diner the other day. She looks like *she* needs a vacation too."

"You're right." He nodded and seemed to come to a decision. "Aurora. You give good advice. You should stick around and give us folks around here some more of it."

"Oh, Tim." She curved her hair behind her left ear. "I don't know…"

"Now, listen here," Tim said, and took her hand in his good one. "You may not realize this, but you've been missed around here."

"Yes, well… I've missed being around here, too." She turned, then winced, but covered it quickly. "Unfortunately Cathy's due back from maternity leave in a few days, so I'll be out of a job."

"Beau, can't you do something about that?"

"What would you suggest? Fire my nurse when she just had a baby?" Beau knew he'd said it a little more harshly than he'd intended. "Sorry, Tim. I'm in a bind, either way you look at it."

"Can't you keep them both on?"

"Not yet. Not enough business to justify hiring two nurses at the moment. We're getting there, but not right now."

"Well, shoot. That's too bad. But there has to be other jobs around, right? Maybe in town?" Tim's sympathy was genuine.

"I'm sure I'll figure something out. The right thing usually happens at the right time, don't you think?" Aurora patted Tim on the shoulder. "In the meantime, I'll call the hand doc in Johnstown and find out when he can see you."

Aurora nodded and placed a hand on her right hip as she left the room.

"Dammit." Tim spoke to Beau, but kept his gaze on their friend as she moved away.

"What?" Beau took a quick look out the door, but she'd disappeared.

"I just wish you could keep her on. She's too much fun to let walk out of here."

"I wish I could, too. But unless Cathy decides she's not coming back I have no choice but to let Aurora go," Beau said.

"Looks like you don't like that idea at all." Tim eyed him closely. "And I don't mean just about the job."

"You're an observant man, Tim." A muscle twitched in Beau's jaw. He could feel it, and he was sure that Tim could see it. "Even if I *could* get her to stay, what have I got to offer her? I can't even give her a job! I've got too much baggage, Tim. I'm not sure I'm over…"

Was he over Julie? He'd certainly been happier lately than he had since her death. He shook his head and sighed.

"Anyway, she's got to *want* to stay. It's her plan to get her life back, and that life is in Virginia."

"It's your job to convince her. There are plenty of jobs in town, aren't there? She could get a job there until you've got enough business to hire her permanently."

Tim looked at him like that was the end of it, but it wasn't. Not by a long shot.

"It's an idea, but she hasn't said a word about finding another job."

"Have you asked her?"

Beau stared at the man. "Asked her what?"

"Asked her to stay?"

Beau shook his head. "It'd be selfish of me to ask her to stay. She needs to decide on her own."

With his good hand, Tim gave Beau a punch on the arm. "Have you lost your mind? The woman of your dreams is about to walk away from you and you're about to let her."

"What am I supposed to do? Kidnap her? Every time I try to talk to her lately something or someone interrupts." Beau shook his head, thinking of this very morning, when he'd made another attempt to talk to her. "As I said, she has to *want* to stay."

Tim leaned forward and peered right at Beau until his pulse jumped.

"Then give her a reason to stay."

Dumbfounded that his patient was giving him romantic advice, Beau simply stared at Tim for a few seconds. "Haven't you been listening? I can't offer her anything here."

"I'm not talking about the *job*, you dope."

"Neither am I…" Beau whispered.

Tim looked at him sympathetically. "You and Chloe. A family. That's what you can offer. A reason to stay."

"I can't expect her to take on a widower and a baby. I

can't even guarantee it will work out, and I have Chloe to think of—it's not just me anymore."

Beau felt the tension in his neck creeping down into his shoulders and resisted the urge to give in to the pain of it. He cared for Aurora but, as broken as he was, could he offer her all she deserved? He wasn't going to beg her to stay. He had *some* pride left.

"Seriously? How long were you married?" Tim's eyes rounded wide, as if Beau had just said something monumentally stupid.

"Ten years. Why?"

"You told Julie you loved her once, didn't you?"

"Sure."

"Did you tell her more than that?"

"Of course. All the time."

"So, you think Aurora only wants or needs to hear it one time that you're interested in her? That you'd like her to stay here? If you want her to stay you need to find a way to talk to her, heart to heart. *Soon.* Before she gets it in her head to take a job in Alaska or something."

Tim stood. Apparently he'd come to the end of his wisdom for the day.

"Looks like you're good to go." Beau stood too. "Aurora will give you the paperwork and let you know when your next appointment is. Glad you came in, Tim. For the hand, I mean. The rest… I'm not so sure about."

"Me, too. I get a nail in the hand and the wife gets a vacation. Go figure." He shook his head as they walked to the reception area.

"It's the mysteries of life that keep it interesting, isn't it?"

"Yes, it is." Tim nodded toward Aurora, who sat at the desk with the phone to her ear. "And that's one fine mystery you ought to be solving right now."

"Tim—"

"You and I both know she belongs here. Her friends and family are here. Her history is here." Tim gave him the once-over. "So are you and Chloe."

Was Tim right? *Could* it work between them? Was he ready to move on after losing Julie? If Aurora stayed for him and things didn't work out, how awkward would that be for both of them?

"Maybe you're reading things that just aren't there."

Maybe he was too. Maybe he had been all along. Maybe his grief had hijacked his brain and led him down a path that really wasn't there.

"Back in the day, because you were so full of yourself and cheerleaders, you couldn't see what a great woman she is."

Beau took a look at her, perched on the edge of the new office chair he'd purchased for her while she chatted on the phone.

"I can see it now, but I can't... I'm not ready... I'm not sure what I can offer her."

"There is no perfect time. No one ever knows when they're ready. The loss of a loved one is always hardest on those left behind. But life goes on. We grieve and we move on. What I've learned about life, Beau, is it's never too late. If you're willing to take the chance. No matter what it is. No matter when it is. It could be a busted water pump, a lame horse, or a woman who needs you."

He clapped Beau on the shoulder with his good hand.

"Keith ought to be back in a few, so I'll finish up with Aurora and then you can take her to lunch or something."

Beau watched him chat with Aurora and her sunny smile for a few minutes, then salute as he left the clinic. There was some recurring pain behind that chipper face she presented to the world. He just hoped *he* hadn't contributed to it.

The bell overhead rang as Tim left and Beau cleaned the room, preparing it for the next patient. In this clinic he never knew what there would be going on at any given moment. He separated the used needles and placed them into the disposal container hanging on the wall.

"I can do that." Aurora made the offer. She'd entered the room, and he hadn't even heard her.

"No problem." He removed the bloody gauze and tossed it into the trash.

"So, it's past lunchtime. Are you going to head out?"

"We kind of lost our lunch hour with Tim, didn't we?" he asked.

"We did. That only gives us about twenty minutes to eat."

"That blows my plan, then."

"What plan was that?"

"I thought we could go out for lunch today."

They needed to talk—he knew that. Tim's words had gotten him thinking more than he already had been.

"Oh, no—not right before Brush Valley Day." Her eyes widened with concern. "There's too much to do. How about we go upstairs and make a few sandwiches or something? We can eat and go over the final touches of our plan for tomorrow. Oh, my, it's *tomorrow*."

She clasped her head with her hands, those blue eyes wide with worry.

"Relax, will you? It's just Brush Valley Day."

"No, it's *not*. It's the cornerstone of your entire business. I've put up notices on the community bulletin board online, on the community TV channel, on Craig's List, in every library in the county, and at Greg's Diner, Ramer's Pub and Grill, and even at the churches. We should be bombarded by people tomorrow."

"I can't believe it. You did all that?"

His eyes popped wide. How had she accomplished all that on such short notice? Was he so self-absorbed that he hadn't even seen what she was doing? Hadn't looked up to notice how wonderful she was and how well she fit into his office and his life?

Tim was right. He'd been too full of himself back then, but now he had no excuses.

"I did." A grin burst across her face. "I want to make a big splash tomorrow. It's the last community gathering before the weather turns and people will be out in droves. There's a steam and gas demonstration, old farm equipment on display...the Fosters are having a tractor-pull, and Karen Clever is having a dog wash for charity."

"What? How did you find all this out?" He stood, forgetting about cleaning the room. It could wait in light of the exuberance she had going on.

That beautiful grin returned. "Easy. Just hung out at the beauty shop for an afternoon and got all the gossip."

"Gossip?" Basing his practice on gossip was not what he'd been thinking.

She stepped closer. "On everyone."

That made him swallow. "What have you heard?"

"I'm not telling you." She pointed to the tray. "Finish up, wash up, and come up. By then I'll have some lunch made and I'll tell you everything."

With that declaration she left Beau with his mind boggled, his jaw dropped, and his heart hopeful. Tim was right. If he didn't at least try with Aurora then he didn't deserve her. He'd loved Julie with all his heart, but Aurora had made him smile again. He was a better person with her in his life. Even if it didn't last—as much as he wanted it to last forever—he and Chloe would be better off for their time with Aurora.

With renewed hope in his heart, he washed his hands at the galvanized metal sink and called to Daisy. "Let's go, girl. We've got some work to do. Make sure you act extra-cute, will you?"

After a hurried lunch and a quick return to the office Beau felt a renewed energy of spirit and heart. There was a chance for him to really make a go of things with Aurora, and the potential for building his practice at the clinic was growing by leaps and bounds with her ideas and her energy.

Aurora hung up the phone with a laugh that caught his attention. "What's going on?"

"Oh, that was Mrs. Kinsey. She made an appointment for Monday." She shook her head and her eyes curled up at the corners.

As she looked at him Beau's heart contracted. He realized he was in love with her. He was a dope for not seeing it sooner and doing everything he could to convince her they were meant to be together.

"What for this time?" He was trying to focus on what she was saying, but his mind kept thinking that he loved her.

"She twisted her ankle at the Legion Hall dance—or maybe it was the Grange Hall. She said she was at both, so I'm a little confused about that. But, anyway, she wants you to check on it."

"Couldn't she come in today? We've got time."

"No." Aurora snorted a laugh and pressed the back of her hand to her nose and mouth as her eyes sparkled with mirth. "She's going to a seniors' Championship Twister tournament. She's in the finals!"

"Oh, my God!" Beau smiled, then gave a big laugh. "I'll bet she's going to twist more than her ankle *there*. You'd better set her a long appointment on Monday."

"I'm sure. I've booked her a double appointment."

Aurora shut down the computer and stood, then put her hand on her right hip again with a muffled groan.

"Hip acting up again?"

"Yes. The chair is great—it's just the up and down stuff getting to me now." She nodded. "Since you did the last adjustment I've cut down on all of my medications, and now all I take is ibuprofen."

"You've made remarkable progress. You know that, right?" Somehow he resisted reaching out to her and taking her into his arms.

"I guess so, but I'm still not ready to swing from the rafters in the barn."

"How about before we leave today you let me adjust your back?"

"No." She waved him off and glanced away. "We have too much to do to get ready for tomorrow. It's not important right now."

"Aurora, it *can't* wait. You're more important than that stuff. *That's* what can wait, not you." Geez, she still didn't understand that yet.

"I don't want you to think I'm taking advantage of you because we work together." She gave a hesitant smile, indicating her insecurity about it.

"That's not possible—especially when I offer."

"It's not really that bad, Beau—"

"Hush." He placed his hands on her shoulders and slowly turned her around. "No one is more important to me than my child…and you."

He took a breath after saying the words that might end

their relationship right now. Or they could be the words that solidified it.

"Please let me help you—let me see inside you, Aurora. When we talk about the tough stuff you shut down. I don't want that. I want to talk about it, bring it out into the light and see it for what it really is."

"What is it, then? *Really?*" Anger sparkled in those eyes. Anger that hid a massive pain.

"You've been hurt. Really hurt. You don't deserve to feel bad about it all, to carry the weight of others on your shoulders." Somehow he had to get through to her. Had to make her see how good they could be together. How good they were already.

"That's not it. You don't understand."

"That *is* it. I understand pain, and I understand anger, believe me."

"Beau. Please don't do this. We have other things to do right now." Tears brimmed in her eyes and two bright splotches appeared in her face.

Though she tried to resist and move away from him, he held her tight. This was the key to her torment, the reason she'd run and was still running now. Very few people saw who she was instead of seeing the things she did for them. Including him.

"I'm as guilty as anyone—and I'm here, right now, in front of you, saying I'm sorry. I know I've been focused on the clinic and getting things going, and you've done so many things for me and with Chloe. I don't know how I'd have gotten through these weeks without you. I'm also telling you now, Aurora Hunt, that I *see* you. I see who you are and you are one very awesome woman."

She gasped, the tension leaving her shoulders, and stared up at him, uncertainty in her eyes. "I don't want you to say those things."

For a second she dropped her gaze, then looked at him again. There it was. In her face. In her glistening eyes.

The fear. Fear drove her actions. Right now she was afraid she wasn't good enough. For him. For Chloe. For anything.

He cleared his throat and placed his hands on her shoulders, ensuring that she looked at him. It was now or never. If she didn't stay, then it was his own fault for not asking.

"We've skirted around this issue several times, but I'm going to say it officially. I want you to stay. Here in Pennsylvania. With me…and with Chloe."

She looked up at him, looked into those amazing green eyes. She couldn't find any deception, only pure honesty in his face, in his eyes, and tears filled her own eyes as she looked up at this man who had done his best to make a life for himself and his daughter, to create his business. And now he was trying to invite her into it.

Only *she* was resisting it. Only *she* was the one denying it was possible. Only *she* could see they wouldn't work.

"I don't know what to say…" That it wouldn't work because he was still in love with his dead wife?

"How about, *Yes, Beau, I'd love for you to adjust my hip, then we can get the rest of our work done*?"

At that, she allowed one corner of her mouth to curve upward as the intent of his words got to her. "Okay. I can go that far for now."

"The rest we'll work on—because you *are* a treasure, Aurora, whether you know it or not."

Once again, he held onto her shoulders until she looked into his eyes.

"There's more?"

"There's always more. Always going to be more. I'm serious about wanting you to stay with us."

The heat of his hands on her shoulders melted into her. She wanted this. Wanted him and baby Chloe.

"But why? There are so many things you don't know about me, about my life, about—"

"I'd like the chance to get to know all of those things, but if you don't stay we can't even try."

He took a deep breath and the energy in him changed. The vulnerability between them was nearly palpable.

"I know you're afraid. I am, too. But together we're so much stronger than we are alone, don't you think?"

That melted her resistance. That made her want to curl up by the fire with him for the rest of her life. But she'd worked so hard to leave this place, to build a life else-where—could she put it all aside and reach out to Beau the way he wanted? The way her heart desired?

"I... I'll...you've given me a lot to think about. Things I never considered when I got here."

Swallowing down the fear was hard, so very hard to do. But hadn't she told Tammie that she wasn't willing to give up just because it was hard?

Here was her defining moment.

Did she want Beau and Chloe more than she wanted to give in to the fear?

"I know. I never expected this either."

A tremor pulsed in his hands and she felt it inside her. He was as uncertain as she was, but at least he was will-ing to try. He was willing to give them a chance. To be a family together.

"We're good together, Aurora. You can see that, can't you?"

His eyes begged for her understanding. His face, the

intensity of it, drew her closer as his hands drew her toward him.

"I want this, Beau. I want it so much. But I'm so afraid." She shook her head. It had to be said. The elephant in the room between them wasn't going away.

"Tell me—what are you afraid of? I can help you."

"I'm afraid of giving up everything I've worked for. My independence. I spent so long living by my parents' plan... When I finally broke free I never wanted to go back. But that stupid accident forced me down another path. One I didn't want but that led me to you. Now I feel so broken I'm worried I'm not good enough for you. What if I'm not as good as Julie? What if our relationship never measures up to what you had with her and we don't work? Then we'll *both* be hurt. And I don't want to risk our friendship."

He drew in a breath, as if she'd slapped him. In a way, she had. But it was the truth. It had had to be said.

He tried to talk, but no words came out of this throat. "Wow. Just...wow."

He released her and paced across the room. With one hand he raked his hair back from his face, then faced her in a flash, shock and pain evident in his eyes.

"I had no idea, Aurora. No idea you thought this way."

Tears overflowed. "I'm so sorry, but I had to say it. I'm just so afraid what we have now isn't going to be as good as what you had with Julie, and you'll be disappointed, and angry..."

Her hands trembled and she clasped them together against her middle as she said the final words of fear that lingered in her heart. The final words that could end her relationship with Beau permanently.

"I'm afraid to lose everything I've worked for. To lose our friendship. My heart has been battered and broken so much already." A ragged breath huffed out of her throat. "I love you and Chloe, and nothing would make me happier than to be with you, but I'm afraid I'll never measure up to what you had. And I'm not sure I'm prepared to take the risk."

Without a word, Beau strode past her and out the door.

Brush Valley Day arrived very early for Aurora. She'd set her alarm for five a.m. as she had so much to do before the festival. Somehow, in these weeks she'd been working with Beau, she'd begun to claim some ownership of the little clinic in her rural home town. Today she wanted to show it off. And not just to help increase Beau's business. If she were being honest about it, she was proud of what they'd accomplished in such a short time.

That thought made her pause.

They'd definitely accomplished a lot in the office and in renewing their friendship. Was she wrong to have balked at Beau's words last night? Why could she throw herself wholeheartedly into her job, yet when it came to happiness she wasn't willing to take the risk?

For weeks she'd been excited about today, but now she wasn't as eager as she'd expected. The conversation they'd had last night had cut severely into her joy. Last night things had gone all wrong. The pain in his face had been caused by *her* words and she wished she'd never said anything.

The ache in her heart wasn't going to go away until they talked again. If he even showed up. If he ever talked to her again.

She needed to focus on what was right in front of her. It was the only thing she could do—carry on with the plan. It might be the last thing she could do for Beau.

She staked out a choice location close to the chicken

stand. Ever the opportunist, she thought she could hand out fliers on esophageal reflux and indigestion while people were in the midst of a digestive flare-up.

Though she thought of all those things, the joy of the day had been dampened and the sun was hardly above the horizon.

Scanning the street for his vehicle, she sighed. If she and Beau were at odds, this was going to be a very long day.

Finally Beau's SUV backed up into the space beside her car and she hurried over to him.

"I'm so glad you decided to come." Trying not to panic, she took a breath and hoped her deodorant was going to live up to its all-day reputation.

"Why wouldn't I? We've been planning this for weeks."

"Well, after last night... I thought you might...not come."

"Never even considered it." Beau squeezed one of her shoulders. "Let's get moving, shall we?"

Beau looked at his watch and gave her that grin of his. There was just a hint of the pain from last night in his eyes. Apparently he'd decided to set it aside for today. For right now, for the sake of the festival, she'd go with it. Who knew what kind of relationship they'd have after that? If any.

"Well. Okay. I'm anxious about getting things set up."

And a lot of other things. She shot him another glance, but he maintained his composure, his demeanor, and she relaxed a little. Maybe they could get through the day on an equal footing before he told her to get out of his life.

"If you can help me with the table, we'll get everything rolling."

"Lead the way."

They worked together to get the display and the sun

shade up before the first events of the day began. For a few hours they tag-teamed, alternating offering flu shots and blood pressure checks, taking down contact information and handing out fliers.

"Wow. Not too many takers," Aurora said, heartily disappointed in the number of people who'd stopped by their booth. "I've only had three BP checks and six flu shots." She plopped down into her chair and shoved her hair out of her face. "This is discouraging. I thought more people would be interested in us. I mean, you. The clinic."

"Oh, just wait until after lunch. People will settle down then, get something to eat, work on their indigestion, then come over to see if we have any antacids."

Beau was looking at the situation a different way than she did.

"We don't *have* any antacids. I never thought of that!"

Beau fished around in a box beneath the table, shook a giant bottle of antacids and sat it in front of her. "We do now. In a moment of clarity I grabbed some from the pharmacy on the way over."

"Oh, you think you're so smart, don't you?"

"I try to be."

Secretly pleased at his thoughtfulness, she felt a warmth pulse in her chest. Could they really do this together? This thing they were already doing?

Before she had any time to mull over that idea, there was a new arrival at their table.

CHAPTER TWELVE

As Beau had predicted, the afternoon saw a flurry of increased activity at their little booth. People were looking for information on a variety of illnesses and there was renewed interest in flu shots.

"I've started an email list for people to subscribe to your newsletter."

"I don't have a newsletter."

"You do now."

"Awesome." Beau patted his stomach. "The smell of that chicken is driving me nuts. How about I go get us some lunch?"

"I haven't had it in years, so I'm overdue."

The first piece of smoky barbecue chicken to hit her tongue brought back so many memories for Aurora that she closed her eyes and squealed.

"Too hot?"

She shook her head.

"Must be good, then."

She nodded her head and silently chewed as memories assaulted her from every direction.

So many things that one bite of food gave to her. Memories of family excursions to the fair, memories of her teenage years, going on dates to the fair, or hanging out with her friends. Memories assaulted her, overwhelmed her. Friends she'd lost track of, family who were no longer with them, events she'd missed.

Pain suddenly hit her in the gut as she chewed. Tears filled her eyes, then overflowed.

"What's wrong? That bad?"

She choked down the piece of food and opened her watery eyes to Beau, now stooped in front of her. "No. I've missed *so* much." She hiccuped in a breath. "Being gone. I've missed it here, but I'd convinced myself I didn't belong here, that my life was elsewhere."

"One bite of chicken told you that?"

"Yes." Again and again memories of years past trickled into her brain, and she placed her hand on his strong shoulder, needing a connection with him right now. "I ran away, and I kept running and running, didn't I?"

"Yes, you did, but you had reasons for it, right?"

"I did. I had to go. I had to get out of here. I had to find my life, to make my life somewhere else—or at least that's what I thought at the time. But now I just don't know."

"You did. Now it's time for you to come home, Aurora. Come home to the people who love you, and miss you, and want to see you here every day." He stayed in front of her, with not a care about the people flowing around them.

"How can I do that when I've hurt people, cut them out by leaving? My friends. My family. I don't want to hurt anyone else. Especially you." She placed her hand on his face. "I've hurt you, and I keep doing it, don't I?"

"Shh, Aurora." He pulled her close and hugged her. "You carry the weight of the world on your shoulders, and you don't have to. Just be *you*, and everything will be fine."

The reassurance in his voice comforted her in the moment.

"When you said you weren't prepared to take the risk you shocked the hell out of me. Everything you've done with your life—building your career from scratch in a new state, returning here and starting again, all the chances you took... But I wasn't worth the risk. I wasn't ready for that and it was a slap in the face."

"I'm so sorry, Beau."

"You were right." He nodded and held her gaze. "But you were wrong, too."

"Er...what?"

"We *are* worth the risk. We're already better than I ever could have imagined. I loved Julie, and I always will, but I'm *in love* with you."

A few seconds passed before the impact of his words sank in. "Really?" She sat bolt upright in the chair and nearly knocked Beau over.

"Yes, really." He cupped her face in his hands and drew her closer for a hard kiss. "I've been trying to figure out a way to keep you here and the answer was as simple as being honest with myself and with you."

"Beau, are you sure? I mean, are you really ready for this? What about Chloe?"

"She's already fond of you and has accepted you, so with time I'm sure she'll love you as much as I do." He cleared his throat and glanced away. "So, Aurora Hunt, will you stay in Brush Valley, with me, with Chloe, and someday be my wife?"

"Beau..." The word was a breath on the air, a sigh from her soul. Everything was in that one word. "Yes, I'll stay. I don't know what I'll do for work, but I won't leave. I won't leave you and Chloe. I love you both so much."

"We'll find a job for you somewhere until the clinic is busy enough for two nurses. I just don't want you to go. I want to give us a chance."

"I want that, too."

Lunging from the chair, she launched herself into Beau's arms and hung onto him.

Someone nearby cleared his throat loudly and a familiar voice interrupted them. "Hey, you two. Just who I was looking for."

Aurora pulled back and wiped her eyes with the heels of her hands, hoping she hadn't smeared her mascara.

"Tim!" Beau stood in front of Aurora, giving her a minute to catch her breath while he still trembled from the effort to control his emotions in the moment. "What can I do for you?"

"I got my dressing all torn up."

He held up his hand. It was *not* the pristine white dressing that he'd left the office with. It was falling off and streaked with smudges of who knew what?

"Come over here before Aurora sees it." Beau led him to the opposite side of the tent. "You just can't stay out of trouble, can you, Tim?"

"You know me, don't you, Beau?" Tim gave a laugh and sat on the chair and began to unwrap the dressing by himself. "I got a new horse who needs some extra attention. Got my dressing wrapped up in the bridle. He spooked, then we both ran around the corral like maniacs until the wrapping tore away. It's all dirty, and I knew Aurora would probably give me hell, so I decided to man up and come to you before she finds out and yanks me around by the ear."

"I wouldn't do that, Tim Verner."

There she stood with her hands on her hips, looking like she would do exactly that, and Beau allowed one side of his mouth to curl up. She was a force to be reckoned with, and he loved her with all his heart. In that moment, as he stood there watching her give his patient a hard time, the broken pieces of his heart were melding back together again.

Yes, he would always love Julie. She'd given him the best piece of herself before she died, and he would honor her and their love all the remaining days he spent on earth. But the earthbound man needed to move on, *had* to move on. With Aurora by his side, he knew he could do it. He could have a good life, raise his daughter, and maybe have a few more running around.

"You most certainly would." Tim barked out a laugh. "I remember you yanking Beau around by the ear in geometry class when you bombed a test and he put it up on the bulletin board. You grabbed him by the ear and had him on his knees until he apologized." He slapped his good hand on his leg. "I'll never forget that."

"Neither will I." Beau rubbed his ear, which suddenly burned from the memory.

Aurora's eyes went wide and she clapped a hand over her mouth. "I totally forgot about that." She stood upright, like every stern teacher they'd ever had. "But I'm going to remember it now if you really did what you *said* you did." She gave him a stern look. "Thanks for the refresher, Tim. Now let me see what damage you did while wrangling a wild horse."

She brushed aside Beau's hands, obviously recovered from the bout with her emotions, but her gaze kept darting toward him. That was good.

He watched Aurora give Tim an earful about bacteria and flesh-eating staph, gangrene, and all manner of ills that would befall him should he choose to ignore her instructions. *Again.*

"Okay. Okay. I'll behave myself." He shook his head and looked at her sheepishly from under the rim of his dusty cowboy hat.

"Your definition of that differs a lot from mine." Aurora snorted and added an extra layer of tape, giving him a dose of the stink eye as she did so. "Don't get it dirty— or I'll be calling your wife to watch you closer."

"Please don't do that." Tim squirmed a little in his seat. "That's really unnecessary."

"Then behave yourself. The longer you keep irritating the wound, the longer it will take to heal."

"I know. I *know.*"

"Then *do* it. What you resist, persists. Have you ever heard that?"

"No. But I get it." Shaking his head, he widened his eyes briefly. "Boy, do I get it."

"Okay. Lecture over." She gave him another look, watching to see if her words had really sunk into his brain. "For now. Don't screw this up before you even get to see the hand surgeon."

"Beau? Can you *do* something about her?" Playful as ever, Tim teased him.

"What? Me? No way. Not touching that one." Beau held his hands up like he was facing a rattlesnake.

It turned into a good-natured argument about who was going to do what. This little moment was just the kind of fun Aurora needed. Another person from her past reinforcing how much she was needed here. How much she was wanted here. Not just because of him and how good they were together.

"Excuse me. Is this a bad time?" A woman stood a few feet away, hesitating.

"This is a perfect time." Beau stood and greeted her, glad that people were still stopping by for a variety of reasons. "I'm Dr. Gutterman. What can I do for you?"

"I was interested in getting a flu shot."

"Great. My nurse Aurora is in charge of those, so I'll place you in her capable hands."

After Aurora had finished up, he approached her.

"I never could have done this without your input and help, Aurora. *Never.*"

"Oh, it wasn't that much. Really…"

She dropped her gaze as a flush colored her neck and face. Though she tried to brush off the compliment, he could see that she was pleased.

"Just take the compliment and my gratitude for what they are."

"What *are* they?"

"Sincere."

"Beau…"

Now she met his gaze, her eyes glistening with the happiness that he'd wanted to see there for a long time. Knowing he'd put it there pleased him. He'd like to spend all his days looking for that ray of sunshine in her eyes.

"It's true."

He leaned over to kiss her cheek, then turned as he heard a familiar little voice. The squeal let him know who was coming.

"Chloe!"

He greeted the toddler with all the enthusiasm that Aurora expected to see—had missed seeing in the men in *her* family. What was so different about him? He was certainly manly, masculine and strong, but he had a soft side when it came to his daughter. It was lovely to see and something in her heart turned.

Was she really looking at this man who'd been her friend for years in the right light? Could he really be a partner to her in work and in her heart? Letting him in could risk heartache again, for both of them, but anything in life that was worth having was worth taking a risk on, wasn't it?

As the thrumming in her chest made her breathing tight she watched as Beau clasped Chloe in his hands, then gave her a little toss in the air, and she knew she was done for. There was no way she was leaving Beau and Chloe.

Nothing was as important to her as they were.

The baby squealed, delighted with the play. Then Beau tucked her against his side, pressed a kiss to her chubby little cheek. The pain in Aurora's chest burst and tears filled her eyes as she watched the man she'd fallen in love with play with his child.

The sun continued to move westward, casting the man in a bronze glow. His shoulders looked broader, his hips leaner, his legs longer, and when he turned to face her with a grin he was more handsome, his hair more golden blond, and his skin glowed in a way she'd never noticed.

When he looked at her that way, with pure joy in his eyes, her heart cramped in her chest and her knees felt weak and trembling.

She was completely, totally, outrageously in love with Beau Gutterman. Hopelessly in love with him.

As he approached, Chloe reached out to Aurora and her heart beat a little faster again. Tears pricked her eyes at the little girl's plea, and she took Chloe from Beau.

"How's Chloe doing today?" She smiled and gave her a kiss.

"She's been a good baby all day, but somehow she knew it was time to see her daddy," said Dolly, Beau's mother.

The woman turned and approached Aurora with an assessing look on her face. Her eyes were the same vivid green as Beau's, and it was obvious where his looks came from.

"You must be Aurora?"

"Yes, I am." With her hands full of baby, she couldn't shake Dolly's hand, so she nodded. "It's been a long time, hasn't it?"

"Oh, yes. I do recall meeting you once or twice when you kids were in school. Beau tells me you've been a godsend to him at the office."

"He does?"

She cast a quick look at the man whose face was unreadable at the moment. Aurora couldn't tell anything of what he was thinking or feeling from the way his eyes were guarded and the firm set of his mouth. All moisture left her mouth as she stared at him.

After a short visit, Dolly took Chloe and placed her in her stroller. "I think I'll take her home before the fireworks get started. They'll be too loud for her."

"Good idea." Beau leaned over and pressed a kiss to his mother's cheek. "Thanks for taking her today."

"It is a joy. She's a good baby, and I love having her."

"You have to tell me, though, if she gets too much for you."

Dolly Gutterman pulled herself upright and raised one brow at her son. "Are you trying to tell me that I'm getting too old to handle a baby?"

A flash of a grin took over Beau's face for a few seconds before he controlled his expression. "No, ma'am. I'd never do that."

"Good. Having a baby around makes me feel younger every day." Her bright look was taken over by a sad grief for a few seconds, as Dolly looked at her granddaughter, who was falling asleep right in front of them. "I just wish things were different. That she had a mom to love her, too."

"She will. I promise." He placed a hand on Dolly's arm and gave a little squeeze. "I'll give you a call when we're all wrapped up here."

"Okay. By then I'm sure she'll be asleep. She can stay overnight. I don't mind at all."

"If you don't mind... Aurora and I have some things to finish up and it could get late."

"Call me in the morning."

She raised her face to his and he kissed his mother on the cheek, then kissed Chloe and watched as they moved away.

Aurora had stood transfixed, watching the conversation between Beau and Dolly.

"Beau!"

A feminine voice called to him, and both he and Aurora turned to look.

"Don't leave yet."

"Cathy?"

Beau placed his hands on his hips and grinned at the woman coming their way. A baby was strapped to her chest and her husband kept pace with them as he toted a diaper bag.

"You look *fabulous*." The awe in his voice was almost tangible. Beau eased the blue cover away from the baby's face. "He's beautiful!"

Despite herself, Aurora was drawn closer to the new family too. This was the baby that she and Beau had delivered together her first day here.

"Oh, he's a beauty, for sure," Aurora said, and the pain, the hurt in her chest dissipated as the baby shifted position and yawned, then settled down again. "How are you doing?"

"I feel great." The look of adoration Cathy cast on her baby was pure bliss. "He's a good baby, and sleeps most of the night."

"That's a miracle in itself," Aurora said, knowing that not *every* baby slept through the night.

"I'm so glad you stopped by." Beau stretched around her and shook hands with Ron, her husband. "Are you ready to come back to work yet?"

Aurora held her breath. Her future rode on the answer to that question. Moisture broke out on her palms and her tongue felt like it was stuck to the roof of her mouth. Her heart, which had just been quiet, now thrummed with anxiety. She waited for Cathy's answer.

"Oh, that's something I wanted to talk to you about." She looked at her husband, then a grin erupted on her face. "While I've been off, Ron got a promotion, and now I don't have to work at *all*!"

Cathy practically glowed as she announced that her dream of becoming a full-time wife and mother had actually come true.

"We never thought we could do it on one income, but now I can stay home with the baby and Ron can bring home the bacon."

Beau cast a quick glance at Aurora, then faced Cathy again. "I'm thrilled for you. You'll have to bring him in for his first round of shots soon, and all that fun stuff."

"I will." Cathy faced Aurora. "I also wanted to thank you both for helping when I went into labor. You saved our lives." Tears overflowed on Cathy's face. "I'm sorry. My hormones are a wreck."

She wiped her face with the baby's blanket.

"Come here." She hugged them both as well as she

could with the baby on her chest. "When I come in to visit, I expect that waiting room to be full."

"I hope you're right." Beau hugged her back.

"With everything that I've heard around town, you're going to be busier than ever. This isn't something I anticipated happening for a long time. But with a new baby, I just want to stay home and rock him, and watch every time he does something. It's so new and wonderful and scary all at the same time."

"You'll be fine, Cathy. You'll both be fine. If I could be a new dad and take care of Chloe with…with everything that went on, you can do it for sure."

His voice cracked as he spoke and Aurora knew he was remembering how Julie had died, and her heart ached for him.

After they'd left, Beau turned to her and grinned. "The job's yours if you want it." He paused. "*Do* you want it?"

With a squeal she wrapped her arms around his shoulders. "Of *course* I want it!"

Beau's arms clasped her tight and the tremor in his muscles reached her heart.

"There's nothing else I want more."

They stowed all the supplies in their vehicles, then Beau faced Aurora and held on to her shoulders as the night deepened and the crickets began their nightly tunes.

"Will you stay with me? I want to hold you tonight." His breathing was fast and hard, matching her own. "Chloe's staying with my mom, and we can have some adult time together."

"Beau…" Without her consent, her hands moved up to clasp his shirt in her fists. Pulses of desire filled her as she eased closer to him.

"We've come so far in our lives alone." He pressed a

kiss to her forehead. "I want to get to know you all over again. And again. And again."

"I do, too." Any remaining pieces of ice and protection surrounding her heart rapidly melted beneath Beau's warmth and his words.

Without another word he swooped down and kissed the living daylights out of her. If that kiss didn't tell her how he felt, then nothing would.

He pulled back. "Aurora, I love you. I love you so much." He cupped her face and waited until she looked up at him with watery eyes.

"I love you, too. You mean so much to me, and I can't stay here without being with you and Chloe. It would kill me."

For a few moments they stood in the twilight, just holding each other, shaking and trembling with need, trying to hold on to these new feelings, new realizations, and new possibilities for them together.

In a flash, Beau brought her against him again and squeezed her. "We're going to be great together. We're going to be a family. The three of us."

"Kiss me. Kiss me like you're never going to let me go."

Reaching up, she guided his mouth to hers. She parted her lips to him and ached with need as he devoured her, driving desire up to the surface.

They explored each other and Beau pressed her against the car, pressing his hips against hers, letting her know in no uncertain terms of his desire for her.

"Let's go. I need you, Aurora. I need you *now*."

He dipped and took her mouth with his again, then they both jumped as lights flashed overhead and seconds later came the resounding boom of fireworks.

"Oh!" Aurora looked overhead at the spiraling lights streaming back to earth. "I'd forgotten about this."

"I hadn't. I knew there were going to be fireworks tonight," Beau said, but he wasn't looking up. He was looking straight at her.

"Oh, really?" That made her smile. "Fireworks?"

"Yes, there are *always* fireworks when we're together." Beau took a breath and pressed his forehead against hers. "Then you'll stay? Stay with me tonight, every night, and build a life with me?"

The fear and the vulnerability in his voice broke her heart. They'd both had their share of tragedies, but together she knew they could build a life, build a business and build on the love they already had for each other.

"I'll stay and love you forever."

EPILOGUE

One year later

FALL WAS AURORA'S favorite time of the year in Pennsylvania. Every year was special, with the leaves in full color, but this year was extraspecial.

Today she was approaching the lake just outside of town, and she admired the afternoon sun glistening on the surface, sparkling and adding a little magic to the day. Leaves scattered by the wind clattered across the road onto the grass and swirled past the crowd gathered there.

Since she'd woken this morning her heart had been in overdrive, and as the horse-drawn wagon she was riding in arrived she felt it hammer in her chest.

The crowd of people—friends and family, some who were both—were gathered at the edge of the lake and waiting for her to arrive.

"Whoa!" Tim pulled on the reins and the horses slowed to a stop.

After getting down, Aurora looked for Beau. There he was, under an arch at the water's edge, looking strong and handsome and so very loving as he waited for her to arrive.

The last year had been a whirlwind of love, of blending

two families, and of her realizing that what she'd needed had been in Brush Valley all along.

"Thank you, Tim." She leaned up and kissed his clean-shaven cheek.

"You're welcome." He cleared his throat. "You're a beautiful bride, Aurora, and I'm grateful that you're my friend, too."

Tears choked her throat as she took the few steps toward her mother, who stood proud and beautiful, wearing a peach-colored dress that mirrored Aurora's gown.

"Are you ready to walk me down the aisle?" Aurora asked.

"You're sure this is what you want?" Sally's voice was choked with emotion.

After a quick look at Beau, she nodded. "Absolutely. Today is the best day of my life."

"I just wish your father were here."

Aurora looked overhead at the bright blue sky and at the way a light breeze teased the trees. "He's here, Mom. He's here."

In minutes she held Beau's hand and the words were spoken that would join them together as partners, friends, soul mates and as family.

Then Beau's lips were on hers and the crowd around them applauded. Beau hugged her with one arm and took Chloe with his other, and the three of them stood together, united as one family, one unit, one love.

* * * * *

*If you enjoyed this story,
check out these other great reads
from Molly Evans*

*SAFE IN THE SURGEON'S ARMS
HER FAMILY FOR KEEPS
SOCIALITE...OR NURSE IN A MILLION?
CHILDREN'S DOCTOR, SHY NURSE*

All available now!

MILLS & BOON®

MEDICAL ROMANCE™

THE ULTIMATE IN ROMANTIC MEDICAL DRAMA

A sneak peek at next month's titles...

In stores from 23rd February 2017:

- **Their Secret Royal Baby** – Carol Marinelli *and*
  Her Hot Highland Doc – Annie O'Neil

- **His Pregnant Royal Bride** – Amy Ruttan *and*
  Baby Surprise for the Doctor Prince – Robin Gianr

- **Resisting Her Army Doc Rival** – Sue MacKay *and*
  A Month to Marry the Midwife – Fiona McArthur

Just can't wait?
Buy our books online before they hit the shops!
www.millsandboon.co.uk

Also available as eBooks.

MILLS & BOON®

EXCLUSIVE EXTRACT

Secret royal prince Dr Elias Santini is stunned
when he rushes to an emergency delivery.
The patient is Beth Foster… and she's
having his baby!

Read on for a sneak preview of
THEIR SECRET ROYAL BABY

'How pregnant is she?' Elias asked.

'Twenty-nine weeks. Her waters broke as we got her
onto the gurney. Elias, this baby is coming and very
rapidly.'

They had reached the cubicle and Elias took a stead-
ying breath.

'What's her name?'

Before Mandy could tell Elias he was already stepping
into the cubicle.

And before Mandy said the name, he knew it.

'Beth.'

She was sitting up, wearing a hospital gown, and
there was a blanket over her. Her stunning red hair was
worn up tonight but it was starting to uncoil and was
dark with sweat. Her gorgeous almond-shaped eyes were
for now screwed closed and she wore drop earrings in
rose gold and the stones were rubies.

They were the same earrings she had worn the night
they had met.

He could remember vividly stepping into her villa

and turning the light on and watching the woman he had seen only in moonlight come into delicious colour—the deep red of her hair, the pale pink of her lips and eyes that were a pure ocean blue.

Now Valerie had her arm around Beth's shoulders and was telling her to try not to push.

For Elias there was a moment of uncertainty.

Could Mandy find someone else perhaps? Could he swap with Roger?

Almost immediately he realised there was no choice. From what Mandy had told him this baby was close to being born.

His baby?

Don't miss
THEIR SECRET ROYAL BABY
by Carol Marinelli

Available March 2017
www.millsandboon.co.uk